NUDGE NUDGE WINK WINK DIE

RIIS MARSHALL

NUDGE NUDGE WINK WINK DIE

RIIS MARSHALL

TURFHILL COURT PRESS

First published in Great Britain in 2017 by Turfhill Court Press

Copyright © Riis Marshall 2017

Riis Marshall has asserted his right under the Copyright, Designs and Patents Act, 1988, to be identified as the author of this work.

This book is a work of fiction. The characters and events portrayed in this work are entirely fictional. Actual institutions and agencies have been included at various points within the narrative as appropriate to the story. The behaviour of fictional characters portrayed as members of some of these institutions and agencies and their personal and political views are not meant to represent in any way the behaviour or political or personal views of any actual members of these institutions or agencies.

All rights reserved.
Without limiting the rights under copyright reserved above, no part of this publication may be reproduced or transmitted, in any form or by any means (electronic, mechanical, photocopying, recording or otherwise), without the prior written permission of the copyright owner (except for brief direct quotations, with full acknowledgement of both the author and their source).

A CIP catalogue reference for this book
is available from the British Library

ISBN 978-1-63587-400-6 (pb)

2 3 4 5 6 7 0 9 8

Turfhill Court Press
4 Robertson Road
Grantham, Lincolnshire NG31 8AQ United Kingdom

info@RiisMarshall.co.uk
www.RiisMarshall.co.uk

Cover design Copyright © Turfhill Court Press 2017

Printed and bound in Great Britain by
Printondemand-Worldwide, Peterborough

This book is dedicated to May, my idea bouncer,
my pal, my wife.

Acknowledgement

I wish to extend my thanks to Rosemary Dickson A.C.P. for her explanation of how modern heart-lung machines are configured and operated.

'I was just following orders.'
Adolf Eichmann

CHAPTER ONE

HER FRUSTRATION AT her not being in control reached its apogee; she raised the fist-sized rock and struck him hard on the side of his head. He fell forward. She pushed him into the water boiling around their knees. He floated, face down, for seconds then his water-logged clothing sucked him under. Now there was nothing for her but to wait until the water subsided so she could escape this black, dripping, claustrophobic prison.

Winifred Hyde-Davies did not believe in teambuilding; she thought it a complete load of nonsense. Teambuilding was for wimps who did not have the balls to take charge of an organization and make decisions. No, the way to run any organization, particularly a large organization, was through power—power wrapped in a velvet mantle of charm if possible but power nonetheless. If charm failed, the true leader raged, threatened, bullied, lied, even blackmailed—whatever it took to get the job done. Destroy totally anybody challenging her decisions or authority. She agreed without qualification with Tonya Harding's affirmation: 'I'd do *anything* to be the winner!'

The exercise began hours ago, now she was unsure how long it had been, with the six kitted out in boiler suits, hard hats, headlamps, spare batteries, water bottles and maps. They were to find their way through the pothole working as a team, from the lower, downstream entrance at the base of a modest limestone cliff to the upper, upstream exit on the other side of the narrow ridge. Their leader assured them it was completely safe even though they were without a guide.

The pothole was a complex affair with many intersecting passages, low crawlways and stream courses. Good use of their maps would see them through; if they cooperated and trusted their judgement they would succeed. I wonder what Human Resource Practitioner, Personnel Person or whatever they're calling themselves these days dreamed up this idiocy?

And she, still a supervisor, certainly not near the top but with a clear vision of her future, was learning how to play the game—of displaying the right body language, of saying the right things, of *doing* the right things, of, at least superficially, being *seen* to be doing whatever she judged her superiors expected her to be doing. Naturally she never articulated this—her personal leadership model—to anybody, definitely not her colleagues and absolutely not her superiors. Thus her ostensibly enthusiastic participation this weekend in the Peak District and her present location trapped in a small chamber in a flooded pothole.

But the hidden agendum was obvious to her: they were not being assessed on their abilities to build a successful team, the aim of their masters was to assess which demonstrated the strengths to be fast-tracked to leadership within a big, complex organization. There could only be one winner; perhaps her ability to judge the true objectives of those in power was improving.

Several glanced to a sky darker and stormier every minute. One turned to their leader and asked about the possibility of flooding. Tick! a black mark for *him*; one down, four to go.

Once into the narrow passage and with their adjusting to the blackness, chilly air and dampness, they moved in single file along the stream. She showed no interest in decision-making; she fell back to last in line and contributed nothing. They walked slowly and unsurely in the streambed, ankle-deep in the gently flowing water, making inane comments about their progress. What was the fuss all about? just keep walking upstream. Sometimes they had to crawl on their hands and knees for a few metres under a low ceiling but still—no problem.

They stood after one crawl into a widening passage. Here they faced their first problem: a tributary, nearly as broad and deep as the one they were following, flowing into their stream. Decision time. Maybe there might be more to this exercise than first imagined, although she still did not think what they were doing had anything remotely connected with management skills. Which way to turn? Arguments began; the five gathered round with headlamps pointed at the map held by one of them, the one now doing most of the talking, and suggesting they follow the stream entering their passage from the left. She backed up several paces and glanced at her map. She touched the arm of the man whom she judged represented her greatest threat and, although the quietest, probably the strongest member of the group.

He backed away and turned to her: 'Yes?'

'Look at this. I think we need to go to the right.'

He looked at the map then nodded: 'Yep – I think you're right.'

She stepped forward and addressed nobody in particular: 'Right. You yahoos can stand around here and argue all day. We're going this way.'

They complained the route she proposed looked longer than their choice, and they should not separate. She said nothing. They waited a few seconds for her response. She turned and the two stepped into the passage to the right. Soon the voices of the four, yammering on about working as a team faded until they were lost in the sounds of water flowing in the rocky streambed.

They continued upstream, walking when the passage was high enough and crawling when it was not. Soon the low ceiling meant belly-crawling in the stream. They sat with their backs against opposite walls.

She looked at the map: 'I think this low bit only goes on for a few metres then opens into another room. Beyond that it looks like maybe another short crawl then a fairly straight walk to the end. If it gets too tight we can always back up and go back to where we left them. Make sense?'

'Makes sense.'

He led. They were now thoroughly soaked. The passage was not tight, certainly not by the standards of experienced potholers: it was a half metre high and a metre wide. They moved slowly forward.

They crawled twenty metres then entered a room the size of the third bedroom in a modern house—bijou as bedrooms go but generous after their crawl. They moved onto a convenient ledge, sitting upright with their backs against a wall and their feet high enough to be out of the water, resting for a few minutes.

While he sat perfectly still she fidgeted, drumming her hands against her hips and banging her heels alternately against the rock behind her feet.

She yelled, not quite a scream but clearly an exclamation more animated than a simple statement: 'Shit – oh shit!'

'What?'

'The water's rising. Hell, when we sat down our feet were well free of it but now it's lapping around our boots. And listen – not much or a gurgle anymore – closer to a roar!'

'Christ! What'll we do?'

'Stupid question, my friend, stupid question.'

'Easy now.'

She shined her light on both passages: 'Easy now, my arse! The water's rising. Must be those black clouds we saw – what's the lovely poetic word, "gathering"? The one we just came through is fully flooded now and the one upstream isn't much better. While we've been sitting here pissing the time away, any escape from this bloody place has been cut off.'

He grabbed her arm; his hands were shaking: 'But what'll we do?'

'Two possibilities as I see it, Roscoe. We wait until the water level peaks, then subsides, hopefully no higher than our chins or if it rises to the ceiling we drown. Simple as that. Oh, yeah – there's a third.'

'Yes?'

'If you think we can hold our breaths for a twenty-metre crawl we can swim out, going back the way we came.'

'Now who's talking shite?'

She sighed and sat back: 'You're right. That makes no sense at all. About all we can do now is turn off our lights to save our batteries, relax and wait.'

'What – just sit here in the dark?'

'You have any better ideas, scheissekopf?'

'Not really.'

They switched off their lights and sat, saying nothing; it was impossible to judge how long. Soon they decided pitch blackness and roaring, deepening water were too overwhelming so they agree to keep one light on.

Her fidgeting stopped; she sat with her back rigidly against the wall, her muscles tense and the water still rising. Her right hand closed around a rock on the ledge next to her right hip and she tightened her grip on it then relaxed—again and again, almost as one might squeeze an exercise ball. It was the only part of her moving. Anger replaced her initial fright—anger bordering on rage about what was happening to her. Her comments grew shorter and her intervals of silence longer.

He was shaking all over and was *not* silent. The quieter she became the more vociferous did he.

When he repeated for what seemed to her the hundredth time his useless question about what they would do if the water rose to the ceiling, she screamed: 'Oh for Christ's sake – would you just shut the fuck up!'

He said nothing for a minute then took off his hard hat: 'Isn't it about time we switched lights?'

She reached up with her left hand to turn on her light while her right hand tightened around the rock.

The water subsided slowly along with the roar until it was again a gently-flowing stream defined by the passage walls. Still she had no idea how much time had passed. She glanced at his body, now exposed by the lowering water level, and kicked his hard hat aside. She took several deep breaths and dropped down to crawl upstream out of the room.

Soon she could stand and walk. A half hour later she squeezed through a narrow bend in the passage and the faint blue light ahead signalled the end of her journey and safety. Ten minutes later she walked into daylight and a setting sun peeking between more billowing grey storm clouds.

Their leader and his deputy greeted her: 'You've made it.'

'Rather obvious, isn't it? What about the others?'

'The four made it back to the lower entrance. We've been waiting for you two.' He looked towards the entrance then again to her: 'Where is he? The others said the two of you were together.'

'He was behind me for a while in one of those low passages. When it opened into a little room the water rose quite quickly. He was gone. Isn't he with the rest of you? When he disappeared, I assumed he turned back. If he's not with you, he must still be in there somewhere. Shouldn't we go in and look for him?'

'We can't – actually. Another storm and more rain coming. I've alerted the local cave rescue team. They'll be here soon, and they'll decide when it's safe for them to go in. We can only hope he's found a spot high enough where the water didn't reach him.'

'So much for teambuilding, then. Gives a whole new meaning to the Cave Rescue game, doesn't it?'

She looked from him to the entrance then to him and paused. She smiled: 'I really hope he's okay.'

They walked over the ridge and their leader assembled them next to the mini-bus: 'Right. First thing is to get you five back to the hotel and a hot shower and some dry clothes. I'll wait for the rescue team then I'll catch up with you. We'll forget about processing the exercise for tonight – we'll do it in the morning. For now, get some rest and I'll see you all later. I'll let you know if and when they find him.'

This must be one of those incidents the military refer to as collateral damage, she thought, settling into her seat for her return to civilization.

CHAPTER TWO

Os DORAN, CLOSE protection security consultant, turned onto final and the deafening silence from the rear seat told him at the very least they were not going to die. He was learning to fly gliders. Today it was not about *flying* them—he was already reasonably good at this, today it was about *landing* them, an entirely different matter. Maybe this is something of a metaphor for life, one only gets one chance at it.

He rolled out of his turn six-hundred feet above the ground instead of where his instructor told him he should be—three hundred. His turn was well-coordinated; it was just that damned height! He extended the airbrakes fully and worked the elevator—up and down, up and down. The nose followed and his speed control went all to hell: instead of his planned forty-five knots, theirs fluctuated from a little too fast fifty to a much too fast seventy.

He kept the brakes fully open and struggled with the speed. He closed them to half when they were twenty feet above the grass and was able to get their speed down to something near fifty-five knots—more or less. Still no sound from behind him. They hit the ground with a resounding thud that did no damage other than to his now quite fragile ego. They rolled to a stop and the right wing dropped slowly to the ground.

Finally, a quiet response from the back seat: 'That wasn't a landing – that was an *arrival*.'

Os said nothing.

They climbed out, pushed the glider to the edge of the runway and waited for the tractor to retrieve them.

His instructor smiled a fatherly sort of smile: 'Great flight except for that last little bit at the very end. Couple more weeks and you'll be ready to go off on your own.'

Os smiled a sonly sort of smile: 'Must try harder.'

Theirs was the last flight of the day. Along with the rest of the fliers, they stowed the gliders and the tug aircraft in the hanger, rolled the big doors shut then walked to the clubhouse to talk about what a great day it had been. The duty pilot stationed herself at the end of the long table to collect flying fees. Some arranged themselves around the table to update their logbooks and others propped up the small bar; pouring coffee or tea, or sipping pints of lager. Many munched on crisps or chocolate bars.

Os sat next to Amanda Stover. He closed his logbook and smiled at her: 'How'd your flying go today, Mandy?'

'First spins, Ossie. Wow!'

'Thought you were gonna die, didn't you?'

'Yeah. Didn't, as you can see, but still scary.'

'Keep at it. Before long they'll get to be fun.'

'Don't know about that. How'd you get on?'

'Flying's coming along okay. Landings still suck big time.'

'Keep at it. Before long they'll get to be fun.'

This banter continued. He shifted uncomfortably on his chair, took a deep breath and turned to face her more directly. His pupils dilated slightly: 'Hungry? I know a pub not too far from here that serves great food.'

'I think that'd be nice,' she smiled as her pupils dilated too and she let out a breath of her own. Some elements of human behaviour are universal.

The Brindle Cow had made the transition from a pie and a pint pub to a restaurant for anybody wanting a quiet, intimate meal. The owners kept the exposed-beam ceiling, working fireplace, wood panelling, age-stained pitch pine floor and most of the original brass fittings but not the fruit machines. They installed no high intensity down lights or television screen the size of a barn door; patrons had to be satisfied with quiet music, either jazz or blues according to the whim of the landlord on the day. Although it was a great place for a first date—or any other date, for that matter—at first neither Amanda nor Os considered whether this meal was a first date or something else.

The conversation through their ordering and starters went well; they discussed gliding in general, spins and landings in particular and attributes of the perfect instructor. Just before their main courses awkward pauses began sneaking into the conversation; it was then both their nonverbals suggested this was, indeed, something like a first date.

Os finished his venison terrine then carefully aligned his knife and fork on his plate. This took a long time: 'So, tell me, what sparked your interest in gliders?'

She finished her deep-fried mushrooms then carefully aligned *her* knife and fork on her plate. This took even more time—talking about flying gliders without mentioning either Bill, her husband, or her two daughters. Her answer was as awkward as his question: 'Well, I decided finally I was ready for some *me* time. And what about you?'

When it was time for pudding and coffee, neither knew any more about the other, although there were many comments about the excellence of the food, the nice music and the ambiance.

Os thought it was time to up the ante: 'I hope you don't mind me asking – er – but I think I can see just the hint of an absent ring on your left hand. Does this mean there used to be a *Mister* Stover?'

Her shoulders tightened and her face reddened, then she relaxed and smiled the tiniest of smiles. Goodness, men are such wimps; I've been waiting for this question for about three-quarters of an hour now: 'Widow. Two years last month.'

'Sorry.'

'No. It's okay. It's the first time I've been asked about it – by a guy, I mean. Really. It's okay.'

'I'm a good listener – if and when –'

'Not ready to talk about it – not just yet.'

She shifted, her pupils dilated and her smile broadened: 'And what about you? Is there? – I mean *was* there? – oh God – this is all going to hell, isn't it?'

They sat back and laughed. The ice had been well and truly broken. They ate their puddings and drank their coffees. Os paid for their meal and they walked to their cars. Amanda fished her keys from her bag.

He opened her door and she climbed in. Their hands brushed: 'Thank you for a very lovely meal, Mister Doran.'

'And thank you for your very pleasant company, Missus Stover. See you next weekend.'

'See you next weekend.'

They waved to each other as they drove out of the car park. Some elements of human behaviour are universal.

A few fliers are at the airfield every weekend, Saturday and Sunday, from the time the gliders are trundled out onto the line to the time they are safely stowed at sunset—winter and summer, rain or shine, windy or quiet. Some fly only occasionally. It is a matter of commitment to the sport; some just want to fly more often than others. Amanda and Os fell somewhere between these two extremes.

Three weeks after their first non-date Os soloed on a Sunday when Amanda was not there to celebrate with him. The week after on a Saturday Amanda managed her first full, three-turn spin from entry to recovery with no assistance from her instructor and when Os was not there to celebrate with her.

Throughout the summer on days when they both flew, they ended it with a meal at the Brindle Cow. Towards the end of the summer Amanda soloed too and they became good friends. These evenings ended as their first except for the gradual progression from that initial, almost accidental brushing of hands and the vaguely-felt tingle accompanying it to a reasonably solid peck on the cheek. Nothing more, and it was enough. It was enough for her because it was as much as she could accept at the time and it was enough for him because he sensed it was enough for her. No need for any commitments—no pressure.

Amanda's assumption before that summer was Commandos and Special Forces men were huge and heavily built—like the bouncers one sees at nightclub doors. This was not the case with Os: at five feet ten and with a slim, wiry build, what set him apart was an intensity, a presence and a taciturn inner strength that manifest itself as supreme confidence with no hint of arrogance.

This became clear one night when they were leaving the pub. Two hoodies appeared when they were near her car, one on either side of them, waving what looked like the biggest knives in the world and demanding their car keys. She later said she had never in her life seen a forty-year-old man—or a man of any age, for that matter—move as fast as he did. His right hand flicked out like a striking snake, catching the right wrist of the yob to his left in a grip causing him to yelp in pain and drop his knife while Os' left hand grabbed his scrotum. In one swift, smooth, coordinated movement he raised him off the ground and pivoted around to his left, pushing her behind him as he turned, slamming the screaming hoodie's head into his mate's stomach. The two wannabe carjackers dropped in a heap; he grabbed both knives and flung them over a hedge far into a neighbouring paddock.

He bent down and whispered: 'If you ever try that again, I'll cut off your balls and feed them to you. Any questions? None? Good. I'm glad we've had this little chat. Bye!'

They drew back against a car, nodded and whimpered.

She touched his arm: 'Remind me never to get on your bad side.'

He turned to her, smiled and dusted off his hands in a clichéd gesture: 'Amateurs.'

He told her he spent sixteen years in the Army in the Special Forces, seeing duty in the First Gulf War, Bosnia and Kosovo then Iraq. He said little about these campaigns other than the Americans had better rations, better body armour and better showers. Following that he worked as a mercenary for a little while. He said nothing about this experience and with any mention of it he started moving into a faraway place where she sensed she could never follow. For the past four years he worked as a private security contractor doing close protection. There was never a Missus Doran although there were two engagements; the life of a career Special Force soldier places extraordinary demands on a relationship. He was learning to fly because it was something he always wanted to do.

⌘

She worked in a building society as deputy manager. Her two children, Louise and Anne, were eleven and nine. She told him nothing more about the circumstances of her husband's death. Following two dreadful years, happy memories of their time together were now gradually replacing the continual thoughts of grief and sadness.

At thirty-four she was in the full bloom of womanhood. She exuded that profound sexuality accompanying fecundity—five feet five, deep auburn hair, flashing brown eyes, a wicked smile. She was bubbly and beautiful, and friendship was fine; he could wait. They sometimes laid stretched side-by-side on the grass next to the runway on sunny afternoons watching gliders take off and land, and, thoughts of flying forgotten, talk for hours about almost anything.

One afternoon during one of these discussions he looked at her and totally out of context asked another one of those, 'Men are such wimps!' questions she anticipated for weeks: 'So, when am I going to get to meet these girls?'

How about next weekend?' she responded—question with a question. 'They've been asking when Mummy is going to take them flying. We could spend the day together.' She had thought this through in advance.

The Sunday went well for all. The girls enjoyed their flights with a total absence of fear children of their ages possess: there were no, 'But I'm afraid of heights!' or 'But it has no engine!' or 'But what if the wind dies?' comments many grown-ups make before their first flights. After flying they visited what was now their local.

The evening ended with Os' seeing them into her car. Without any pecks on cheeks, he shook Anne's and Louise's hands gently and gallantly, and wished the three a good night.

Amanda drove in silence for a few miles, finally responding to the mysterious whispering from the back seat: 'So, what do you think, girls – did you enjoy the day?'

'Is Ossie going to be our new daddy?' Anne asked — more fearlessness.

Amanda paused and concentrated on the road: 'No, darlin', Ossie isn't going to be your new daddy. Your daddy will always be your one and only daddy. No, sweetheart, Os is just a friend of Mummy's. We both like flying and after flying sometimes we like to go to the Brindle Cow for a meal. But we're just friends – honest.'

Anne blithely accepted this protest too much; Louise was not convinced. Until now Amanda avoided this question. Women can sometimes be wimps, too.

CHAPTER THREE

Winifred, now divisional Director, Paediatric Surgery and Specialist Medicine, St. Gildas Royal Infirmary, Manchester, was on target to become the youngest ever chair of the board of a large NHS Foundation Trust hospital—a career progression carefully crafted when she was at university and followed consistently until now. She never let anything interfere with it, certainly not this: over the past three months mortality rates for thoracic surgical procedures in her division were well above target. She needed answers before she submitted her quarterly performance reports.

She never failed to achieve any agreed objective on time and was never seen to lose at anything, no matter how mundane or trivial. Supporting this was an instinctive ability always to shift the blame for failure conveniently onto the shoulders of either someone threatening her next promotion or in the direction of a troublesome subordinate. Her primary tactic was her thoroughly unsentimental capability to reduce anybody who challenged her to a snivelling wreck with razor sharp sarcasm or, failing this, naked, shameless bullying. Her honours degree in Economics and Accounting included no courses in medicine or surgery but this never hampered her rapid ascendancy in the organization.

But this situation was extraordinary: this was not some silly administrative error, the failure of somebody working for her to deliver a thoroughly meaningless report on time or somebody's lack of compliance with a minuscule budget allocation, this was a routine surgical procedure inexplicably gone wrong. Responsible individuals identified, blame apportioned, appropriately mawkish apologies offered to grieving parents, lessons learned; it was time to schedule a meeting.

Winifred never entered a room to chair a meeting, she arrived. Although everyone around the conference table was on the same level as she within the formal organization or subordinate by only one tier, everything communicated clearly she was in control. It was *her* meeting: matrix management writ large.

She bustled through the door at precisely the scheduled time and pushed it shut behind her without breaking stride—its closing just short of a slam. The seat of power at the end of the table farthest from the door was vacant and awaited her. She sat down, flipped open her folio, looked at everyone around the table and held eye contact with each in sequence until they looked away. It was a full minute before she spoke. Machiavelli would have applauded.

'Ladies and gentlemen, just what the fuck is happening here?' to the Divisional Director of Anaesthetics/Theatres/Critical Care, the Deputy Chief Nurse, the Head of Quality, the Deputy Director of Workforce, the Head of Education and Training, the Head of Theatre and Post-Op Nursing, and the Chief Pathologist.

People shifted in their seats, papers rustled on the polished hard-wood, bottles of water were opened and glasses filled. Nobody spoke.

'PS and ASD, for Christ's sake, we're losing patients to pulmonary stenoses and atrial septal defects – routine stuff – twenty, thirty minutes on the pump – two, maybe three hours skin-to-skin and we're losing them! We've lost five in the last quarter – one more than the whole of last year. Just what the hell's going on?'

Silence still and minimal eye contact.

'Who's screwing up? Cardiology? Pre-op? Anaesthesia? Perfusionist? Post-op? Just who the hell is killing these patients?'

She nodded to the Pathologist: 'Doctor Sharma?'

He opened a manila folder, touching his right index finger to the bridge of his glasses, raised them slightly and swallowed twice. He read in a monotone without looking at her: 'Complete post mortem results indicate death in all five of these cases was caused by massive hypervolemia resulting in acute hyponatraemia followed by the onset of rapid, irreversible cerebral oedema. In every case the severity of the defect was fully consistent with pre-op diagnosis. There is no indication the surgical procedures themselves contributed materially to mortality.'

He closed the folder and looked at her with the same lack of passion expressed in his reading.

'Thank you, Doctor Sharma. So – the cause of this massive hypervolemia?'

'My guess is –'

'*Guess?*' She looked around the table then settled again on him. 'You think the parents are going to be satisfied with a *guess*? You think when the press get hold of this I can placate them with a *guess*? "Well, ladies and gentlemen, we've called this press conference to announce that we have absolutely no idea who's been murdering the little children who come to us for life-saving surgery, but we *guess* –?"'

She paused with the timing of a master of stand-up comedy, slapping the table with each word: '*Who – the – fuck – is – killing – our – patients?*'

She straightened her shoulders, placed her palms on the table at either side of her folio, raised her eyes to stare directly at the ornately-framed photograph of Florence

Nightingale hanging on the wall facing her then ceased all movement except quiet, measured breathing.

Silence: no papers shuffled, no water poured, no water sipped. After an appropriate pause, the Head of Theatre and Post-Op Nursing spoke: 'The most likely cause of hypervolemia post-op in a heart patient is infusion with water rather than isotonic fluid and the most likely cause of *massive* hypervolemia is the pump was primed with water instead of Hartmann's.'

'Are you telling me, Gillian, the bloody perfusionist filled his bloody heart-lung machine with bloody water instead of Hartmann's and killed five of our patients?'

'No, Winifred, I'm suggesting in the absence of any other information, that is the most likely cause. Whether he accidentally or deliberately primed his machine with water instead of CSL is a question we can't answer sitting here and –'

'Why the hell would he do *that*? Christ he's been doing this job for what – at least eight years now? What kind of screw-up are we talking about here? Was he just not paying attention? Is he going through his fucking mid-life crisis? Is he turning into some kind of serial killer? Is he doing his Beverley Allitt impersonation?

'Doctor Sharma, is this hypothesis consistent with your findings?'

'Yes, Winifred, it's highly likely.'

'Any other possible causes?'

'The anaesthetist's, recovery room's or intensive care's drips are possible causes but based on the volumes involved they're not likely.'

She looked around the table: 'Does anybody here have anything else to offer?'

The Deputy Chief Nurse raised a timid hand: 'I've known Bill Stover for the entire time he's worked here and under the assumption Doctor Sharma's conclusions are correct, I'd bet my life that he neither made a mistake as monumental as this one or did he do this deliberately. There must be something else. I think –'

Now there was no basis for anybody's doing any more *thinking*; she knew the cause and the person responsible: 'This meeting is adjourned,'

She turned to the Deputy Director of Workforce: 'Jeffery, I'll want to suspend Stover until this matter is cleared up, but not just yet. I'll need to think about the timing of it for now.'

She closed her folio with a slap and left the room.

CHAPTER FOUR

HE PUSHED INTO Amanda's opening front doorway: 'Trevor LaFarge of the *Manchester Evening Gazette* –'

She shrieked, shoved him away and slammed the door then threw both bolts. She screamed—a scream of pain and rage, and collapsed in a heap with her back to the door. She sat for five minutes, then jumped up and ran, locking the kitchen door, closing and locking every window, drawing every curtain; halting her two-year journey out of darkness and in an instant returning to the afternoon when two detectives arrived informing her of her husband's death.

She made two calls when her shaking subsided, the first to the building society. She apologized to her workmates and told them an emergency with the girls meant she needed to stay home for the day. The second call was to Os.

'What I'm doing right now can wait. I'll be there in about half an hour. Sit tight.'

He opened the letterbox flap and called to her. She let him in and he hugged her tightly then led her to the sofa: 'Need a coffee or a cup of tea?'

'Coffee would be nice. Instant will have to do. I've never really learned to work that fancy –' and she started crying again.

'I'll figure out how it works. You look like you need *real* coffee, instant just won't do.' He patted her gently on the shoulder.

She heard the coffee maker gurgling as he walked back into the room. Her eyes filled with tears again: 'Bill loved his coffee.'

He sat down next to her and took both her hands in his: 'Okay. Easy does it. Tell me about it.'

She shuddered. For the first time, she talked with him about Bill and his work: about how he loved what he did with a passion sometimes making her jealous. She expressed her bitterness and hatred for everybody involved from his boss to the reporters and tabloid editors, squeezing his hands and hammering them against her thighs in rhythm to the wrongs she described. She blamed the surgeons for not defending him; convinced, as was Bill, the problem was with the IV fluids; he had not made mistakes; they hounded him to death for something he simply did not do.

When she paused he stood up and returned with two coffees: 'Right. Tell me about what happened today.'

Suddenly: 'Trevor LaFarge! I know him! He was the one who stood up at the press conference and asked if Bill had been arrested. Until then nobody had mentioned him by name.'

'Sounds a lot like managed news to me. It happens all the time, especially with politicians. Somebody wants to leak something or blame somebody for something, so they prime a reporter to ask a leading question during a press conference. Never mind that for now. You sit tight and take it easy. Be your old self when the girls come in from school. I'll have a chat with Madame LaFarge. I can promise you he'll not trouble you again.'

'A bit like the hoodies?'

'A bit like the hoodies.'

They drank their coffee in silence. He stood up: 'There's an almost full pot of coffee there for you. Next time I'm here I'll show you how to work the machine. I'll see you soon.'

He kissed her on the cheek. They hugged; he left.

A brief trawl of the internet led Os to Trevor: where he worked, his home address and mobile number. Just after sundown he parked his car across from his flat. He decided a surprise meeting in his front room would maximize impact, so he picked the lock on the front door and went in, found a cold soda in the fridge, sat down comfortably on the sofa and waited. Much of good security work is waiting and watching, and Os was very good at security work, ready to wait all night.

Trevor opened the door and switched on the lights at nine-thirty. He looked amazingly calm seeing a stranger in his front room sipping a soda in the dark: 'So, who are you and what do you want?'

'Draw the curtains and sit down, asshole. We need to talk.'

Trevor stood perfectly still.

Os sat up straight on the edge of the sofa and motioned him to a cheap, imitation Barcelona chair in black opposite: 'I said, "Sit down, asshole!" What bit of that didn't you understand?'

Whether it was from total surprise or because of something in Os' voice suggesting he was somebody to be taken seriously, Trevor complied. His calmness looked to be ebbing but he still managed to display a little dignity: 'So – who are you and exactly what do you want?'

'You paid a visit to a woman named Amanda Stover this morning?'

'I never discuss stories I'm working on and, anyway, what's it got to do with you?'

'Amanda Stover's a good friend of mine – a very, *very* good friend – and I want you to stay far, far away from her.'

'But – let's suppose I was thinking about doing a story on Amanda Stover and just suppose you were a very good friend of hers, I still don't see why this is any business of yours.'

'I can see you're not getting my message. I guess I'm not explaining myself very well.'

Trevor, leaning back uncomfortably in his reclining chair looking up as Os stood, towering over him: 'Okay, okay. No problem. I'm off her case. Promise.'

'Right, let me put it this way. I'm in constant contact with the lady and even more so since today. Whatever is her business you just made *my* business. You don't know me and you don't want to know me.'

He stepped even closer: 'Now – to make my point clearly.'

He reached down and squeezed a nerve point in his shoulder. Trevor screamed, then: 'Okay, okay!' as he rubbed his aching shoulder.

'Thank you for seeing things my way. I'll let myself out. You must hope you never see me again because when people upset my friends I get angry. Don't make me angry – any angrier than I already am. You've probably heard it before, but you wouldn't like me when I'm angry. Goodnight, Mister LaFarge.'

He drove home and rang Amanda. He told her about his meeting and, despite his warning Trevor off, he might contact her again: 'I'll keep an eye on him to see whether he behaves himself or not. I doubt it. In the meantime, hang in there.'

He almost said: 'Kiss the girls for me.'

CHAPTER FIVE

TREVOR PICKED UP his mobile and punched in a speed-dial number for his contact with the Greater Manchester Police: 'Hello, Detective Sergeant Quinn.'

'Hello, Trevor. What can I do – off the record, naturally, for better relations between the Great British Gutter Press and the GMP?'

'Flattery will get you everywhere – off the record, naturally. I need a favour.'

'Shoot. Well, sorry – that's usually in poor taste on my patch. What you want?'

'I need some information on a truly scary guy I found in my flat this evening.'

'Well, to start with you're going to have to give me more to go on than "truly scary". What's this guy look like, what was he doing in your flat and why, exactly, should I give a shit?'

'Remember that Stover case a couple of years ago?'

'Yeah, I remember. The hospital tried to blame it on Stover but he denied everything. To tell the truth, there wasn't one shred of evidence linking him to those deaths. Poor chap killed himself. What's this truly scary guy got to do with it?'

'I went around to talk to his widow. Follow-up piece, you know. She went ballistic, slammed the door on me, knocked me down the bloody steps, screaming like a banshee. When I came home tonight this dickhead's sitting in my lounge telling me to keep away from her. I don't know what his connection is but I think he means business.'

'You still haven't told me what you want from me.'

'See if you can track this guy down. Let me know who he is. Maybe CCTV of his car driving away, car reg, you know the kind of thing and –'

'Tall, short, black, white, heavy, skinny, well-dressed, hoodie? Give me some help here.'

Trevor described Os in as much detail as he could recall beyond 'truly scary' and the time he left the flat. Quinn told him to leave it with him and he would check him out when he had some time, probably within the next couple of days. Trevor's describing him as 'well over six feet with the build of a heavyweight boxer' helped Quinn's investigation not at all.

He decided to stay away from Amanda Stover until he knew more about Os. He was genuinely impressed this man found him so quickly.

Quinn asked him a few more questions about his visitor: 'From what you've told me he might be either military or ex-military – maybe high end security work. I'll check out the usual suspects who live or work in this area starting with the obviously limited description you've given me. He's probably just a friend of Stover's widow – I can't see her hiring a mechanic to scare you off. When I come up with some names I'll ring you and you can come around a look at a few photos we have on file. In the meantime, it'd probably be wise for you to back off until we know who this guy really is.'

'Thanks, Quinn. My thoughts exactly. Appreciate your help.'

CHAPTER SIX

Os WANTED TO help now he knew the story behind Bill's death—at least from Amanda's perspective. His close protection work for celebrities, politicians and a few high profile people in the business world helped him understand some of the pain Amanda and Bill experienced. Some celebrities court paparazzi, even giving them advanced notice of the time they are leaving that quiet, out-of-the-way, intimate restaurant in the early hours, but most want to get on with their lives with as little interference as possible.

Os felt ordinary people—whatever that meant—should be left alone. Freedom of the press considered, there was no public interest in long-lens photographs covering several inside pages of tabloids of the two girls in a schoolyard as had happened with the Stover family. It was a violation of person at least on the scale of one's being burgled or mugged and yet it was well within the law. It was time to kick some well-deserved ass.

He rang a nerdy and brilliant computer whiz: Brian—two Ps—Snapp and arranged a meeting. He wanted help to find out as much as he could about Bill's death. In the time he had known Amanda, he watched her move slowly out from behind the walls she built around her and the girls—protection from the big, bad world. And he had seen her snap swiftly behind these walls the instant Trevor knocked on her door. Did Os love her? Probably. Was she a friend in need? Definitely.

What he wanted to do was not just to move her back out from behind these walls but help her get to a place where she would never have to think about further retreat: to give, in the words of the current cliché, 'closure'. To help her he needed to understand fully the circumstances and for this he needed first to know the players. This is where Brian could help him.

There is an aphorism one can make a connection between oneself and anybody in the world with a maximum of six links. So when Os' sister received her Duke of Edinburgh Award from The Man himself, Os' links to, for example, Mao Zedong might look like this: his sister to Prince Philip to The Queen to Winston Churchill to Joseph Stalin to Chairman Mao. What he had in mind was to start with the names he already had on his list: Amanda, Bill, Winifred and Trevor, then with Brian's help and this amazing linking device known as the World Wide Web, start making connections.

These connections are buried deep within myriad computer systems intrinsic to the fabric of twenty-first century life—internet searches, websites visited, extant emails, forgotten emails, files deleted from hard drives, files *not* deleted from hard drives, file copies of letters, minutes of meetings, diary entries, airline and hotel bookings, train journeys, car services, wine purchases, visits to GPs and Casualty departments, and credits and debits to various accounts.

Brian was an expert: a hacker extraordinaire, capable of uncovering this hidden information. Starting with nothing more than a name, even just a surname, he could expose a trail through, as he called it, 'the luminescent aether' few others could follow. But he possessed a further skill just as important for Os and this was his ability to cover his *own* tracks. Just as users leave trails, so do hackers, but not Brian; when asked about this, his recurring comments were either: 'This won't hurt did it?' or: 'I'll be out before you know I'm in.'

In addition to his being the paradigm hacker, he was also a talented programmer. He developed an application that married traffic and content analysis to artificial intelligence and used a spider to trawl the 'net looking for subtle connections between seemingly unrelated data. He called it *Proust V1.0* and it relieved him of much of the tedious attention needed to make sense of the huge number of bits, bytes and pixels burning up his aether every nanosecond of the day.

They met at the 'I of Providence', an internet café on Portland Street near the Britannia Hotel in Manchester. Brian was his usual, chubby-faced, grinning, manic self and his dress sense had not improved. Other than their being about two inches too long and generously baggy, his dark blue cotton trousers were unremarkable. This is where 'unremarkable' ceased. The shirt was a garish mixture of colours, either Ocean Pacific—vintage seventies—or Hawaiian; Os was not sure. Except for the tails hanging out and the collar, the rest of it was concealed under a jumper that was a leftover from a fifties *Bisto* poster or something he received from an old auntie for Christmas.

The nerd pack in his left shirt pocket, filled to capacity with pencils, gel pens and a stylus or two—in prelapsarian days it likely would have included a slide rule—pushed the left side of his jumper out as though he was harbouring some alien parasite ready to burst from his chest and take over the world. The hippie sandals were cool except for the white socks. He needed a haircut and his facial hair was too long to be designer stubble and too short to be a beard. His attaché case, black plastic with bright red handle and latches, looked like something carried by a mobile hairdresser.

'So Ossie long time no see as they say how's everything going these days in the close protection security business? whoops! guess I'm not supposed to mention that in public am I? well heck let's just start again so long time no see how's everything going these days?'

'Hello, Brian. I see you've stopped taking the tablets again.'

'Not funny not funny those tablets really helped and anyhow I've been off them for almost a year now and – heck it's nice to see you what can I do to help?'

Os looked around the crowded space; not sure whether the patrons of this busy place were staring at them because of Brian's tailoring or his mad repartee: 'Let's grab a coffee and go somewhere more private.'

They ordered takeaway lattes and carried them across to Piccadilly Gardens where they found a quiet bench. Brian opened his case and pulled out a Samsung Netbook. While he was waiting for it to boot up he sipped his latte and whistled and hummed. His right heel moved up and down like he was driving a treadle-operated sewing machine. Os tried hard to ignore this knee vibrating at the periphery of his vision.

Brian hit a couple of keys: 'Right oh inscrutable one tell me what you need.'

He typed while Os talked. He paused occasionally to ask a question but otherwise his chubby fingers flew over the small keyboard like lightning.

When Os finished he waited a few seconds until Brian paused: 'Let me ask you a question.'

'Yep?'

'If you're so good at hacking, I have to assume there are at least a few others in the world as good as you are –'

'Let me interrupt you right there big guy *almost* as good.'

'Well, okay, *almost* as good. Sorry. So what's to stop them from hacking into *your* computer and finding this stuff you've just entered?'

'Good question Ossie good question the answer is I never connect this baby to the internet if I want to upload anything to the 'net I take just what I need from this machine and copy it to my PC on a removable hard drive and go from there once a year I copy everything I think's important to new hard drives burn all the old ones throw them in the canal and start over.'

'Wouldn't it be simpler just to install a firewall?'

'Another good question but as you've heard me say I can get through any firewall in existence and if I can so can maybe one of those guys who's almost as good as me so at the end of the day firewalls are useless except for guys like you who don't know much about computers sorry but that's life I mean some guys like you are very good at killing people with one finger but not very good with computers whereas guys like me are very good with computers but totally useless when it comes to killing people with one finger ¿Qué?'

'Yeah, reckon that makes sense. So now – I've given you everything I can think of to get you started. Is this a good place to meet when you have something?'

'Yep this is just fine coffee's great give me a couple of days I'll ring you.'

They said their goodbyes. Brian closed his Netbook, put it in his case and started walking towards Piccadilly Station; Os hailed a taxi to take him back to his office. By the time he reached it he decided he would tell Amanda nothing about what he was doing until either he was convinced he had totally quashed any interest by Trevor in her or her story or until events made it necessary she be told.

He sat in his office thinking about what he wanted to do next. It might be useful to spend some time in the library looking through newspapers for the months they were investigating under the assumption even well into the twenty-first century not everything had been digitized; maybe he could help Brian by providing some good old fashioned paper support.

CHAPTER SEVEN

TREVOR SAT AT his desk trying to come up with a creative explanation for his source of information for a hot story he was working on. His source was not that at all, rather a series of hacked text messages between a local MP and his mistress. Quinn rang to suggest he come in to look at some photos. He logged off his PC, left the usual, thoroughly inaccurate and meaningless sticky note on his keyboard and drove to the station.

Now books of mug shots have been consigned to the dustbin of history; Quinn sat him in front of a monitor and brought up a series of images of 'truly scary men' 'about fortyish, dark hair with just a hint of grey, six feet to six feet four, broad shoulders, angular face, unsmiling'. Trevor naturally was not able to identify Os Doran. He did, however, identify one who 'looked a little like him', not definite but maybe; perhaps it was the intensity of the non-smile.

Trevor nodded and Quinn whistled: 'Not good news, my friend, not good news at all. His name is George Barr, well, that's the name we know him by, whether it's his birth name or an AKA is still in some doubt. He's a loner – not connected directly with any crime families or gangs in the area. We think he's been responsible for at least three contract killings over as many years but nothing's stuck, not enough evidence – no witnesses willing to testify – you know the story. There are some indications he's worked as a mercenary in central Africa but, again, nothing concrete. My advice is you walk away from this one. Seriously.'

'Seriously?'

'Yep. Messing with this man could get you killed and from what we know, it might take you a couple of days to die. Your description as "scary" is right on the mark. Go home. Forget about this Stover case. Forget about any follow-up story. Think about taking a nice, long holiday – go to the South of France and work on your novel or something. Change your name, move to Canada or New Zealand or someplace, have plastic surgery – anything but messing with this guy!'

Trevor, highly motivated investigative reporter, decided to ignore Quinn's advice. He went back to his office, finished the article on the MP and his mistress, submitted it to his editor, updated the sticky note on his keyboard then went to a neighbourhood where at least a few pub landlords might be able to tell him more about George Barr than had DS Quinn.

CHAPTER EIGHT

Os SIGNED INTO Manchester Central Library, St Peters Square, opened his folio for inspection by the people on the desk then walked to the newspapers archive section. He filled out requisition slips for papers he wanted to look at—national and local, broadsheet and tabloid. Several digital microfiches arrived a few minutes later. He located a viewer, loaded in the first fiche, settled comfortably with his open notebook and went to work.

Good security work is about being able to predict what might happen—what potential adversaries are planning. Only by being able to anticipate what *might* happen can one prepare, and this preparation must go well beyond the obvious; it must include, as far as possible, the unobvious. It must begin with accurate information about the adversary. If Os were hoping to stop Trevor LaFarge and anybody else bothering Amanda ever again, his work needed to be built on a sound understanding of these people, whoever they were—what they were capable of and their likely actions.

He looked at photos, scanned lurid headlines, read text carefully and worked through various papers and sequences of articles from Winifred's first press conference to Bill's suicide. He recorded reporters' names and dates of publication, everyone who offered evidence at the coroner's inquest, surgeons and remarks by anybody who commented on the affair in print. He found references to IV fluids but neither names of suppliers nor their spokespersons although he was confident Brian could easily fill in these blanks.

He made detailed notes, particularly the sequences of various articles and comments. When he finished he was convinced, as was Amanda, whatever happened, Bill was not at fault; through all the information in front of him there was nothing any rational person could describe as 'evidence'. He was not ready to agree with her the IV fluids had been mis-labelled, but he thought this likely. What he expected next was Brian's help to support his contention with emails to and from various parties, and perhaps file copies of letters, phone logs and diary entries—potentially incriminating waste lurking undeleted in the electronic trash bins of the new millennium.

Os owned a house on quiet, tree-lined Hawthorne Lane in Wilmslow he used variously as a bolt hole, safe house and base for operations he was not keen for anybody to know about. He set up one bedroom as an incident room where he could spread out his notes and draw flowcharts and record the results of solo brainstorming sessions on a huge whiteboard. His communications systems consisted of a cardboard box full of pay-as-you-go mobile phones with unregistered sim cards, and a couple of encrypting satellite telephones even the folks at Chelmsford, Digby, Vauxhall Cross and Fort Meade knew nothing about.

The internet connection linking his PC to the rest of the world used software routing all his traffic through an encrypted network of dedicated servers displaying the server's IP address on the Log Files rather than his. He could create fictitious IP addresses and locations, and change these at will.

He spent two hours organizing his notes then rang Amanda and asked about coming around for a little chat: 'As I said earlier, I don't know whether we've heard the last of Mister LaFarge, but my guess is he'll try to contact you again – people like him don't just go away. I have a couple of things I want you to think about.'

'Why don't you come around for tea? Spaghetti Bolognaise okay?'

'Spaghetti Bolognaise's just fine. I'll bring some wine.'

'Great. See you in about an hour if that's okay.'

'See you then.'

He pulled two mobile phones from the cardboard box and drove to the Stover residence.

The four of them enjoyed a leisurely meal followed by real coffee—Amanda had learned to work the machine—and the usual family film. When the girls were tucked up for the night, the two of them sat side-by-side on the sofa.

'Right, Ossie Doran, you've been your regular great-to-be-around self this evening but a little quieter than usual. Mind telling me what's going on?'

'I think you're probably going to hear more from LaFarge or some of his friends and if and when that happens then I'll see to it. In the meantime, until we know something about the ifs and whens, there are some things you can do to prepare – some things to make it just a little harder for him to surprise you.'

'But how can I prepare if I don't know what's going to happen?'

'Good question. Remember, this is what I do for a living – keeping ne'er-do-wells off balance. Granted I don't think he's out to do you any more harm, he's just thoroughly annoying. But you've had enough thoroughly annoying in your life over these two years and you don't need any more. He doesn't yet know the meaning of thoroughly annoying.

'Here's what I want you to do over the next few weeks. I want you to stop using your landline for outgoing calls and screen all incoming calls through voicemail. You and I – and your mum – will communicate using these pay-as-you-go mobiles, turning them on only at pre-arranged times and always turning them off when not in use.

'When we go flying we fly the same weekends and travel together in my car. We don't send emails to each other or to anybody else – we text with these new mobiles. If I think *these* have been hacked, we burn them and pay another visit to the cardboard box. You and your mum vary your routes for school runs.

'And – finally – I'll follow you randomly when you drive anywhere, and I'll spend time, also at random, parked outside your houses.'

He sat back: 'Any questions?'

'Not really. It's just –'

'Just what?'

'Well, it's just – it doesn't seem fair. This man totally destroyed my life once and now he's doing it again! Why should *I* have to disrupt *my* life when he's the one who gets paid for messing me about?'

'Not fair. You're absolutely right. But I can assure you it won't last forever. Once I get my hands on him –'

'Okay. Enough self-pity. Wanna go flying next weekend?'

'Great idea.'

He looked at his watch: 'Time for me to go. Busy, busy, busy. You know how it is – the work of a close protection security consultant is never done.'

They stood up together and held hands—for the first time tightly—when they walked to the front door. He turned to her and she slammed him back against the door and thrust herself against him. A peck on the cheek was clearly not part of her plan.

He whispered: 'I have a better idea for next weekend if you're interested. Instead of going flying, how would you like a couple of days in London? You could use the break.'

'I think that's a wonderful idea.'

They kissed again and she ground against him even harder: 'I hope you'll be bringing your friend. I think it's time for me to meet him.'

'Yes, he'll be there. I call him "Mister Happy".'

CHAPTER NINE

Winifred went back to her office after her meeting with Doctor Sharma and the others, consulted a small notebook secreted in one of the inner pockets of her attaché case then picked up her phone. She would not entrust this message to the post or even email.

When her party responded she said: 'We have a problem.'

CHAPTER TEN

THE SENIOR SURGEON spoke to Bill without turning from his work: 'Let's go on bypass.'

Bill unclamped the venous line and adjusted the flow, then: 'We're on bypass.'

Venous blood returning to the heart from the body through two major veins, the superior and inferior venae cavae now flowed into cannulae inserted in these veins then into flexible plastic tubing leading to a reservoir mounted on Bill's pump console. From the reservoir it flowed into an oxygenator where, as in the lungs, adding oxygen and removing carbon dioxide turned it from venous into arterial blood. A roller pump returned it to the patient through more plastic tubing; here it re-entered the patient's body through another cannula inserted in the femoral artery. It coursed 'backwards' up the descending aorta and the aortic arch as far as the aortic valve. During its ascent it streamed from this major artery into the entire arterial system, delivering oxygen to the body.

The heart-lung machine is an amazing creation of the human mind. Pundits refer to it simply as 'the pump'. It replaces a patient's heart and lungs during operations so surgeons can make repairs to the heart or surrounding major blood vessels. On bypass these major organs are isolated completely from the patient's cardiovascular system while the pump maintains full blood flow to the entire body, but especially to the brain that cannot survive without irreparable damage if deprived of oxygen for more than about three minutes.

Apart from more effective oxygenation technology and some electronic gadgetry, this machine has changed very little since it began to see service in operating theatres in the late fifties and early sixties in the last century. And the one element unchanged over these sixty years is the perfusionist, sometimes referred to as the 'pump technician', sometimes as the 'heart-lung machine operator' and sometimes most grandly as an 'extracorporeal circulation technician'. Although surrounded very closely by a dozen of the most thoroughly competent individuals regularly gathered in one room and totally committed to their joint work, his job is one of the loneliest in the world.

Bill changed into scrubs at six forty-five in the morning on a typical workday and trundled the console and perfusion system into the operating theatre. There is nothing impressive or even vaguely interesting about the console other than to the uninitiated—a stainless steel box on wheels comprising roller pumps, a few switches, dials and gauges.

He positioned the console out of the way of people going about their various duties. Then he set the perfusion system—clearly more impressive than the console—on top of it. The perfusion system is a thoroughly complicated assembly of mostly transparent plastic components in various sizes and shapes, some enclosing bits of arcana relevant to their functions. Flexible, clear plastic tubing, part of it concealed within sterile wrappers, joins all these components.

Bill primed his machine with one and one-half litres of an isotonic fluid: Hartmann's solution, sometimes called 'CSL'. He removed a unit of CSL from a supply cabinet and recorded the batch number in his notebook. Before he emptied this unit into the reservoir, he held up both the unit and the entry in his notebook for inspection by the circulating nurse. After she confirmed the information he recorded agreed with the information on the label, he transferred the solution to the machine. The nurse repeated this confirmation for all three units. By now surgeons had entered the theatre, were gowned and gloved, arranged themselves at the table and began the operation.

He moved the pump to directly behind the senior surgeon then arranged a stool, sat down comfortably, turned on the oxygen and one of the pumps circulating fluid through the machine then noted the level in the reservoir.

Now his workday truly began. He quietly said to the senior surgeon: 'We're ready to go on bypass,' then sat back and waited until they were ready.

Later the surgeon turned to him: 'We're ready for the lines.'

Bill reached for the one part of this system still enshrouded in a sterile wrapper, opened it and carefully exposed a coil of plastic tubing with fluid coursing through it. The surgeon manoeuvred it up and onto the table with no danger to the integrity of the sterile field. Bill placed a clamp on the venous line and sat back again. He said nothing; he was asked no questions.

It was a simple as this: from the time the surgeon ordered him to go on bypass until the patient came off, anywhere from ten minutes to eight hours according to the severity of the defect and the nature of the repair, he sat silently attending his machine. He and his machine were a unit with one aim: to maintain the patient's blood pressure and volume. And despite the apparent complexity of this mass of gleaming stainless steel, pumps, plastic gadgets and tubing, he achieved this doing nothing more than maintaining the fluid level in the reservoir by making minor adjustments to the speed of the roller pumps. He might have opted for an electronic monitoring system to do this automatically but preferred to do it manually, arguing this kept him alert.

Later the surgeon spoke, again without looking away from the field: 'Let's come off bypass.'

Bill clamped the venous line: 'We're off bypass.'

When they were satisfied the heart was functioning normally, they removed the lines and handed them back to him. He wheeled the pump into the corridor, took a break then began the rest of his work for the day.

This was as important although more mundane. He took the pump back to his workroom, drained the system, disassembled the unit and discarded the plastic parts. Then he moved to a small clean room where he assembled a complete, new system comprising disposable sterile components and plastic tubing. He checked this assembly carefully to ensure it was in order for the next operation, clearly as critical to the patient's safety and recovery if not quite so spectacular as activities in the theatre.

Work as a perfusionist suited the introspective, unassertive to the point of timidity, left-brained Bill Stover, able to focus fiercely on the job at hand—totally immune from any distraction and with meticulous attention to detail. His work was his life—other than reading, occasional hill walking and time with his family. He was a thorough romantic and each time they successfully repaired a serious heart defect in a baby sent away to live a long and normal life, he was moved. Entered the theatre at a quarter to seven in the morning, he knew not whether he would leave the hospital at two-thirty in the afternoon or midnight. He liked it this way. He was very good at his job. He loved his work and he never made mistakes.

CHAPTER ELEVEN

Arnold Hohenzollar, salesman, Sutton Millhouse Medical Products and Winifred's contact there, looked at her with an awkward fusion of a wink and a leer: 'So, Winnie, just what's so serious a problem we can't deal with it by phone or email?'

They met in a small coffee shop on Carthusian Street near the Barbican the day after her meeting with Doctor Sharma and the others. She was attending a one-day conference on the implications of medical ethics for non-medical hospital staff.

They ordered their skinny lattes, exchanged a few pleasantries then got down to business.

She hated being addressed as 'Winnie' but accepted it graciously from anybody capable of regularly handing her brown envelopes stuffed with cash: 'Contaminated IV fluids or, more to the point, incorrectly labelled IV fluids and, specifically, sterile water labelled as Hartmann's. Any possibility this is happening?'

He had tried to bed her so far without success but had not given up all hope. He shifted uncomfortably, studied his latte intensely, fiddled with his spoon then looked back to her: 'Well, yeah, I suppose it's *possible*. Why the concern?'

'It looks like our pump technician might have infused several patients with water accidentally. We've lost five we shouldn't have in recent months. Based on his work habits, it's likely he didn't screw up. So – Arnold – did you or didn't you?'

'Wow! Yeah – well – we've tagged some water with CSL, Ringer's and NSS labels accidentally. Only a few units got out of the factory. We were able to recall most of them on the QT but I guess you *might* have ended up with a few.'

'For Christ's sake why didn't you let me know? I *might* have had a few? How many are a *few*? Ten, a hundred, five hundred, a fucking thousand, how many? My stats for this quarter are looking like crap! I'm not a happy camper – not by a long shot.'

He played with his spoon some more then moved on to a serviette, quickly turning it into not very imaginative origami: 'Hell, it's just a tempest in a teacup. Maybe a thousand – maximum two. No harm done. I didn't say anything because I thought it would blow over –'

'And now I'm stuck with a big pile of it! Old buddy, if I'd wanted to shovel other people's shit for a living I'd have gone to work for those people who empty septic tanks.'

'No problem – not really. There's absolutely nothing written down – no paper trail. Although we can estimate a window, even *we* don't know the batch numbers or the exact total. Stonewall it. Hell's fire, *you* didn't do anything wrong. This isn't *your* fault. Just ignore it. Blame it on the technician. Who's to know?'

She sipped her coffee: 'Yeah, I suppose that'll do. Blame it on him – poor son of a bitch. Nobody's going to take his word over mine and, anyhow, he can't *prove* he didn't do it. Problem solved.'

She went back for the afternoon session. The next speaker's address was titled, *Maintaining appropriate relationships between buyers and vendors: not just the letter of the law but the spirit also*. The day had turned out fine after all.

The dynamics of hospital operations are complex. Here, perhaps more than in any other organization is the distinction between the formal and informal so profound.

From the start of the twentieth century practitioners considered the ideal structure for business organizations growing bigger and more complex. The obvious model was the military with strict chains of command, orders issued by individuals to subordinates and each person at each level receiving these orders from one and only one superior

But this was cumbersome. They thought there must be a better model and devised many, all based on the assumption an individual could receive orders from different superiors according to the nature of the order. The result was mass confusion and a model that never worked very well. Originally it was described as 'functional management' and although the principle remained the same, many imaginative name changes through the years never resulted in anything that worked any better.

This is the way hospitals are organized: nurses, technicians and others working with patients are responsible to their line managers for all things relating to administration but they take orders for patient care from medical doctors and surgeons.

Bill's line manager was Patricia Borochek, Head Nurse, Paediatric Surgery and Specialist Medicine and her boss was Winifred. Patricia was responsible for signing his time sheets, agreeing his holiday requests, assuring his attendance at training courses, completing his annual assessments and approving petty cash vouchers he submitted.

But for everything connected with the operation of his heart-lung machine he reported to the surgeons he supported. If they decided he should attend a conference or a training course, he did so, although expenses were paid from the budget managed by Winifred. If they decided he should be supported by an assistant or awarded a pay rise, it happened. If they decided he should be replaced, it was done immediately.

Herein is the fundamental difference between acute care hospitals and other organizations. To answer the question about whether Bill primed his pump with the wrong solution, within the context of the hospital organization, it was not an issue of good practice, it was a matter of responsibility to the Trust Board: it was a question addressed by administrators and not medical practitioners. To whom was he accountable? to the surgeons from whom he took direction within the theatre, naturally, but beyond this, to Patricia? Jeffery Coyle, the Deputy Director of Workforce? Bharat Patel, the Head of Quality? or Winifred? The formal organization chart decreed he was responsible to all these managers. But the dynamics of the informal organization ordained his responsibility was to the one wielding the most influence and power outside the operating theatre: Winifred.

Backhanders are standard within many industries involving specialized equipment and materials. Procurement contracts are costly for equipment produced in small quantities with high manufacturing costs like heart-lung machines and aircraft carriers, and for supplies low in cost but consumed in high volumes like intravenous fluids and bullets. In either case, large amounts of money are involved.

One assumes buyers purchase first according to specification then price: several vendors submit tenders all to specification and the rational buyer selects the vendor offering the lowest price. This is a reasonable assumption in an ideal world; in the real world it is often different. Customers write specifications deliverable by ideally just one vendor or, at most, a few. The preferred tender is accepted, naturally. The vendor pays a generous commission to the salesperson who brokered the sale who then returns a portion of it to the person who wrote the specification. Both parties benefit at the expense of the customer, in this case the hospital patient or as is more likely the government agency paying the bill. Everybody involved is happy with this arrangement except the end user who is ignorant of the whole process but nevertheless pays handsomely for it.

Winifred was one of the members of the committee writing specifications for most of the specialized purchases made by St. Gildas Royal Infirmary and, as with many other negotiations she was party to, results were usually according to her wishes.

The annual contract for the hospital's entire range of sterile intravenous solutions was awarded to SMMP, had been for the seven preceding years and was likely for the following year. Winifred and Arnold were benefiting nicely from this and were keen to see this relationship continue for a long time.

CHAPTER TWELVE

W‌INIFRED SUMMONED THE Deputy Director of Workforce to her office the next morning: 'Right, Jeffery, I want Bill Stover off site immediately, suspended without pay and all his records pertaining to operations collected and brought to my office. After I've had time to digest all this, I'll want to speak to him later this afternoon, I'll text him, but in the meantime I don't want him anywhere near a patient. I want him out of this bloody building!'

Jeffery thought about arguing this action was premature but decided against it. His aim was to get out of the room and her presence quickly. He nodded his assent: 'Yes, I'll see to it immediately.'

He went deep into the bowels of the building where all the equipment and supplies needed to keep St. Gildas Royal Infirmary running smoothly were prepared, stepped through the door into Bill's workroom and without any greeting began the conversation with an abrupt: 'Bill, we need to talk.'

'Oh, hi, Jeffery. Wow! This sounds serious, what can I do for you?'

'This *is* serious, Bill. I'm not really sure how to explain it. Sit down.'

Bill wheeled the perfusion unit he was checking to one side, pulled a stool from under a work counter, settled on it and motioned Jeffery to the chair at his desk: 'Can't be *that* bad, Jeff. Sit down.'

Jeffery shook his head then paced back and forth in the narrow space between them. He did not explain anything: 'I've just come from a meeting with Winifred and she's instructed me to suspend you without pay and order you off hospital premises immediately.'

Bill stared at him and was silent for a few seconds. He lifted his hands and shrugged his shoulders; he smiled. He thought this must be either a monumental misunderstanding or an elaborate practical joke. He assumed the latter: 'Not me, man. I'm the most well-behaved guy in the whole of the universe. I pay my taxes, I vote regularly, I don't fiddle my expenses, I'm nice to my kids and dog, I don't even hardly ever beat my wife –'

'Listen – will you please just listen!'

'Yeah, okay. You've got my attention and now you've got me worried. Tell me.'

Jeffery did *not* tell him: 'You are to be suspended immediately without pay and you are not to come onto hospital property until further notice. I have been asked to remove all your notebooks and take them to her office. She'll want to meet with you this afternoon to tell you what happens next. Keep your mobile close by, she'll text you –'

'What the hell's going on?'

'I can't say any more. Winifred'll tell you and –'

'But what about my work? We have a full schedule for next week and I have a lot of work –'

'She'll handle all that. I don't know. All I know is I have my orders –'

'But, Christ, why is this happening? What's –'

'Please. I can't tell you anymore. I can't help you. You'll find out about it later when she –'

He jumped up; the stool teetered then clattered to the floor. He ripped his jacket from the hook on the back of the door so violently the loop on which it was hanging tore, stuffed his mobile phone and pen into his pockets, and walked out the door leaving the perfusion unit only half checked.

Jeffery looked through cabinets and desk drawers, collected what he assumed were the appropriate records and notebooks, closed the workroom door then delivered these materials to Winifred's office and informed her PA it had been done. Fifteen minutes elapsed since he entered Bill's workroom.

A thoroughly bewildered Bill stomped out the hospital's main entrance door with his head down and his shoulders slumped; his feet hit the pavement hard, moving at a pace that was almost a run. He navigated the horseshoe-shaped forecourt then crossed the car park, dodging visitors and staff along the way. As he neared the street he slowed to a normal pace.

What to do now? I can't go home yet, Amanda'll know something's wrong. He did what he always did when he needed to do some critical thinking, he headed for the nearest coffee shop. He ordered a large cappuccino and a huge slice of carrot cake then located a small table at the back in the quietest corner he could find.

He ate the cake and drank some coffee. Ever the optimist—he was the paradigm glass half-full guy, he concluded when he met Winifred, whatever the misunderstanding, it would be corrected and he could go back to work. End of story. He planned to hang around the coffee shop until he went home at a reasonable time, spend as routine an evening as was possible with his family under the circumstances, tell them he was looking at a really heavy day tomorrow, kiss them all goodnight, go to bed, arise early and go to work. Problem solved. Neither Mandy nor the girls would need to know; he would be back on the job by the end of his workday. Whatever cheery face he could assume at home would do.

His phone buzzed and he read Winifred's text to come to her office at two-thirty for a meeting. He ordered another cappuccino.

CHAPTER THIRTEEN

WINIFRED ORDERED BILL, when he came in for their meeting, to enter the hospital through the main entrance, sign in as a visitor—complete with temporary name tag hung on tape around his neck—and come directly to her office without going to the canteen, gift shop, locker room, his workroom or anywhere else. He was to speak to no one before their meeting. He complied.

She was what most people describe as 'street smart'. Some people spend hours studying manuals on body language and non-verbal signals. They learn how to read these broadcast by others and they practise sending controlled ones of their own for all their face-to-face encounters. For Winifred these skills came naturally. She knew instinctively when to terrify somebody from the moment of confrontation or instead to charm the unfortunate individual until she could move in for the kill. She chose the latter tactic for this meeting.

He walked up to her PA's desk at two twenty-five: 'Hello, Vanessa,' he greeted her with the best smile he could muster under the circumstances.

She indicated, making only the most cursory eye contact and without speaking, he should sit next to a man who looked like he was selling something. A few minutes later Winifred opened her office door, walked over to the salesman, smiled, introduced herself and shook hands with him, ushering him into her office without a glance at Bill.

He picked up a magazine called *Health Care Management* from a low table and thumbed through it without finding anything interesting enough to distract him. Most of it seemed to be taken up with colourful and persuasive full-page advertisements for things hospital administrators must buy to make their hospitals world class.

At three forty-seven she opened her office door. In one smooth movement she ushered the salesman out of the office, spoke briefly to Vanessa, returned to her office and closed the door. Again she made no eye contact with Bill. He was merely annoyed by this treatment at first but as he waited he became more and more angry. He thought about confronting Vanessa or even walking across the room and knocking on Winifred's door then hesitated. He could wait if she could so he settled back in the chair and stared at the wall directly above Vanessa's head. Although she never looked at him, the more fiercely he stared the more she fidgeted; at least he was getting *her* attention if not Winifred's.

At four forty-one Winifred opened her door and nodded across the room for him to enter. She pointed towards a very low, upholstered armchair next to a coffee table, pulled a straight-backed wooden chair across from the small conference table and sat facing him. She looked down comfortably at him, he looked up uncomfortably at her. A stack of his notebooks occupied the centre of the table between them.

She stared at him for a few seconds then spoke gently, almost in a whisper—her voice was non-threatening: 'I have a problem, Bill, and I don't know what to do about it. I hope you can help.'

'Winifred, I don't have the faintest idea what you're talking about.'

'In the last quarter we've had five deaths from either pulmonary stenosis or atrial septal defect – one more death from these minor defects than all last year. Bill, how would you explain this?'

'Why me? Why are you asking me this when I'm not the expert? I'm a pump technician. I run the machine. I'm not a surgeon.'

'Well, you see, that's my problem. I *have* asked. Well, not the surgeons because they're out of town this week, but the pathologist. His expert conclusion is these patients were transfused with water instead of isotonic fluids.'

'I still don't see what this has to do with *me*.'

Her reply was even gentler, if this were possible: 'Doctor Sharma tells me the only way this could have happened is through your pump – you primed with water instead of CSL.'

He relaxed a little and his apprehension lessened. He kept accurate and complete records, he followed procedures rigorously, he never strayed from these, even under sometimes intense pressure in the theatre. Logical, left-brained Bill Stover was confident he was not part of this problem: his meticulous notebook entries would support his argument.

He glanced down at them: 'I prime my machine with Hartmann's solution. Every unit is recorded. Before I put it into the machine, I ask the circulating nurse, or somebody else if she's busy, to check the unit *and* my notebook entry. Occasionally the anaesthetist will pass me a syringe and ask me to infuse the contents into the reservoir. When this happens I also enter it in my notebook. I never deviate. I never take shortcuts. You know all this, Winifred – you've observed our pump cases. I never make mistakes!'

Her world view suggested by now he would be expressing the slightest hints of doubt but she saw none. It was time for her to apply more and slightly less gentle pressure: 'But do you expect me to believe you're right and Doctor Sharma's wrong? A moment ago you reminded me you're not a doctor, now you're trying to tell me you're right and the doctor is wrong.'

He picked up one of his notebooks and turned pages until he came to details for one of the cases they were discussing. He held it up to her: 'Look. Here are my entries with times and ticks to indicate the units were checked by somebody else.'

She looked at the entries for several seconds then back to him. As she spoke she leaned forward and, although still seated, began slowly invading his personal space. She deliberately moved closer to him than people in Western society consider reasonable—starting to threaten him: 'William Stover, you must have made a mistake. Either you accidentally primed your machine with water thinking it was CSL or you realized your mistake and falsified these entries. You fucked up!'

Bill sometimes commented he would never make it as a Ninja: he was not very good at handling unpleasant confrontations. But he made no mistakes—he was confident.

He looked directly at her: 'I *did not* make any mistakes. I *did not* prime my machine with water. *There has to be some other explanation!*'

'There is no other explanation.'

She leaned even closer and stared, expecting him to look away. He did not look away. For the first time in years, she broke eye contact before her opponent. It was a trick he learned during a training session, something she seemed not to be familiar with. It is almost impossible to maintain direct eye contact with another person for more than a few seconds, particularly during a disagreement. The ruse is to stare, not at the eyes but at the bridge of the nose. Even from the distance of only two feet, the difference is not apparent.

He leaned back and put the notebook down: 'I did *not* make a mistake.'

She sat back and was silent for a few seconds. She lost this battle but, as they say, not the war—she was still fully in control: 'Mister Stover. I am formally suspending you immediately and without pay. You are to refrain from entering any hospital premises, nor are you to try to speak with any hospital staff, managers or surgeons. You are not to have access to any of these records you maintained in your work. Due to the serious nature of this situation – the deaths of patients, it may be necessary for me to involve the police. I strongly suggest you consider retaining legal counsel immediately.'

She ushered him to the outer office, instructed Vanessa to ring for a security guard to escort him out of the building then ordered him to wait. Without looking at him again, she walked back into her office and closed the door.

As he stood waiting for his escort to arrive he felt he was the subject of some bizarre psychology experiment. During the first half of the twentieth century, researchers at universities across the Western world but mostly in France, Germany and America conducted a series of experiments designed to try to help them better understand the working of the human mind. Some were instructive, some merely interesting and some genuinely weird.

One involved a small group of undergraduate volunteers gathered in a room presumably to be part of a study on short-time memory. The researcher conducted a relaxed discussion and wrote a single digit number on the blackboard then erased it a few minutes later. Members of the group were asked to recall the number later during their discussion. All but one were told in advance to give an incorrect answer. That individual, as expected, answered correctly. It was not research into short-time memory, rather an experiment in group dynamics. The true aim was to observe the behaviour of group members as the one tried to convince the others they were wrong while they were to argue the contrary. Arguments were sometimes upsetting for individuals offering correct answers, particularly if they were unassertive or not comfortable with confrontation. The experiment was traumatic — potentially damaging to fragile psyches and had to be abandoned.

He was unsettled by his meeting with Winifred but still firmly convinced he was right and there was another explanation. He knew he was going to have to go home immediately and explain to Amanda what was happening. He was confident he would not need the services of a solicitor.

CHAPTER FOURTEEN

Winifred rode the lift down five floors to Bharat Patel's office after her meeting with Bill. Interesting, she thought, I can see a clear, statistically significant positive correlation between one's perceived status in the NHS and the floor on which one's office is located. His PA ushered her into his office immediately.

He did not look up but continued tapping his keyboard: 'Be with you in just a second, Winifred. Please sit down. Must get this done now while it's only a tiny bit overdue.'

He smiled, clicked his mouse a couple of times then looked at her. He, like Arnold, dreamed about one day taking her to bed: 'Hi. What can I do for you?'

'Hello, Bharat. I have a problem and I think you can help me.'

'Always ready to help any of our friends whose titles begins with "Divisional Director" –'

'This is important –'

'Of course, of course. What do you need?'

She reminded him of the discussions during their meeting two days before. With no reference to Bill, she said: 'In view of the sensitive nature of this matter and just to remove any possibility of contaminated or mislabelled IV fluids ending up in circulation, I think it would be wise for you to dispose of all units of sterile water, Hartmann's solution, lactated Ringer's and normal saline in the hospital and re-order. And to my thinking, the fewer people who know about this, the better. I can bury the costs without too much trouble. Ring Arnold at Sutton-Millhouse. He'll arrange to deliver replacement fluids immediately and remove our existing stock.'

'Yes, certainly I can see to it. Two questions, though, how soon and why – precisely?'

She leaned towards him and let her impressive décolleté take control of the meeting: 'In answer to your first question, as soon as possible. Today. Staff don't think anything unusual's happening when you suddenly recall supplies from the floor – in matters of quality, you do it all the time. And in answer to your second question, I think it best to keep this *totally* off the record because were there to be even the remotest possibility solutions had been contaminated, questions might be asked about your incoming inspection procedures and we wouldn't want that, would we?'

He shivered, moved his eyes from her breasts to her eyes, back to her breasts then to her eyes again: 'No, of course, we, indeed, would not want *that.*'

'Good. That's settled then? Thank you. I *know* you can take care of this.'

She stood up, winked at him and left his office. He shivered once more then rang Arnold.

One wins every battle and thus the war when long-term strategies are subsumed under solid tactics. This was Winifred's mantra. There is a possibility people of the British Isles would speak French today had Napoleon had at his elbow a tactician of her calibre. In addition to these skills, and her thoroughly intimidating body language and non-verbal signals, she was strikingly beautiful. She was five feet, nine inches tall with long, always carefully coiffed, natural blonde hair. She turned heads when she entered any room. These attributes were enhanced by tastefully scanty, extremely well-fitting underwear and *very* expensive, professionally-tailored clothes setting off her spectacular figure. Men she confronted were often reduced to trembling, mumbling ruins. When discussing her numerous assets one of Bill's male colleagues commented: 'Articulate speech is difficult when your tongue is hard.'

Women hated her.

She scurried through her outer office with a terse, 'No calls!' to Vanessa. She pulled a pay-as-you-go mobile phone from her attaché case, one of three she kept for calls such as this then consulted her little notebook: 'Hi, Trevor.'

'Hello, Winifred. It's always nice to hear from you.' He was in the queue not far behind Arnold and Bahrat, and so far with no better luck.

'This is an exclusive for you – but you *must* wait 'til Tuesday next to publish any of it. This will give you a little time to dig up some background filth.'

'Fire away.'

'Okay. On Tuesday I'm calling a press conference to inform the world we've experienced an unusually high number of deaths in our paediatric heart surgery unit. Sad – *very* sad. We've identified the cause and it turns out our senior perfusionist, a man named William Stover, is responsible either through deliberate malfeasance or gross negligence. In either case, he has been suspended until further notice and the police have been called in to investigate.'

'Dynamite stuff. Why wait 'til Tuesday?'

'You know how these things work. I need time to pull this all together and manage everybody here who's involved.'

'How do you want me to play this?'

'Play it any way you want just as long as you put the blame squarely on Stover and take all the pressure off the hospital. We didn't have anything to do with this, the hospital's not to blame, the surgeons aren't to blame. We'll naturally offer the standard contrite apologies – lessons will be learned, etcetera, etcetera, but I want St. Gildas' reputation to emerge unscathed. Capisce?'

'Yeah – capisce. No problem. Thanks for the tip. I owe you.'

'Of course you owe me, you twat – you *always* owe me!'

She gave him some details about Bill, his wife and children, his time at St. Gildas and the straightforward surgical procedures he made go horribly wrong. She rang two more tabloids and offered them the same exclusive.

She ordered Vanessa to bring her some coffee then pulled a textbook for theatre nurses from her bookcase describing the full range of congenital heart defects from the lesser such as patent ductus arteriosis to the most serious such as transposition of the great vessels, their symptoms, corrective surgical procedures and prognosis for survival to adulthood. She sipped her coffee while committing the information on pulmonary stenosis and atrial septal defect fully to memory then poured a second coffee and rang one of her contacts with the police.

CHAPTER FIFTEEN

BILL WALKED FROM the bus stop to their three bedroom, mid-terrace house still thinking the glass was half-full and still confident he could fix it. Winifred was a proper harridan but she was no match for the surgeons; when he was able to speak with them all could be explained. By the end of day Monday everything would be fine.

He worked irregular hours: sometimes three eighty hour weeks in a row followed by three of twenty. His monthly wage was level: he was not paid overtime but compensatory time off; even without his being paid beyond this suspension, he could manage all right without pay for a couple of weeks because he had enough hours banked to cover it—assuming, of course they paid him what they owed him to date. Tonight, though, he *must* tell Amanda. He was never good at hiding anything important from her for more than a few hours and certainly not for an entire weekend. He wondered whether it would be helpful to email Doctor Tournabel or might it be wiser to wait and speak with him directly on Monday.

He never walked through the door at the same time two days in a row but he never worked weekends: Saturday and Sunday were proper family time. He usually looked forward to these but he dreaded this one. He tried to make the evening as normal as possible. They found a family film on the telly, made up two big bowls of popcorn—toffee for Amanda and Louise, butter and salt for Anne and him. He expected to tell Amanda everything after the girls were in bed; convinced no matter how normal he tried to appear, within a minute after 'The End' flashed on the screen and the girls were tucked up, she would confront him with something like: 'What've you been up to?'

This is exactly what happened.

He told her about his conversations with Jeffery and Winifred, and reasserted his confidence all would be explained when he was able to discuss it with the surgeons on Monday. They would not tell the girls; daddy was sometimes available for the school run when cases were rescheduled at short notice.

CHAPTER SIXTEEN

DOCTOR ALEJANDRO TOURNABEL, Chief of Surgery and Senior Paediatric Thoracic Surgeon at the St. Gildas Royal Infirmary bounced into his office at six-thirty Monday morning fresh and tanned from his week-long conference in Houston, Texas, and ready to go to work.

He greeted his secretary with his usual cheery: 'Hi there, Molly, sweet Molly!' then stopped mid-bounce when he realized Molly was anything but sweet: 'Why the long face, Mollypet? I haven't been back long enough to give you any grief, have I?'

'No, doctor, but things are in a state. Miz Hyde-Davies has cancelled all your pump cases and suspended Bill Stover and –'

'Whoa – bummer! Reckon I'd better check this out with her, right now.' He turned and left the office almost as briskly as he had entered but with not quite so much bounce.

He sped past Vanessa's vacant desk and opened Winifred's door without knocking. She prepared well for the battle she knew was coming; he was expected.

'Right, Win; wanna tell me what the hell's going on here.'

'Oh, good morning to you, too, Alex,' she replied with the sarcasm used to unbalance anybody with significant power approaching her for a serious confrontation. Outside the office she was either 'Miz Hyde-Davies' or 'Winifred' and he was either 'Doctor Tournabel' or 'Alejandro', they were only 'Win' and 'Alex' to each other. Unlike Arnold, Bharat, and Trevor, he *had* succeeded in bedding her, clearly to his pleasure at the time but much to his dismay when he realized later blackmail was also one of her tactics. Missus Tournabel knew nothing about this and the good doctor was concerned to see it remained this way: 'Again, Win; what's going on?'

'This relates to the five PSs and ASDs we've lost in the past three months. Doctor Sharma puts it down to hypervolemia and the only reasonable cause is Stover primed his pump with water instead of Hartmann's.'

'I think you're talking out of your amazingly beautiful ass. Bill Stover doesn't make mistakes.'

'How else can you explain it?'

'I have no idea; I'd have to think about it but –'

'We *have* to account for it somehow. What do you suggest?'

This conversation continued; neither conceding any ground to the other. She finally succeeded in pushing through her proposal: 'Okay – here's what I want to do. We pull Stover out of the loop—just for a couple of weeks, mind you. Draft a technician in from University to cover your cases. Give me some time to investigate this fully. This'll also give me some time to prepare in case some grieving parents get to thinking too much about it. Before *that* happens I think we need to get the police –'

'The *police*?'

'Yes, the police. We need to pre-empt any action by the press. If we call the cops in before the press get wind, we'll have demonstrated we're taking this very, very seriously. Cover all bases. No stone unturned, etcetera, etcetera. You know the drill. And I think we need to call a press conference ourselves –'

'Yeah. But the *police*, the *press*?'

She had her way. He seconded a pump technician from the University Medical Centre and rearranged his surgery schedule for the next fortnight. She would call in the police later in the day and schedule a press conference for the next day. He also agreed it was better he should have absolutely no contact with Bill until this issue was resolved. After all, the reputations of the hospital *and* the surgical team were at stake.

CHAPTER SEVENTEEN

THE POLICE CAR parked on the street was unremarkable other than one seldom appeared in this quiet suburban neighbourhood. Bill stepped through the door to see two uniformed officers and a thoroughly traumatized Amanda. It was as one sees in film and television drama: he confirmed his name and where he worked, and although he was not under arrest he needed to accompany the officers to the station to help them with their enquiries. He was even helped into the back seat of the car with the stereotypical hand on top of his head. As he was led out the door, Amanda asked if she should contact a solicitor and he said he thought it might be a good idea.

In the interview room the traditional cassette tape recorder was absent, replaced by a camera with a winking red light mounted high in one corner. He assumed it recorded both video and audio. He was not searched or fingerprinted. During his initial processing he answered the obligatory questions: his name, age address, place of work, marital status and a few others. He refused to provide a DNA sample voluntarily and declined offers of tea, coffee or water.

He based his preparations on what he saw on TV. I'll ask no questions or volunteer any information, I'll answer with the absolute minimum number of words and if they want more they will have to ask for it. I must try my best not to lose my temper even if provoked.

Two men entered the room fifteen minutes later and introduced themselves as Detective Chief Inspector Singh and Detective Sergeant Quinn. I wonder which one is the good cop and which one is the bad cop, as they sat across the table from him. Maybe I've been watching *too* many films. DS Quinn frowned and said nothing while DCI Singh did all the talking. I guess Singh's the good cop.

He consulted a brown manila folder: 'Right, Mister Stover, do you know why you've been brought here?'

'Not really.'

'Absolutely no idea at all?'

'No. I asked the officers who brought me in but they refused to tell my anything other than that I needed to come in to help with your enquiries into some deaths at St. Gildas.'

'What can you tell us about the deaths of –' he consulted the notes in his folder and read off the names given him by, Bill assumed, Winifred, '– patients at the hospital where you work?'

'They were all patients who had open heart surgery.'

'The dates?'

'I'd have to consult my notes to give you the exact dates.'

'Anything unusual about these patients?'

'Not really. They all died, of course, but you already knew that.'

'Of course. My question is, was there, to your knowledge, anything unusual about the deaths of these five particular patients?'

'Not that I can tell you. You would have to ask the surgeons or the pathologist?'

'But do you have an opinion, Mister Stover?'

'No.'

The questioning continued with Bill offering no more than monosyllabic responses. He knew the DCI's covert aim and he was determined not to make references to heart-lung machines, priming fluids or hypervolemia. He doubted Singh knew much about heart-lung machines, priming fluids *or* hypervolemia and if he wanted to discuss these, he would have to ask. He did not ask; he decided to change tactics: 'You declined to volunteer a DNA sample. Can you please tell me why?'

'I have absolutely no idea why I'm being asked these questions about these deaths and I have absolutely no idea what my DNA has to do with anything relating to them.'

'But if you have nothing to hide, Mister Stover, why would you refuse this request?'

'It's precisely *because* I have nothing to hide that I'm refusing.'

Singh paused and fussed with the folio, opening then closing it. About now the good cop is going to ask the bad cop to lean on me. But, no, Singh continued with another change of tactics: 'According to your Divisional Director, Paediatric Surgery and Specialist Medicine, these patients shouldn't have died – their surgical procedures were quite straightforward and they all should have survived. Something must have gone wrong and we've been asked to investigate and find the cause. Even though you're not a surgeon, with the experience you have you must have some idea why –'

'And I've told you,' he interrupted, 'you're asking the wrong person –'

'– and I'm asking *you*.'

'And I've told you I can't help you.'

Singh decided he was wasting his time. The interview continued for two hours with nothing more being achieved. Throughout, Bill's behaviour, both verbal and non-verbal, was consistent with somebody who had nothing to hide. He *may* have made a mistake and he *may* have been careless but he certainly was not lying. Singh further assumed since he refused the DNA sample he would also refuse to volunteer for a polygraph; Singh did not trust polygraphs, anyhow.

'Okay, Mister Stover, we're going to terminate this interview for now. We'll make arrangements for a car to take you home. We may want to speak with you again in connection with this matter. Thank you very much for your cooperation.'

The two uniformed officers drove him home. He was pleased they did not speak; he was exhausted by the interview and had no interest in making small talk. He thought he handled the whole thing well. On the ride back he wondered what was going to happen next.

They turned the corner and he immediately knew what was happening next, but it was so far removed from his experience it felt more like a dream than reality. In front of his house at least two dozen photographers and reporters on the pavement blocked access to his driveway. They surrounded the car and snapped and flashed as it stopped. He saw no television set-up with video cameras, fur-covered microphones on the ends of long poles or satellite dishes on tops of vans; he assumed these were free-lancers looking for photos they could sell to the tabloids.

Was he annoyed by this intrusion? perhaps, but he was baffled. His confusion was about why all this interest was shown in him, only one member of an extensive team, and compounded by how these paparazzi—if that is what they were—found out about his trip to the police station and the origins of the incident causing this in the first place.

The two officers exited the car and moved to the rear nearside door where he was sitting. The photographers crowded around—jostling each other none too gently for position but the officers pushed them aside and escorted Bill towards his front door. He looked straight ahead until they crossed the threshold and slammed the door in their faces. Amanda grabbed him and they hugged tightly for what seemed like a full minute.

She had been crying: 'What's happening, Bill? I don't understand what's happening, Bill.'

'We'll talk about it later, sweetheart. We need to make some plans for getting the girls home from school,' he said as he turned to the officer he assumed was the senior of the two.

He nodded in return and with some obvious sympathy said: 'Close your curtains. Don't open your front door. Don't answer your phone. If you must go out, ring for a taxi to come around to the back. If you have relatives nearby go and spend the night there. They'll hang around for several hours if they think they'll see some activity but otherwise they'll get bored and go looking for greener pastures.'

Anger replaced helplessness. Amanda sensed the tension rising in him and squeezed his hand tightly before he exploded. He calmed down but his 'thank you' to the officer was perfunctory bordering on rude. The policeman had nothing to do with his predicament but he was ready to strike out at anybody who came near. The officer stepped out and they slammed and locked the door. They ran through the house ensuring every door and window was closed and locked, and curtains were drawn. The knocking continued.

Bill switched the telephone to voicemail: 'We'll use mobiles for the next few days. Right now I think we should do as he suggested. Pack a couple of cases and take a taxi to collect the girls then go to your mother's at least for tonight. They must be real idiots if they think we're going to answer that!'

He led her up to their bedroom and for a few minutes they sat on the bed and held each other without speaking then: 'Right, Mandy – sweetheart, time to get moving. Ring your mum then ring for a taxi. I'll try to explain what I think's happening on the way to school. We'll make up some story for the girls. I just hope these bastards haven't found their way over there, too.'

Amanda said nothing as she picked up her mobile to make her calls.

They packed cases for themselves and the girls, and carried them down to the kitchen. Amanda pulled the door curtain aside to look for their taxi and screamed at the face looking back at her. The camera flashed; she dropped the curtain.

Bill stepped to the utility cupboard and pulled out a galvanized bucket: 'Right. I've had just about enough of this shit!'

He moved to the sink, filled the bucket with hot water, moved back to the door and nodded to her to open it. She drew back the Yale lock and yanked the door open. He doused three very surprised paparazzi with water hot enough to get their attention but not hot enough to do any permanent damage. They screamed; she slammed and locked the door. For the first time since he came back from the police station she smiled. They heard the muffled voice of a clearly *very* angry photographer: 'I'm suing you for assault and grievous bodily harm! I'm going to the police! I'm going to the European Court of Human Rights'

'Go ahead, you fucking moron, call anybody you like!' He seldom swore in front of Amanda, *never* in front of the girls and never used the 'F' word in their hearing. He peeked through a gap in the curtain and concluded they all had either given up and gone elsewhere or at least moved around to the front of the house.

Their taxi arrived a few minutes later and nobody disturbed them while they loaded their cases in the boot. Bill kept looking behind them on the way to school to see if they were being followed by any motorbikes changing lanes recklessly with pillion riders taking pictures. He did not see any.

They held hands tightly. Bill thought carefully about what he wanted to say—something totally inane such as, 'I have absolutely no idea what's going on,' would not do; he had thought and said this too many times already. He tried to put his left brain to work and try another approach: 'Right, sweetheart, let me take you through this from the beginning.

'Over the past three months or so we've lost five kiddies we shouldn't have. They didn't die on the table but all within about one day post-op. This is highly unusual because deaths from these conditions are extremely rare.'

'But, darlin', I don't see what this has to do with you.'

'I'm coming to that, Mandykins. I'm coming to that.

'Sometimes patients just die and there's no obvious explanation. Once in a while, for example, for some unexplained reason – nobody knows why – the instant the anaesthetist puts the mask on the little guy's face, he arrests.'

'But I *still* don't see what this has to do with *you*.'

'Well, this time the pathologist concluded they died because their IVs contained water instead of something called "isotonic fluid". It's kinda complicated to explain so we'll just leave it at that. Somebody made five mistakes and these resulted in five deaths.'

'And they think it was *you*!?'

'They think it was me.'

'And why do they think it was you?'

There the loop was closed and Bill was back to: 'I have absolutely no idea.'

They arrived at the school, having decided they would tell the girls Daddy had a few days off and they were going to have a little holiday at Nana Shirley's house even though Nana Shirley only lived about fifteen miles from their home. They collected the girls and Bill continued to look around for paparazzi but saw no suspicious-looking characters lurking about in the bushes. Anne and Louise were variously happy about a visit to their Nana's and disappointed they would still have to go to school every day. They never thought to question why they were travelling by taxi and not in their own car. Bill told Amanda he would wait until later to retrieve their car in the dark of night.

When they were finally settled for the night—Anne on the sofa in the living room, Louise in the conservatory, and Amanda and Bill in the guest bedroom—they resumed their conversation. Amanda put aside the magazine she was not reading: 'Right, Doctor Stover, what else can you tell me? What did they do with you at the police station?'

'I've been thinking a lot about this – well, hell, I *would*, wouldn't I? – and whichever way I go I keep coming back to the same conclusion.'

'And that is, my sweet?'

'Either some serial killer sneaked into ICU in the middle of the night and pumped a unit of water into each of these – possible, I guess, but not likely with our CCTV system and seriously competent security guards, or the units I hung up were mis-labelled.'

'That possible?'

'Possible, I guess. I supposed it's happened a few times in the history of the world.'

'But why blame it on you?'

'Well, hell, Mandy, they have to blame it on somebody. They can't just shrug their shoulders and say, "Shit happens," and let it go at that. You know how these things work: muck flows downhill and stops with people like me at the lower end of the food chain.'

'Whoa, big fella. Whoa! Sounds like my daughters' hero, the greatest daddy in the whole universe is feeling sorry for himself and given up the fight. Stop right there, pardner! Nobody, but nobody, messes with my man! Think, just think – where do we go from here?'

They thought about their options and decided to try to contact Doctor Tournabel in the morning despite Winifred's orders on the contrary. They did not sleep very well.

CHAPTER EIGHTEEN

BILL RETURNED FROM taking the girls to school in the morning and an agitated Amanda met him on the doorstep: 'I have bad news – well, it's probably bad news.'

'Oh, yeah?'

'I've just heard on the news the hospital has called a live press conference at nine-fifteen.'

'So where you get this "probably' shit," white man? It's bad news for Christ's sake! You know they're going to blame it on me. I can't bloody win, can I?'

'Let's just wait and see what they have to say.'

They poured coffees and arranged themselves in front of the television. Following brief reports concerning the worsening situation in the Middle East, an earthquake in Turkey and a visit of the Deputy Prime Minister to a pasty factory in Cornwall, the presenter announced they were going to a press conference at the St. Gildas Royal Infirmary in Manchester. The cameras went to live feed: Alejandro, Winifred and Singh filing solemnly into the room crossing in front of a huge St. Gildas logo prominently displayed on a blue background. They manoeuvred behind a table covered with linen in the same shade of blue on which three microphones stood. Cameras snapped and flashed as the three sat and Winifred, in the centre, picked up a sheet of paper containing her notes: 'Ladies and gentlemen, we've called this press conference to announce progress in our investigation into the unexplained deaths of five of our paediatric surgery patients. I'll have a brief statement then we'll entertain questions.

'Over the past three months five of the little children – tiny, tiny babies – who come to us from all over the country for life-saving surgery have died in mysterious circumstances. While you are correct in assuming that no open heart surgical procedure is minor or routine under any circumstances, procedures carried out on these five assume risks much lower than for many others. In short, these five should not have died! We are naturally saddened by these deaths and our hearts go out to their grieving parents.

'On Friday last I ordered an investigation into these unexplained deaths in order to determine the cause and learn lessons so this need never happen again. Now I'd like to ask Doctor Alejandro Tournabel, our Chief of Surgery and Senior Paediatric Thoracic Surgeon to explain to you what we think has caused these unfortunate deaths and whether they could have been prevented. Doctor Tournabel?'

'Thank you, Miz Hyde-Davies. I shan't go into all the technical details surrounding these sad deaths. What I *can* tell you is we are confident they were caused by the infusion of the wrong intravenous solution, either accidentally or deliberately by a person or persons yet unknown. To this end, we have asked the police to investigate and we have offered our full and complete cooperation to identify and prosecute the person or persons responsible. Now I think DCI Daljeet Singh would like to tell you about progress he and his team have made in their investigation. Detective Chief Inspector?'

'Thank you Doctor Tournabel. As you can appreciate we are in the very early stages of our investigation. We are examining paper records including diaries, notebooks, logbooks and other relevant documents. We are conducting a thorough analysis of telephone records, emails and, naturally, information stored on computer hard drives. Finally we will be interviewing a number of individuals – hospital employees – whom we think may be able to help us with our enquiries. Miz Hyde-Davies?'

'Thank you, DCI Singh. Now we are prepared to take your questions.'

She only acknowledged those reporters she was confident would enable her to manage carefully this information flowing live into viewers' bedrooms, living rooms and kitchens. In the beginning, most questions addressed technical minutiae then they moved on to congenital heart defects and the special problems related to performing surgery on children. The theme gradually shifted to the specific details connected with the wrong IV solutions.

When she decided the time was right, she looked across the room then nodded: 'Yes, Trevor?'

'Trevor LaFarge, *Manchester Evening Gazette*. Is it true you have arrested one William Stover, a perfusionist in your paediatric surgery unit and charged him with deliberately tampering with the IV solutions Doctor Tournabel is referring to?'

'While it is true DCI Singh has questioned one hospital employee as part of this investigation, at this time I am not prepared to name that individual, nor can I confirm any details such as whether he has been arrested. Further I cannot confirm whether the police are interested in questioning anyone else in connection with this particular line of enquiry. Thank you very much, ladies and gentlemen. We will schedule further press conferences as our investigations yield more information.'

All three stood up and turned as the questioning continued and the multitude of cameras snapped and flashed them out of the room.

'Oh, Bill,' said Amanda.

'Oh, shit!' said Bill, '*now* I know what's happening – now I know, "Why *me*?" Hardly worth a call to Tournabel now, though – better just talk to a solicitor.'

CHAPTER NINETEEN

BILL AND AMANDA trawled the internet looking for a solicitor. They had no experience—basing their decisions on the proximity of offices and the impressiveness of website homepages. They chose the first with whom they could get an appointment in the afternoon, prepared a list of questions they thought might be helpful, ate lunch, dressed and left for their meeting with Raeburn Chalmers, Solicitor.

'There is not really much I can do unless you are either arrested and charged with something or sued by grieving parents. Should this happen, I should be pleased to represent you. I can't prevent these actions by any sort of pre-emptive motions, restraining orders or injunctions. If and when your employment is terminated, I can represent you at a tribunal hearing. It's probably best if you don't try to contact anybody within the hospital.

'I can do nothing about harassment by reporters or paparazzi unless you're arrested or they inflict actual bodily harm on you, your wife or either of the girls. I can, of course, assist you in bringing charges against newspaper publishers if and when they published libellous or scurrilous articles about you or members of your family but this would only be resolved after years of litigation and many hundreds of thousands of pounds in costs.'

'So, in precise legal terminology, I'm fucked.'

'I'm afraid so.'

Human beings can sometimes come to terms with terrible things facing them when they can put names to them—the unknown becomes slightly less frightening even if still mostly unknown. For Bill everything at last made sense: he primed his pump with sterile water labelled as Hartmann's. There was no way he could prove this and watching the press conference convinced him Winifred had succeeded. Now he and Amanda could move forward and try to build a defence for the challenge they were facing.

They went back to the house determined to formulate a plan for whatever was coming. There were things to do. First, despite all advice on the contrary, Bill must contact Payroll to see about payment for his banked hours: they needed to pay the bills. Amanda would increase her work hours. Every evening he would take a taxi to their house to collect any post and check their voicemail for messages. Even though taxis would stretch their budget, by travelling alone and not in their own car they might reduce chances of reporters finding them and tracking them back to Shirley's house. Except for occasional grocery shopping and school runs, they would go dark, staying in the house. This was short-term. Surely within a few days somebody from the hospital would contact them to tell them what was to happen next.

He was picking up his mobile preparing to ring Payroll when it vibrated — a text message from Winifred ordering him to come to her office at two-thirty in the afternoon following the same procedure he used for his last visit. On the way to the hospital he came to two conclusions. First his career as a perfusionist, certainly at St. Gildas and probably everywhere else, was finished; he assumed when he came face-to-face with Winifred she would terminate his employment. Second, the closer he came to the hospital the angrier he became. But this was not preparatory to a rampant outburst, instead it was a hot, seething, well-controlled undercurrent.

Thus he arrived at the hospital and calmly walked through the main entrance ignoring the reception desk where he had been ordered to sign in as a visitor. He walked directly to the lift to Winifred's office, entered at two twenty-seven and walked straight to her door.

A startled Vanessa looked at him: 'Miz Hyde-Davies is not ready to see you yet, Mister Stover.'

'Fuck you, bitch,' he said coolly and gently. He opened Winifred's door without knocking.

'Ah, Mister Stover, how pleasant to see you. Please sit down, we have several matters to discuss.'

He did not sit down, he did not pace about. He stood perfectly still with his hands at his sides: 'Let's save the small talk and get right down to it. You've won, I've lost. It's as simple as that. I'm not sure what, exactly, is going to happen next but I *am* sure of one thing and that is that you've got your way. You and I are both fully aware I made no mistakes – the labels were wrong. But that doesn't matter now, there's absolutely no way I can prove that.'

'Correct, Mister Stover; I have, indeed, won. But then I'm sure you're aware I *always* win. You will, of course, be paid for all hours owed to date and any holiday time accrued. I've instructed Payroll to credit your account before close of day today. And, as you have anticipated, your employment with St. Gildas Royal Infirmary is formally terminated effective today. Under the circumstances it would be unwise for you to sue for any termination pay in lieu of notice. And, naturally, it is impossible for me or Doctor Tournabel to provide you with any kind of favourable reference. Should you wish, I can ask somebody from Security to accompany you if you need to remove any personal property from your locker or workroom. Other than that, I think we're finished here.'

'Not quite.'
'Oh?'

'One question, Winifred, one question – why me? Why have you chosen to dump this on me? You know I have always done my job to perfection. I've made no complaints, I've made no demands. I've never upset anybody. Why me?'

'I wouldn't expect you to understand any of this but the simple answer is it has nothing to do with *you* – it's nothing personal.'

'But what's it have to do with, then?'

'It has to do with the way society operates. When things go wrong people need to be able to blame somebody – people need scapegoats – people need acts of revenge directed not at the organization but at an individual.'

'So, I've been sacrificed for the greater good?'

'Well, put, Mister Stover, well put. Perhaps you *do* understand. You wouldn't expect *me* to shoulder the blame – or the hospital – or the surgeons – or the suppliers, would you, if there were another way?'

'But is there no such thing as honour or integrity? Is there no honest acceptance of responsibility?'

'Your silly sentimental view of the world has gotten you nowhere – *will* get you nowhere. Honour, integrity and the acceptance of responsibility get you nothing – nil – zip – nada. The only thing that matters is power – the power of gold, the power of subtle persuasion, the power of naked authority, the power of the gun. Do you really think these patients – these *children* – mean anything more to me than a means to my end – to my place in the grand scheme of things – to *my* power? It would make no difference to me whether the organization I headed made bricks or toilet rolls, fixed broken pushbikes or broken babies' hearts.'

He made no further appeals to any of the characteristics that in his world-view raised human beings above the rest of the animals on the planet.

He turned and she taunted him with one last insult: 'Try living in the real world for a change. At least try preparing your children to deal with reality somehow better than you have.'

He stepped across to an open shelf and picked up a magnificent twenty-centimetre Lalique Lotus vase in a pale shade of bluish green. He hefted it then tossed it back and forth between his hands several times. As he drew back his arm to throw it against a glass-fronted bookcase she said: 'That would cost you far more than the salary we owe you. You may want to think again.'

Without saying anything or looking at her, he put the vase down gently on the table and left her office closing the door quietly behind him. She was right, of course: even in this she alone held the power. He checked his current account balance at an ATM, confirming he had been paid what he was owed then left the building. Now he needed to be near his beloved Mandy more than he needed cappuccino or carrot cake, so he looked for a taxi.

When he arrived at Shirley's he told Amanda about his meeting with Winifred. He was too sad and angry to go into any detail—simply that he had lost his job with no appeal to possible reinstatement. They agreed for the moment they could achieve nothing by analysing any of it; they could make no meaningful plans for their future. They would just have to wait to see whether he was to be interviewed further by the police and how they were to be treated by the press. So, nothing more was to be said about it until something happened—or at least until morning.

⌘

The next morning Amanda said she would take the girls to school by taxi: 'While I'm gone, my darlin', maybe you should go out for a walk. Put on a silly hat and sun glasses so the paparazzi don't recognize you.'

'Not funny.'

'I'm serious. The walk'll do you good. Get out and get some fresh air. You like walking – you're always saying you do some of your best thinking when you're walking. Stray as far as you like, stay as long as you like. I'll be here when you get back.'

The taxi arrived, she kissed him goodbye and shepherded the girls into the car. He donned his disguise, closed the front door and went for a walk.

Walking turned out not to be very good advice. Passing a newsagent, he came face-to-face with himself. The photo was one taken when he climbed out of the police car after they drove him home. His face covered most of the A-board; he looked startled and very angry. 'DOCTOR DEATH!' screamed the headline, 'MORE PHOTOS INSIDE!' He picked up the tabloid and tore through the pages. What he found on page five was worse: a photo of Anne and Louise taken with a long telephoto lens. They were playing in the schoolyard with their friends and everything in the image had been carefully blurred except for their two faces, accentuated within clearly focussed circles. Here the three-column headline asked if these two were 'The Daughters of Doctor Death?' Finally, Bill acknowledged, the glass was half empty.

CHAPTER TWENTY

BILL ARRIVED AT school with the girls and saw the police car and two officers moving a gaggle of reporters to the far side of the street. Thank God for small favours. But this was no consolation for what happened next. Their head mistress approached the car before he finished helping then out.

She greeted Anne and Louise with a terse: 'Hello, girls,' she greeted him with an even more terse: 'Mister Stover, we have a problem we must address this morning.'

'Yes, Miss Gregg, how can I help?'

'I'm afraid I'm going to have to ask you to remove the girls from school from today.'

'And you've decided this because?'

'Because of all the disruption your – situation – is causing the other pupils –'

'My *situation*! What, pray tell, has – my *situation* – have to do with anything and what precisely is my *situation* anyhow?'

'Please don't make this awkward for me, Mister Stover. You know exactly what I mean.'

'No, Miss Gregg, I have no idea what you mean. Please explain it to me.'

'Your involvement with the murders of these five little children and –'

'Murders? *Murders*? For Christ's sake, Miss Gregg, what papers do you read?'

'Mister Stover – language, please!'

'Who's said anything about *murder*?'

'Well – the police –'

'The police have never said anything about murder.'

'But –'

'Okay, okay. Let's start again. Forget for the moment about the disruption you're talking about, what do *you* think? Forget for the moment you're a head mistress – what do *you* believe?'

'What I believe has absolutely nothing to do with this. This is about the safety of the children in my care and –'

'What you believe has *everything* to do with this. Hell's fire, woman –'

'But the other girls are starting to call your girls "Daughters of Doctor Death" and those reporters keep crowding around when they are in the playground and –'

'– and you do nothing to stop it? What about the safety of *my* girls? I thought with all the upset they're going through at least here at school things would go on as normal.'

'I'm sorry, Mister Stover, but I've made my decision. Perhaps when this is all over –'

'Yeah. Well, perhaps when this is all over, when they visit me in The Scrubs I can read stories to them.'

'I'm sorry; I'm really sorry.'

'Never mind. You're not sorry – not really. You've simply eliminated a little problem from your daily life and now you can get on with things as normal. Don't worry. You and your children are safe. Doctor Death and his daughters won't trouble you again.'

Hell is being subject to torment and not knowing how or when it will end. The convict being burned at the stake or suffering the death of a thousand cuts knows at some visceral level the excruciating pain will eventually end. The political prisoner or the victim of the Inquisition knows not when the torture will cease. This was Bill's conclusion in the weeks following his termination. Not only had their entire world been turned on its head, reporters and paparazzi hounded he and Amanda. They surrounded Shirley's house; they followed them everywhere they went, whether by car, taxi or bus; they congregated outside school and the building society; they knocked on the door at all hours, they phoned round the clock. A few even waited outside the family home apparently under the assumption a once-in-a-lifetime photo opportunity awaited when Bill arrived each night to collect the post.

Aside from the sometimes claustrophobic jostling and their concern about the long-term effect on the girls, it became almost something of a game. In the end it wasn't intrusions from a bunch of sad, obnoxious gits that created hell for them, it was the continual reminders of their collective feelings of helplessness: their complete lack of control over their lives and their total lack of knowledge of when—or *how*—it would end.

The location of their safe house was compromised so they moved back home, at least that would take some pressure off Shirley and she could have her house back. And moving home provided the girls with a little comfort, they would be in their bedrooms—their own little sanctuaries. Although the reporters were annoying, the family was getting used to having them around.

Initially Bill was enraged by what he read in the tabloid that published the photos and headline on the A-board, particularly those of the girls inside. He questioned whether it would be better to ignore them completely or read them all to see what the world of great British journalism was saying about them. He opted for the latter and each day purchased a copy of every paper in the shop carrying any information about events at the hospital. His collection was becoming impressive.

Now they ate breakfast together, Amanda took the bus to work, he drove the girls to school then collected his newspapers and went home to the empty house. At the end of the day the routine was reversed. They never went out together; Bill made midnight grocery runs to a nearby twenty-four-hour supermarket.

Their new routine worked until this Monday when Miss Gregg excluded them. Both girls sobbed while Bill belted them securely into their seats. Miss Gregg turned and walked towards the school entrance. They drove off past the two police officers and the gaggle of reporters; Bill thought about trying to say something light to cheer the girls up but he could think of nothing.

He drove to the newsagent's shop and found a parking space directly opposite the door. Because he could see them clearly while he collected his papers and paid, he left them in the car. He wanted to get them home quickly and concluded this would save time. He looked around and spotted no photographers when he entered the shop but within the two or three minutes spent collecting his papers and moving to the checkout they surrounded the car and started snapping pictures of the terrified girls.

Seething achieved nothing, he wanted their attention. He picked up a cigarette lighter and a tin of lighter fuel, and asked for a carrier bag for his purchases. He exited the shop and put his left arm through the handle of the bag. He approached the car with the uncapped tin in his right hand and the lighter in his left. One photographer turned towards him; Bill soaked the front of his jumper with lighter fuel and flicked the lighter into flame. The man jumped back and screamed. Bill smiled at him and whispered: 'If I ever see you near my family again, I'll set you on fire. Do you understand?'

'I'm calling the cops. This is illegal. You can't do this to me.'

'I've just done it, you fucking asshole. Call anybody you want. I'm past caring.'

'But you can't –'

'You still haven't answered my question, motherfucker,' he said even more gently as he squeezed the tin and sprayed his crotch: 'You wanna push me some more?'

The photographer jumped back: 'I'm cool, I'm cool. No problem.'

'Good. I'm glad we've had this little chat,' he smiled and looked to the others. 'You see, fellas, I'm having a really bad day – a really bad week, as a matter of fact. And when I have really bad days I get seriously angry and when I get seriously angry I tend to go a little crazy. Dare I say "*mad*"? yes – I think "mad" is the operative word. Now if you want to call the cops and complain about this, go right ahead. But I think it might be a much better idea if you all just went away.'

He bared his teeth and snarled like a dog, stepping towards the others, waving his fuel tin and flick, flick, flicking his lighter. He pivoted, ignited the lighter and directed a stream of flaming fuel at the brick wall next to the newsagent's shop. The photographers turned and trotted away. He climbed into the car and drove home.

 Earlier they sat the girls down and tried to explain as well as possible in seven and nine-year-old syntax what had happened to Daddy and why those silly people who publish newspapers were saying all those things we know aren't true and over the next few days – well – we're just going to have to put up with some bother by these photographers. If we just try to ignore them, in a little while they'll go away.

They hadn't gone away, if anything their presence was becoming more intrusive. Bill wondered if it would do any good to have a chat with Singh; he had shown what seemed to be some sympathy towards Bill's plight. He decided it would be a waste of time.

He took the girls into the house, closed the curtains and tried to calm them down. This was difficult because he, too, needed some calming down. They turned on the telly, trawled the channels until they found a programme about how a massive, modern ocean liner is built and settled themselves on the sofa—three-in-a-row—with a plate of ginger nuts and big glasses of fruit juice.

They were just getting to the part where the huge funnel was being lifted onto the ship by an even huger crane when his question about contacting Singh was answered for him. The two officers who delivered him to the police station on his earlier trip appeared when he responded to their knock: 'Mister Stover, we have to ask you, once again, to accompany us to the station to help us with our enquiries. You are not under arrest but we need to speak with you.'

'Oh, not again! Can't this wait until my wife comes home? There's nobody here to see to the girls.'

'No, sir, I'm afraid we need to see you now. Isn't there somebody – a neighbour, a relative – to sit with them?'

He stepped outside and closed the door: 'No, there's nobody here to help. Not my problem. Your problem. If you want me to go with you now, then arrest me and bring some bloody social worker or somebody around to watch the kids. What the hell kind of operation are you folks running, anyhow? I tell you, I'm not moving!'

'Well then, sir, perhaps you *and* the girls can accompany us to the station –'

'Great. What the hell're you gonna do, handcuff us all and throw us in the back of your bloody car? Maybe blue lights flashing and siren screaming? Why aren't you out there catching crooks or hassling hookers or whatever it is you're supposed to be doing?'

They agreed to send around an unmarked car and drive to the station well within speed limits and with no blue lights flashing or sirens wailing. A WPC took the unhappy girls to a lounge and Bill was taken to an interview room. In a few minutes Singh and Quinn entered the room.

Singh's folder seemed to have grown noticeably thicker: 'Thank you for coming in to speak with us, Mister Stover. We –'

'I'm really getting tired of this shit. I've lost my job – I've lost my *profession*, my kids have been kicked out of school – they're in tears most of the time, I'm getting hassled by paparazzi and the papers are calling me a murderer. What – just what the fuck do you want from me?'

'I understand your concern but –'

'No you *don't* understand my concern, Mister Singh –'

'That's Detective Chief Inspector Singh if you don't mind –'

'I *do* mind! What the hell're you gonna do now, charge me with refusing to address you by your proper title? Tell me, just tell me – *what the hell do you want from me*?'

Singh repeated the information provided by Winifred that the only reasonable causes for the five deaths under investigation were Bill's errors.

He started to repeat the details from Doctor Sharma's report when Bill interrupted: 'Let's pretend I'm Poirot or Columbo or Jessica Fletcher, maybe even Inspector Lynley or Wycliff or Frost –'

'Please, Mister Stover, this sarcasm will get us nowhere.'

'No – what *you've told me so far* is getting us nowhere. Let me ask you a question.'

'Usually it's *us* who ask the questions –'

'But you haven't asked any questions, have you? You've just told me what I'm supposed to have done. I've cooperated. I'm sitting here voluntarily. You haven't had to arrest me. So – let me ask you a question.'

'Go ahead.'

'We're still back to my original question, the one nobody's ever even tried to answer for me. Of all the people at the hospital involved with surgery on these kiddies, why does it necessarily come down to me and *only* me? Dozens and dozens of people, for Christ's sake! Have you interviewed them all? Have you interviewed *any* of them? Doctor Tournabel, the anaesthetists, the scrub nurses, the circulating nurses, the recovery room nurses, the IC nurses, the dieticians, the volunteers who push around the trolleys with colouring books on them? Have they *all* been in here for questioning? Why is it out of all these people you think I'm the only one responsible?'

'In our business, just like on the telly, we look for "opportunity, means and motive".'

'But hell's fire, that's just my point. You're assuming, to quote some more telly, "There's been a murder; there's been *another* murder." What's your evidence these deaths have been other than sad accidents?'

'According to Miz Hyde-Davies –'

'You're not fucking her, too, are you?'

'I'll ignore that –'

'Well, somebody here at this station probably is. Anyhow, if you're going to analyse this from *your* prospective, just what the hell was my motive – what on God's green earth would make you or anybody else think *I'd* want to kill anybody, let alone my patients?'

'But Miz Hyde-Davies said –'

'She would say anything to anybody anywhere that would keep her looking squeaky clean. She'd shop her own mother as a brothel keeper if she thought it'd make her look good. She knows absolutely nothing about open-heart surgery, or any other kind of surgery, for that matter, she's a bloody accountant. Any technical jargon she spouts she probably read in the *National Enquirer*.'

'I don't understand.'

'Look at the facts – look at *all* the facts for Christ's sake. Look at the entire surgical process from start to finish, then ask yourself once again if the only – *evidence* – you have that points to me is not, in fact, evidence at all. The only thing pointing at me is Brenda Big-tits' index finger!'

The interview continued for another hour with no progress. Every time Bill asked a specific question about evidence, Singh's response was to refer to his notes and quote Winifred. Bill suggested maybe the IV fluids were mis-labelled and Singh replied he had asked her about that possibility and her response was that, based on St. Gildas' stringent quality assurance procedures, *that* would have been impossible.

Quinn asked Bill why he was so jumpy and why he was swearing so much if he had nothing to hide. Bill's response was to say nothing and stare at him until he broke eye contact, then: 'I told you why I'm jumpy. My whole bloody life's going down the dunny quick-time because of something I didn't do – something you have absolutely no evidence I did – something that probably didn't even happen the way you think it did – and you refuse to investigate it properly.'

Singh tapped the manila folder with his index finger while Quinn stared at the wall above Bill's head. Bill waited a minute or so then pushed back his chair and stood up: 'Right, either arrest me and charge me with something – or whatever it is you do – right now or I'm outta here. I'm having no more of this bullshit. And I'll tell you this, too. If you *do* want me to come in here again, you're going to *have* to arrest me. And if you *do* come for me, I'm not opening the door to you, so you'll have to bring along one of those battering ram thingies you use sometimes. I'm gone.'

He turned and walked out the door. Neither Singh nor Quinn said anything. He collected the girls from the lounge where the WPC had been waiting with them then the three of them took a bus back home.

He spent the rest of what was left of the afternoon getting the girls calmed down again. They were comfortably settled back on the sofa and he had started to prepare their tea just as Amanda arrived from work. They were fine when she gave them their usual cuddle but everything fell apart when she asked them what kind of day they'd had. As they tried to tell their story they became more and more hysterical; they had not cried like that since the year before when Mister Macavity, their cat was run down in the street in front of the house. Bill stood with a vegetable knife in his hand and a dish towel over his shoulder, looking on helplessly from the kitchen doorway while the three women who were his entire life hugged each other and cried.

He turned and threw the knife and towel into the sink, stormed across the kitchen to the back door: 'I gotta get out of here. I'm going for a walk.' He slammed the door behind him.

The house was dark when he crept into the kitchen at eleven-thirty. Amanda left the door unlocked as he expected. He climbed the stairs, undressed and slid carefully into bed beside her. She was not asleep: 'Feel better, now?'

'Not really – not really, babes.'
'Where you been?'
'Walking – just walking.'
'We need to talk, we can't go on like this.'
'I know, sweetheart. We'll talk tomorrow. We need to organize some home schooling for the girls and I think it'd make sense if I tried to find some kind of job. Keep my mind off things.'
'We'll talk properly when I get back from work tomorrow.'

They held each other tightly. Now it was his turn to tremble and sob. She held him even tighter without saying anything more until he fell asleep.

CHAPTER TWENTY-ONE

THEY SETTLED INTO *another* new routine over the next week. Shirley arrived during breakfast to stay with the girls. Amanda went to work and Bill went job hunting. Both returned in the afternoon and after tea they worked with the girls on their reading, maths and science. They ignored their long-term future and concentrated on their getting through the next day and only the next day—that was enough. Next month and next year would have to wait. The gaggle of reporters shrunk slowly.

Bill needed a job; pay for his banked hours at St. Gildas was almost exhausted. And he must do something to occupy his time; sitting around the house all day was driving him mad. He correctly assumed any prospective employer interested in legitimate references was out of the question; what he needed was either casual, agricultural or agency labour—maybe even a security guard: folks who were not too concerned about one's job history. For half his applications he told the truth and for the rest he made everything up, complete with bogus references. Whatever they were looking for, he was their man. Well hell, at least I'll find out whether they really check histories or not. Applications for these jobs were always made in person—no telephone calls or email enquiries, indeed, one of the competency tests for applicants was whether they could complete the written form with a minimum level of cogency and breath without mechanical assistance.

He tidied himself up—but not too tidy: chinos, reasonably clean trainers, hooded cotton jumper over open-neck checked cotton shirt and dark blue baseball cap with the New York Yankees baseball team logo in white. Unlike most applicants, he did not wear jeans and he removed the cap when he went in for his interviews. He soon learned telling the truth did not work: immediately he listed his last employer as 'St. Gildas Royal Infirmary', interviewers made the connection with Doctor Death and he was out the door.

He switched to Plan B and on his written applications described himself as having moved recently to the area from Lincolnshire where he worked in a vegetable preparation factory in the Fens. He thought about referring to actual companies but decided that, too, was a waste of time. The only truths on his applications were postcodes for the Fens, his name, National Insurance number and bank details; he needed these last three to get paid.

His first two interviewers said he reminded them of Doctor Death but that must just be a coincidence and he would hear from them within the next week. Miss Parris, Human Resource Executive at his third interview, never made the connection and she told him to report to a ready-meal factory in Ashton-under-Lyne for an induction session the next Monday morning at ten. His assignment was as a 'factory operative' on the night shift starting the following Wednesday evening at ten-thirty. He had to arrange his own transportation for his induction but the agency mini-bus was available for his night shift work, collecting him and returning him to the end of his street.

He discovered working the night shift in a food factory was not much fun. He stood beside a conveyer belt to his left where a line of plastic trays flew past. In front of him to his right was a big stainless steel tray full of mushroom risotto and directly in front of him was a digital platform scale. His job was to pull the next available empty tray from the belt, place it on his scale, fill it with risotto to the weight of 120g +5g/-0g and return it to the belt. There were five people in a row, he was third; he was supposed to fill every fifth tray. The belt started moving promptly at eleven. By half-past midnight the woman factory operative behind him was bombarding him with a constant stream of obscenities because in his effort to meet the weight tolerance he was filling fewer than every fifth tray and she, presumably, was tasked with filling the trays he missed. He assumed she must have a great deal of experience as a factory operative.

Most of the screaming stopped by two in the morning because he was hitting his target of one in five trays but now he had another problem: somebody called his 'line leader' stood directly behind him and bombarded him with a constant stream of obscenities because most of his weights were well outside the +5g/-0g range. Bill assumed he must have a great deal of experience as a line leader— no doubt promoted from the ranks of factory operatives because he was able to scream and swear better than all others. He thought about turning around and punching him in the face but decided he could hold out until their meal break; maybe he would do better with experience.

The only other interesting thing that night happened during his meal break at three o'clock. He went through the serving line in the canteen, paid for his sandwich, chips, apple and coffee then moved to a seat at an empty table. He sat down and was arranging things on his tray when a man set his tray down opposite him: 'This table's for cookhouse. Nobody sits here but cookhouse.'

Bill looked at him, waved his fork gently and smiled: 'How'd you like me to rip your eyeballs out and shove 'em up your ass?'

The man said nothing, picked up his tray and moved to another table. Wow! only been here a few hours and already I'm speaking the language like a seasoned pro.

He finished his lunch and went back down the stairs to the production area. He pushed his tray through the hatch into the scullery but kept his fork in the pocket of his white coat in case he met anybody from the cookhouse on the way down.

The rest of his shift was without incident. He clocked off at seven, threw his concealed weapon in a rubbish bin, climbed into the agency bus at seven-fifteen and walked through his front door at seven minutes past eight. He said: 'Hello, munchkins,' and kissed the girls, kissed Amanda, poured himself a coffee and, unlike the rest of his family, sat silently on a stool at the bar in the kitchen rather than at the dining room table.

'How was your night, darlin'?'

'I'm tired.'

He said nothing more. He drank his coffee, stood up, kissed the girls and Amanda again, climbed the stairs, set his alarm and went to bed.

He adapted to night-shift work quickly because of his irregular hours at the hospital. He was almost always in a foul mood when he came home but he usually hid it until he went to bed. When he wakened at teatime he came down with a smile and hugs for his three girls. Each evening he helped the girls with their home school work until they went to bed and he went off to work.

From the time he got into the agency mini-bus on the way to work until he disembarked in the morning, often he said nothing at all, neither to his fellow bus passengers nor any of his workmates. He responded in monosyllables if spoken to but initiated no conversations of his own. He acquired the reputation of somebody with a miserable disposition who was better left alone. Nobody from the cookhouse bothered him and since he gained minimal competency in filling trays to the required weight, his line leader said nothing to him other than to assign work. Screaming from the woman behind him on the line diminished to a level he could tolerate. Nobody addressed him as 'Doctor Death'.

He coped well enough for two weeks then one morning the bus driver handed him an envelope containing a note from Miss Parris asking him to attend a meeting in her office at ten o'clock. Great! How the hell would she like it if I asked her to a meeting at my house at two in the morning?

She invited him into her office promptly at ten and directed him to sit down. She seemed anxious and never smiled: 'Mister Stover, we have a problem.'

Her 'we' confused him because, although he knew *he* had some really heavy ongoing problems, he could not see how these affected her. Maybe it's the royal 'we' all human resource practitioners use to promote feelings of togetherness, team spirit and workplace camaraderie. I wonder how much time *she's* spent on the nightshift in a food factory.

'How can I help you, Miss Parris?'

'It seems you haven't been totally truthful with us concerning your previous employment.'

'So?'

'I really don't think that's an appropriate response to my statement. What I mean to say is you lied about your employment history.'

Bill assumed he was in trouble and this was probably the end of his employment with this agency: 'Well, heck, doesn't *everybody* lie about their previous employment? Don't you folks assume everybody always lies on job applications?'

'We assume that many CVs include a bit of "creative adjustment" to start and stop dates, typically to eliminate brief placements not related to applicants' fields of expertise and naturally we expect them sometimes to inflate the importance of contributions to their previous employers' businesses but you, in fact, have never worked in a food factory at all.'

'I do my job. You've had no complaints from –'

'We have, in fact, received a complaint from the factory where you're placed.'

'So what kind of complaint is it? It doesn't have anything to do with the cookhouse does it?'

'No, it has nothing to do with the cookhouse. It has to do with the fact that you are the man the newspapers call "Doctor Death". You are the man responsible for the deaths of those five babies at St. Gildas Royal Infirmary. According to their complaint, you may be a murderer!'

'I guess this means I won't be going in tonight or for the rest of the week.'

'No this means you're never going back there again.'

'Okay. Well, then, I'd better get moving and look for another job. Two questions – when will I be able to collect what I'm owed through last night and may I use you for a reference?'

'In answer to your first question, you'll be paid for hours worked and your current account will be credited on the usual date. In answer to your second question: "in your dreams, mate". Now get out of my office.'

'Thank you, Miss Parris, it's been nice doing business with you.'

She had no Lalique vases in her office so Bill closed her door quietly and went home to bed.

He did not tell Amanda Doctor Death had struck again. He went off at the usual time, ostensibly to work. Instead, he wandered in and out of several late-night cafés drinking coffee and finally settled for the night in the accident and emergency department of a hospital in Oldham. It was busy enough he attracted no undue attention so long as he moved about and did not fall asleep or look like he was dossing. What was he going to do next? The obvious answer was to move on to another agency and make up another work history.

If he went back out every morning after breakfast telling Amanda he was scheduled for training sessions on hygiene or health and safety, assuming he found another night-shift job soon, maybe—just maybe—he could get away with it. It was worth a try; he was putting intense pressure on her and Shirley with his miserable disposition and outbursts of temper. He worked hard to keep smiling in front of the girls but he was not always successful. He was near his breaking point and assumed they must be too.

It worked. On the second morning of his faux training, he landed an agency job as a security guard in a small business park in Gorton starting the following Monday night. Problem solved. Between late-night cafés and Casualty departments he made it successfully through the week—neither Amanda nor Shirley suspected a thing. Major Jackson interviewed him. The agency prohibited their wearing uniforms except on site so he went off to work each night in his civilian garb. This time his CV included security work in Liverpool and Preston for several agencies and security firms. He wondered how long this work would last before Doctor Death arrived.

His job was to wander all around in and out of office buildings checking doors were locked, coffee pots were off and nobody was cruising the car park trying to steal any of the few cars parked there through the night. Every hour he checked in with Sergeant Kenneally at a desk in one of the buildings but otherwise he was left alone. Nobody screamed at him; nobody said much of anything to him and this suited him. With his master key he could sneak into empty offices and have little naps, as long as he made his rounds according to schedule and reported to the desk more-or-less on time. He thought his fake employment history might keep him in work a little longer than at the food factory because he encountered fewer people during the night.

This worked for three weeks. Amanda and Shirley assumed he was still a factory operative filling little plastic trays with mushroom risotto all night long; they certainly did not say anything to indicate otherwise. He was coming home in the morning in a slightly better mood. Then one night Sergeant Kenneally handed him an envelope containing a note from Major Jackson demanding his presence in his office at ten the following morning to discuss a matter of some importance.

It was déjà vu all over again: his meeting with Major Jackson ended as had that with Miss Parris. He was running out of temporary employment agencies and potential workplaces.

He secured work in a waste recycling plant after a few more nights in cafés, and hospital waiting rooms, and a few more ten o'clock training sessions. There were no induction sessions for this position: training was strictly on-the-job. Another agency bus collected him at the end of his street at the usual nine-fifteen. Amanda and Shirley were still under the illusion he was a factory operative.

He stood beside a conveyor belt on which a never-ending stream of mixed recyclable waste whizzed past. He was to pull almost everything off the belt and into appropriate chutes, leaving unrecognizable bits of plastic, metal or wood to travel to the end into some kind of purgatory for non-recyclable stuff. The belt moved fast —

faster than the risotto line and his linemates were far more adept at screaming and swearing than his old friends in the ready-meal factory. They were also much uglier, many of them much bigger, and they smelled much worse; he decided waving forks at them would not be a good idea. Not only did his workmates smell bad, his entire work area reeked of a sewage/garbage fusion and the noise, even with the little blue rubber things they gave him to stick in his ears, was overpowering.

He coped through sheer bloody-mindedness during this his first night as a recyclable waste management technician until an hour after returning from his lunch break. Then he lost it. At four-thirty he stepped back from the line, walked the length of the belt along the grated steel walkway ignoring screams and swearing, went down the grated steel stairway and across the filthy floor into the changing room, threw his hard hat, wellies, gloves, ear plugs and smelly yellow boiler suit in a heap against the wall and went out into the yard.

He did not clock off; he was too numb to care about the money they owed him. The main gate was locked and the perimeter wall was topped with razor wire. The gate was not, so he climbed over it and dropped down the outside to freedom. He was eight miles from home but that was okay—the walk would give him time to think and he needed the walk more than he needed a ride in a mini-bus. Now he would have to tell Amanda everything.

'Wow, you smell, darlin',' she kissed him. 'Bad night?'

'Terrible night, babes. I'm a wreck. I'll just take a coffee up with me while I shower. Don't really feel like talking now. See you tonight. Tell you all about it then. Kiss the girls for me, please.'

He waved to the girls as he passed the dining room door: 'Hi, munchkins. Love you.'

He was sleeping soundly when she came into the darkened bedroom after work carrying two coffees. She usually let him sleep until teatime but today she sat on the edge of the bed and waited until he started to stir: 'Hello, sleepyhead. Sleep well?'

'Yeah, babes. I was dead to the world.'

'You smell a lot better now. Ready to tell me just what's going on?'

He told her everything since his meeting with Miss Parris.

Amanda never interrupted, neither to criticize what he did nor query him for any more details. She did not suggest she knew what was happening nor did she comment that she felt anything other than he was simply struggling to stay positive and get on with his life. She was appalled, not because of his decisions, rather because her quiet, gentle husband had borne these horrible experiences alone and not told her about any of them. In the end they laughed about his escape over the gate and his long walk home.

She kissed him: 'Well, it's over now. Come on down and have some tea with us. Spend the evening just hanging out with your girls. We'll go to bed early – you look like you could use a few more hours' sleep. Tomorrow night after I get home we'll figure out what we're going to do next.'

CHAPTER TWENTY-TWO

THE CORONER OPENED the public inquest without summoning a jury. Witnesses called included Doctors Sharma and Tournabel, and St. Gildas' Chief Anaesthetist, Divisional Director of Anaesthetics/Theatres/Critical Care and the Deputy Chief Nurse. The coroner did not call Winifred or Bill. Under English law either could have volunteered information as someone with an interest in the proceedings but she had already made her case through the media and he felt his testimony would only anger him further and would not change anything. The coroner ruled the deaths were due to accident or misadventure. Winifred attended; Bill did not.

After adjournment, paparazzi surrounded Winifred when she descended the steps in front of the courthouse. She reached the pavement, stopped and held an impromptu press conference—impromptu for the reporters, certainly, but carefully rehearsed by her. She reiterated the message that everybody at St. Gildas was deeply saddened by the deaths, their collective hearts went out to the families of the victims and that lessons would be learned. When Trevor LaFarge asked the same question he asked at the press conference and she responded with the same answer, it was open season on the Stover Family once again.

It is not within the jurisdiction of the coroner to decide who is responsible for a death; *that* is the duty of the tabloids. This was Bill's observation as he scanned the papers reporting the hearing.

Now the pressure increased; the notoriety generated by the coroner's decision brought the story back to the front pages. Bill stopped reading the papers; what he read infuriated him too much. They agreed Shirley would keep away for her own peace of mind. The girls stayed indoors. Their only forays through the ranks of the reporters surrounding the house were when Amanda travelled to and from work and Bill went out late at night for groceries. They stopped answering their door and the telephone.

He visited the police station and chatted with Singh who told him the police could do nothing about reporters so long as they caused no damage or assaulted a member of the family. He suggested Bill retain a solicitor to petition the court for restraining orders to keep them a specified minimum distance from the house and from their persons when they went out but Bill replied this cost more than they could afford.

Bill sometimes disappeared into himself to think about one of his projects—whether it was a Wendy house for the back garden or his dream of someday learning to fly. When he went quiet the three women in his life knew he was off in a place of his own but he would return—he *always* returned. Back in a couple of hours, typically in time for tea. Then he was their loving husband and daddy again: tickling, teasing and telling his really terrible jokes.

But a week after the inquest Amanda noticed he stayed away longer, sometimes much longer—lost in his own world for most of the day. It was so obvious the girls were asking: 'What's wrong with Daddy?'

She had no answer—it was time for the two of them to have one of their talks: 'I know what's bothering you. It's just I don't know how to help.'

'I don't know what to do, babes. I try to look to the future, to when this will all be over and I can't see the end – I don't know what's going to happen to us – I don't know what's going to happen to *me.*'

'The only thing I can say is we – the two of us, together – will beat this thing. Somehow, sometime, it'll all be over. Until then we have to hold each other, support each other – lots of group hugs, lots of popcorn on the sofa.'

'But will that be enough, babes? I don't know if that'll be enough.'

'It *will* be enough, darlin', it's what we have!'

Now the fantasies started to intrude. In the beginning they were fairly unimaginative: walking up to the nearest paparazzo, grabbing his camera and smashing it against a convenient wall. This was against the law; he knew he would be arrested but he did not care. They became more ambitious: he pictured himself going out the kitchen door, picking up two bricks, walking down the alley to the cross street, around to the front and bashing a couple of them in the face. Next he thought about buying a shotgun, walking out the front door and mowing down as many of them as he could before the police came around and took him out. Maybe taking his shotgun into the hospital and blowing first Vanessa's then Winifred's face to unrecognizable pulp. Getting his hands on some hand grenades, walking into the police station and blowing himself up along with Singh and Quinn. He was angry and bitter, and so far he had not vented any of it in front of his family but he was rapidly losing control. He knew it, he felt it.

The final insult was the letter. Two weeks after the inquest, along with the usual poorly articulated ramblings in equally poor handwriting calling him a baby killer and a few obscenely gross money offers from the red tops for his exclusive story on why he became a serial murderer of children was one with the return address of a firm of solicitors. It informed him a civil class action suit was being brought against him by the parents of the dead children stating he was in breach of his duty of care to them and charging him with manslaughter by gross negligence.

He rang Shirley, asking her to come over as soon as possible. An emergency had come up and he needed to go out for a little while. She arrived by taxi an hour later.

He thanked her, kissed the girls, pushed through the phalanx of paparazzi and left in the taxi.

CHAPTER TWENTY-THREE

BILL WALKED FROM the warm, bright afternoon sunshine into the cool, peaceful darkness of the church. He moved past people milling around the narthex admiring the ancient stonework and dark carved wood, and the group of children enjoying themselves, probably on a school trip. He walked forward along the nave and sat in a pew near the altar. He sat silently looking from the altar to the high, dark ceiling and back. He breathed slowly, evenly and deeply.

He had not prayed for a long time, just as he had not believed for a long time. Although he felt deeply there must be some kind of master plan behind the universe and everything in it, years earlier he rejected what he referred to as 'that man with a long white beard declaring today one person was blessed with a natural ability to play the piano beautifully while another was cursed with an incurable cancer'. When he prayed it was not to that man but to this master plan, whatever its form. He thought about his life, his beautiful family and his future. He concluded he had no future. He sat quietly for an hour then stood and walked slowly back down the nave to the narthex. He found the low door to the narrow, winding stone staircase leading to the tower parapet, stepped through and closed it then began climbing the two-hundred and eleven steps.

William Bragg Stover died as the result of his highly inelastic collision with the York flagstones below the West Front of the church. He calmly stepped off the tower parapet and assumed a position skydivers describe as 'semi-frog'. He fell from the parapet to the flagstones, 44.50 metres, in 3.01 seconds and collided falling at 29.54 metres per second—146.00 feet, 3.01 seconds and 66.09 miles per hour in old money. These computations are based on Newtonian mechanics and take no account of air resistance; his actual time was slightly greater and terminal velocity slightly lower. Relativistic mechanics would not improve the accuracy of calculations at this speed.

Television news readers and newspaper reporters described his death as 'instantaneous' although this is inaccurate, certainly in any mathematical sense; it is sufficient to say it was quick. The collision itself did not cause death, rather it was massive trauma to the organs enclosed within his intracranial and thoracic cavities.

When he climbed onto the parapet all his rage and bitterness were gone; replaced by an overwhelming sense of emptiness and sadness. He left no note. His only regret as he fell was the distress his death engendered in the people strolling around inside and outside the church, particularly the children. The flagstones were undamaged.

CHAPTER TWENTY-FOUR

OS WAS A tracker—proficient in the art and science of tracking humans. Now he was interested in a different sort of tracking: the trail a bag of Hartmann's solution made from its creation to its end. Bill Stover's death was the culmination of a labyrinthine chain of events beginning when he primed his machine with incorrect IV solutions. The tracks Os was seeking were not those of a plastic bag filled with clear, sterile liquid but those of the people involved in its travels.

The cultures of organizations determine these paths. All organizations but particularly business organizations and political parties, evolve according to the personal objectives of people in power within them, not just those at the top with formal authority but those throughout who wield significant degrees of personal power. When Os sat down to wait for Brian on their appointed bench in Piccadilly Gardens carrying two lattes and his folio, he wanted to understand the culture of St. Gildas Royal Infirmary and the behaviour of people in positions of personal power such as Winifred. He expected Brian to provide him with a back sighting from her desk to the place where the bags were filled and labelled.

Brian arrived a few minutes later. Now his jumper looked like it came from M and S, circa nineteen-seventy-five, and the white socks had been replaced by orange and even brighter orange argyles. His nerd pack was more prominent than during their last meeting; Os wondered why any woman would want to go through the bother of breast-implant surgery when two of these would do the job nicely.

They went to work: 'So, what do you have for me today? Hacked into anything worthy of my attention since last we met?'

'"Since last we met" that's a great line almost poetic loads and loads of seriously interesting stuff is it really true at Commando college they teach you to kill people with a credit card? "Commando college" is that onomatopoeia or alliteration I never remember which one?'

'Alliteration, Brian, alliteration. If I said, "I'm gonna cut off your goolies: 'Snip, snip'," the "Snip, snip," would be onomatopoeia, and I never went to Commando college. There's no such thing as Commando college and I wasn't a Commando anyhow. What do you have for me?'

'Well I started with Winifred Hyde-Davies really posh name by the way do you know the origin of the word "posh" –?'

Os touched him gently on the arm: 'Calm down, my friend, calm down and try to stick to the subject –'

'Sorry oh reticent one sorry it's just that well you know words *fascinate* me and – I did a thorough search of anything to do with her and there are a lot of emails to and from her to an outfit called Sutton-Millhouse Medical Products – we'll call it "SMMP" for short – and particularly to a guy named Arnold Hohenzoller who seems to be a sales rep or something and since they supply St. Gildas Royal Infirmary well heck it looks like they supply every hospital in the country with intravenous fluids – we'll call them "IV fluids" for short – I think that's a good place to start turning over rocks to see what crawls out and maybe you'll want to check out Bharat Patel the quality control guy at St. Gildas and Stanley Kowalski – how's *that* for a name? – he's some kind of quality assurance honcho at SMMP and maybe even Victoria Schaffner I think she's

Hohenzoller's boss sales manager excetera – anyhow they're all on this flash drive and –'

'And for you, my sartorially challenged young friend, I have a whole raft of names of reporters from various papers I'd like you to check out – see who talked to whom, and when. It'd be really helpful to know precisely *when* these guys learned certain specific details about what was going on and how much of it they just made up.'

Brian gave Os the stick with the hundreds of emails he collected and in return Os handed him the sheaf of notes he made while examining the newspaper articles he reviewed during his trip to the library.

'Let me ask you a question. If somebody communicated with somebody else by mobile phone – let's say two years ago, is there any way for you to find out what they talked about or is that beyond even your amazing skills?'

'Good question well not really a good question because you already know the answer is "Yes" but it's kinda tricky.'

'How so?'

'Well as we all know our friends in high places MI5 MI6 JSSO CIA DHS NSA you know the people of whom we're not supposed to know anything about anyhow this is one the conspiracy theorists are right about our friends not only monitor *all* these communications but save them to their amazingly huge hard drives deep in the bowels of the earth and they keep them forever I can get in to look at them sure I can but –'

'So, what's the problem?'

'The problem is they keep track of how many times these files are accessed and their systems are good *very* good even I can't get in and out without alerting them remember the good old days when cash tills were those big ornate cast brass mechanical things where the sale

116

amount popped up on white tabs in that glass window across the top you know the kind you see on the end of the counter in the general store in the cowboy movies –'

Os touched him on the arm again: 'What's this have to do with covert surveillance and hacking into government files?'

'Patience – patience making my point with an analogy here or maybe it's a metaphor or even an allegory never mind as I was saying this till had a panel on the front the owner could unlock and lift up and behind it were mechanical counters that recorded the number of times the drawer was opened and the amount of money rung up when the keys were pushed so at the end of the day he could compare total sales with the cash in the drawer but there was another counter that counted the number of times the panel was opened so he would know if somebody had been under the panel messing with the other counters sort of like checking up on the checker-upper.

'Anyhow our pals at Digby and Fort Meade have counters just like those attached to their systems if I sneak in even for just a few seconds I can do it a couple of times before the red lights start blinking but I have to be quick and I have to know exactly what I'm looking for –'

'So, we can't just go fishing, we have to be looking for very specific information – dates, precise times, names?'

'Got in one got it in one any more questions for today?'

'No, I reckon that'll do for now.'

They exchanged a little more information, finished their conversation and their lattes, said their goodbyes and left the Gardens.

CHAPTER TWENTY-FIVE

OS WENT BACK to his incident room, drew some more lines and boxes on the ever-expanding flow chart on his big white board and thought about what he wanted to do next. His approach to Arnold was different from his confrontation with Trevor. Now he had no facts, only assumptions, and he had no idea what Arnold knew about the deaths. What he *did* know, based on the emails on the flash drive, was he and Winifred had communicated frequently during this time. Os knew medical products suppliers spend huge amounts of money schmoozing and promoting their wares to doctors, hospital administrators, NHS executives and huge numbers of bureaucrats and politicians in prospectively profitable decision-making positions. He based his plan on this knowledge.

He represented an American firm opening a chain of private hospitals across Britain catering exclusively to the needs of the super-rich. It was all very hush-hush and he headed a team his employer called 'The Pathfinders'. His specific job was to establish lines of communication with potential suppliers.

After several cryptic voicemail messages, Arnold rang him: 'Mister Gilrey? Arnold Hohenzoller here, Senior Sales Executive with Sutton-Millhouse Medical Products. How can I help you?'

'Thank you very much for returning my call, Mister Hohenzoller –'

'Arnold, please – Arnold will do nicely –'

'Arnold – then. We need to meet, privately, *very* privately, of course, to discuss potential contracts with your firm. As you can well understand, due to the nature of our enquiries, we have to be quite circumspect –'

'Of course, of course – at a time and place convenient for you, naturally.'

'I'm at the Dorchester. Tomorrow afternoon – two o'clock? – the Promenade would suit me nicely.'

'Fine, Mister Gilrey. See you at two. I'm sure you'll be pleased with what we at Sutton-Millhouse Medical Products can offer you.'

I'm sure we will, thought Os, more than you can imagine.

Os checked into the Dorchester the next morning registering as Thornton Gilrey. Other than his overnight bag and fake passport, the only thing he carried was a very expensive-looking attaché case. At two o'clock he exited the lift to The Promenade and spotted Arnold. They shook hands and moved to a small, intimate table.

He removed a leather folio from his case, opened it, pulled a pen from his jacket pocket, clicked it twice, looked down at his notes, paused then smiled. These theatrics took a long time: 'Right – to business.'

Without revealing the tiniest detail about his employer or the number and possible locations of these planned private hospitals, he laid it on with a trowel; hinting contracts with the approved supplier would be *huge*. He continuously emphasized 'supplier' in the singular and this looked to affect Arnold like Pavlov's bell; soon he expected him to start salivating—fantasizing about the massive commissions coming his way.

In equally oblique rhetoric, Arnold hinted at the potential 'finder's fees' awaiting the individual responsible for writing and signing off the agreed purchase specifications.

Now both men sat back, and their body languages suggested they agreed—a win-win result had indeed been achieved.

Os sipped his coffee, meticulously touched his napkin to his lips and gently moved on to Phase Two: 'Now, we must consider the matter of quality.'

Immediately Arnold shifted to a defensive position — shoulders forward, arms crossed, pupils slightly dilated, respiratory rate increased: 'I can assure you, Mister Gilrey, that our quality assurance and quality control procedures are amongst the finest in the industry – world class, as a matter of fact. Not right now, obviously, because of the confidential nature of our discussions, but at an appropriate time in the future, we shall be pleased – nay, delighted – to provide you with suitable references confirming the high standards to which all our products are manufactured and distributed.'

'Of course – of course. Please forgive me if my question suggests any criticism of your operations. Surely you understand this is such an important part of my job. It's just that –'

'Yes?'

Os gradually leaned closer and his voice dropped almost to a whisper: 'Well, as you can appreciate, we've done our homework and – I'm sorry – this *is* rather awkward – but a couple of years ago there was an incident reported in the papers – without consulting my notes it was – if I remember correctly – the St. Gildas Royal Infirmary in Manchester – something about the possibility of some deaths resulting from contaminated IV fluids – I believe you were the supplier in question.'

Arnold's body language was a mess. He was on the horns of the proverbial dilemma: he clearly could not deny SMMP was St. Gildas' supplier but anything he said would sound like a denial. He was silent. He shifted uncomfortably and swallowed several times. He fiddled with his spoon. He made the least possible eye contact:

'Yes, yes, you *have* done your homework. Yes, indeed. Certainly we were – as we still are, as a matter of fact – sole suppliers of intravenous solutions to St. Gildas. I can assure you the matter was investigated fully not only by our quality assurance executive but also St. Gildas' head of quality and there was absolutely no evidence of any problem with our products.'

Os watched him squirm then moved on to Phase Three: 'I know this isn't the way it's usually done but – a few minutes ago you generously offered to provide my team and me with references. Would you be able to introduce me to somebody on the senior management team at St. Gildas who was intimately involved with this issue – somebody familiar with the incident and one with whom I might discuss it in detail? I'm sure you understand the importance of this with respect to the *huge – long-term contracts* – under consideration here.'

He glanced at his watch, snapped his folio shut and stood up: 'Goodness, is that the time? Terribly sorry, Arnold, but I *must* cut this short. I'm scheduled to make an important phone call to my office then on to another meeting. I'm sure you understand.'

Arnold's relief was so obvious Os struggled to keep from smiling. The poor wretch had been offered an opportunity to escape before he lapsed into total incoherence. He stood up too, mumbled his thanks for the opportunity to do business with Mister Gilrey and his team, and commented he would make arrangements for him to meet somebody from St. Gildas at his convenience. As Os entered the lift he saw him moving frantically towards the impressive bar at the far end of the Promenade.

CHAPTER TWENTY-SIX

HEAVILY FORTIFIED WITH copious amounts of the finest spirits available at the bar in the Promenade, Arnold clutched his mobile phone preparing to make two calls on which his career and personal fortune probably depended. Any feelings about the possibility of his conversations being recorded by secret government agencies were overridden by his concern for survival. He was descending swiftly towards the lowest level of Maslow's pyramid. The first call was to his boss, Victoria Schaffner. The more he struggled to characterize his meeting with Os in terms of potential contracts for SMMP, the less coherent he became.

She interrupted him: 'So – let me get this straight, Arnold. You spend an hour and a half with a man you've never met before who promises you business that'd generate enough in commissions for you to retire to the Caribbean in decadent luxury but the only thing you know about him is his name – you don't even know who he represents or what, exactly, he's planning to do except for a vague song and dance about a chain of private hospitals and a never-ending stream of purchase orders. Then he starts talking about product quality and before he's finished the two of you end up discussing the St. Gildas fiasco and a few minutes later he's out the door?'

'Yep, that's about it.'

'My friend, you'll certainly never have haemorrhoids 'cause you're a perfect arsehole! Do you have even the vaguest idea about what's happened? You schmuck, you've most likely just been had either by an undercover reporter or a private investigator acting for Amanda Stover. Christ, you're an idiot of the first order! And I'll bet you didn't even get a kiss before he slipped it in.'

Arnold raised his glass to signal the bartender for another drink. She heard nothing except his heavy breathing: 'Okay, okay, whatever damage has been done has been done – there's absolutely nothing we can do about it. About the only thing you *can* do is stay away from this bozo. No phone calls and *certainly* no meetings. My guess is you won't hear from him again 'cause you've given him all the information he needs to move forward with his project, whatever it is –'

'But I didn't give him anything!'

'You gave him *everything*! Well, I assume you didn't give him everything – you didn't give him a blow job, did you? Well maybe you did, hell, you'd do anything to close a deal.'

'No – no blow job. I assure you.'

'Christ, you're so thick! Irony – irony. You don't do irony, do you?'

He suffered her tirade in silence, broken only by *her* heavy breathing, then: 'Right, I'll get one of our people to run a check on this guy, *if* we can find out who he is, and see what he's really up to. In the meantime, try not to do anything else stupid. Goodbye.'

He took another gulp of his whisky and punched Winifred's number into his mobile. This conversation was more or less like the one with Victoria and by the time it ended he was in dire need of another drink.

CHAPTER TWENTY-SEVEN

THE ANSWERS TO Os' questions lay deep within the maze of Sutton-Millhouse Medical Products' organization. He was confident of this; somebody within SMMP knew about the release of defective IV fluids and had ordered the cover-up. Kowalski had probably not issued the order but knew who did, so his next meeting needed to be with him. Time for some traditional black ops work.

He located Stanley's house near SMMP's headquarters in Milton Keynes, loaded some tools of his trade into his car and arrived there just after sundown. He parked across from the Kowalski family home and watched them through the windows until he judged their evening meal was finished and they were settled into their weekday evening routine.

A woman answered the door: 'Missus Kowalski, sorry to trouble you at this late hour. Melvin Gibbs, SMMP Security. There's been an incident at our offices that requires Mister Kowalski's immediate attention. Is he available?'

'Yes, certainly, Mister Gibbs. I'll get him for you.'

She left him standing at the open door and returned a few seconds later with Stanley following her closely: 'Mister Gibbs, how can I help you? Sorry, do I know you?'

'No, sorry, Mister Kowalski, I'm new with the team. This is urgent.'

He shook hands with Stanley and urged him out through the door and closed it quietly. Immediately it was shut he gripped his arm and pulled back his coat far enough to display his holstered Glock 17: 'No heroics now and we can get this over just as quickly as possible and get you back to your family with little harm done.'

'Just who the hell are you and what do you want? There must be some mistake –'

'No mistake. I need some information you can give me. Now shut up. We're going for a little ride.'

A thoroughly terrified Stanley allowed himself to be led to the car.

Os drove in silence occasionally looking across and glaring at his prisoner to keep him cowering. They travelled through the suburbs into the countryside until Os located a complex of derelict farm buildings. He followed the potholed dirt track far enough to be out of sight of passing traffic. He dragged him out of the car and across the yard then kicked open the door of one of the buildings, shoving him in and ordering him to wait. His training and experience suggested his captive would do as he was told; he was confident there was little possibility of his being waylaid by a kung-fu kick or Stanley's trying to run.

He returned carrying a large holdall and a portable electric lantern. Now he wore surgical gloves. He pulled a scarred wooden chair into the centre of the room, motioned Stanley to sit down then secured him to it with gaffer tape. His arms were pinioned to his sides and his legs were strapped to the chair legs but he was not gagged.

He made a feeble protest but he was shaking so badly it could be heard in his voice: 'There must be some mistake. I haven't done anything. Who are you and what do you want?'

Os said nothing; he hummed tunelessly and smiled as he removed things from his holdall and aligned them carefully on the workbench, making certain Stanley could see everything. These included a blowlamp and a cigarette lighter, several pairs of pliers and cutters, a long steel bar, a scalpel, a pair of secateurs, a bottle of bleach and a tasar: 'Oh, there's been no mistake. You are, in fact, Stanley Kowalski and you are involved with quality assurance with Sutton-Millhouse Medical Products and you have worked in this capacity for the past five years?'

'Yes, but?'

'Well, then, there's been no mistake. I need some information and I'm sure you can provide it for me.'

'But what? What's going on? Are you some kind of corporate spy, is this industrial espionage, do you want information on how we make some of our products, are you one of our competitors? What do you *really* want?'

Os ignored him. He lit the blowlamp then adjusted it. The clear, blue flame was bright in the darkened room, its roar more menacing than the flame. He picked it up in his left hand, the scalpel in his right and turned back and stood over him. Stanley could feel the heat on his face and see the tiny, shiny blade reflecting the light. His bladder let go and his trousers darkened.

He pleaded: 'Please – please, what do you want? *I don't know what you want!*'

Os turned off the blowlamp and put it and the scalpel on the workbench then turned back to him: 'Here's what I need to know – here's what I need to know. A little over two years ago you produced some intravenous solutions with the wrong labels.'

'We were able to recall all of them before –'

'All of them, Stanley, *all of them*?'

'Well – not quite *all* of them. A few bags got out.'

'A few?'

'Well, as far as we could tell, a couple thousand.'

'A couple thousand. Doesn't sound like "a few" to me.'

'Well, there was no harm done.'

'No harm done? Can you tell me with every confidence absolutely no harm came to any patients?'

'Well, not really. Of course I can't tell you that, but –'

'Just so long as the blame for any problems wasn't dumped on your doorstep everything was fine?'

'Well – yes, I guess you could put it that way.'

'So what you're telling me is that even if a few patients died, everything's fine as long as SMMP didn't get the blame?'

'That's the way the world works, isn't it?'

Os relit the blowlamp and again leaned over him waving the scalpel: 'No, that isn't the way it works in *my* world. Now, simple question – who at SMMP ordered the cover-up?'

'I can't possibly divulge that information. It might mean the end of my career.'

'If you don't, it might mean the end of your eyes, my friend.'

He moved the lamp and scalpel to within a few inches of his face.

Stanley screamed: 'Alright, alright. Please, please don't hurt me! Take it away, please take it away!'

Os put the things back on the bench: 'Talk to me.'

'The man who ordered the cover-up was Gordon Milne, our director of operations. Please don't hurt me, Mister Gibbs; I was just following orders.'

'Interesting – isn't that exactly what they said at Nuremberg?'

'Now, will you please let me go?'

Os hummed as he collected his tools and returned them to the holdall then put it in the car along with the lantern. He came back and removed the tape, rolling it into a ball, kneading it and tossing it from hand to hand: 'Okay. I'm outta here. I strongly suggest you sit without moving for at least a half hour before you even *begin* to think about walking back home. I also strongly suggest you don't mention any of this to anybody, particularly

Mister Milne or any of your workmates. You shouldn't even mention this to your wife – you can use the time while you're walking to think something up. You've no doubt heard the cliché, "I know where you live." Well, it should be pretty obvious from our little adventure tonight that I do, in fact, know *exactly* where you live. Were I to need to call on you again, I might not be so accommodating. You don't ever want me to visit you again, now, do you, Mister Kowalski? You don't need to answer that. No? I thought not. Bye.'

Os walked to his car and drove back home. Stanley did as he was told and waited what he estimated to be one-half hour—it was closer to ninety minutes—before he began his long walk home.

CHAPTER TWENTY-EIGHT

TREVOR LaFARGE ENTERED the Flayed Ox, a pub in Cheetham Hill, hoping to look at George Barr. Whether he wanted to meet him or not depended on whether he was the man who confronted him in his flat or somebody else. Trevor was here based on a tip from a landlord at another pub near this one. If he were the man who had confronted him in his flat then he wanted absolutely nothing to do with him. If, however, as he was coming to believe, George was a different person, he thought he might be able to hire him to track the mysterious stranger down.

Although a seasoned gutter press reporter and used to scary meetings with people unfriendly to his style of reporting, he was still nervous in this place he would never refer to as 'his local'. It was a public house detectives entered only in pairs and into which uniformed officers never ventured except under extreme circumstances. He ordered a pint of bitter and nursed it standing at the bar positioned so he could see patrons as they came and went. He waited.

An hour later and half-way through his second carefully-paced pint he saw George come in. He walked to the bar two men away from Trevor and ordered a lager. He emanated an aura that frightened Trevor even more than had the man who visited his flat. While *he* just looked stern, George looked vicious and while that man projected a quiet strength, George made one feel he might enjoy hurting people. And he was even bigger than Trevor had imagined from his photo. Perhaps Quinn was right: moving to Canada might be a more sensible option than confronting this man. He waited until it was clear George was alone and, based on his body language, not expecting to meet anybody.

Trevor moved away from the bar, past the two intervening drinkers and slipped in next to him: 'Mister Barr?'

'Who the fuck're you? Waddya want?'

'My name is Trevor LaFarge and –'

'Who the fuck are you and what kind of name is "LaFarge" anyhow? You some kinda fuckin' Roosky or Pollock or somethin'?'

'I need some – you might be able to – the landlord over at the Oubliette said – well – you might be interested in some work – pest control work. He said you sometimes do contract pest control work.'

'Did he now?'

This conversation continued for several minutes— Trevor stumbling over his words and George revealing nothing more about himself beyond his liberal use of that universal noun/verb/adjective/adverb of uncertain etymology.

At last Trevor constructed a meaningful sentence with only a few awkward pauses: 'Okay, Mister Barr, maybe my information is good and maybe not. I need some work done for which I'm prepared to pay cash and maybe you do this kind of this work or not. If not, just tell me to go away and I'll do that and you'll never see me again. But if you're interested can we sit down and talk about it?'

George nodded and they moved to a quiet corner table. George sat with his back comfortably to the wall and with a decent view of the room. This left Trevor sitting uncomfortably with his back to the crowd.

'Right, Trevor LaFarge – hee, hee, what's this *pest control work* you need done?'

'Well, it's not really pest control work as we usually know it; I just want you to find somebody for me –'

'Then what? Legs broken, acid in the face, dog poisoned, wife beat up, house torched, goolies cut off or something more?'

Trevor shuddered and his pupils dilated; this man was not speaking meaningless banter or in clichés—Trevor believed he actually *did* these things to people: 'No, nothing like that. I just want him found and I want to know his name. I'll take it from there.'

'So, how the fuck'm I supposed to find him if you don't even know his fuckin' name?'

'Well, Mister Barr, that's what I want to pay you for. I'll give you as much information as I have and you see if you can find him for me. I'll pay you for your time, whether you find him or not.'

'So what's to stop me from just takin' your money and disappearing into the fuckin' sunset?'

'Absolutely nothing, but a guy's gotta start somewhere.'

'Sounds like you wanna find this dork real bad.'

'You might say that. Interested or not?'

George said he was interested. Trevor described Os in the little detail he had. His intimate contact with George made Os' appearance seem less frightening—his height and weight diminished along with the fear. He included Quinn's comment Os was probably ex-military, possible Special Forces, Commando or SAS and George said this might help with his search.

He gave him Amanda Stover's address and a photo: 'But she has absolutely nothing to do with this search, I'm only interested in him. You must leave her out of this.'

'So why tell me about her at all?'

'Well – I know she's a friend of his, don't ask me how, I just know. I don't know how close they are but maybe, just maybe if you checked out her place you might find him hanging around. Hell, Mister Barr, I'm not trying to tell you how to do your job – I just thought it might help.'

He told George his confrontation had been in the Manchester area although he could not assume this meant this mystery man lived there, and he looked a little like George himself.

'Right, Trevor LaFarge, not a fuckova lot to go on. Meet me here next week this time and we'll go from there.'

'So, how much money you want up front?'

'Nothin' tonight.'

'Nothing?'

'Naw, we'll talk about it next week.'

Trevor stood up and reached out to shake hands with him. George glared at him and snarled. Trevor was uncertain whether the snarl was real or an element of his public persona; he assumed the former. He left the pub as quickly as he could without looking like a man running for his life. George quietly sipped his lager.

CHAPTER TWENTY-NINE

Victoria Schaffner, Sutton-Millhouse Medical Products' senior sales executive finished her demolition job on Arnold then took several calming, deep breaths. She sensed the possibility for a train wreck of major magnitude. She rang her director of operations and heard his voicemail message telling her he was out of the office, then rang his mobile: 'Hello, Gordon. Vicky here. Sorry to interrupt you whatever you're doing but we need to talk. This is urgent. Sounds like a great party, by the way. Where the hell are you and how quickly can we get together?'

'Ah, bit of a problem, there. Hold on for just a moment 'till I find a quiet spot – that's better. Right. What's the matter?'

'We need to talk and we need to do it in person, not by phone. Where are you and how soon can I see you?'

'Well, in answer to your first question, I'm at a party at the Health Secretary's country place in Buckinghamshire. Quite a rock pile. Big, old and imposing – bit like me, one might say – eh? Not too far from Aylesbury. In answer to your second question, it looks like this'll go on into the wee hours, if not all night. Look, if this is *really* important why don't you drive over? Lot of important people here and I just can't get away. Can't this wait?'

'No, this *can't* wait! I don't want to say any more now. Give me some directions and I'll see you in an hour or so.'

'Sounds rather mysterious. I'm intrigued. See you then.'

Victoria was responsible for negotiating and securing some of the biggest contracts for medical supplies in the world. She had an uncanny ability to anticipate possible problems—some even suggested she might be psychic—coupled with a gut feel for situations where 'things just did not look quite right'; when she predicted an impending disaster or even a little bump on the road to a signed agreement, SMMP senior managers and executives paid attention. Her annual pay packet consisted mostly of commissions and exceeded all but those of her chief executive and a couple of directors; she had no interest whatsoever in a place on the board.

Sans Soucis, the country home of the Right Honourable Darwin Cantwell, MP and Secretary of State for Health was quite a rock pile indeed. Victoria was suitably impressed as she negotiated the sweeping gravel approach looking for a convenient space to park among the assorted Bentleys, Rollers, DB14s, Range Rovers, high end BMWs and Audis, a couple of Porsches, Jags and even a Bristol Blenheim scattered about apparently at random; about the only ones absent were Lamborghinis and Ferraris. A career as an elected servant of the people can't be too shabby a way to earn a crust.

She collected a flute of champagne from a sparkling silver tray supported by a motionless white-coated waiter standing to attention near the entrance and sipped it while she moved through the crowded rooms looking for Gordon. She recognized some Members of Parliament, a few lords, two footballers, several intellectually challenged TV celebrities, a shamelessly self-promoting businessman who hosted a popular television series called *Bullying Losers For Fun and Profit*, a gaggle of lobbyists for the healthcare industry, the ambitious director of marketing for one of SMMP's generally unsuccessful competitors, three cabinet ministers in addition to Cantwell himself and the chief executive officer of World-Universal

News Corporation, the publishing empire whose stable included the cream of Britain's totally tasteless tabloids. The only one missing seemed to be the Prime Minister.

She finally located Gordon and without saying anything other than a whispered, 'Come with me!' clutched him by the arm and dragged him out through the French doors, across a veranda and down wide steps into expansive gardens.

Steering him to a convenient bench in a secluded nook, they sat down: 'Oh, hi, Gordon. Nice to see you. And you, too, Vicky, yeah, great to see you. Enjoying yourself? Yes, thank you. Great party. Come here often?'

'Sarcasm doesn't become you, Gordon, and I am genuinely sorry for disturbing you but I told you this is important.'

'It must be. What's up?'

'Remember that Stover incident a couple of years ago?'

'Not really. Who the hell's Stover? Refresh my memory.'

'The mis-labelled solutions. Surely you remember *that*!'

'Oh, yes. Christ! Why now? I'd assumed we'd buried that one forever.'

'Me, too – hadn't even thought about it for yonks – but good ol' Arnold Numbnuts just had a meeting with some guy asking truly awkward questions. I don't know what's going on but –'

'Shit! That information in the wrong hands and –'

'– and we're all going down the toilet quick time – well, hell, you don't need to remind me. Anyhow, bitching about it won't do us any good. We've got to find this mystery man and figure out what he's up to before the proverbial hits the fan. If it does, a lot of us are gonna be covered in it.'

'So, other than noting a significant number of scatological references dotting this conversation, what, exactly, do you want me to say?'

'Say you can make this go away. Call in some favours. With your alliances in the corridors of power surely you can connect with a fixer who knows somebody who knows somebody who can find this guy and warn him off. You know the drill.'

'Okay, leave it with me. I'll have a word with Cantwell and –'

'Cantwell? Why involve him?'

'Well, hell, Vicky, he's as much a part of this as you and me. He needs to be warned. Besides, he probably knows more fixers than anybody in Westminster.'

'But –'

'I'll see to it! As soon as I know anything I'll let you know. There's nothing more you can do in the meantime. Relax. Have a few more drinks. Mix. Rub elbows with the great and the good assembled here. Everything's under control.'

'Isn't that the last thing Custer said before the Battle of the Little Big Horn?'

'No, I think the last thing he said was: "Look at all them fucking Indians!"'

'That's exactly what I mean. You haven't convinced me everything *is* under control.'

Victoria gave him the little information she had: the name 'Thornton Gilrey' they assumed was false, and the time and location of Arnold's meeting with him. Gordon assured her people Cantwell knew could track him down; with the plethora of CCTV cameras, facial recognition software and fingerprint databases permeating twenty-first century society, he was bound to have left enough of a trail for them to follow.

CHAPTER THIRTY

DARWIN LIVINGSTON BEDFORD Cantwell was ideally suited for a life in politics. Born into an upper-middle-class family of independent means, enrolled at a public school followed by studies in Economics and Political Science at Cambridge then elected to the safest seat in the country as the youngest Conservative ever to enter Parliament, he was utterly devoid of empathy for anyone other than like-minded fellows, with no sympathy for anybody and endowed with an arrogance ensuring supreme confidence under every circumstance, he might be described as the 'perfect politician'. Received wisdom among many Conservatives was he was destined for greater things, possibly even residency at Number Ten.

A sign on the wall prominently facing all who entered his office in Richmond House proclaimed: 'I have three rules for life: Rule #1 – I am the Boss, Rule #2 – The Boss is always right, Rule #3 – If I am ever wrong, see Rule #1.' People who knew him intimately commented this sign was the only indication he had any sense of humour even as they acknowledged this was, in fact, one of the principles he lived by. An American might have remarked: 'He thinks his shit don't stink.'

Rule Number One worked well most of the time with an occasional need to refer to Number Two and *rarely* to Number Three. Although he would not acknowledge he had done anything wrong—he *never* admitted to his having done anything wrong, he was, nevertheless, confronted with a situation he might characterize as 'one of those very rare occasions'.

The fixer he chose for this assignment was a retired detective chief inspector from the Met, Milford Cleeland, who, in addition to his being the paradigm of discretion, was also known never to ask awkward questions beyond his need to know. 'Need to know' in this case did not include any information on why Darwin wanted to locate this mystery man. He delivered his report in an A4 envelope to Darwin at a coffee shop on Great Peter Street. Darwin asked no awkward questions of his own under the principle 'need to know' works both ways; he knew enough about Milford's methods to conclude he likely obtained CCTV images from the Dorchester and identified his target using a facial recognition system.

The man calling himself 'Thornton Gilrey' was a private close protection security contractor named Oswald Doran based in Manchester; home and office addresses, and landline and mobile telephone numbers were included. Milford's notes indicated Doran was squeaky clean except for a stint as a mercenary in central Africa—the details of which were scant. On many weekends he flew gliders. Darwin considered this information. The good news was he was not a reporter trying to disinter an incident that should have stayed buried forever. The bad news was the possibility he was investigating this for someone who was: a reporter, somebody writing a book about the healthcare industry or the NHS, or William Stover's widow. In any case, he needed to be scared off.

He placed another call to Milford and arranged a second meeting at the coffee shop. They found a table and ordered cappuccini. Darwin handed the report back to him: 'Right, Milford, good work so far but I need more.'

'Okay, Mister Cantwell, what next?'

'I want you to bring in a couple of heavies to pay our Mister Doran a visit. Two things. First, these men aren't to know *anything* other than his name and location – absolutely nothing about the whys and wherefores. Their simple message to Doran is to stop bothering people and to stop asking the kinds of questions he asked during his meeting at the Dorchester. They can demand his solemn promise to behave and we both know that won't mean anything – especially to a man like Doran. The only actual result will be to let him know certain people are aware he's trying to go to places he shouldn't be going.

'Second, I don't want any more rough stuff than absolutely necessary – only if he fights back – and then only enough force to allow your men to get away. I don't want his house trashed or his car torched. I don't want him beaten up or kneecapped, I don't want his cat or budgie killed, I just want him warned off. According to your report he's a loner with no family or even any close friends that he associates with regularly. Maybe he has a girlfriend. If he does, I want you to make clear they are not to touch her or even go near her. Understood?'

'Understood. Timeframe?'

'Just as soon as possible.'

'Usual arrangements?'

'Yes. Ring me when it's done and we'll meet here.'

'Done.'

Darwin handed Milford an envelope containing cash in payment for the work done to date and they went their separate ways.

CHAPTER THIRTY-ONE

OS PARKED ON the street close to his terraced house, shut off the engine and sat quietly for a few minutes. He had returned from dropping off Amanda and the girls after a nice day of flying and their usual meal at the Brindle Cow. Three weeks had passed without incident and Trevor had not bothered her. Without telling her what he was doing, he shadowed her several times during the school run and saw nobody following her. He was still thinking about his approach to Gordon Milne; he would wait until he and Brian exchanged more information before he made his next move.

He closed the car door and collected his flying bag from the boot. He squeezed the fob to set the alarm when a man materialized from the shadows thirty feet in front of him. When the man stepped into the light, Os could see him pointing a large-bore revolver: 'Doran?'

'Yeah – who's asking?'

'Put your hands where I can see them. Now! You tooled up?'

'No.'

Os raised his hands slowly above his head and turned around far enough to see a second man behind him also thirty feet away. He was holding a sawn-off shotgun. Os was in no position to defend himself. He stood still, absorbing details about the two: their sizes, builds, accents and clothing: 'What do you want?'

'You've been askin' the wrong people the wrong kind of questions.'

'I ask a lot of people a lot of questions. It's part of my job.'

'Shut up and listen, nobhead.'

'You still haven't told me what you want.'

'You had that meeting at that hotel in London a while back.'

'What of it?'

'Well, the people you was askin' about don't like you askin' all those questions about their business.'

'And you still haven't told me what that has to do with you two.'

'You must be thicker'n pig shit, Doran. Those people are friends of ours and they told us to have a quiet word with you and that's just what we're doin' now. That ain't too hard to understand, now, is it?'

'So what if I don't listen and do what you tell me?'

'Well then I guess we'll just have to come back here some night when you're asleep and blow your fuckin' head off. That answer your fuckin' question?'

'Guess so.'

'Right. You been warned. Now you just stand very still without movin' for about an hour so me and my friend here can get away then you can go in your house and have a wank or do whatever you want to do. You can call the cops if you want but I don't think it'll do you no good. Maybe we'll see you again, Doran. You better hope not!'

Os stood perfectly still as the two turned and walked down the street and out of sight. Both were tall, over six feet and of stocky build. Both were Caucasian, bearded and dressed identically. The accent was definitely not Mancunian—possibly East of England. Both wore jeans and classic black leather motorcycle jackets. Os read the name on the backs of their jackets: 'Sons of Damien' when they passed under a streetlamp. This was reinforced minutes later when he heard two big bikes—probably Harleys—thunder into life down the street. Not too clever, really, wearing their colours on a job.

⌘

He brewed coffee—relaxing as he came down from the adrenalin rush. No harm done: he came away from the confrontation intact and now it was time to figure out just what was going on. He did not think Trevor sent these two goons around; that is, unless he was in communication with either Arnold or Stanley and he doubted this. No, it was probable Arnold told Victoria about their meeting and this information rolled up the chain of command to somebody who issued the order, possibly Milne or maybe someone even higher. In any case his enquiries certainly had come to somebody's attention. This suggested he had gone to, in the words of an American he knew in Iraq, 'somewhere he hadn't otta bin'. Good. Maybe it was time for some action. He needed to do some more flowcharting and talk to Brian but in the meantime he could do a little surfing of his own and maybe find out something about the Sons of Damien Motorcycle Club.

He booted up his PC and logged onto Google. He found links to forum posts about a gang based in North Lincolnshire called 'Sons of Damien'. Their headquarters were on a farm near Upton between Lincoln and Gainsborough. His search yielded some press reports suggesting possible links between them and several recent murders and arson attacks. He concluded they might not be very nice people but going after them now was likely premature; they were probably, as had been Stanley, just following orders.

Somebody with clout decided to send him a message. Since 'they', whoever they were, knew his name and address, and details of his meeting with Arnold, they might also know about his relationship with Amanda. Now it was time to confront Milne, his highest link in the chain, but he also needed to think about organizing some protection for Amanda, the girls and Shirley.

CHAPTER THIRTY-TWO

OS LEFT NO voicemail messages—he kept phoning until his party answered in person: 'Good morning. This is Arnold Hohenzoller, Senior Sales Executive, Sutton-Millhouse Medical Products. How may I help you?'

'Hi, Arnold, Thornton Gilrey here. How are you this morning, mate?'

Arnold sputtered for a few seconds and was silent for even longer, then: 'Mister Gilrey – really didn't expect to hear from you – I – er – following our first meeting – discussions with my manager – we – well, *she* decided – in view of the importance of potential contracts with you – she wants to be party to any conversations or meetings we have. I'm sure you understand. May I put you on hold for a moment?'

Os waited in silence for a minute, then: 'This is Victoria Schaffner, Mister Gilrey or whatever the hell your name is. Just who the hell are you and what the hell do you want?'

'Hello Miz Schaffner. Ah, we meet at last. Finally I've got past the monkey to the organ grinder. Or maybe you're just another monkey. Is Gordon Milne really the organ grinder or is he just another monkey, too?'

'What do you want?'

'Well, I think it's time you, Mister Milne and I had a heart-to-heart talk –'

'About *what*? *Just what the fuck do you want*?'

'Well, Miz Schaffner, you see, this's why we need to talk. I think you already know what I want to talk about. And the fact that you're screaming at me the way you are suggests you're well aware of what I want.'

'Okay, you've got my attention. Please say no more. You want to meet with Gordon and me. When and where?'

'Well, Vicky, may I call you "Vicky"? Fine, you may call me "Thornton" if you wish. Or not. Well, let's say we meet tomorrow at noon in Campbell Park, the Skeldon Roundabout on Silbury Boulevard, you know where I mean, under that really interesting sculpture, "Chain Reaction" I believe it's called. We can find a nice quiet spot in the park where we won't be bothered and well away from prying eyes and nosey parkers. Okay? And I think it would be wise not to include any of your other colleagues at this meeting – in view of the sensitive nature of this matter. I'm sure you understand.'

'Fine. Fine.'

'Oh, and –'

'Yes –'

'As you may have already gathered, I'm rather good at my job although, admittedly you don't quite know yet what my job is. Please inform Mister Milne it would be unwise to bring anybody else along to our meeting, say, for example, any members of the Sons of Damien –'

'I don't have the faintest bloody idea what you're talking about.'

'I'm sure you don't, but I'm certain Mister Milne does.'

'Goodbye!'

Victoria slammed the phone down, stormed out of her office and up two floors, ignoring the lift, strode into Gordon's suite and rushed into his office over the protests of his secretary.

She stood glaring at him with her arms folded until he finished his telephone call: 'We have to stop meeting like this, Miz Schaffner. People are starting to talk. What can I do for you –?'

'You said you'd make it go away and it hasn't gone away!'

'What the hell're you talking about?'

'The Stover thing. You told me Cantwell'd make it go away and it hasn't gone away.'

'All right, all right. Stop babbling and tell me what's happening.'

'I just got off the phone with Gilrey or whatever the hell his name is –'

'What?'

'He rang Arnold to ask for a meeting. Arnold wet himself then passed the phone to me. Gilrey's demanding a meeting with you and me, and he hinted he knows something about the Stover thing. I don't know whether he's bluffing or not but from what he says my guess is he's not – well, not entirely.'

'But why *me*? Where'd he get *my* name? And to think of it, where'd he get *your* name?'

'I have absolutely no bloody idea but we need to deal with this man before he does any more damage.'

'Calm down – calm down. So when and where're we supposed to meet?'

'Tomorrow. Noon. Campbell Park. He wants to talk with you and me and nobody else.'

'Shit! Cantwell said he'd see to this but obviously he hasn't. You go back to your office. I'll ring him and dump this back in his lap. Obviously his fixer didn't fix anything. Maybe he can think of something. I'll get back to you as soon as I know what's going on.'

CHAPTER THIRTY-THREE

OS DROVE TO Milton Keynes at six o'clock the next morning and conducted a recce of the area. There were plenty of nooks and crannies where miscreants might hide but approach roads were open and level, and visibility was good across the park. He planned for his confrontation with Schaffner and Milne assuming although they were competent in the world of shady procurement deals, backhanders and perhaps even blackmail and honey traps, they probably had no experience at all in the world of kidnap or violence—actual or threatened. He had no photographs of either. He organized no backup; he thought it unlikely either was a physical threat.

At eleven-thirty he drove along the road next to the park twice, looking carefully for suspicious characters but saw none. He parked a quarter mile away, off Silbury Boulevard, hid the key and fob under a stone jammed against the front offside tyre and walked to the sculpture. He left his Glock in the glove box. He anticipated an unfriendly confrontation and knew the intimidating value of a pair of dark glasses: he wore his Ray-Ban Aviators.

The two arrived a few minutes later, parked next to the bus shelter near the roundabout and walked towards him. He stood next to the sculpture and assessed them as they came closer. Victoria's body language hinted she was unsure of herself; this was consistent with the situation and Os assumed this was as it should be. Gordon on the other hand appeared confident—sure of himself—and to Os this meant either he was such a cocky son of a bitch he thought he could emerge from this meeting as a winner or something else was happening.

He read the situation correctly but failed to react in time. Something was out of place; something was not quite right. His experience with high profile clients—people who moved in the highest circles—provided him with something about their dress sense and Gordon was not dressed like the director of a big business organization—he was dressed more like a detective. Os confirmed this a second later when he glanced down at his shoes: heavy, rubber-soled cop shoes, but by then it was too late.

The woman stopped five paces from him, reached into her handbag and pulled out a small, shiny pistol he did not recognise. She dropped her bag and held it in both trembling hands pointed at his chest. She was too far away for him to disarm her; although it was clear she did not do this kind of thing every day, she had been coached well. He moved one small step closer to her and she moved one big step back. He could not see whether it was cocked or not.

'Right, Doran. Hands up and stand perfectly still.'

For somebody who's obviously an amateur she's doing okay, he thought. He turned to the man, also five paces away pulling what looked like a 38 Special from a shoulder holster.

Her use of his name confirmed he had let himself be led into a trap: 'I take it this isn't Gordon Milne and I'll bet this isn't even Victoria Schaffner.'

'Right on both counts, Mister Doran, this *isn't* Gordon Milne, but I know who *you* are, and I guess you didn't get the message the other night, so apparently what we have here is a failure to communicate.'

'Shame. I was looking forward to meeting them both. And you two are?'

'Piss off! Maybe my friends are right, you really aren't too clever.'

He kept the revolver pointed steadily at Os' right knee while he made a call on his mobile.

'Okay, we've arranged a little ride into the countryside for you. I'm afraid it may not be too comfortable for you but one way or another we must get your attention. I hope you'll understand.'

A dirty white van of uncertain age and lineage came around the roundabout and pulled onto the verge next to the sculpture. The two Sons of Damien Os had already met, this time sans their colours, climbed slowly out. They were both smiling as they approached him cautiously. Although they were big and powerful, with Os' experience he could have taken them both down if it were not for the two weapons pointed at him, one in the hands of a possibly seasoned law officer and the other in the hands of an obviously nervous woman.

He let himself be handcuffed and patted down professionally by the man who was not Gordon Milne; that he was cuffed with his hands behind him also suggested the man was trained as a policeman. The two goons threw him none too gently into the back of the van and slammed the door also none too gently. He could hear their final instructions from inside.

'Right, I'll be along tomorrow morning to ask him some questions. In the meantime, you should soften him up a bit. But be careful – not too much softening, if you know what I mean. He needs to be able to give me some answers.'

'And after that?'

'Well after that – after all, he knows what we all look like and –'

The two giggled. He heard more muffled conversation then the two climbed into the van and drove off.

In detective and murder mystery television and film drama, the captive riding in the back of the van cleverly keeps track of travel times, roughness of roads, turnings, sounds like railway carriages being shunted conveniently nearby or foghorns on quays and thus communicates a location to rescuers. Os did not need to do this because where he was going had nothing to do with his getting out of the trouble he was in. And there was nobody looking for him. Instead he needed to think about what he was going to do when they arrived. He also needed to figure out who the cop was. Whatever was going to happen to him was probably going to be unpleasant.

Survival mode kicked in. He needed to get the cuffs in front of him so he could work on them. Thank goodness these were traditional chain cuffs and not hinged; he would have struggled to escape from speedcuffs, especially if they had been applied rear stack. He rotated his wrists so his arms were straight behind him and his hands were back-to-back. Then he pulled himself into a tight ball and rolled around on the floor; he had not practised this since training sessions a long time ago.

With the cuffs manoeuvred down his back and legs then under his feet and into his lap, he twisted his wrists once again until his palms were facing. He removed his sunglasses and went to work. Shame to ruin a pair of classic Aviators but needs must. He broke off one wire temple and used it to pick the locks. He worked hard with this, too. He rubbed his wrists, sat back comfortably and planned his next move.

He had two choices: either wait until they arrived at their destination he assumed was their headquarters or try to get them to stop the van before they reached the farm. He chose the latter.

The back of the van was clean: no convenient tyre irons, rope, pieces of wood or anything else he could use as a weapon. Never mind; he could deal with these two, particularly since they expected him to have his hands cuffed behind his back. He made another assumption that turned out to be accurate: although they were big and strong they were not very fast and certainly not very bright. He also had an advantage: while he was hidden in the darkness, when they opened the door they would be looking in from full daylight. They were moving smoothly and at high speed, probably on a motorway or a duel carriageway. He was ready.

He started yelling and swearing while moving from one side to the other, slamming into the walls with his full weight. After a minute of this mayhem they stopped. He heard the passenger get out and come to the back while the driver stayed in his seat. Os stood up and grasped the cross-frame member under the roof above his head and waited until the man opened the offside half door and looked inside. While he was framed in the light and peering into the dark, Os swung forward hanging from the frame and kicked him full in the face with both feet. He crumpled to the ground in a heap—dazed but not unconscious.

He would live to fight again but Os had a minute to deal with the other before he recovered. He climbed out the door, ran to the front on the nearside, around the front and slammed the door into the driver climbing out. He was jammed halfway out the door and Os head butted him, breaking his nose. He, too, dropped to the ground but not unconscious. Os ran to the back to the first man now trying to get to his feet. His second kick to the face— one Chuck Norris would have been proud of—dropped him again and this time he stayed down. Os moved back to the front and repeated this manoeuvre with the driver. Not bad for two minutes' work.

He dragged the two off the verge, down into some bushes and next to a stock fence overgrown with nettles.

He laced one arm of each through the fence and secured them with the cuffs. Dock leaves rubbed on his arms eliminated most of the stinging where he brushed the nettles; as it turns out at least this old wives' tale is true. He climbed up the bank and into the van, waited a few minutes for the rush to subside then drove back to his office.

When he debriefed himself, as he always did at the close of a contract, he asked himself why he had been so careless, and his only sensible answer was he let himself become personally involved. Refusing to become personally involved with people he was protecting was not the same as ignoring their feelings, rather it meant not allowing these feelings to upset his timing or interfere with his making good decisions. He concluded his love for Amanda and the girls had drawn him into a level of personal involvement he was usually able to avoid.

CHAPTER THIRTY-FOUR

OS EXCHANGED THE number plates on the van with some he kept for just such purposes and parked it on a street a little distance from his office. He travelled by the next available train to Milton Keynes then boarded a bus to Campbell Park where he retrieved his car and drove back to Manchester. Between Google Search, Earth and Street View he located the farm that was the base of operations for the Sons of Damien: a rambling, motley collection of interconnected farm buildings surrounded by overgrown fields just to the west of Upton. It would have been nice to have the time for a proper reconnaissance but what he planned needed to be completed before the night ended.

Into the van he loaded gear to stow a heavy motorbike securely and a few other things he might need. He left home at sundown, drove for an hour and a half, parked the van off the road in a grove of trees and walked a quarter mile to the farm. He scouted the ground surrounding the buildings, considered possible escape routes and located what he judged to be the weakest points of entry.

There were people about so there was nothing more to do but wait with no idea whether they would all eventually leave and go to wherever motorcycle gang members go when they are not hanging out at their headquarters or if some lived there. He sat comfortably and securely in nearby bushes, and watched and listened to riders fire up their bikes and roar off. He wondered whether anybody was waiting for the two to return with their captive in the van or that assignment was nothing out of the ordinary for these outlaws.

At midnight he heard no more activity and judged all those who were leaving for the night had gone. He needed to confirm either the complex was deserted or locate anybody still there and, if so, whether they had gone to sleep or were just chilling out. He needed to make a big noise and see if anybody responded. He worked his way around one of the buildings to the disassembled steel framework of a utility building stacked up against a wall along with the sheets of rusted corrugated steel that had originally covered it.

He used a fence post to lever the frame members away from the wall far enough they crashed to the ground with a noise that certainly would have come to the attention to anybody on the farm. He scurried back to his hideout and waited. Nothing happened. Over the next half hour he did this with two more piles of suitably noisy building materials. Still nothing happened; he assumed the farm was deserted.

Two areas interested him: their armoury and their workshop. He put on his gloves, rummaged around through rooms one might euphemistically describe as 'living quarters' and his searching led him to an impressive collection of firearms. He selected three for his project: a Colt 45 calibre model M1911A1 semi-automatic pistol, a Webley Break-Top 455 revolver and a break-action 12 bore sawn-off double barrelled shotgun of unknown make. These latter two were possibly the ones he faced two nights before. They all looked well-used and he hoped police departments across the country had ballistics reports on file implicating these in various crimes. He gathered them along with ammunition for each and moved on to the shop.

A big sliding door identified the shop and he wandered around between twenty massive, powerful and shiny Harley-Davidsons. The one he chose was a FLSTC Heritage Softail Classic with fringed white leather saddlebags and custom deep-purple candy paint job; he wanted something memorable. He found a board full of keys above a workbench and identified the one for his ride. He went back to the rooms where he started his search and located a Bell full-jet helmet with tinted visor and a leather jacket with full Sons of Damien colours across the back, both almost in his size. Everything was moved to the door and piled there. He confirmed the bike would start easily and the door was unlocked.

He retrieved the van, returned and reversed it up to the door, slid the door open, positioned the board he was using for a ramp, walked the bike up into the van and strapped it securely in its cradles. Then he loaded the rest of his gear into the van, slid the shop door shut and drove out onto the road. He was doing well so far but he still had a great deal to do before sunup.

The route he chose from Upton to Manchester included many miles on motorways and duel carriageways. He drove west from the farm to the A1 where he parked the van in a lay-by screened from the road by trees. He unloaded the bike, put on his helmet and leather jacket then headed for Manchester. On his journey he stopped twice for fuel at motorway services being careful to expose his bike, its number plate and his colours to whatever CCTV cameras were looking his way.

He arrived in Cheetham Hill at three. Earlier in the day he identified three pubs in the area known to be the locals for constantly warring gangs. Still managing to conduct his business in full view of cameras, he rode into the car park of the Oubliette and blasted two big windows out of the front of the building with his shotgun. He rode to the Baited Bear and emptied six 455 calibre rounds from his Webley into windows across the front of the building. Next he defaced the sign hanging over the door of the

Flayed Ox by firing seven 45 calibre rounds from his Colt into it.

On his return journey he stopped twice for fuel. He stowed the bike in the van and drove back to the farm, arriving just before five o'clock. He drove past once looking for signs of life before he returned the bike, helmet and jacket, and arsenal to their rightful places. At five-thirty he slid the door shut and began his drive home. Whether members of the gang eventually discovered some of their gear had been borrowed did not concern him.

He loaded a pushbike into the van and drove to Snake Pass on the A57 above Glossop, parked it along a deserted section of the road, replaced the number plates, set fire to it and rode his pushbike down the winding road to Glossop where he boarded a train to take him back home.

It was time for answers to some questions. Did Gordon Milne engineer his failed abduction or was somebody else pulling the strings? Who was the detective, was he serving or retired and was he a key player or simply an enforcer? Would another visit to Trevor give him any more useful information or was he just the hack reporter Os assumed he was? Would it be worth spending some time with Winifred? And finally, if things were heating up, at some point these people would probably threaten Amanda. What did he need to do to protect his girls? Maybe it was time to schedule another session with Brian.

CHAPTER THIRTY-FIVE

TREVOR STEPPED UP to the bar in The Flayed Ox, ordered his pint of bitter and waited for George. He came in a few minutes later and they moved to a table. Trevor tried to look calm and in control but failed miserably; he kept his hands firmly locked to the edge of the table to stop their shaking. His eye contact with George was totally out of sync with his speech and his attempt to keep the conversation flowing with at least a minimum of jocularity was a complete waste of his time.

'So, George – Mister Barr – have you – do you – can you tell me who my – ha –mystery man is?'

'You gotta be fuckin' kiddin'! No name, no picture, nothin' but, "maybe he's ex-military, maybe he's in Manchester and maybe he got a fuckin' girlfriend".'

'Well, I said it's not much to go on but you said –'

'Right, alright, I know what I fuckin' said,' as he pulled a bent and soiled photograph from his shirt pocket. 'Here. Take a look at this. Reconize him? Any these blokes him?'

Trevor took the photograph, laid it down next to his pint, re-clamped his hands to the table's edge and looked closely. It was of twelve men in jungle camouflage fatigues posing for the camera under some palm trees. The sun was bright, the bare ground was more red than brown and in the background he could see several round mud huts with conical thatched roofs. The men were all holding what looked to him to be Kalashnikovs. He immediately recognized George. He looked carefully at the other faces and spotted Os. He sat very still and stared at the image for a few seconds then handed it back to George.

He pointed to him: 'There, that's him. I recognize him. Yeah, that's definitely him.'

'Fuck! Him? That's fuckin' Ossie Doran. I've been looking for him for a long time. I was told he was in Birmingham. I got a fuckin' score to settle with him. An' he's here – he's here in Manchester? Can you find him for me? I want you to find him for me.'

'Well, Mister Barr –'

'What – "Well, Mister Barr?" – well, I give you his fuckin' name. Now you find him for me!'

'But all I wanted from you was his name and you've done that and now I'll pay you as we agreed –'

'No, Trevor LaFarge, it don't work quite like that.'

'I don't understand –'

'The deal's off. You find 'em and you tell me where he is –'

'Then?'

'Then what happens then is none a your fuckin' business.'

'But I need some information he has and –'

'But nothin' – shit! But what happens to him will happen to you if you don't do what I tell you.'

The conversation continued and with each exchange Trevor lost more control of the situation. Thoroughly terrified by George's not-so-thinly disguised threats of violence if he refused, he agreed to return in two days and provide him with Os' address, definitely, and phone numbers, possibly. As he left the pub he was reminded of Quinn's advice about a move to Canada's being good for his health.

CHAPTER THIRTY-SIX

OS WANTED TO protect the girls and do it quickly. He sent Amanda a text message telling her he needed to speak with her urgently after work. She returned his message and he arrived at the house around seven-thirty in the evening. The girls were settled on the sofa watching television.

She sat him at the dining room table and poured him coffee: 'So, why all the mystery, Ossie? We –'

'"Aidie". My closest friends call me "Aidie".'

She took his hand, winked at him and smiled: 'So now I'm one of your bestest friends, Aidie, one of your inner circle?'

'Something like that. Well, heck, you've agreed to my dirty old man invitation to a weekend in London, so – yeah, I guess that makes you one of my bestest friends.'

She smiled again and squeezed his hand: 'Tell me something – why "Aidie"? And anyhow you're not *that* old.'

'Well, it's my middle name, well, not "Aidie" but "Aidan". And thanks for that.'

'Okay – *Aidie*, what's up?'

Until now, he told her nothing about what happened, the warning visit, the attempted kidnap or his midnight ride. Now he told her everything, only omitting his thoughts about the scale of the cover-up. He hesitated occasionally, giving her time to respond or ask questions but she said nothing; she just looked more and more intense as he talked. Her silence was confusing him; he was not certain whether she was pleased with his actions or sad she was being reminded of the terrible events of the past.

He tried to respond to what he thought she was thinking: 'I told you I'd see to Trevor LaFarge and that he wouldn't bother you again but when I started looking into it – well, there just seemed to be more and more to it – more people involved, more twists and turns. And being the person I am, I just decided to follow and see where it led.'

'So, why, exactly, are you telling me now?'

'Well, my almost abduction yesterday – more amateurs – the detective, or the man I assume was a detective, wasn't an amateur by any stretch of the imagination but the two berks he hired to do the job – Wow! Aside from all that, though, somebody somewhere with some serious levels of clout is involved and I'm starting to think since they've come after me they might soon be coming after you.'

'So, what, Aidie, my new bestest friend, do you suggest?'

He told her it made sense to send Shirley and the girls away, somewhere far away, and he asked if they had any relatives in Canada, America, Australia or New Zealand where they could stay for a couple of weeks.

She squeezed his hand again: 'Do you think all that's really necessary?'

'Yes, I think so,' and now he squeezed *her* hand.

She rang Shirley and they discussed the three of them going to stay with Shirley's sister in Toronto. They confirmed their passports were in order and early next morning went to a high street travel agency and booked a flight leaving Heathrow mid-day the following day. They paid cash for their tickets, went home and packed. Shirley was bewildered that things were happening so quickly, and Amanda assured her everything was fine, and without giving her too much detail, told her what Os had discovered about the events leading up to Bill's death. Although Shirley was not fully convinced of the need for these drastic actions, she agreed to the move. The girls were excited about a mysterious two-week break from school all the way to Canada.

Os collected them the next morning. They loaded their cases into the car, exchanged lots of hugs and kisses with Amanda then left for the airport. They followed motorways for their entire trip: out of the city and onto the M6, finally exiting the M25 near Heathrow.

He spotted the car tailing them somewhere near Stoke-on-Trent; these were definitely *not* amateurs. He would not have been able to lose them without some evasive driving, upsetting his three passengers and delaying their arrival, so he maintained his speed and they continued their journey as though everything was normal. They drove south and he planned their exit from the car and into the terminal. While on the M25 he quietly told Shirley what he wanted her to do when they stopped. She confirmed all their documents and tickets were safely in her handbag and told him she was ready.

He switched to the lane leading to the taxi rank at Terminal Four with their tail following, now two cars behind. Os whipped into an empty slot and stopped. There was no space for the other car so they double-parked, still two cars behind. Shirley jumped out, opened the rear door, unsnapped the girls' seatbelts and hurried them into the terminal through the nearest door. Once they were inside and within the ring of heavily armed uniformed police they would be safe; no matter how good these men were, it would be impossible for them to snatch somebody from the check-in hall.

Immediately Shirley closed the rear door Os pulled out of his slot and sped out the exit ramp just as an attendant was approaching, no doubt to tell him he was not allowed to park there. He was ready for some evasive driving should he need it. Both men left their car to follow the three into the terminal; Os' quick departure caught them out. They ran back to their car when they saw him drive away; in his mirror he saw police coming at the two from several directions. Unless they had some official identification or at least something that looked official they would be occupied for a while.

He drove casually around the loop, parked in a short-stay bay, collected the cases from the boot and met the three inside while they were queuing to check in. He stood in the queue with them until they were handed their boarding passes then followed them to Security as far as he was allowed. With more hugs and kisses they waved goodbye and were on their way.

He wandered around the terminal for half an hour, leaving through Arrivals. He paid for his parking ticket and walked to his car, looking around for his tail. He saw none and wondered whether they were still nearby or had been detained by the police. He exited the complex onto the M25 and homeward.

During his return journey he never exceeded the speed limit and stopped twice. He ordered coffees and nursed them casually sitting in services restaurants. His aim was to see if the two men were still tailing him. When he left the second restaurant he was puzzled he had not seen them. He doubted they were still being held by the police at Heathrow so either they were not very good at their jobs or something else. The 'something else' frightened him because he realized they might not have been after him but the girls. Now he exceeded the speed limit by a great deal in his rush to get back to Amanda.

He double-parked in front of the house and his fears were confirmed when he touched the front door and it yielded; not only was it not locked, it was not latched. Fight or flight response activated in the direction of fight; he silently stepped into the hall, listening for any sound telling him someone was in the house. He heard none. Even as he knew she was not there to answer him, he called to her anyhow. Furniture was disturbed, some ornaments were broken and several pictures were askew but although the ground floor rooms had not been thoroughly trashed it was clear she had struggled. More carelessness; damn! she should have been with them on their airport run. Now he must move fast and he must stop making stupid mistakes.

CHAPTER THIRTY-SEVEN

GORDON MILNE WAS in the eye of the storm where for now it was completely calm, oblivious to the whirlwind enveloping him. Other than Victoria's hysterical outburst in his office, he knew nothing about anything that occurred over the past seventy-two hours connected with what he used to casually refer to as 'that little inconvenience', from Darwin's aborted attempt to make Os stop asking awkward questions to Amanda's abduction.

He never heard of Milford Cleeland or the Sons of Damien and he knew nothing about what was going to happen to him in the next few hours. Since he heard nothing further from Victoria or Darwin, he assumed all was quiet and the problem had been addressed; now things could get back to normal. He returned from a long, delightful and successful lunch where potentially profitable promises were made over many nudges and winks, and a couple of fat brown envelopes changed hands while extremely expensive vintage cognac flowed freely. In days gone by, costly Cuban cigars would also have been smoked. It was a glorious afternoon.

CHAPTER THIRTY-EIGHT

OS MADE TELEPHONE calls using a series of interesting names and even more interesting accents, starting with the SMMP central switchboard. The first gained him Gordon's direct line; the second, his mobile. Obtaining a home telephone number and address were a little harder; his friend Brian could easily have done all this for him but time was tight.

He spoke with Gordon's secretary pleading he needed to deliver a surprise gift his wife had purchased for him while she was in London but when he arrived in Milton Keynes he discovered he had lost the address and if the gift didn't arrive in time he would absolutely positively lose his job. Hearing this sad, sad story, she was almost in tears and when Os put the phone down he had the address he needed. He stowed some gear in the boot, put the Glock and two loaded magazines in the glove box and headed for the Milne residence on Linford Lane in Willen.

He pulled off the street and onto the gravel approach; swinging around until he was facing the street. He was impressed by the house; the medical products business must reward its lackeys handsomely. He snapped a magazine into the Glock and stuck it behind his belt in the middle of his back, walked to the door and rang the bell.

When she opened it: 'Missus Milne?'

'Yes?'

He grabbed her by the arm, pushed her inside, slammed the door, towed her into a big, impressively-furnished reception room and shoved her down onto one of three Chesterfield sofas tastefully arranged around the fireplace. He pulled the pistol from his back and waved it around: 'Listen carefully.'

'What – who?'

'Quiet! Don't say anything, just do what I tell you. Anybody else in the house – anybody around at all? maid? cook? gardener? pool cleaner? fitness coach? toyboy?'

'No. But what –?'

I need to speak to your husband – *now*!'

'But he's not here!'

'I can see that. Ring him, wherever he is. Tell him to get here now. Tell him it has to do with Bill Stover. Tell him my name is Gilrey – *Gilrey* – and I'm pointing a very big gun at you and unless he gets here soon –. He'll get the picture.'

'But –'

'Do it – now!'

She picked up her mobile from a side table, punched in a speed-dial number and waited for a response. When Gordon answered she was reasonably calm when the conversation began but as it continued she became more hysterical until finally she was screaming incoherently.

Os took the phone: 'Milne!'

'Yes, what do you want, Gilrey?'

'I want you here – now!'

'And if I refuse?'

'Then she dies, and she dies very slowly. Is that clear?'

'And if I ring the police?'

'Then she dies anyway but maybe just a little quicker immediately I hear a siren or see a car that's not yours disturbing the gravel in front of your very imposing house.'

'Don't hurt her. Please don't hurt her. She knows nothing about this. I'll be there in maybe thirty minutes.'

'If you're not here in forty-five minutes I start removing her fingers, one-by-one and if you're not here in an hour and a quarter I start on the eyes. Is that clear?'

'I'll be there. Don't hurt her.'

Os sat down on a facing sofa and glared at her. He drummed his fingers on the rich, red leather, looked at his watch repeatedly, tossed the pistol from hand-to-hand, crossed and uncrossed his legs, smiled at her occasionally, sighed loudly and hummed off key. She sobbed throughout but said nothing—no begging, no questioning. He was not a cruel man: he was not tormenting her for his pleasure but to impress Gordon with the seriousness of his intentions; Os wanted her to be a trembling wreck when he arrived. It was working well.

Thirty-five minutes later Gordon screeched in off the street, crunched to a noisy stop and stormed in. Os calmly and silently waved the pistol at him and signalled him to sit next to his wife. Gordon took her hand and sat down without speaking. He looked as though he was still suffering the effects of the sixty-year-old cognac.

He looked at Os and even under these extreme circumstances appeared to be trying to maintain some level of dignity and control: 'What do you want, Gilrey?'

'Come on, Milne. We're well beyond all that. You know exactly what I want.'

'I don't understand –'

'In short words that I'm sure you *will* understand. Where have you taken Amanda Stover?'

'I still don't understand; I don't have the vaguest idea what you're talking about –'

Os stood up, grabbed her by the arm and pushed the barrel of the Glock against her elbow.

She shrieked and Gordon screamed: 'I don't know where she is! I didn't do it. I think I know who might have but *I* didn't do it!'

'Who, Milne, who?'

Os pushed her back down on the sofa.

Gordon sat back and recovered some of his composure. He swallowed twice. He hesitated and breathed deeply: 'Darwin Cantwell, the Health Secretary.'

Os grabbed her and pushed the pistol into her elbow again: 'Do you seriously expect me to believe the Health Secretary's involved in this?'

Gordon was pleading now. He was terrified by Os' response but his non-verbals suggested he was telling the truth—or at least his version of it: 'Do you really think I'd make this up?'

'Probably not.'

He paused, then: 'Now, here's what you're going to do. You're going to tell me where I can find him. Then the two of you are going to sit here quietly – without moving for two days if that's what it takes. He may be at home, he may be in Westminster, he may be in Whitehall, he may be in bloody Bali on a conference. You're not going to try to warn him. You're not going to try to contact the police. You're not going to try to contact *anybody*! If you do, when I'm finished with him, I'll be back. Do you understand?'

Both Milnes shuddered then nodded; they relaxed a little now Os' attention was elsewhere.

Os relaxed a little himself: 'Okay. Few more answers and I'm out of here for now. First question. Kowalski said you personally ordered the cover up. That true?'

Gordon looked at him like a vicar who had just been caught snorting cocaine in the vestry: 'Yes.'

'Hohenzoller told Schaffner and she told you I was sniffing about?'

'Yes.'

'Then you told Cantwell and he sent in the heavies?'

'I guess so.'

'What do you mean, you *"guess so"*?'

'Well I mean I told Cantwell. He said he'd fix it. I don't know what happens after that. He never comes back to me with any details.'

'"*Happens*", "*comes*" – interesting choices of words, Milne. Maybe Freud was right after all. Suggests to me you do this all the time. Great set of ethics you operate under, Gordon – you and all your crowd. People die – kids die – and it's okay if they can't pin it on you. Blame it on somebody else way down the food chain and things'll be just fine – the money keeps on rolling in. Or maybe it's the power. Money or power, which is it?'

Gordon shrugged; Os stood up: 'Cantwell and where he's likely to be. Ring him and tell him there's been a new development and you need to see him urgently. Find out where he is. Tell him you'll meet him wherever, it's important.'

Now?'

'Unbelievably stupid question. Now!'

He handed the mobile to Gordon and again put the muzzle of the Glock against her elbow: 'Careful, now. Be *very* careful.'

CHAPTER THIRTY-NINE

Os ARRIVED AT *Sans Soucis* at sundown, parked under trees on the approach road and walked to the grand entrance. According to Gordon, Darwin was home and he was alone—conveniently his wife was at their flat in London and the live-in couple who were housekeeper and gardener were away for the evening. Gordon sounded suitably hysterical over the phone and the Secretary agreed to see him, assuring him there was absolutely nothing for him to be concerned about.

When the door opened Os was not as gentle as he had been with Gordon's wife: he slammed Darwin against the wall and punched him hard in the stomach: 'Where've you taken Amanda Stover?'

As Darwin slowly recovered from the punch he regained some of his composure: 'I have absolutely no idea what you're talking about, Mister Doran.'

'Wrong answer!' Os punched him again. 'I'm not a happy man. I want to know where she is and I want to know now. Right now.'

With this punch Darwin dropped to the floor and curled into the foetal position. He moaned: 'I don't know where she is.'

'But you know who does.'

'No, I *don't*.'

'This isn't getting us anywhere. Apparently I'm not explaining myself very well.'

Os pulled him to his feet and dragged him through the house, out back to the shed where the gardener kept his tools. He kicked open the door, pushed him inside and slammed it. Darwin was silent. Os switched on the lights, swept the workbench clear of tools and everything else on it and shoved him onto it on his back. He found some rope and tied him securely, spread-eagle fashion. Although Darwin's pupils were dilating, he was becoming tense and he looked clearly like somebody who was not in control of what was happening to him, he still projected the arrogance fundamental to his personality: 'Do you know who I am?'

'Oh, well, heck, let's see, does that mean you don't know who you are or is it some sort of rhetorical question suggesting I should know who you are but I, in fact, don't?'

'This is not a joking matter! I don't know what your game is but I can assure you you are making a very big mistake. I am a member of Parliament and a minister in Her Majesty's government and –'

'And *what*, Mister Secretary? What, precisely, are you going to do now – here?'

Darwin continued his demands: 'Release me immediately before you find yourself in more trouble than you're already in. Surely you know that in *my* position, with *my* authority, I can bring the full force of the law down upon you and –'

'Well, now you see, as far as I can tell, your position is flat on your back tied to a workbench in a shed way out in the country where, as they say in the B movies and hackneyed TV drama: "Nobody can hear you scream".'

'But surely a man with your experience knows how these things work. You've been asking the wrong people the wrong kinds of questions. You're in over your head. You're going places where –'

'Let me finish it for you: "Places where I shouldn't be going." Can't you think of a better line than that?'

Os paused. He started rummaging around in a dark corner of the shed then back to the bench.

'What are you going to do now?'

'Oh, now we're going to engage in a little game of "questions and answers". I'll ask questions and you give me answers. Each time I'm not happy with your answer, something unpleasant will happen to you. I don't know whether you're familiar with this game or not, but I can assure you by the time we're finished here, you will be.'

'Who are you, really? Who are you and why? You're a fool if you think I'm going to answer any of your questions. You're making a big mistake!'

'Well, you already know who I am. You addressed me by name at the door. You may be able to help me understand how you came by my name. The "why" is maybe a little more complicated. Perhaps we'll talk about it as we play our game. For now, though, I ask and you answer. Simple.'

Os removed Darwin's shoes and socks: 'Nice shoes, by the way. Bespoke? West End? Jermyn Street, maybe? Look like it. Must have cost you a bundle but, hell, never mind, taxpayers are good for it – put it down to expenses. ¿Qué? Maybe not taxpayers, maybe backhanders from your pal Milne. And so it goes.'

Darwin was still adamant: 'I'll tell you nothing!'

Os went back to the corner, moved some rakes and spades aside and wheeled a petrol-powered mower to the bench. He found a spanner and removed the spark plug, located some electrical wire and a pair of cutters, cut two pieces of wire each ten feet long and stripped twelve inches of insulation from all four ends. He wrapped the bare end of one wire around the head of the engine; the second to the spark plug lead and both were secured with electrician's tape. The other ends of the two wires were wrapped around Darwin's big toes.

When he realized what Os was planning, all arrogance drained out of him. He screamed: 'What are you doing?'

Os said nothing. He reached for the starter pull cord then stopped: 'Where have you taken Amanda Stover?'

'I don't know. I had nothing to do with it.'

Os pulled the starter cord slowly out to its full length. For every second revolution of the crankshaft, Darwin's legs convulsed with the high-voltage shock. He moaned: 'I don't know, I don't know.'

Os let the cord retract then pulled it three times rapidly. Darwin screamed as he bounced painfully on the bench: 'I don't know! I told you I don't know!'

'But *you* gave the order. You know who took her.'

'I don't know.'

Os pulled the cord five times. Darwin screamed even louder and beat the back of his head on the bench. His bladder let go. He was pleading, sobbing: 'Please stop. Please stop. I don't know. I don't know.'

Os reached for the cord again. Darwin screamed even before he touched it: 'Wait, wait!'

'Well, now, maybe we're getting somewhere. I told you you could help me. Shame about the trousers. So, who did it and where is she?'

'His name is Milford Cleeland, retired Met DCI. He does jobs for me. He fixes things. I don't know where he took her. He doesn't tell me—need to know. You know how it is –'

'So, what you're telling me is that even if I left one of these wires on your toe and wrapped the other one around your soaking wet scrotum and tried to start my mower – and tried and tried and tried – even if I did it for hours on end, you still couldn't tell me where this Cleeland took her?'

Darwin whimpered: 'No. Please, please, no more – no more. I really don't know.'

'Well let's try a different question. Where do you *think* he took her?'

'What I do know is he keeps himself at arms' length – he doesn't do anything heavy himself. He has some people who do it for him.'

'Who? Where? What *people*?'

'I don't know for certain. Just some men. Several times he's hinted about a motorcycle gang, I think – up in Lincolnshire somewhere maybe. Believe me, that's all I know.'

'So where might I find this Cleeland? Never mind for now; I'll look for him later.'

He had the information he needed; Cleeland's whereabouts could wait. He thought it would be a startling coincidence if there were two separate motorcycle gangs from Lincolnshire involved with this project; a safe assumption was Amanda was being held at the farm, or if not there, somebody there would know. It was time to move.

'I think I'll just leave the Right Honourable Gentleman here to think about what a very naughty boy he's been. I'm sure over the next few hours he'll be able to slip his surly bonds and make his way back to his grand house and find some dry trousers.'

Over the wholly contrite yet vociferous objections of the Secretary who still had electrical wires wrapped around his big toes, Os turned off the lights, closed the door, walked to his car and headed for Upton.

CHAPTER FORTY

Os REACHED THE farm at midnight. He parked in the same grove as before. Now in addition to the loaded Glock he strapped a Gerber Mark II combat knife to his leg, stuffed the second magazine for his pistol in his sock and worked his way to his hideout. Thinking about his carelessness of two days ago, he planned this assault with more attention. He assumed somebody was minding Amanda so he would have to disarm and disable at least one and probably two—maybe more. Next he needed to find her then get her out. More of a challenge but he had done this sort of thing before. His advantage was he already knew something about the layout.

He was fresh out of convenient stacks of building materials so he put a bullet into the nearest window. That should get somebody's attention. The door somebody came out of was, he assumed, the one closest to where she was held. A man, not quite as large as the two he had already met but at least as ugly and mean-looking, and maybe a little slimmer emerged from a door near where he knew the armoury was located. Good, a visit to the armoury would be helpful. The man stepped outside, out of the light, and stood quietly for a few minutes, looked around then went back inside. Maybe they were used to having shots fired through their windows in the middle of the night.

Carrying half a brick he picked up on the way, he walked across the deserted yard and up to the wall next to the door. When he was ready he threw the brick through the window he had already attacked. The hole he made this time was much bigger and the man was out the door almost before the falling glass stopped tinkling. Os stepped behind him and brought him down with a rabbit punch. He pulled him away from the door, closed it quietly, dragged him across the yard and into a shed, found some rope and tied his feet and hands securely. The lower half of the man's shirt made a convenient gag.

Next he went through the door, closed it behind him and stood perfectly still listening for signs of other minders. Hearing nobody, he worked his way to the armoury where he picked up a sawn-off shotgun and a pocketful of cartridges. He moved silently through several rooms but found no sign of Amanda. It was time for more. He stepped behind the door he thought led to more interior rooms and blasted out another window with the shotgun. If nobody comes running now, there's nobody else here.

He waited for half a minute then heard footsteps. This time he wanted his opponent awake so he could tell him where she was. When he stepped into the room Os grabbed him from behind with a sleeper hold and held the compression until he stopped struggling and began to sag. Os dropped him to the floor on his back, put his foot on his neck and waited for him to begin to recover.

When he did, Os bent over him: 'Where's the girl?'

The man shook his head and Os pressed down harder with his heel on his windpipe: *'Where's the girl?'*

Now the man waved one arm feebly in the direction of the door he had come through while he pointed his other hand frantically at his throat.

Os reduced the pressure on his neck: 'How many of you in here? Hold up fingers.'

The man blinked rapidly as he inhaled deeply and held up two fingers.

'Two of you? No more?'

He nodded. Os dragged him upright and jammed the barrel of the shotgun in the middle of his back: 'Show me the girl.'

The man led him through two rooms to a padlocked door. He pulled a key from a nail on the wall, removed the padlock and started to push it open. Amanda screamed when she heard the activity and only stopped when she recognized Os. He lowered the shotgun to the floor and put the man in another sleeper hold, this time not stopping until he was unconscious.

He dropped him in a heap then hugged her tightly: 'I'd ask you if you're all right but that'd be a stupid question. Let's get out of here.'

She said nothing; she just hung onto him as he led her gently through the labyrinth to the outside. He walked her to his hideout in the bushes: 'You just sit here. I need to see to these two and do something else then we're away.'

Still not speaking, she sobbed and mumbled and trembled and held him. He slowly untangled her and placed her hands in her lap: 'It's okay. Everything's okay. You're safe now. Sit tight; I'll be back soon. As a friend of mine says: "I'll be back before you know I'm gone." I promise I won't be long.'

He went back into the building and dragged the still unconscious man out into the yard and well away from the collection of buildings. Then he went to the shed where he found the other man awake now and terrified. After Os untied his feet, he allowed himself to be docilely walked to a spot next to the other.

It was clear both had lost any interest in fighting. Os retrieved more rope from the shed and tied them tightly together, back-to-back—hands and feet then wrapped more rope snugly around their necks; any struggle would result in their chocking themselves. He went into the shop, pushed a rubbish bin next to a rack stacked with tins of paint and set fire to it, collected Amanda from the hideout and they walked slowly towards the car. She was dirty and shaken but apparently unharmed. He still asked her nothing about what happened or how she felt, and she said nothing.

By the time they reached the car, the workshop was well alight. He helped her into the car, climbed in and locked the two of them in. He reached over and took her hand. She turned, buried her head in his shoulder, wrapped her arms around him and sat perfectly still. They stayed this way for half an hour, only stirring when they heard the sirens of fire engines attending the blaze.

She was sound asleep when he gently shifted her head and shoulders comfortably back against her seat. He went into the boot and stowed his weapons then changed the number plates as he had done with the van. He returned to the driver's seat carrying a baseball cap for Amanda and an Australian bush hat for him. She stirred when he put her hat on but did not waken. He pulled both hats down low over their eyes. The drive from the farm to the safe house in Wilmslow was made as far as possible on B roads under the assumption there would be fewer CCTV cameras.

They reached the house at four o'clock. He tried to wake her, but she jumped when he touched her arm. He squeezed her hand and kissed her on the cheek and when she calmed he led her into the house. Without turning on any lights he sat her on the sofa and sat down beside her with his arm around her shoulder. She snuggled against him and went back to sleep.

About a half hour later she stirred and opened her eyes: 'Where are we?'

'We're in my secret hiding place where nobody can hurt you.'

'Good. I like that.'

She closed her eyes for a few seconds then she was awake: 'Where are we, Ossie, – I mean, Aidie?'

'I told you we're in my secret hiding place.'

'I know you said that but where *are* we?'

He explained it was a house he used for some of his work; when one of his clients needed to disappear for a little while: 'In the films and on TV they call it a safe house.'

'Oh, you mean like in the spy stories? Does that mean you're a spy, Aidie? Imagine that – my new bestest friend is a spy!'

'Well, yes, it's a little like in the spy stories but, no, I'm not a spy. Look, I need to go out for a little while and buy some groceries. I want you to go to bed and try to sleep until I come back then we'll have some breakfast. After that, I'll explain everything.'

He carried her up the stairs and into a bedroom at the back of the house, laid her on the bed and covered her with a blanket. She let him care for her as she dozed off. He bent down and kissed her on the cheek again: 'When you're staying in a safe house, there are some safe house rules.'

'Yes, safe house rules.'

'Rule Number One – Don't turn on any lights.'

'Don't turn on any lights.'

'Rule Number Two – Don't answer the phone no matter how many times it rings.'

'Don't answer phone – rings.'

'Rule Number Three – Don't answer the door to anybody.'

'Don't answer door – anybody. That's a lot of rules, Aidie, I'm not sure if I can remember all those,' and she was asleep.

He changed his jacket for a quilted blue and yellow affair with 'University of Michigan' emblazoned across the back and a huge yellow 'M' on the front. The bush hat was replaced by one that might have been worn by a cricket umpire. He drove to a twenty-four-hour supermarket, paid cash for enough groceries to keep them fed for a week, returned to the house, parked the car in the garage and stowed his purchases in the kitchen. He looked in on Amanda and she was still asleep. He retrieved the Glock from the car, stretched out on the sofa, put the pistol under a cushion next to his head and went to sleep just as the sun was coming up.

Her screams woke him at nine. From habit he grabbed the Glock and ran up the stairs into the bedroom. She was sitting upright on the bed with the blanket clenched tightly in her fists and pulled protectively around her shoulders, staring at the wall and screaming: 'No! No! No! – No! No! No!' Os dropped the pistol, wrapped his arms around her and drew her face in against his shoulder. He held her this way until the screams morphed first into sobs then into silent trembling.

When the trembling subsided: 'Safe house – remember – safe house, Mandy. Nobody can hurt you now. You're safe.'

With his foot he slid the weapon under the bed out of her sight.

'Right, Doctor Aidie says his patient needs a good, long, hot shower followed by a good, long, leisurely breakfast followed by a good, long, relaxing stint on the sofa, maybe watching some thoroughly mindless daytime TV. Towels are in the cupboard in the bathroom and there's a big, fuzzy dressing gown hanging on the bathroom door. Hand me out your clothes. By the time you're ready to get dressed, all traces of the Sons of Damien will be gone.'

'Sons of Damien?'

'I'll explain over breakfast.'

She stood up and he pointed her towards the bathroom door. She walked in, closed the door then opened it slightly a couple of minutes later to hand him her clothes. He collected the Glock, went downstairs and put her things in the washing machine. He knew enough about the needs of people released from captivity to understand the shower was more than a device for washing away dirt: it was a mechanism for cleansing the psyche. He expected her to stand under the steaming cascade for a long time. He was proved right when she came downstairs in the dressing gown more than an hour later.

'Right. Full English, continental, eggs Benedict, buttered brown toast with Chef Aidie's special six-fruit fruit salad, three-cheese omelette, what's your pleasure, Madam?'

'Full English, if you please, sir, I'm famished.'

'Full English it is, then,' he said as he handed her a cup of coffee. 'Have a seat and we'll chat as I cook.'

CHAPTER FORTY-ONE

TREVOR LaFARGE, UNLIKE Gordon, was fully aware the maelstrom he was being sucked into had the potential to destroy him. He had enough worldly wisdom to know he either must do exactly as George Barr ordered or suffer some yet undefined horror—*or* move far away very quickly. His work as a tabloid reporter provided him with stories of things happening to people who did not obey commands issued by individuals from this part of the city.

He recognized the holes in the sign over the door of The Flayed Ox as having been made recently by bullets of considerable calibre and he shuddered as he counted them. He went through the door for this third and hopefully last ever meeting with George feeling like a man walking to his execution; the analogy was not lost on him. The seven holes focused his terror. Nice neighbourhood; I never, ever want to come here again.

George was not a happy man: 'You been workin' on this for two fuckin' days and all you got is his home address and a fuckin' phone number!?'

'That's all I have.'

'I don't know whether to believe you or not, Trevor LaFarge.'

'I can't find him, Mister Barr. Honest. I can't find him. He's not in the phone book, he's not in the Yellow Pages, he has no website, he's not on Facebook and when I Googled "Oswald Doran" it returned no pages – absolute zero. He's supposed to have an office somewhere in Manchester but I can't find it. I waited at his house for two nights and he never came home – he never came around. Sorry – it's all I can do.'

'And you ain't seen him at all?'

'No, I haven't seen him. I even paid a computer nerd I know to hack into his phone and his voicemail but for two days he's never phoned anybody and nobody's left him any messages.'

'I don't believe it! He got a fuckin' girlfriend?'

Trevor began to shiver. He had no desire to involve Amanda Stover in this; she did not deserve the attention of Barr simply because he was looking for Ossie Doran. He waited until the shivering subsided then swallowed too many times and blinked too often before he answered: 'I don't know whether he has a girlfriend or not.'

'You're fuckin' lyin'! How'd you like me to take you out the car park and break both your fuckin' elbows?' Where's his girlfriend live? She got any – hee, hee – kids?'

Now Trevor's instinct for survival overcame any noble thoughts about protecting Amanda; he gave George addresses for her and for Shirley.

'That's better. Now we're getting' somewhere – two for the price of one. That ain't so bad now, is it? Anything else you got for me?'

'No, Mister Barr.'

'Sorry?'

'No, Mister Barr!'

'Good. Now – one more thing.'

'Yes?'

'If you *do* happen to see Doran I don't think it'd be a good fuckin' idea to tell him I'm lookin' for him. Got that?'

'Yes.'

'Louder, Trevor La fuckin' Farge.'

'Yes!'

'Oh, by the way, what's the name of that rag you work for?'

'*Evening Gazette – Manchester Evening Gazette.*'

George stood up and drained his glass: '*Manchester Evening Gazette*. That's all for now. If I need anything else, I'll get in touch at the *Manchester Evening Gazette*. Maybe meet your boss. Maybe the three of us can do lunch.'

He slammed the glass down on the table, turned and walked out. Trevor stared at the far wall and sat without moving for ten minutes. He was a rabbit transfixed by the headlights of an approaching car. Finding Ossie, telling him all and throwing himself on his mercy seemed like a better option than his having further dealings with this madman. The long-overdue follow-up piece on Bill Stover's widow his editor had been hounding him for was ignored—it could wait; his highest priority was trying to figure out not just how to stay alive but to emerge from this affair with all his body parts intact and in full working order. Right now he was not optimistic.

CHAPTER FORTY-TWO

DARWIN'S FRUSTRATION WAS not his lying on his back in urine-soaked trousers in the dark tied securely to a workbench and with electrical wires wrapped around his big toes, it was his total lack of any control over what was happening to him. He struggled. Doran tied him well and he achieved no more than rubbing his wrists and ankles raw, causing the muscles in his arms and legs to cramp, and making the back of his head hurt each time he banged it on the bench in anger.

He alternated between useless struggles and intervals of exhaustion. His immediate concern was soon his gardener would find him in this embarrassing position. One must maintain, always, a certain level of decorum in front of the servants.

Modern synthetic ropes have two properties making them less than ideal for tying someone to a workbench for a spot of torture and that is, unlike good old-fashioned hemp or sisal, they stretch a little and knots, even properly tied, slip a bit. Darwin thrashed about on the bench and along with dawn slowly brightening the shed he felt his wrists a little looser in his bonds. Now instead of flailing about haphazardly, he concentrated on his right wrist; pulling hard against the rope, loosening it even more.

His only anchor for this exercise was his left wrist and both burned with the effort. When the first sunlight glinted through the dirty windows, he slipped his right hand free. This done, he released his other three appendages, climbed stiffly off the bench, removed the wires from his feet and put on his shoes. He closed the door and limped damply back into the house, ignoring the untidy state of his gardener's workplace.

First a shower and change of clothes, then he went to work, disregarding any concerns about the security of landlines or mobile voicemail systems. Now he was the baron in his castle issuing commands to his vassals, expecting immediate and total obedience. No more clandestine mutterings across tiny tables in trendy coffee bars on narrow streets in London, now there were audiences in his library at his country estate.

He rang Gordon. He cradled the phone between his chin and shoulder, and rubbed his still-stinging wrists, waiting for an answer. He became angrier with each unanswered ring and when Gordon finally responded his face was as livid as the rope burns on his arms.

'Do you know what time it is?'

'Is that supposed to be a rhetorical question, Milne, or is this just another instance of my having to do your job for you?'

'What do you want at this time of the morning, Darwin?'

This casual response under the circumstances removed any attempts at civility by Darwin.

'What I want, you fool, is an explanation! What I want is your snivelling arse here in my library within the hour so you can tell me why, precisely, you sent a madman around to my house last night to assault me! What I want to know is why a tiny incident of absolutely no consequence whatsoever that happened over two years ago has suddenly resurfaced under the most awkward of circumstances. What I want is answers and I want them now!'

'Sorry, I can't. I've a very important meeting with –'

'Yes, you bloody well *can*. You have nothing – absolutely nothing – more important than dealing with this now! I'll expect you here within the hour!'

He slammed the phone down: 'God save us from grammar schools.'

Next he rang Milford and his demands were similar. He was busy assessing damage at the Sons of Damien's farm one hundred miles away and he needed two hours to drive to *Sans Soucis*. Unlike Gordon, he was fully awake and fully aware he had failed miserably on this assignment, and of the possible damage to be wreaked on them all by Os Doran. He attended a comprehensive.

A thoroughly rumpled, unshaven, sleepy-eyed and penitent Gordon arrived forty-five minutes later and was shown into the library. He stood and waited uncomfortably while Darwin sat imperiously behind his George II desk and ignored him.

Until this unfortunate unpleasantness involving Doran, their relationship had been one of mutual benefit—one might even have described it as 'cosy', at least insofar as *any* relationship with Darwin could ever be described as 'cosy': in return for huge, unrecorded, cash contributions to the Conservative Party and his re-election campaigns, SMMP was favoured with many continuously recurring, obscenely over-priced, long-term contracts to supply hospitals and doctors' surgeries throughout the country. Naturally both parties were pleased with this arrangement and unhappy at the prospect of its coming under scrutiny by anybody capable of bringing it to the attention of the great unwashed masses.

Darwin continued ignoring Gordon until Milford, reasonably un-rumpled but smelling slightly of smoke, arrived then they both were seated like naughty schoolboys summoned to the headmaster's office; he glowered at them across his desk. The only things missing were the black gown and birch. When they left two hours later, given a choice they probably would have preferred canings to the verbal abuse heaped upon them, particularly now both Doran and Stover had disappeared without a trace.

Gordon's orders were to go to his office and behave as though everything were normal; but to report immediately anything in the least out of the ordinary.

'Do you think you can do *that* without mucking it up?'

'Yes, Darwin.'

'So, what are you going to do if Oswald Doran rings and asks for a meeting?'

'Ring you immediately.'

'And what are you going to do if the window cleaner who comes into your office isn't somebody you recognize?'

'Ring you immediately.'

'That wasn't so difficult, now, was it?'

Milford's orders were to search for Doran and Stover using the considerable resources available to him but not to approach them or try to contact them; he was merely to report their whereabouts to him.

'Do you think you can do this without mucking it up?'

'Yes, Mister Cantwell.'

'Do you think you can do this without burning down any more buildings or having anybody else beaten up and handcuffed to a fence in the middle of a patch of nettles?'

'Yes.'

'And what, exactly, are you going to do if you locate either of them?'

'Not contact them but ring you immediately.'

'As of this moment, I'm taking charge of this project. I'll find these two and put a stop to this nonsense, since clearly you two can't. Good day!'

After the two shuffled dejectedly out of the library he consulted a small notebook hidden in a secret compartment in his desk and made note of three *very* private phone numbers. The first call was to Assistant Commissioner of the Met, Leslie Grant-Stubbs, an acquaintance from school and Cambridge, to schedule an urgent meeting for late in the afternoon in London. The second call was to Wallace Weymouth, Assistant Director-General of MI5, another friend from school and Cambridge, to schedule an urgent meeting for early evening in London.

Then he rang the third member of this small circle, Marmaduke Beattie, owner and Chief Executive Officer of World-Universal News Corporation, the publishing empire whose tabloids represented seventy-three percent of all daily and Sunday newspapers sold throughout Britain. Gordon's company advertised heavily in Beattie's papers, and they in turn were highly supportive of Darwin, his fellow Conservatives and his caring, innovative yet cost effective management of the NHS, not only throughout their editorials but also routinely within their biased news coverage.

In return the Office of Fair Trading looked favourably upon all Beattie's mergers and acquisitions, actual and proposed, usually concluding 'too many differing points of view in the Nation's newspapers will only serve to confuse the reading public'. Americans would have described this tripartite relationship as a 'circle jerk'. His meeting with Beattie was slightly less urgent and could wait until the following morning.

CHAPTER FORTY-THREE

DARWIN AND LESLIE met in a small, private suite in Leslie's club in Pall Mall. The labouring classes might describe his request as 'calling in a favour' but these men preferred the far more genteel 'quid pro quo'. If Milford petitioned one of his still-serving colleagues under similar circumstances, his request usually involved an exchange of cash, but within *these* corridors, information, influence and power were the media of exchange. Leslie held his lead crystal tumbler of twenty-five-year-old Macallan Single Malt between his hands and caressed it lovingly: 'You sounded distressed on the phone, Darwie, this *must* be urgent. How can I help?'

'I need a man found and seen to, Stubbsie.'

'Must be more specific, old boy, when you say, "seen to", what, precisely, do you mean?'

'I mean I want him arrested and charged with something – anything – and put away where he won't cause me any more annoyance.'

'What has he done?'

'He's been asking embarrassing questions about things that are absolutely none of his business.'

'And by "embarrassing questions", you mean –?'

'Oh, don't be obtuse. Let's just let it go at that!'

'I mean, what has he done to justify his arrest?'

'Nothing, really, well nothing we can lay at his door –'

'But I need *something* to work with –'

'Terrorism. What about terrorism. Terrorism's popular right now. He's a threat to our national security. Will that do? He's ex-military, he knows about weapons and explosives, he's a torturer, an arsonist and probably a kidnapper.'

'Yes, that should do it.'

Over more well-aged single malts, Darwin provided Leslie with information on Os including his background and recent activity, omitting any references to Milford's involvement, Bill Stover's suicide or his encounter with the lawn mower. He included Amanda's address with no information other than the suggestion she might be his girlfriend.

Leslie said it would not be too difficult.

'We'll plant some Semtex in his house, then inform our friends in Manchester who will subsequently get a search warrant from a sympathetic judge, alert the media and conduct a dawn raid complete with battering rams, much shouting and flash photography. Having done that, everything will fall nicely into place. The newspapers will plaster his photo – you do have a photo, I assume – all over A-boards throughout the land, TV presenters will solemnly warn audiences he's extremely dangerous and should not be approached then everybody will be looking for him. What with all this European Court of Human Rights balderdash, nowadays it's far harder to fit somebody up and make it stick but this should work out fine – it'll be like the old days.'

He smiled. They exchanged a few more pleasantries, drained their glasses, shook hands and Darwin went on to his next meeting. He and Wallace met in a small, private suite in Wallace's club in Saint James's Square. Wallace held his lead crystal tumbler of thirty-year-old Balvenie Single Malt between his hands and caressed it lovingly: 'You sounded distressed on the phone, Darwie, this *must* be urgent. How can I help?'

This meeting was conducted like the earlier one with only a few differences in the detail: Wallace would create a bogus dossier with details of Doran's involvement in recent plots to overthrow democratically elected presidents of several central African republics and place it in MI5's files. Then following the discovery of Semtex in Doran's residence, the security services would go onto full alert in their search and apprehension of this dangerous man. The other difference with this meeting was Darwin's consumption of so much single malt through the afternoon and early evening lessened somewhat his sense of urgency for locating and detaining Oswald Doran.

Before Darwin made his call to Marmaduke Beattie he tried to recall details of the Stover incident. Although it was clear Stover's carelessness had resulted in the deaths of five children, none of them was a member of a family of any importance so he thought little about it. Gordon assured him there was no possibility whatsoever SMMP were implicated and that was the end of the affair. Darwin's only lasting memory was Beattie's lurid headlines and carefully crafted articles placing the blame solely with Stover. He had no memory of his suicide. Darwin suggested Marmaduke carry out a similar review of the facts of the case before their meeting.

They met over breakfast the next morning at the Savoy River Restaurant in Carting Lane. They were used to be being seen together, so anybody observing their quiet conversation would not think anything out of the ordinary. Darwin needed substantially more from Marmaduke but this did not concern him. This relationship was not based on the sentimentality of old school ties; it was pure pragmatism—each had something the other coveted. Cantwell wanted favourable publicity—continually—and Beattie wanted to increase his market share—continuously: the paradigm symbiosis. They placed their orders and with only a few pleasantries, Darwin moved straight to the single item on his agenda; even for a man of his tastes, it was too early for single malt whisky: 'Duke, I need some publicity for a project I'm engaged in.'

'You're *always* looking for publicity for some project.'

'This is serious – extremely serious.'

'Everything you do is serious – what's so special about this one?'

'I need you to create what I think military tacticians refer to as a "diversion". I want anybody revisiting this Stover affair to be looking anywhere except in *my* direction.'

'Nothing we can't handle. What'd you have in mind?'

He proposed a series of headline articles about terrorist suspect Oswald Doran who had been under police surveillance but had disappeared without a trace along with Amanda Stover. Whether she was his hostage or a willing accomplice was unclear. These could be supplemented by background articles about his murky past, his work as a mercenary in darkest Africa and his association with other known terrorists. Darwin did not discuss his two earlier meetings but suggested it might be helpful for Marmaduke's reporters to liaise with their usual anonymous sources within the ranks of the police.

'Yes, I can get my staff to put something together. Do you want to have a look at it before we publish, or will you be happy with whatever we decide to go with?'

'Anything you do will be fine. You know I always trust your judgement in these matters. Timing is essential – I want this issue before the public just as quickly as possible.'

'We can have this out in all the morning editions tomorrow.'

CHAPTER FORTY-FOUR

AFTER BREAKFAST AMANDA and Os sat on the sofa until mid-afternoon chatting and drinking coffee. He talked about what he had done and what happened to him. Then she talked about her abduction: her struggles with her captors and her terror. He watched this drift into a catharsis—a regression gradually through a stream of consciousness to the events of two years before when heartbreak over months ended in the loss of her Bill.

A corollary to Murphy's Law states: 'It's always darkest before it's completely black'. In Os' world, when things were quieter than he expected this usually meant something bad was about to happen. This was one of those times: it was too quiet. Now they were secure in his safe house, but it could not last. He needed to take the fight to them; he and Amanda could not just sit here and wait.

Only a few people knew about this house; he used it rarely for clients and then never revealing the location—driving them here in the dark and by indirect routes. He was careful any communications in or out were by pay-as-you-go mobile phones and these he destroyed at the end of each job. He scanned anybody brought here beforehand for tracking devices or subcutaneous chips.

He leased the house for cash through an agency based in Geneva. They were the registered owners of the freehold, and rates and utility bills were channelled through them. Through the letterbox were freebie newspapers and junk mail directed either to 'The Occupier' or 'The Homeowner', nothing more. But the people stalking them had access to resources ensuring their eventually being found—likely sooner rather than later.

He needed answers. Tactically, how soon would these people discover them, and the nature of the attack? From what happened so far, they acknowledged no limits. Strategically, to whom could he deliver the information he gathered to expose what was turning out to be a massive conspiracy of silence connecting the worlds of big business, national politics, the gutter press and maybe the police?

What began as an unfortunate accident, possibly nothing more than somebody's turning the wrong valve somewhere on a production line ended in the deaths of an unknown number of people. The fault was not in the incident, although this was bad enough, it was in the subsequent deliberate, carefully constructed silence.

He moved. He changed number plates on the car again. Now he wore a bulky, quilted, dark green jacket with 'Slippery Rock' emblazoned in white across the back and 'The Rock' in big white letters on the front, and a green baseball cap with a white 'S' on it pulled low over his eyes. He gave Amanda a beeper; even with somebody's breaking down the door she could push the button and alert him.

'Remember Aidie's safe house rules. Draw the curtains at sundown before you turn on any lights.'

She winced when she saw him check the magazine in the Glock: 'Is that really necessary?'

'Afraid so. Different world – different game – different rules.'

He hugged her gently and she clung to him without moving for a minute and with her head buried in his shoulder. Then they kissed. When they drew apart she blew softly in his ear: 'I'm still waiting for my dirty weekend in London.'

He smiled.

He rang Brian before he left. He was happy not having to leave a voicemail message: Brian was not noted for prompt responses and now Os was on the move he needed information immediately.

'Good afternoon Brain – two Ps – Snapp, public relations consultant installer of hack-proof firewalls and artificial intelligence expert no job too large no job too small ring me for a confidential consultation and quotation how can I help you?'

'Hello, Brian, what's the "artificial intelligence expert" bit all about?'

'Oh hi Ossie long time no see or more accurately long time no hear I just added that bit about AI sounds impressive doesn't it and by the way there's no such thing as a hack-proof firewall but the ones I can build for you are as good as it gets world class we public relations consultants like to refer to it as "literary licence" in our promotional literature what've you been up to – 's everything okay?'

'Slow down. No, everything's not okay. I need some help.'

'You must be desperate if you're ringing or are you just trying to avoid spending any more of your hard-earned cash on coffees?'

'No time on this one, I need some information in a hurry. And remember, I'll buy you all the coffees you want – sticky buns, too, if that's your pleasure.'

'No sticky buns thanks anyway they muck up my keyboard but maybe next time some of those American hot dogs in toasted buns with lots of mustard on 'em I'd like that.'

'American hot dogs it is then. I need you to find out as much information you can for me on a detective chief inspector from the Met named Milford Cleeland.'

'Cleveland? I need to write this down.'

'No, Cleeland, C-L-E-E-L-A-N-D, Milford Cleeland.'

'Funny way to spell "Cleveland" what's he done?'

'Never mind what he's done, but if you can get his address and phone number for me. Maybe some of his contacts. I think he's retired but he probably keeps in touch with some of his pals who are still serving. I'm not sure but it's likely his base of operations is in London. Oh, and check out any communications he has with a motorcycle gang in North Lincolnshire called the Sons of Damien – and Darwin Cantwell, Health Secretary. Anything you can do to help is appreciated.'

'Wow! interesting company he keeps Damien and Darwin – Darwin and Damien – alliteration I remember now Damien and Darwin dangerous duo of dastardly deed doers not bad eh?'

'You need to get out more.'

'If you ring me back tomorrow about this same time 's that okay?'

'That's fine. And I promise American hot dogs next time. See you, mate.'

He parked two streets away from Amanda's house and walked casually along past it, looking for any signs anybody was watching. He saw none. He walked to a cross street, around to the back and went in. Nothing looked to have changed. He reversed his path back to the car and drove to his house, strolled around the same way as before, eventually entering through the kitchen door.

He sometimes referred to his lifestyle as 'travelling light', to a casual visitor it looked like a show home decorated to interest prospective buyers, an interior designer describing it as 'minimalist' and a psychologist noting the absence of anything personal on display.

It had been trashed; nothing smashed, but chairs and sofa overturned, drawers tipped onto the floor and bedding thrown about. He was not sure whether this was another warning or they were looking for something to help find him. They discovered nothing useful. Everything connected with his work—weapons, computer files, paper records and clothing—he kept either in his office, the safe house or in a not-too-nearby lockup. Personal items were a few clothes, his toothbrush, razor and a part-used bar of soap—enough to provide his DNA but not much more. He thought about ringing the police to report a break-in but he could do that anytime, claiming he was on holiday and had no idea when it happened.

He left through the kitchen door and walked along the alley to a cross street, this time turning away from the street fronting his house. He walked two blocks before crossing back to the front street and beginning his walk past his house. One-half block from his house he spotted the only car with anybody in it, a man sitting reading a newspaper and with a clear view of his front door. Of itself this was not enough to suggest he was watching the house but if he were still there hours later he probably was; how much time can one spend sitting in the dark in a car reading a newspaper?

Os went back to his car preparing to wait until after dark to return to see if the man had moved. While he waited he made two phone calls. The first was to a freelance investigative reporter, Sally Madison Tomlinson—by-line: 'Madison Tomlinson', 'Sally' to her friends. He provided her with protection during one of her projects when she asked more questions about the business of a shady property developer than he thought appropriate. She lived and worked from an old farmhouse near Hollow Meadows on the A57: her quiet refuge from the slings and arrows she often dodged in her work. She was totally fearless and scrupulously honest, two attributes earning her accolades from many and death threats from a few. If anybody could tell the world the story he wanted told, she could. She agreed to see him the next evening.

His second call was to Paul Adler, a comrade he served with in Bosnia and who now worked for MI5 in some unspecified capacity. Any time Os asked him what, exactly, he did in defence of The United Kingdom of Great Britain and Northern Ireland, he was met with a wink and a: 'need to know, my friend, need to know.' He rang Paul at home under the assumption although the hypothesis governments of the Western world monitor everybody's telephone calls all the time might be unproven, it was safe to assume all calls made to and from Thames House certainly were.

They began, as they always did, with a routine they created many years before as a windup for any potential listeners analysing content: 'The fat lady sings at midnight.'

'Elmo Lincoln, nineteen-seventeen.'

They snickered every time when they pictured some poor soul sitting in a secret room somewhere deep in the bowels of an intelligence-gathering operation hearing this exchange made again and again through years during telephone calls from locations all over the world—trying to figure out what it meant and whether these messages suggested any serious threat to the security of Western democracies.

'So, Paul, how's everything these days in the world of secret intelligence gathering or, as some say, spying on innocent citizens going about their lawful business?'

'Spying? Spying? Wash your mouth out with soap, Oswald Doran. Sorry, mustn't use names. Nothing to do with me, mate, remember, I work in public relations. It's been a while. How're you doing?'

'Not good – not good. I've stumbled into something that keeps getting darker and darker the deeper I go. What started out as a favour for a friend is turning out to be much, much more and I need some help of the kind you might be able to provide. Think of it as a public relations consultancy project. Yep, that's it – the wheels are coming off my PR project and I need your help.'

'I don't have the faintest bloody idea what you're talking about. And does it have anything to do with a woman? It always does.'

'Well – not *always*.'

'Almost always but never mind. Tell me all about that bit later.'

Os spent the next fifteen minutes telling him about everything happening to him and Amanda, and his real aim to expose not only the cover-up but the specific high-profile people responsible for it. He wanted an acknowledgement—not a meaningless, snivelling, 'lessons will be learned' apology—but a full *public* acknowledgement from them.

'Wow! For a bloke who's supposed to blend into the woodwork and do his job without being noticed, you certainly *have* been noticed. So what do you want from me, really?'

'Two things. See if the waves I've been making are rocking any boats anywhere within your organization that's not supposed to exist and second, point me towards one person—anybody—you work with whom I could trust when I'm ready to go public with this. You know what I mean. Oh, yes, and another thing –'

'You said "two things", mate –'

'Well, hell, so I lied a little bit. If I need some dependable muscle, can you ID a reliable contractor or two who might be able to watch my back for me?'

'You don't ask for much, do you?'

'Well, naturally, I know I can depend on you. Remember what the Americans used to call us: "The dynamic Duo".'

'Yeah – well, enough trips down memory lane. I'll see what I can do – in my spare time, of course. Remember, even *I'll* start a few boats rocking if I ask the wrong people too many of the wrong kinds of questions. Where and when can I contact you?'

'I'm trying to go dark so let me ring you at home in a couple of days. That okay?'

'Fine. When you're ready.'

'See you, pal.'

Now he strolled back down the street, checking on his watcher and thinking about his options. He had several, ranging from the modest—ignoring him totally: simply driving back to the safe house and forgetting about him, to the extreme—making him disappear permanently: sending his own oblique message to whomever sent him. He chose another: following him and maybe tracking him back to his employers. He moved his car to where he could see both his quarry and his front door then settled back comfortably.

Waiting silently for hours is about as boring as it gets, even for a competent operative such as Os. He waited and he thought about another, potentially more interesting option. He removed his Slippery Rock disguise, left the car quietly by the nearside door, walked down the street half a block keeping well in the shadows, crossed over to the other side and began walking briskly toward his house. He entered his front door then strolled through the house, turning lights on and off moving from room to room, ensuring he could be seen from the street. He did this for an hour then went to the first floor turning off lights behind him until he closed the curtains in the front bedroom and switched off the last light. Then he left quietly by the back door and returned to his car. His ruse worked: fifteen minutes later his watcher started his car and drove off.

He followed him to the car park of the Flayed Ox and parked on the street under a tree near the entrance. He put his disguise back on, waited, then at ten-thirty crossed the car park, smiling as he counted seven bullet holes in the sign.

He pulled his hat down low, came through the door, stopped to look around and decide which way he wanted to go, then moved through the crowd to the far end of the bar where he could stand with his back more or less to the wall and see much of the room and most of the patrons. Keeping his head down, he ordered a pint of Guinness then leaned back against the wall.

Just like every other expert in law enforcement, intelligence gathering or high-end security work, he was sceptical of anything looking like a coincidence—when things seemed somehow connected, they probably were. His watcher was chatting with Trevor and George and this was not an amazing coincidence, it suggested something more complicated.

That the man who had been watching his trashed house until an hour ago should be sitting in a seedy pub Os shot up a couple of nights earlier together with a troublesome tabloid reporter he challenged recently and a man from his tormented past was not the result of some chance encounter, there must to be more to it. His problem was he had no idea how these events and these people were connected. Now he thought a confrontation was not the best way to act: he chose to watch and wait.

His conclusion was either Trevor or George located his house and the watcher was put there to report when he returned. Trevor's assigning somebody to watch his house made no sense at all. And exactly why George should be looking for him now was something he could not answer; they had gone their separate ways several years before under terrible circumstances and he hoped never to see him again. Three questions were still to be answered. How Trevor was involved in this, were they the ones who turned over his house and how were these three connected with the SMMP cover-up, Bill's death and Amanda's kidnap?

He left the pub and drove to his lock-up, assuming his watcher reported he was home in bed. If George and maybe others were coming for him he must prepare. He changed into black jeans, jumper and baseball cap. Along with his Glock and Gerber, into a holdall he put a second pistol, two more magazines, a box of 9x19 jacketed hollow point cartridges, a second knife, a small torch, a black rip-stop Nylon military poncho and his Slippery Rock outfit. He loaded this into his car and drove back to the house.

He parked a half block from the house one street away, walked up the back street and into his rear garden. With one knife strapped to his leg, a Glock in his belt behind his back and a second magazine in his sock, he settled himself comfortably into a dark niche between the garden shed and the wall with the holdall beside him and the poncho draped over him. The streetlamp shone a little light on the garden, but he was in complete darkness and nobody would see him unless a torch was pointed directly at him. He sat back with his eyes closed to condition his night vision and waited.

An hour later he heard a car stop at the end of the back street, its door open and shut then move around to the front of the house where it stopped again. He heard and then saw the watcher enter by the gate and move to the kitchen door. He assumed George would go to the front and the two would enter simultaneously. Soon he would know whether they planned to storm the house like a TV or film SWAT team and rush to his first floor bedroom hoping to overpower him before he could react or sneak in expecting to immobilize him while he slept.

George Barr was not the brightest soldier in the battalion and enjoyed screaming when he attacked; Os never decided whether this was to intimidate the enemy or to psych himself up for whatever he thought was coming. Here Os assumed they would enter silently: no reason to alarm the neighbours and call attention to themselves.

He guessed correctly. After waiting two minutes, probably to let George get into position, the man picked the lock on the kitchen door, entered, leaving the door open behind him. There was no sound from inside the house for three or four minutes then George's screams were loud enough to awaken anybody asleep the length of the street.

'He ain't fuckin' here! Where the fuck is he? *He ain't fuckin' here*! He's supposed to be here and he ain't fuckin' here.'

Os could not hear the other side of this conversation but assumed the watcher was trying to placate him. It was not working. He heard them stomping down the stairs and out the front door. With both doors open, he heard snatches of conversation. George was not a man to be near when things were not going well for him: indeed, he was the paradigm of, 'You wouldn't like me when I'm angry', now he was clearly *very* angry, and Trevor and the watcher were his targets. The watcher was to blame because Os was not discovered in his bed and Trevor was to blame simply by his being Trevor and his being there.

Os was prepared but he was not ready for a fight with George because he expected it to end in the death of one of them; this was *not* the time. Were he to be asked, his reply would be he hoped there would never be a right time. Maybe tomorrow when he met with Sally and spoke with Paul, the things happening might start to make sense. He chose to sit quietly in the dark until the car sped off then he went back to Amanda. He let himself in quietly and was pleased she did not waken when he looked in on her; she must really feel safe in his safe house. He closed her door and went to his own bed.

CHAPTER FORTY-FIVE

A BUSY NIGHT at the Doran residence, indeed. One hour after their departures, two men dressed all in black and wearing balaclavas parked nearby, walked up the back street, through the garden to the kitchen door and went in.

'Guy must live alone. Whew! Look at the state of this place. Not much of a housekeeper.'

'Not our problem, mate. Let's do this and get out of here.'

They taped two blocks of Semtex to the underside of the sink with gaffer tape.

Before leaving, one punched a number into his mobile: 'Done.'

CHAPTER FORTY-SIX

AMANDA AND OS sat watching the morning news and enjoying another of his expertly-cooked breakfasts, this time, eggs Benedict: 'Breaking news, this just in. At five-thirty this morning, members of an elite squad of the Greater Manchester Police force, acting on an anonymous tip from a member of the public, raided the terraced home in Old Trafford of Oswald Aidan Doran, discovering a large quantity of explosives hidden in his kitchen. They met with no resistance and the whereabouts of Mister Doran are not known.

'Police have warned the public he is believed to be armed and extremely dangerous. He is thought to have been responsible for several recent violent assaults and at least one arson attack. He is wanted in connection with a number of suspected terrorist plots. Interpol have also issued warrants for his arrest in connection with crimes against humanity and atrocities committed during a failed coup attempt several years ago in Chad by a war-lord in the Southern province of Logone Oriental.

'He may also be connected with the disappearance of Amanda Stover, who has been reported missing from her home in Stockport and has not been seen for several days. Police have not confirmed the two incidents are related.

'According to a neighbour of Doran, who wishes to remain anonymous, he lived alone, was not known to have any family or close friends, was quiet and kept himself to himself but was seen to come and go at odd hours and did not seem to have regular employment.

'Police have asked anyone spotting Doran not to approach him but to immediately ring the number at the bottom of your screen.'

'Wow, Aidie, you've been a busy boy. The things you get up to when you go out all by yourself in the middle of the night! By the way, what time was it when you got in last night – or was it this morning?'

'Don't ask. But we know for certain we've finally got their attention. I love it when a plan comes together.'

They trawled the channels, and the BBC, SKY News, Look North and West Midlands Today all reported the same story with no variations except for the pictures. The BBC presented an artist's sketch with Os frowning and looking *very* scary, SKY offered a photo of him in a dinner jacket during one of his higher-profile security assignments and ITV showed him with several of his comrades somewhere in the desert in Iraq with everybody's faces blurred out but his. In a few hours CNN would likely pick it up.

'Well, Mister Doran, what do we do now?'

'Well, Missus Stover, I'm thinking about that. Two things. This evening I'm due to meet an investigative reporter whom I'm hoping will put all this together and tell the world everything we've discovered. Then I'm going to ring a friend at MI5 who can probably get us to somebody whom we can trust to protect us until this is all over. Then –'

'Then what, exactly?'

'Then – we wait and see.'

'Wrong answer. I don't believe you. I've known you long enough now to know you're not really a "wait and see" sort of a guy.'

'Ah, well then, you've seen right through my disguise. No, we're not going to just wait and see. Based on how long Sally –'

'Sally?'

'Yeah, Sally Madison Tomlinson, my reporter friend. She's –'

'She? Madison? Madison's a pretty sexy name for a girl. You and she ever an item?'

'A lady shouldn't ask!'

'I'll ignore that. Is she, was she –?'

'No, she isn't and no she wasn't. She's just somebody I trust.'

'Don't know whether I believe that or not. Mind if I come along tonight?'

'Rather you didn't. She lives over near Sheffield so I'll only be gone about three hours tops. But I won't know how close they are to finding us until I talk with Paul.'

'Now you're scaring me. What, exactly, do you mean by "finding us"? Are you telling me these people are not only out looking for us but are near to finding us? Even here? Even here in Aidie's safe house?'

''Fraid so. It's not a question of whether they will but *when* they will. Relax. They can't be that close just yet. We probably have a day or so. Anyhow I'll know better tonight and then we'll decide.'

'I'm not convinced.'

At sundown Os changed the number plates once more. This time his disguise comprised an orange and white track jacket with 'Texas Longhorns' across the front and the white silhouette of the head of a cow with really long horns across the back, and an orange and white baseball cap with 'U T Longhorns' across the front and a little white silhouette of the head of a cow with really long horns on either side. He reminded her to draw the curtains after dark before turning on any lamps and to keep the beeper with her.

He drove the M67 to Hyde then onto the A57 at Glossop then across Snake Pass towards Sheffield.

An hour later he located Sally's remote farmhouse near Hollow Meadows. He locked his car and looked around wondering how this woman prevented any of the many enemies she made through the years from finding her and doing her serious damage.

He asked her about this, and she winked and smiled: 'You'd be amazed, well, no, Ossie, you wouldn't be amazed because you know about these things, but between some infra-red sensing devices dotted about and my friends, Messrs Colt, Purdey, Smith and Wesson, I'm pretty secure here.'

'But you know full well IR sensors can be detected and bypassed.'

'Someday I'll show you my system. You're absolutely right, no system's totally full proof, but I trust mine. And if you remember, a pile of empty paint tins strung on a tripwire still works. By the way, I ever tell you about the ultimate burglar alarm I'm thinking about building?'

'Nope.'

'Right. I might set this up so if somebody *does* get in through a window nothing happens until they're well inside. Then about a minute later a shotgun loaded with a blank goes off and a spotlight comes on shining on a big sign hanging from the barrel. On the sign is written: "There is another shotgun somewhere in this house. See if you can find it." Good idea, nicht wahr?'

'Good idea, but I still worry about you up here in the middle of nowhere on your own.'

'I appreciate your concern but, trust me, I'm fine. Speaking of "fine", it sounds like you're not. Tell me about it.'

He spent an hour giving her all his information: names, dates, what Kowalski, Milne and Cantwell told him, his trips to the farm and his attempt to exacerbate some of the ongoing gang wars in Manchester. He also referred her to Brian and suggested he could provide her with hard evidence such as email messages to support her investigation. He told her he would ring Brian later to tell him she would be in touch.

'But if he questions who you are, mention American hot dogs, alliteration and onomatopoeia, and he'll know you're genuine.'

'Funny company you keep, Ossie.'

'Ignoring his weird dress sense, he's a real whiz with these typewriters that plug into the wall. Trust him, he'll give you some good information.'

He told her he and Amanda were going into hiding, probably later that night, he would contact her in a couple of days and not to believe everything she heard on the news. She told him to keep his pecker up and be careful. He drove back to Wilmslow and smiled as he listened to the ever more strident news reports on the radio. If these were to be believed, he was just short of being a baby murderer and serial killing cannibal. He wondered what tomorrow morning's newspapers would have to say about him.

At the safe house he first rang Brian and updated him. He spent no time asking for information because now there was little Brian could give him that would be helpful; he needed nothing more than a home address and phone numbers for Winifred. Brian hummed and whistled for a few seconds then gave it to him. Os told him Sally would be in touch and to give her everything she asked for; she would be looking for hard copies of incriminating emails.

'Sally can she kill people with a credit card too maybe in her case it's a Biro – ha-ha.'

'Say "Goodnight", Brian.'

'Goodnight Brian talk to you soon Ossie take care I'll wait for your call.'

Next he rang Paul: 'Hello, Ossie. I don't know what you've done. Well I know what you've *told* me you've done, but you've really put the cat amongst the pigeons.'

'What I've told you is exactly what I've done. Nothing left out.'

'Well the boats are truly rocking tonight. No time to talk. If they've connected me to you they'll be after me, too. Keep this short. They're coming for you. They have this super amazing traffic and content analysis program called *Orwell* and they've located your safe house. It didn't take them long, did it? If the information I have is right, some contractors are coming for you in the early hours. Get out of there and get out now! You could stay and try to fight but they'd just send more. Take the satellite phone with you and try to ring me tomorrow at exactly this time. I'll wait for your call. If we're both safe we can talk then. Go.'

'Thanks, mate. I owe you big time.'

He turned to Amanda: 'Okay, you're right, no more "wait and see". As of now, we're outta here. I have a clever plan. Tell you about it on the way.'

'Time to stop by my place and collect some clothes? I'm getting a little tired sitting around in these same things all day long.'

'No time. Where we're going we should be able to find you some. Whether they'll fit or not is another matter but we can't risk going anyway near your place. I don't want to alarm you but –'

'Save your breath, Aidie, I'm already seriously alarmed.'

They took the holdall, Os' various disguises and the satellite phone, turned on a few lights and left. On the drive she put on the Slippery Rock disguise. He told her about his conversation with Sally and within a few days she would have given her story to the media and the conspiracy of silence—the massive cover-up—would end. Although it would not return her husband she would, at last, have some sense of vindication. She said nothing.

Three quarters of an hour later they arrived in Altrincham and cruised around looking for the intersection of Dunham and Devisdale Roads.

'Mind telling me what we're looking for, Aidie?'

'Well, I was kind of saving that for a surprise.'

'I'm all out of interest in surprises. Just tell me what's going on.'

'Remember Poe's *The Purloined Letter*?'

'Not really. I was never a great fan of Poe – I'm more of a Balzac and Bellow sort of a girl. Enlighten me.'

'Well, to make a long story short, if you want to hide something, where's the best place to hide it?'

'I never read Balzac or Bellow. Just kidding. Bill wanted me to try some Joyce once but I lost it after about half a page. No, I'm quite happy with Cookson and Cartland. I give up – where's the best place to hide something?'

'Right out in the open. Or more accurately, right in the midst of the people who are looking for you.'

'So?'

'So, we're going to kill two birds with one stone, so to speak. Or, actually three birds.'

'So?'

'We're going to hide out in the home of Bill's archenemy Winifred Hyde-Davies.'

'Aidie, I'm really in no mood for jokes and there's nothing remotely funny about her. Actually, the mood I'm in right now, I'd gladly strangle her myself.'

'No joke. We're taking the fight to the enemy. Now! And maybe you *will* get the chance to strangle her. But only if I can watch.'

'Not funny. I still don't understand –'

'Trust me.'

'So what are these three birds?'

'One – we hide out where nobody will think to look. Two – we capture the one person who started all this. Three – we get our hands on a high-value bargaining chip, a high-profile hostage. Make sense?'

'Interesting way you make your living and I don't like the idea at all.'

'Trust me.'

'You already said that and I didn't believe it last time either.'

They located Winifred's house: a modern, three-storey maisonette in a cul-de-sac filled with high-end cars. Good—separate entrance, separate alarm system, no need to buzz a neighbour and pretend to be delivering a pizza; people in this part of town probably never order take-away pizzas anyhow. They parked not directly in front of her entrance but in a shadow under a big tree.

'Okay, first things first. There are probably lots of CCTV cameras around here so we have to look like we belong. It's almost midnight, week night. Maybe she's home, maybe not. If she's not home, great – we just casually walk up to the front door, look like we're struggling a bit with our keys while I pick the lock, step inside, disable the alarm with this magic electronic thingy I just happened to have here in my pocket, then we pour ourselves a drink and wait for her return.'

'And if she's home?'

'I'm working on that.'

'And how will we know?'

'We keep it simple. We just ring her landline and see if she answers. If she does, obviously she's home. If it goes to voicemail then we try her mobile while looking at her windows to see any lights going on or off. If she doesn't pick up either her landline or mobile, we'll assume she's not home.'

'You still haven't told me what we're going to do if she's home. How do we get in before she rings the police?'

'You stand well back in the shadows while I get in and disable her. That done, I'll tell you to come on up.'

'But?'

'Remember, I do this for a living.'

He rang Winifred's landline. A light came on in a window on the first floor and she answered. Os switched his mobile off and motioned Amanda to stay under the tree. He waited until the light went off then stood still for another minute. He crossed to the door, picked the lock, opened it, stepped inside then closed it. Amanda heard the alarm for five seconds then silence. The light came on again for two minutes then went off. Amanda waited; she shivered.

Five minutes later Os opened the door and signalled her to come across the car park and into the house. Amanda held his hand as they climbed the stairs. She was still shivering.

Winifred was taped securely to a white Barca chair — genuine, unlike Trevor's chair, thought Os — with brown packaging tape. Her smashed mobile and laptop lay at her feet; a dishtowel was stuffed in her mouth. Amanda walked up to her, bent down and slapped her hard across the face twice. Winifred whimpered briefly then glared defiantly at her. Amanda slapped her, again and again, until she broke eye contact. She had stopped shivering.

Os positioned two chairs from the dining table in the large, open-plan room directly in front of Winifred and sat Amanda on one of them.

'Easy now, Mandy. Plenty of time for that. We've probably got at least twenty-four hours before we're on the move. You'll get your chance.'

'Sorry, Aidie – it's just that –'

'I know. We'll I don't know – really. But just be calm for now.'

He sat on the other chair, pulled the knife from its sheath, laid it on the floor between their chairs and faced Winifred: 'Okay, here're the rules. I'm going to take this gag out of your mouth. You're not going to scream. If you do try to scream, I'm going to stuff this gag back in your mouth and cut off one of your fingers. Understand. Nod your head – up and down – if you want to keep all your fingers; shake your head – back and forth – if you think I'm bluffing. Oh, hell, maybe I'll just go back to the car and leave you alone here with my friend. What'd you think of that?'

Winifred's pupils dilated, she struggled against the tape and whimpered. Os removed her gag.

'Who the fuck are you people and just what the fuck do you want?'

Os smiled and winked as he turned to Amanda: 'What do you think? Should we tell her or just let her keep guessing as we cut off bits of her or – well, you tell me, it's your show.'

'Oh, I don't know, let me think. I know – we'll ask her some questions and we'll decide what to do if we're not happy with her answers. Make sense?'

'Makes sense to me. Take it away, Missus Amanda Stover.'

Winifred gasped when she heard the name: 'What do you want?'

Amanda slapped her again: 'Wrong. We're asking the questions, remember. Want me to slap you again? No? Then shut your bloody mouth and speak only when spoken to. Okay, let's try it again. Remember Bill Stover who used to work for you?'

'Yes.'

'Louder, if you please.'

'Yes!'

'Okay. Remember what happened to Bill Stover?'

'I had to terminate his employment.'

'Well done. You're doing fine – just fine. So why, exactly, did you have to terminate his employment?'

'You know why for Christ's sake. Because he –'

'Because he *what*?'

'Because he – because he –'

Amanda picked up the knife and waved it in Winifred's face. Os adjusted his position to intervene if necessary but Amanda was calm and controlled.

'Because he *what*, Winnie – *fred*? Go ahead, say the words. Tell me what he did. Oh, goodness me, you're sort of – what is it they say? – "on the horns of a dilemma" aren't you? If you tell me what you told the world he did then you and I both know that's a lie. And if you tell me the truth? Either way you're in deep do-do with the widow of the man you killed – a woman who happens to be facing you at the moment holding a very long and very, *very* sharp knife. Wow! Wouldn't want to be in your shoes, now!'

Her torment continued for two hours. By then all defiance was gone. She seemed genuinely surprised they made contact with all the people they had and their version of the incident was correct in every detail. She was terrified because of the unknown: she was uncertain whether they planned to torture her, kill her or do something else yet undefined.

Os made a thorough recce of the house looking for other mobile phones or laptops, and netbooks, ipads, pagers or the like. He decided to keep the landline active and the voicemail switched on. He switched the alarm system back on. He went to the car and returned with the holdall and satellite phone. Amanda sat throughout staring down at Winifred still taped to her chair and with neither of them saying anything. Os finished his chores, checked Winifred's bonds, moved both chairs back from her five more feet then sat on the other chair next to Amanda.

'Okay, it's almost light and I have to go out for an hour or so. Now here are some rules even more important than safe house rules. The obvious is not to answer either the phone or the door. I'm going to gag her again. Do not remove it. Keep your distance from her. Clear?'

'Understand.'

'Now, I'm going to leave the Glock here with you. I'll show you how the trigger safety works. If she tries to move or if you have any doubt at all, shoot her through the knee. Can you do that?'

Both Winifred and Amanda shuddered then Amanda nodded feebly.

'I'm deadly serious. This woman murdered your husband and *she will kill you, too, if she gets the chance*. Do not give her that chance. Clear?'

'Yes.'

'Right. I'll be back as soon as I can. No mystery, I just need to get a few supplies to keep us going for the next twenty-four hours or so, then this'll all be over. Which disguise you think I should wear?'

'University of Michigan. Yes, I like Michigan.'

He showed her how to hold and fire the pistol, laid it on the floor beside the knife, put on his UM gear, kissed her on the cheek and left.

He returned in an hour carrying a plastic bag with the name and logo of a pharmacy on them. Amanda had not moved; she sat perfectly still staring at Winifred. Winifred tried to maintain unbroken eye contact but failed; she was clearly more terrified of Amanda than of Os. He put the Glock back behind his belt, checked her bonds again, removed her gag and made a pot of coffee.

When the coffee was brewed he asked Winifred if she wanted a cup: 'Piss off, whatever your name is.'

'Well now, that's not very polite. The name's Doran, Oswald Doran. I suspect you'll remember it. And it's going to be a long day so I suggest you calm down and try to be nice to us. You already know a bit about Missus Stover here, but you don't really know anything about me. About the only thing that should interest you is that I don't take kindly to people who are mean to my friends and you have been very, very mean to my good friend, Missus Stover, here. So, I understand you think of yourself as something of a hard woman but believe me, you don't know the meaning of the word.

'Maybe if we have a little time later I can describe an adventure your good friend Darwin Cantwell had while in my company a couple of days ago. It involved a lawn mower, some electrical wires and some bare feet and, oh yes, some urine-soaked trousers. So, if you're interested – although I'm sure you don't keep a lawn mower here in the house, you do have a source of electrical power and no doubt we can scare up some wire if you want to see just how hard you are. What say – want to have a go? No? Well, then shall we try it again, would you like coffee?'

'Yes, I'd like some coffee. Black, no sugar, thank you.'

'Now, see how easy that was.'

Os returned from the kitchen in a few minutes with three coffees. Amanda still had not moved. Winifred asked if she could go to the toilet. Os nodded and removed her tape. She stood up and stretched then moved towards the bathroom. Os followed her. She looked at Os then at Amanda then back to the bathroom door.

'No, Winnie, doesn't work that way. You're dealing with me now. And the door stays open. You'll just have to get used to it.'

Os stood near the open door.

'What're you – some kind of pervert, Doran?'

'That's Mister Doran, if you don't mind, or even if you do mind – or Ossie if you prefer. And oh, don't flatter yourself into thinking this is some kind of game. If you're lucky you'll get out of this alive and with all your bits still in place. If you misbehave on the other hand –'

'All right, all right. I get the message.'

She finished and washed her hands then Ossie marched her back to her chair. He reached for the roll of tape: 'Is that really necessary?'

'That's a truly stupid question. If you're not happy with this tape I can slice open the soles of your feet so it will hurt a lot if you try to run away. So – your choice, some tape or something else – you decide.'

Winifred acquiesced. Os re-applied the tape then Amanda held the coffee for her to sip. Os paced around the room, looking out the windows as the sky lightened then returned to the two women in the middle of the room.

'Sun's coming up. It's going to be a long day and who knows what the night will bring? Anybody for breakfast?'

CHAPTER FORTY-SEVEN

WINIFRED LIKED TO think of herself as a realist, the paradigm pragmatist—unsentimental, cynical. She valued nothing except her own power. She respected power in others and thus, despite her fear, held a grudging regard for Os and the power he held over her. But she was terrified of Amanda, probably because as a woman she knew the behaviour throughout history of women wronged.

Os, she assumed, valued her as a hostage and would treat her reasonably well; she could expect no such treatment from Amanda. When he was nearby she appeared to relax slightly even taped to her chair; when he was not she feared for her safety. Os sensed this and every time he left the room he sat Amanda facing her with the unsheathed knife on the floor beside her. Amanda sat erect with her hands resting demurely in her lap, staring at Winifred, smiling at her, glancing down at the knife then back at her again and again until she whimpered then looked away.

CHAPTER FORTY-EIGHT

OS DECIDED NEXT to speak with Brian.

'Hello, Brian.'

'Oh hi Ossie boy there's sure a lot of stuff about you on the news a lot of stuff I didn't know about you for example I had no idea you were a terrorist and that you kept loads of explosives in your house and that you were a serial killing cannibal and all that other stuff it's amazing what you don't know even about your closest friends so what's happening now?'

Os replied as he stopped for breath: 'Need to ask you some questions.'

'Fire away well maybe "fire away" isn't the best thing to say under the circumstances I mean –'

'Brian!'

'Yeah sorry.'

'What can you tell me about a program called *Orwell*?'

'*Orwell*? Wow! *Orwell*'s this super secret super powerful software the Chartered Institute for Management of Human Resources invented well although they developed it they didn't have any computers with enough memory and hard drive storage to run it on so they let MI5 and MI6 beta test it for them –'

'So what's it actually do and why is it so secret? And if it's all so secret how is it you know all about it?'

'Oh first things first it's the ultimate in traffic and content analysis all you have to do is input names of two people any two people in the world and if there's any connection between them any connection at all *Orwell* will flag it up –'

'Are you telling me if they entered "Ossie Doran" and "Lord Lucan" it would show no result but if they entered my name and your name it would connect us?'

'Yep but wait ladies and gentlemen there's more you see the way it works is they set up all these spiders that crawl not only the internet but every data base they can get their hands on – or get their 'bots on if you will ha-ha – and they run everything they find through this massive traffic analysis routine so if they typed in "Ossie Doran" they could find out what kind of sausage you bought for your last barbeque and whether you wear Y-fronts or those tiger-striped bikini briefs and if Maggie Thatcher went to a fancy dress party in nineteen-eighty-four dressed as Arthur Scargill they would know about it there's some indication they have linked it to some seriously powerful hacking routines too so they can spider all sorts of government data bases and private email files and – wow! it's great.'

'So why would the CIMHR people develop something like this?'

'Well I don't know but I think it's because you know human resource and personnel people think everybody always lies on their CVs and their job applications and interviews so I guess maybe they thought if somebody's looking for a job they just type in their name and scan in their CV with their OCR and get a printout then they don't really have to interview them so that saves them lots of time and they can reject all the applicants faster and more efficiently without interviewing anybody and that's what computers are all about saving time and effort.'

'So what you're telling me is if they entered my name it would flag up you and Amanda, where you both live and details like that about all my friends and associates?'

'Yep that's about it I know about it naturally because it's my job to know about programs like this even if everybody else thinks it's really top secret and it really *is* top secret anyhow because it's so powerful and the government can use it to spy on people and oh shit if you're thinking what I think you're thinking that means if they're looking for you they're looking for me too –'

'That's right.'

'Oh my what do I do now I mean where can I –?'

'It's okay. Calm down. I have a clever plan.'

'It'd better be a clever plan because I don't wanna die and even though we're good friends I never hid any of your explosives in my house for you and I didn't know anything at all about that cannibal stuff and –'

'Right, listen up! You're not going to die. Here's what I want you to do. I want you to pack your laptop and your toothbrush in a little case and go to the St. Gildas Royal Infirmary and –'

'But that makes no sense because that's where this all started and won't they be looking for me there and –?'

'That's my point my friend, they will be looking for you everywhere *but* there.'

'Oh I get it sort of like Sherlock Holmes in *The Purloined Letter* and they won't be looking for me there hiding in plain sight right out in the open good idea should I wear a disguise I have one of those Tam O'Shanter fancy dress party hats with the ginger hair sticking out all around it and they wouldn't recognise me in that and –'

'No. Maybe your New York Yankees baseball cap pulled down low over your eyes but no tartan Jock hat. Now listen carefully. You may be there for a day or so until this all shakes out. What I want you to do is wander through the corridors where there are lots of people about. Go into the canteen from time-to-time and just look like you're a visitor waiting for somebody. Read a newspaper. No problem. When it gets late and most visitors are gone go to Casualty and hang out there, again looking like you're waiting for somebody. Just be careful not to work your laptop in places where they tell you not to. My guess is in the canteen it will probably be okay. The important thing is to try not to draw attention to yourself –'

'Do you think they'll have those American hot dogs in the canteen?'

'I have no idea but they might. Anyhow, you just hang around there until – probably tomorrow about this time or maybe a bit later – by then I think it'll all be over. Okay?'

'Well okay if you say so I'll do the best I can I'll just wait for you.'

'Take care, Brian.'

Os walked back into the two women: 'Okay, Mandy, I'll take over here for a while. You may want to have a shower and lie down for a couple of hours. If I'm right we may be a little busy over the next twenty-four hours or so.'

She stood up, stretched and walked into the bathroom without speaking. Winifred looked at him; he looked at her. When he stared at her, her body language changed subtly: her confidence was draining away, drip by drip — minute by minute. When he was satisfied with her level of submission, he relaxed, sat back and went back to thinking about their options. He sat this way for three hours, not moving, until Amanda came back — showered and rested. He glanced at his watch, stood up and nodded to her.

When she sat down he squeezed her shoulder gently then walked into the bedroom to the satellite phone and his call to Paul: 'Right, ready to rock 'n' roll. Any good news for me?'

'Well, yes – well, at least I *think* it's good news. I've been in contact with a colleague at MI6 who works at

Hanslope Park. You won't know him but I trust him. He's been in the field and he knows his way around. He's high enough in the organization to make some decisions on his own *and* he has the ear of our Assistant Director General. I've convinced him you're one of the good guys and not the terrorist the papers make you out to be. I know this probably sounds like something out of a film but he's agreed to see you and keep you out of the way until this's sorted. This is all *seriously* off the record, etcetera, etcetera. You need to go to Hinton Airfield, a skydiving field off the M40 not too far from Milton Keynes – busy on the weekends, deserted during the week.'

'Yeah, matter of fact I know where it is. Landed there on my Silver Cross Country. Why there?'

'No reason other than it's convenient to Hanslope – that's where they'll be taking you by the way – and it's not too far from the motorway. Plan to be there at five in the morning. Just park next to the first hanger you come to on your right when you come in. He'll come in and meet you.'

'Sounds all very mysterious.'

'Sorry – it's the best I could do without getting myself in trouble.'

'No worries, mate. I owe you.'

He switched off the phone and went back into the other room: 'Right, let's get her ready for bed. It's a two-hour drive to where we're going and I want to be there by three at the latest.'

'Ready for bed?'

'Well, that's not quite what I meant. I'll walk her to the toilet. When she's done, she goes back on the chair then I'll show you.'

He untaped Winifred and led her to the bathroom: 'It's going to be a while before you get a chance to shower so you'd better wash your face and brush your teeth.'

'Where we going?'

'That'd be telling, wouldn't it?'

When she finished he led her back to the chair and taped her into it. He picked up the carrier bag from the pharmacy, rummaged through it, and removed a hypodermic syringe and box labelled *Dormicum*.

Both women spoke simultaneously: 'What are you doing?'

'Well I thought Miz Hyde-Davies here just might have a bit of a problem sleeping so I figured this would help. It certainly will help *us* because it'll reduce the possibility she'll cause any problems for us during this long and potentially eventful night.'

He opened the box and removed the phial, pulled the instruction pamphlet out and read it, removed the syringe from its sterile packaging, uncapped the phial and drew up a five milligram dose, humming quietly as he did.

'Tell me, you're not suffering from any of the following are you: obstructive pulmonary disease, renal failure, hepatic impairment? No? I thought not. Well I'm not quite sure of the dosage but, heck, who cares? I reckon this'll be close enough. If this doesn't knock her out why we'll just have to give her some more. If it turns out to be too much then – such is life.'

He opened a sterile wipe, swabbed the inside of her arm, located a vein and injected the drug. Winifred complained but did not struggle.

He removed the needle, rubbed her arm and smiled: 'Now that didn't hurt much, did it?'

As she drifted off to sleep, they moved to the kitchen, looked through the refrigerator and cupboards, found the things they needed and made some sandwiches and coffee. They sat quietly while they ate and talked about nothing of importance. She was curious about what they were doing and where they were going but knew him well enough by now to recognise when he would rather not be asked.

At one o'clock. they loaded their gear into the car, untaped a groggy, uncomplaining Winifred, strapped her into the back seat and left for the airfield.

CHAPTER FORTY-NINE

THEY ARRIVED AT the airfield at three and drove slowly past, stopping a quarter mile beyond. Os reached back and pinched Winifred hard on the leg and was pleased she did not respond.

'Must've got the dosage right – at least the minimum anyway. You wait here while I have a good look around.'

He walked to the field, keeping close to the hedges and fences, then made a thorough recce of the area. Convinced there was nobody around he returned to the car, drove to the hangars and, contrary to his instructions from Paul, parked within a small grove out of sight to any but the most careful observers. At three-thirty he cracked both front windows, the better to hear any unusual noises then they settled back to wait.

Although he assumed Paul's information was correct and help was on the way, he also prepared for the possibility of an ambush by arriving early and hiding the car. The early arrival was to allow time for the car engine to cool and thus reduce the potential of their being spotted by somebody using heat sensing equipment. Unfortunately his timing was off. At four-fifteen six silent, competent-looking men all carrying Kalashnikovs surrounded them, with Darwin and Milford standing nearby. Even in the faint dawn light Os thought he could see their smiles. He was reminded of Brian's comment about 'checking up on the checker-uppers'.

Darwin was in charge: 'I assume it is unnecessary for me to order you two out of the car with your hands well above your heads. I believe this is the first time in my life I have had the opportunity to articulate the well-worn and over-used cliché: "Ah, Mister Doran, we meet again."'

Os opened the car door slowly and carefully, keeping his hands clearly in sight, slid out, stood up and raised his hands.

He nodded to Amanda 'Easy now. Just do as they say.'

He looked at Darwin and smiled: 'Yes, Mister Secretary, we meet again. I take it this means communications between Mister Adler and me have been intercepted, possibly compromised through your very impressive *Orwell* system?'

'You are *very well* informed, indeed. And I see you've brought the beautiful Ms Hyde-Davies with you. I assume you have not harmed her.'

'No, I can assure you that, aside from a mild sleeping draught, she is well and, apart from a few slaps by Missus Stover, she has not been mistreated. I think you understand the reasons behind Missus Stover's anger.'

'Enough of this fatuous banter, Doran! Your plans have come to naught. By now Mister Adler and Mister Snapp are in our custody, Ms Tomlinson is dead and within the next few hours you two are going to die in a mysterious explosion.'

He nodded to Milford; he signalled the six who surrounded Amanda and Os, keeping enough space between them and the two to prevent an attack by Os. They began a fast walk to the far end of the runway with Darwin and Milford a short distance behind the others. It was light enough now Os could see their destination: a small, breeze block building with a sloping tin roof.

They opened the door and pushed the two inside. Darwin approached and held up a parcel the size of a brick with a mobile phone taped to it: 'As you can see, this is a fuel bunker: a sturdy breeze block shed enclosing a large steel tank filled with aviation fuel – what most people refer to, I believe, as "avgas". We are going to close and lock this heavy steel door and attach this device. Sometime within the next few hours, Mister Cleeland here will make a call to the mobile affixed to this devise which will cause it to explode and this entire little building, along with its contents to be engulfed in a huge and no doubt impressive ball of fire.

'Now, as you are well aware, using modern forensic techniques, not only the cause of this massive explosion but the two incinerated bodies found therein would suggest some sort of foul play. I, however, as a Minister of Her Majesty's Government, have enough influence at appropriate levels within the establishment to ensure the conclusions of any such inquest will be that this was an unexplained accident and since there was no loss of life, no further investigation is called for. Oh, and by the way, any attempts to open this door or tamper with the lock or hinges in any way will cause this to explode. Is this all clear?'

'Quite clear. Shall we just get on with it?'

'Stiff upper lip to the end. Very impressive. Still – too bad I do not have the time to discuss this matter with you in greater depth. I am certain we could find a lawn mower somewhere nearby. Good day, Missus Stover – Mister Doran.'

They slammed the door. Amanda and Os heard the hasp closed over the keeper and the padlock snapped shut, and further noises—the bomb's being attached, probably with gaffer tape, then silence.

'Well, Aidie, *that* didn't work very well, did it? I assume you have a Plan B up your sleeve.'

'Not really. I guess Brian was right, *Orwell* is indeed an impressive bit of software. I'm sorry to have involved my old friend, Paul, and I'm genuinely sorry about Sally. Meanwhile, we need to figure out how to get out of here.'

'But – what he said about the door –?'

'Oh, we won't go near the door.'

'But –?'

'The roof, Mandy, the roof. Roofs of fuel and ammunition bunkers are always designed as their weak points. Any explosions blow *up* rather than *out*. Safer for anything nearby like other fuel or ammunition bunkers, aeroplanes, people and things like that.'

'So?'

'So we forget about the door and think about the roof. You just sit in the corner and relax. I know – "That's easy for you to say, mate!" We wait for a little while until we're sure they're gone then I start to work on this roof.'

CHAPTER FIFTY

TWO MEN PARKED in trees next to the A57 one-half mile from Hollow Meadows. Using their night-vision goggles, they worked their way across darkened fields to the paddock behind Sally's farmhouse. Their NVDs helped them locate the infrared sensors she had installed. They placed their own infrared light sources to allow them an uninterrupted path to the kitchen windows at the rear of the house. They were not looking for a tripwire.

The tripwire they were not looking for was attached to many empty tins in sizes from one-half litre to twenty-five litres perched precariously on the roof of a small shed. When they fell the clatter wakened Sally and probably her nearest neighbour a quarter mile away. With surprise gone, the two smashed in a window, crawled through as fast as they could and ran up the stairs to her bedroom door. She was ready.

The lead man kicked open the door and she blinded him with the beam of a two million candle power quartz halogen spotlight then destroyed his right kneecap with a charge of number four buckshot from a 12 bore Purdey double barrelled shotgun. This blew him backwards against his partner and they tumbled down the stairs, landing in a heap at the bottom. The injured man screamed; the other waved his arms frantically. In the glare of her spotlight she blasted his right elbow with the discharge of the other barrel of her very expensive, custom-made weapon.

With the two now screaming she calmly turned on a lamp, dressed and reloaded her weapon. She went down the stairs, stepping carefully over the two, no longer screaming, just moaning continually. She turned on several lights, laid the shotgun on the large, cluttered kitchen table, and pulled a Colt M1911A1 and a loaded magazine from a drawer. She looked briefly at the magazine, snapped it into the pistol, pulled the slide back to cock it and chamber a round.

With the safety off she laid it carefully on the table and faced the two men: 'Well, now, gentlemen, mind telling me just who the hell you are and who sent you?'

'Fuck you, Bitch.'

She picked up the pistol and pointed it at the man with the injured knee, the man who had spoken: 'Wrong answer, Scumbag!'

She shot him through the other knee: 'Now, let's try that again, shall we? Who the hell are you and who sent you?'

When she dragged them into the barn and all four knees and all four elbows had suffered irreparable damage, she was convinced they did not know the name of the person who hired them, only their target and they would be paid in cash at a pub in Cheetham Hill when their unknown employer heard on the news about her untimely death by persons unknown. She administered the coup de grâce to each with her Colt 45 and buried them in a five-foot-deep hole under the dirt floor.

She doubted anyone would report them missing and since she expected to end her days on this farm, it was unlikely anybody would be digging up her barn floor without her permission during her lifetime. She also anticipated, correctly, it would be several days before their employer, whom she abduced to be either Darwin Cantwell or Milford Cleeland, discovered they had not completed their assignment; nor would either of them report the incident to the appropriate authorities.

CHAPTER FIFTY-ONE

AMANDA SAT IN the corner with her back against the block wall; Os lay on his back atop the fuel tank with his feet against the corrugated steel roof. The sun was up with enough light creeping in so they could dimly see the space around them. The rafters were steel angles; the panels secured with screws.

He looked for seams: spots where two panels overlapped with screws going through both panels. He wanted a joint where four sheets—the top corners of the lower row of panels and the lower corners of the upper row— overlapped. Any screw here protruded less deeply into the rafter and was likely a little weaker. It was still too dark to see the joints but he felt for the overlap. He found the juncture of four panels, adjusted his position and began kicking at the panel topmost of the four.

He felt the panel flexing with each kick but the screw was not loosening. He rested for five minutes and tried again. Now he felt the corner of the panel beginning to yield. With one mighty kick he heard the screw pop loose and a little light shone through the space between the overlapping panels. He rested for another five minutes then kicked some more and the two screws above his first success gave way.

In a half hour he loosened enough screws to bend the panel far enough away from the rafter to create a space big enough for them to crawl through. He helped Amanda up onto the tank, crawled out onto the roof and pulled her up after him. They dropped down to the grass and moved around to the side of the building unseen from the hangars. They sat and rested without saying anything for a few minutes.

He patted her arm and smiled: 'Plan B, Mandy.'

"Bout time, Aidie. But we're still not out of here.'

'No, but I'm working on it. You wait here while I have a look around. I'm hoping this is like our club and is deserted during the week. One never knows, do one? Sit tight.'

He patted her arm once more, stood up, looked out around the corner of the bunker and, keeping close to the hedges, started working his way towards the hangars and other buildings. He walked around the area and saw nobody. Convinced they were alone, he relaxed and started thinking about finding transportation, then decided flying made sense. Well, why not? A powered aircraft—as some of his friends said—was like a glider except for that big fire hazard hanging off the front end. And even if Darwin and Milford thought they escaped the bunker, they certainly would not assume Amanda and he would be flying anywhere, let alone back to Manchester.

He needed to see if Brian had made it to St. Gildas or if, as Darwin said, they captured him. Having assured himself flying was a good idea, he walked along the rows of aeroplanes tied down around hangars looking for one he thought competent to fly. Well, it was not so much a question of flying it, almost anybody could do that, it was a question of *landing* it—that last little bit at the end.

He made a second circuit adding more depth to his search: looking inside cockpits and at fuel gauges. Most master switches needed keys, the yellow Piper Cub did not. And the float fuel gauge on the J3 Cub told him its tank was full, or nearly so. So far, so good. He knew enough about the good ol' Cub to think it might be easy to fly. But, look Mummy – no flaps: a *lot* like a glider but with no airbrakes. Could he cope with that? Well, it was a case of a long, low approach with good speed control—his speed control on approach was decent these days,

maintaining height with good use of the throttle and—
and this was a pretty important 'and'—a seriously long
runway. Worth a try.

He walked to the bunker without sneaking close to the
hedges: 'Okay, Mandy. Plan B is "Go!"'

'Oh, yeah, Aidie. Don't know whether I like the sound
of that. What'd you have in mind?'

'Just you wait and see.'

He took her hand and they walked to the Cub. As he
began to remove the tie-down ropes, she walked around
the little yellow aeroplane looking at it, then him, then
back to the plane: 'Are you thinking what I'm thinking
you're thinking?'

'Probably. Ever had a ride in one of these?'

'No. Have you?'

'Nope. But there's a first time for everything. Can't be
all that hard, can it?'

'I really don't like it when you say that!'

'Trust me, I'm a close protection security consultant.'

'And I like *that* even less.'

He opened the two-piece door, latching the top half to
the underside of the wing and dropping the bottom half
down against the fuselage. He stood and looked at the
cockpit and the sparse instrument panel then stepped
around the wheel and strut to the cowling. He twisted the
quarter-turn fasteners and opened it for an even longer
look. He checked the oil level then closed and secured the
cowling. Next he climbed into the front seat, settled comfortably and spent several minutes playing with the stick,
the throttle, the magnetos switch and the rudder pedals.
Then he climbed out and did the same pre-flight check or
DI he would have done with his glider.

'Right, I think we're ready. Let's get you into the back
seat and we're away.'

She climbed in without saying anything. She secured her seatbelt—just a belt around the waist, unlike the five-point harness she used in the glider. He confirmed the mags switch was off then cracked the throttle and opened the fuel cutoff.

He smiled at her again: 'I want you to hold the stick full back and push your heels hard on the brakes. No starter on this grand old lady. I've never started one before so this is kind of scary. As soon as she starts and I climb in, you can release the brakes, let go of the stick and I'll take control.'

'Trust me, I'm a deputy manageress in a building society.'

He rotated the propeller several times, pulling it around until it was in compression just beyond top dead centre. He came back to the cockpit and switched the mags to 'Both'. Balancing himself, he grasped the prop towards the outer end of its trailing edge, pulled it down sharply and stepped back away from it. It rotated twice, the engine coughed, smoke puffed from the exhaust then everything was quiet. He repeated this three times and still the engine did not start. He set the switch to 'Off' and looked once more at the panel: 'Bit of a problem here.'

'Yeah I can see that. It doesn't seem to want to start. What next?'

'Good question and I think I have the answer. This shiny knob here has "Primer" stamped on it. Fancy that!'

He unlocked the primer, pumped it four times, closed and locked it and tried again. This time the engine chuffed into life. He climbed in, secured his belt and closed the bottom half of the door as he pulled the stick full back in his right hand, applied the brakes with his heels and adjusted the throttle with his left until the tachometer was indicating eight-hundred rpm. He waited until the oil pressure was reading green and watched until the oil temperature also came up to green. He closed the top half of the door, reached back and squeezed her left foot gently. Then he forgot totally about his passenger and concentrated on his flying.

He looked at the windsock and was happy the light wind was nearly straight down the runway: not much of a crosswind. He taxied to the downwind end. Here he turned ninety degrees to look out and confirm there was, as he expected, no aircraft on final.

He opened the throttle, kicked the rudder and began their run. When they were aligned with the runway and starting to roll he opened the throttle to 'Full'. He remembered once watching a Cub take off and recalled seeing the tail come off the ground almost immediately the plane was in motion, so he eased the stick forward until he could see some runway over the nose.

With full throttle and no significant crosswind, what they experienced was like taking off in a glider on aero tow: all he did was keep the wings level and fly straight down the runway until they lifted off the ground. When the airspeed reached forty knots he eased the stick back just a touch and they were airborne. He looked down and saw the right wheel still spinning but slowing as their shadow dropped away. Not too bad for a newbie, now let's go home.

With no charts to consult, they followed the motorway network north. He began their climb to five-thousand feet, turned west and spotted the M40, then banked right until he was aligned with it. When he was rolling out of their bank he looked back to his right at the field just as the fuel bunker was blossoming into an impressive column of orange fire topped by roiling black smoke. He tapped on the window and Amanda looked.

She smiled and raised her voice over the noise of the engine: 'Plan B?'

'Plan B! Next stop, Birmingham.'

Having done only a little cross country flying in his glider and none in power, he had no idea how many CAA regulations he broke flying at five-thousand feet directly through heavily trafficked airspace around Birmingham and Manchester, but never mind. He doubted Darwin, even with his extremely high opinion of himself, had the power to scramble a squadron of Eurofighters to shoot them down.

He adjusted the throttle and stick to maintain altitude and fly at a civilized sixty-five knots, squeezed Amanda's foot once more and they continued north. His feet were cold and he thought hers might be too; he found the 'Cabin Heat' knob on his right below the panel and pulled it out. He loved flying his glider but this was fun; maybe someday when he had the time he would learn to fly power properly.

His destination was the Woodford Aerodrome not far from his safe house in Wilmslow. This former British Aerospace facility was originally an AVRO factory with a proud heritage: it was where Lancasters, Shackletons and Vulcans, among other famous aircraft were built.

He was going there because he was familiar with the area, because he knew it comprised at least two seriously long runways—hopefully long enough for his first ever solo, tail dragger, no flaps, power landing and, despite its proximity to Manchester, was adjacent to open country on its southern and western boundaries. He was not certain whether it was still deserted after BAE ceased operations, but he hoped so. Also, he had very little idea what they were going to do once they landed but he was working on it; whether this was part of Plan B or the start of Plan C was yet to be decided.

They passed over Birmingham still flying at five-thousand feet and their leisurely sixty-five knots. He located the M6 toll road north of the city and turned a little to the west to keep it in sight as they flew on. His fuel seemed adequate at about one-half tank and the old Continental A-40 engine made him feel like they were really flying.

Just north of what he concluded was Crew, the M6 turned gradually west and here they left the motorway and flew directly north. In the distance he could see the city and south of it Manchester International Airport. He looked to the east of it and spotted Woodford. It was time for adrenaline to start pumping.

When they were ten miles out he reduced power and began a slow descent. He had no real measure of how high above the ground they were but when he judged them to be at two-thousand feet, he levelled off. He looked for smoke to get some idea of wind direction but saw none; he looked for a windsock when they approached the field but saw none either. Maybe the place is deserted after all. With no indication of wind direction he had no choice but to assume it changed little since Hinton—not perfect but it was all he had.

The runway he used for takeoff was into a light wind blowing from about two-hundred and fifty degrees so now he chose the runway with a huge twenty-five painted on the end of it. Wow! even from this far away it looks really long. At two miles out he throttled back further and went through a series of checks he hoped would get them safely onto the ground. Approach speed? how about forty-five knots? Trim for that? done. Carburettor heat? on. Landing gear? fixed. Flaps? none, dammit! Anything else?

no, that will do. There was probably more to it but he could not think of anything.

He throttled back further to bring them down to one-thousand feet and spotted, finally, a rubbish fire in a back garden. It was their lucky day! the wind was still light and still coming from around two-hundred and fifty degrees: almost straight down the runway.

Now he started talking to himself out loud—a carryover from his student days. Most neophyte glider fliers do it for six months after they have gone solo: 'Eight hundred feet above the ground – let's make it one-thousand feet; one-thousand metres upwind from the touchdown point – let's make it a mile. Two average English fields away from the runway – nobody really knows what that means so here, over this far field boundary looks okay.

'Now, keep the speed at forty-five knots and adjust the throttle to keep us at one-thousand feet. Remember, the stick is the speed control and the throttle is the up-and-down control. Fly downwind parallel to the runway keeping the speed steady and let the height come down to around five-hundred feet. So far, so good.

'In a glider I turn onto base leg when the touchdown point is at about forty-five degrees behind me. Not today, Aidie, remember we have no airbrakes. So keep flying at five-hundred feet and forty-five knots until the touchdown point is way, *way* back behind us. There, that looks about right. Now, crisp, well-banked turn ninety degrees to the left. Watch your speed. Roll out, wings level.

'Almost even with the end of the runway, another crisp, well-banked turn to the left and roll out to line up with the runway. Now just keep lined up with the runway and reduce the throttle until we're maybe one-hundred feet above the ground. Easy does it. Wow! we're awfully close to those houses and train tracks. Let's open the throttle a little and gain some height. Never mind. Speed steady at forty-five knots and now we've crossed the boundary and we're into the field. A row of bushes and small trees but we'll clear them easily. Past the trees now and almost over the tarmac.

'Over the tarmac. Chop the throttle. Nothing to do now but keep it straight down the middle of this gloriously long runway. Now the tarmac is starting to look like tarmac – ease the stick back and just try to keep it from landing. Closer and closer and closer. Stick back just a little more – keep it flying, keep it flying, keep it flying.

'Gently, but not gentle enough. Shit! A pretty impressive bounce and we're flying again! Never mind, just hold everything – don't panic – plenty of runway ahead of us. Another bounce, this one not nearly as impressive as the first and once again we're airborne. Hold everything and wait for this old girl to stop flying. One more really gentle bounce and now we're down – all three wheels firmly on the ground and we're starting to slow down. Well, done, Aidie!'

He smiled, pushed Carburettor Heat to 'Off', opened the throttle and taxied them to the far end of this beautiful runway. Their adventure was not over yet; they needed to hide themselves quickly, probably in the trees at the far end of the runway in case somebody on the field noticed their arrival. They rolled off the runway onto the grass and to the boundary fence. He closed the throttle and switched the mags to 'Off'. He probably was supposed to idle the engine for a few minutes to let it cool down gradually but they were in a hurry. He opened the two door panels, removed his seat belt, climbed out and helped Amanda with hers. He closed the panels, patted the fuselage of the little yellow aeroplane then they ran for the boundary fence.

CHAPTER FIFTY-TWO

Os LOOKED FOR a weak point in the chain-link fence topped with barbed wire. They moved to a corner of the field near a road where they could hunker down between a small brick shed and bushes overhanging it. They rested for a few minutes then he studied the fence. The three strands of barbed wire topping it were angled outward: designed to keep people out, not in. All three were loose. He moved mid-way between two posts and started yanking on the top strand until he drew some slack in it. He kept pulling until it hung down below the top of the chain-link. Pulling on the lower two strands gave them a barbed-wire-free space six feet long. He climbed over, helped Amanda over and they were clear of the airfield and hidden in the bushes.

She touched his hand: 'So, you've added yet another talent to your already impressive list. What next?'

'Well, we need to get to somewhere safe and see what's happened to our friends. Brian? well, Brian's just Brian and even if they're holding him I doubt they're going to hurt him. Paul? again, I know him and he can take care of himself. The really bad thing that's happened is Sally – she was supposed to be the one person capable of telling the world about this mess. Since she's gone I'm not sure where we go from here. In the meantime I still think the best place to hide out is St. Gildas and I'm working on Plan C to get us there without detection.'

'And just how're you going to do that?'

'Just watch and learn – watch and learn. You sit here and rest. I'm going to have a look around that farm over there. I'm genuinely sorry about leaving that Cub to the elements. I hope somebody at the field sees it and takes pity. Back in a little while.'

He worked his way along the hedgerow, around behind a large house, possibly a barn conversion, standing alone along the road and surrounded by a large garden.

It was deserted. Still keeping within the shadow of the hedges he moved around the far side and out towards the road to check out a complex of farm buildings across the road. Even in mid-afternoon it, too, seemed deserted until he spotted a well-kept farmhouse behind the buildings. It clearly was *not* deserted. When he retreated into the hedges he spotted the 'For Sale' sign in front of the barn conversion. Might it be empty?

He moved along the hedges to the back then, keeping well-hidden from the road, moved across the garden to the back door. A look through the window into the kitchen confirmed the house was empty and the only likely visitors would be estate agents and prospective buyers. A great place to hide out for a while, even overnight, until he decided on their next move. Still keeping close to the hedgerow, he went back to Amanda and returned with her.

He rattled the kitchen door then turned to her: 'Don't happen to have a kirby grip handy, do you?'

'Matter of fact, I don't.'

'Shucks, woman. In the films and on the telly the girl *always* has a convenient kirby grip stuck in her hair.'

'Sorry.'

'Never mind, we'll just have to improvise.'

He walked around the area between the back of the house and the garage looking for a piece of wire or anything else he could use for an improvised lock pick. He scanned the area around the rubbish bins near the fence and found what he was looking for—a rusty paper clip. He bent it into an interesting shape and went to work on the lock. A paper clip is not the best lock-picking tool in the box; he needed several minutes. He opened the door and stepped in, listening for an alarm and looking for motion sensors. He found neither so he nodded to her; she came in and closed the door. They wandered over all three floors to confirm they were alone then returned to the kitchen.

'What next?'

Well, I'm ready to kick off Plan C but for this I need a telephone.'

'There's one in the front hall. Wonder if it works.'

'Worth a try.'

Os picked up the handset and smiled: 'We have lift off!'

He dialled 999 and was connected almost immediately: 'Nine-nine-nine. What's your emergency?'

'Woman's fallen. Doesn't look like she's breathing. Please help, oh, please help me?'

'What's your name and location, sir?'

'My name? Oh, my name's Thornton Gilrey. Location? Oh I don't know the name of the road. It's behind the old BAE factory in Woodford. By the fence. Service gate. Please help. She's not breathing. I don't know her name. I was just walking along the road and I found her there by the gate.'

'Where're you calling from, sir?'

'Empty farmhouse just up the road. Door was open. Nobody around – I left my mobile at home.'

'Okay, sir, just stay on the line. We have your location. We're dispatching an ambulance and two paramedics. They should be with you in – ten minutes – you stand out next to the road and when the paramedics arrive you can show them where the woman is. Are you okay with that?'

'Yes. Oh, yes, please. Just get here quickly.'

He laid the phone gently on the carpeted floor and motioned Amanda to keep quiet. They stepped away and he instructed her to walk back along the road to just beyond their escape corner to the service gate. When she heard the ambulance arriving she was to lie down and pretend to be unconscious. He would do the rest.

He picked up the phone: 'Are you still there?'

'Yes, sir, I'm still here. The ambulance will be with you in about five minutes.'

He signalled her to leave by the kitchen door and walk up to the gate. He held the phone and waited: 'I hear the siren! I hear the siren!'

'You're doing great, sir. Just great. Now, put the phone down and walk out and stand next to the road.'

He waved frantically when the ambulance approached, pointing up the road to where Amanda was lying. It passed him and he ran behind it to the gate. The two paramedics opened their doors, climbed out and moved towards Amanda. Os stepped behind the man, disabled the radio affixed to his collar, put him in a gentle chokehold and whispered to him: 'Right, sir, please listen carefully. Don't struggle. I don't want to hurt you so if you and your partner just keep calm everything'll be fine. You okay with that?'

The man nodded and relaxed somewhat. Os loosened his grip but kept the hold in place. His partner was bending over Amanda and was not aware of what was happening until Os raised his voice: 'Miss, I want you to move away from my friend here, keep your hands away from your radio and move over to the fence.'

The startled woman looked to her partner then complied.

Os looked to Amanda when she opened her eyes and sat up: 'I want you to remove the radio she has pinned to her uniform. Gently, we don't want to hurt her, we don't want to hurt *anybody*. Now I want you to open the rear doors and find some straps – any straps we can use to tie these nice folks up for just a little while. Can you do that?'

Amanda emerged from the ambulance holding bright orange straps that looked like part of a mountain rescue kit. Not a lot of mountains around here, he thought, maybe they need these up in the Pennines. He instructed her to stretch the woman's arms out at shoulder height and strap them to the fence. When this was done he removed the man's radio and put them both in the cab. Then he pulled the man to the fence and secured him by both arms. Neither struggled.

'I'm really sorry to do this to you two, you've done us no harm, but we have to help a friend who's in trouble.'

He looked at their name badges: 'Pauline, Colin. It would take too long to explain, so as soon as we can have your uniforms and your vehicle we'll be off. It's a nice, warm day and somebody should be along to release you before too long.'

He turned to Amanda: 'You first.'

They loosened Pauline's straps so she could take off her green and yellow paramedic's boiler suit. She was a little taller and slimmer than Amanda so the fit was not great but it would do. They strapped her to the fence again and repeated the process with the Colin, who was a little shorter and stockier than Os. Never mind; needs must. They climbed into the ambulance, reversed into the area in front of the gate and drove along Old Hall Lane towards Chester Road, planning to drive to St. Gildas.

They had gone less than a mile when Os realized driving around in a stolen ambulance was a daft idea. Leaving two very startled and semi-naked paramedics strapped to a chain link fence on a rural country road was not in itself daft; their uniforms might turn out to be useful. But it would not be long before they were discovered and shortly after that the loss of their vehicle would be reported and a search initiated. He assumed it was equipped with a satellite tracking device and he was confident it could be identified quickly by any police helicopter from the big number painted on the roof. No, they needed something less conspicuous.

The nearest hospital with an accident and emergency department was Stepping Hill, four miles from Woodford. They drove into the area adjacent to the A and E entrance and parked their ambulance in a slot between two others. Side-by-side they walked casually through the automatic doors and kept walking until they found a corridor that was not crowded, then looked for a vending machine. Os went through Colin's pockets and extracted enough change to buy two coffees. They stood against the wall beside the machine sipping their drinks and chatting quietly—looking just like a couple of paramedics on a well-deserved break.

She looked at his name badge and smiled: 'So, Colin, my darlin', what next?'

'I have a clever plan, Pauline, my sweet'

'And that is?'

'Well, I've concluded we need something less likely to attract attention than that what we come in.'

'So how do *we* do that?'

'You just stand here looking just as nonchalant as you possibly can while I find us some wheels. Won't be long.'

He handed her his half-finished drink then wandered through nearby corridors until he found the door to a male staff locker room. It was going well for him: the room was unoccupied and most lockers were secured with the familiar round Yale combination padlocks one often sees in locker rooms. He moved from one to the next, unlocking each, opening the locker and looking for car keys. On his third attempt he found a set of keys with a Volvo fob attached. All three lockers closed and locked, he stepped into the corridor and walked back to Amanda. He had been gone less than ten minutes.

'Okay, Missus S, it's time to go.'

They dumped their unfinished drinks in a bin and walked back through Reception and out into the car park. They wandered around and Os clicked the fob until they heard the chirp and saw the lights flash on a bright blue S60: 'Madam, your chariot awaits you.'

'Well done, Mister D. Thank you very much. I'm impressed.'

'Nothing but the best for you, M' Lady.'

They drove to the lock-up. He thought it would not be under surveillance because their pursuers assumed they died in the explosion; he looked around carefully for mysterious men sitting in cars reading newspapers and found none. He loosened a wooden trim strip next to the door and removed a spare key from a space hollowed out on the underside. Once inside he put a Glock 17 and a Model B Uzi carbine in a holdall along with spare magazines and plenty of 9x19mm cartridges for both, a Gerber, a duplicate of his magic electronic thingy for bypassing alarm systems and keypad locks, four pay-as-you-go mobile phones, several credit cards and some cash. He put this bag in the boot then closed and secured the door to the lock-up.

He slipped the key under the trim strip, hammered it back in place with a rock and climbed into the car: 'Before we go on to St. Gildas I want to have a look at Sally's place; just in case our Mister Secretary of State for Health doesn't have his facts straight.'

She settled back comfortably in the seat and closed her eyes: 'I could get used to this. Much roomier, smoother and quieter than that little yellow aeroplane.'

CHAPTER FIFTY-THREE

DARWIN FELT CHIPPER this Thursday morning. He ordered his driver to bring the car around for his drive to Westminster and his attendance at the weekly Cabinet meeting. They had lost track of Snapp and Adler—two minor actors in the drama being played out, but Doran, Stover and Tomlinson—their three stars with top billing—would trouble them no more.

He rang Milford: 'Status report?'

'Not good news I'm afraid, sir –'

'May I remind you, I don't pay you for bad news, I pay you to deliver *good* news? Now what, pray tell, is going on?'

'Two things. First the fire investigation team report that, although the explosion seems to have been the result of some kind of bomb or booby trap, no bodies were found –'

'Of course no bodies were found, you idiot. They were not *supposed* to find any bodies.'

'No, I'm not quite sure you get my meaning, sir. I mean *no bodies were found.*'

'Are you telling me those two escaped?'

'That, sir, appears to be the case.'

'And?'

'And the two contractors dispatched to see to Madison Tomlinson seemed to have disappeared.'

'Mister Cleeland, before the day is out, before the sun goes down – as the plebs might put it – I want these three found and delivered to me at *Sans Soucis* by my return this evening. Is that clear?'

'Yes, sir. Absolutely.'

'And may I add another expression sometimes used by the great unwashed masses: I want them delivered to me dead or alive! Is that clear?'

'Yes, sir. Absolutely.'

'This has gone on far too long. It must end today!'

He was no longer feeling quite so chipper; Milford's assurances certainly did not encourage him. He decided he could no longer delay what was inevitable: it was time to warn the Prime Minister about possible consequences. Their private secretaries arranged for him to ride with the PM in his car travelling from Westminster to a factory in Narborough immediately following the Cabinet meeting and his audience with the Queen. Darwin sat in silence while the two were driven up the M1 and the PM read, shuffled and signed an impressive sheaf of important-looking papers.

Near Hemel Hempstead, he organized these papers into a tidy stack, straightened his tie and looked up: 'Yes, Darwie, how can I help you?'

He spent the next twenty minutes describing the Stover incident and his part in it, omitting his encounter with the lawn mower and his connection with Milford. Ostensibly he was seeking advice on how to deal with it, at a visceral level he was asking his boss to make certain it went away. The PM, as always, appeared genuinely concerned.

'Well, I don't know what I can do to help – really. Let me think about it and get back to you. Naturally I'll back you one hundred and ten percent if any of this comes to light.'

They approached Toddington Services just north of Luton and the PM signalled his driver to leave the motorway. Adjacent to Burger King he stopped the car, got out, opened Darwin's door and stood to attention.

Darwin climbed out and the PM leaned across and shook his hand: 'I'll be at Chequers this weekend. Ring me Sunday afternoon around two on my private line. We'll talk.'

The PM straightened up and went back to looking at his papers; the driver closed his door and they drove off onto the northbound carriageway.

CHAPTER FIFTY-FOUR

HARRISON, 'HARRY', MABE retained Detective Sergeant Raymond Quinn to provide information—usually routine but sometimes ad hoc—useful to him in the conduct of his business managed from his local, the Baited Bear in Cheetham Hill. DS Quinn was not happy with this arrangement but discovered, too late unfortunately, one did not resign from Mister Mabe's organization. He was known, technically and legally, as a 'bent copper'.

Harry asked Raymond to help him identify the person responsible for the destruction of three large, plate glass windows fronting the establishment a few nights earlier. Harry was trying to be as helpful as possible by giving Raymond an envelope containing three relatively undamaged slugs dug from the woodwork behind the bar. These were full metal jackets and Harry hoped Raymond's access to the forensic laboratories of the Greater Manchester Police would provide evidence linking this weapon to other crimes and thence to the possible perpetrator(s). He had an arrangement with the landlord that the CCTV system was normally inoperative, the better to hamper any enquiries by police into the comings and goings of his fellows; this arrangement was in place the night of the attack.

Raymond returned the day after to deliver his report: 'Ballistics on the slugs will take about two more days but I've had a look at the CCTV images from nearby streets and I'm puzzled.'

'It ain't your job to be puzzled, Quinn, that's my job. Your job is to tell me what I need to know. Capisce?'

'Yes, sir, Mister Mabe.'

'So?'

Raymond shifted uncomfortably and swallowed twice: 'Well – the CCTV images from around the time show a man on a big Harley-Davidson wearing Sons of Damien colours – that's a club in North Lincolnshire –'

'I know who the fuckin' Sons of Damien is!'

'– and the PNC check confirms the bike belongs to a man named Cedric Fettle. Helluva name for a biker. What?'

'So what's so bloody puzzling about that?'

'What's confusing me is he's not trying to hide his identity – it's almost as though he wants to be recognized.'

'Well, shit, most of them bikers is dumb muthafuckers. Maybe he just doesn't know no better.'

'Or, maybe he's deliberately trying to start something.'

Harry hammered the table with his fists until their pints started dancing towards the edge. Raymond winced in time with the blows.

'Now just why the fuck would he want to do *that*?'

'I have no idea. That's just my opinion.'

'Well, if they want a bloody war, then war it'll be. Teach 'em fuckin' farm boys to fuck with Harry Mabe!'

It was a busy day in Cheetham Hill pubs. Simultaneous with Harry's and Raymond's meeting, Milford sat down with another crime boss, Edmund, 'Eddie', Voigt in the Oubliette. Unlike Raymond, Milford was not in the employ of Mister Voigt, to the contrary Milford sometimes sub-contracted work to Eddie and his confederates for situations where discretion was crucial. Mister Voigt and Mister Mabe were not the best of friends. In fact, this lack of amity often increased dramatically the workload of members of the Greater Manchester Police assigned to keep the peace in this part of the city. Mister Voigt was curious about the loss of the two big pub windows several nights previously, but identification of the person or persons responsible was not high on his list of priorities.

Milford provided Eddie with all the information he had on Os, Amanda and Sally including their home addresses, landline and recent mobile telephone numbers, photographs, a few known associates, last known locations and that they were proving difficult to find and detain. He omitted any information concerning his interest in these three, or anything linking them to the Stover incident or the Secretary of State for Health.

Eddie made some notes in a small notebook then reached for the photos: 'So what's the brief?'

'The brief, quite simply is I want them to disappear without trace as soon as possible.'

Eddie was silent for a minute: 'So this Doran character. This the same Doran's on the news lately – this baby-killin' terrorist cannibal?'

'Yep, the same.'

'So, if he's such a bad-ass and half the fuckin' cops in Britain lookin' for him, why you need me for this job?'

'Well, I can't tell you too much – bit of bother for a public official who must remain nameless – what I *can* tell you is this isn't straightforward. The news reports aren't totally accurate – something of a smoke screen until this man's found.'

Eddie thought about this then his demeanour and his tone of voice moved from relaxed and well modulated to tense and very angry.

'Sounds like you're not tellin' me everythin'. You know I don't like that one bit. Hate goin' into anything without knowin' what I'm goin' into. And you know bloody well that ain't the way I operate. So either you tell me what I need to know or you can fuck off!'

'Okay, sorry. Doran is ex-Special Forces – career – and he's good. Twice I've been close to him and both times he's got away.'

'So why'd you not just do 'em when you had 'em?'

'Good question, but my employer didn't want that.'

'Your employer must be a fuckin' moron. What is he, some fuckin' derivatives trader or politician or somethin'?'

'Something like that. Point is, I want them done now – all three of them.'

'The usual?'

'The usual.'

This terse and cryptic agreement signalled the deal was done: Eddie's pest control experts would take on this assignment and upon completion Milford would see to the transfer of a pre-agreed amount of either heroin or crack cocaine from GMP evidence storage to the Oubliette. Eddie acceded to a certain amount of flexibility in this arrangement: should appropriate quantities of the hard stuff not be available, he was prepared to accept the equivalent value in either cannabis or Ecstasy in lieu of. He glanced at his notes and the photographs, stuffed them into his shirt pocket and the meeting was adjourned.

CHAPTER FIFTY-FIVE

AMANDA AND OS travelled across Snake Pass to Hollow Meadows and Sally's farmhouse. He drove past, looking across the field, hoping to see signs of life. He saw none. *These people are starting to piss me off, maybe it's time for an all-out, frontal assault.* He stopped the car two hundred yards from the house, reached into the holdall on the back seat and pulled out a Glock. He checked the magazine, snapped it back into place and drove up the dirt track to the house, turning the car in the cluttered yard so it faced the road.

He left the motor running: 'Looks like the place's deserted. I'm going to have a look around.'

'Shouldn't we have parked up the road in the trees and sneaked around the back?'

'Naw, the time for sneaking around is over. It's go for broke!'

He walked up to the door. When he knocked he reached back and pulled the pistol from his belt. The door snapped open and he confronted the very impressive 45 calibre bore of Madison's Colt while she the business end of his Glock 17.

She smiled: 'Is that a gun in your hand or are you just glad to see me? What I believe the Americans refer to as a "Mexican standoff". Hello, Ossie. What's new? Oh, and what's with the green boiler suit? Doesn't fit very well. You look like a paramedic.'

'I'm *supposed* to look like a paramedic, Sally. Long story. Tell you about it on the way. Understand you had a spot of bother the past day or so.'

'Nothing I couldn't handle, as I reminded you last time we met.'

'So, "the reports of your death are highly exaggerated", as they say.'

'Would seem so. What now?'

'I have a clever plan. Listen up, please. I'd like to put you and Brian in a place where you can work uninterrupted until you pull this together and take it to whomever. Make sense?'

'Makes sense to me. I'll get my coat, my case and my laptop. Okay If I bring my friend Mister Colt here? Still not comfortable with these new-fangled plastic things.'

'Mister Colt's welcome on our adventure. Shall we go?'

He introduced the two women then moved the holdall to the front seat so the two could sit together in the back.

'It'll give Mandy the chance to tell you all about this from the beginning. By the way, you ever hear of a reporter named Trevor LaFarge?'

'That effen toe rag? I'm surprised somebody hasn't done him in by now. What's he up to this time?'

She booted up her laptop and added to her notes while she asked specific, detailed questions about everything from Bill's initial suspension to their arrival at her house.

She was fascinated by Trevor's involvement: 'He'd sell his little sister to Arab slave-traders if he thought there's a lurid story in it. That sounds just like his style, ask a pre-arranged question during a press conference and get somebody's name out in the open – whether there's any truth in it or not. Don't know much about this Hyde-Davies character yet but, yes, he's done this sort of thing before for a price. She must be a real piece of work. He probably thinks he'll be rewarded with, shall we say, "the sweet fruits of her gender" in return for his help. By the way, you haven't told me where we're going, have you?'

'I'm saving it for a surprise. You'll see.'

'Don't like the sound of that, my friend.'

'It's okay. Anyhow they think you're dead. Trust me.'

Amanda patted her arm: '"Trust me." That's just what he keeps telling me and look where it's got us.'

Sally slapped the light tan leather seat beside her: 'Nice wheels. What kind of mileage you say you get with this baby?'

'Didn't say. Doesn't matter. Did I mention we just borrowed it for a while?'

They drove in silence while Sally typed. They reached the crest of Snake Pass and began the long, winding drift down to Glossop; Os looked in his mirror at the two women: 'So, Sally, when you finish this Pulitzer-Prize-winning exclusive, who you gonna call? Certainly not one of Beattie's rags?'

'You really know how to hurt a girl, don't you? No respect! You soldier blokes are all alike. No, it's going to the only editor I trust, the only one's not in bed with the Tories *or* Labour – Livingstone Stanley, the *Evening Tribune*, this country's last really independent broadsheet.'

'Incredible name for an editor, incredible name for anybody. With that name he must have gone through hell in school, almost as bad as "Oswald".'

They drove into St. Gildas' car park, parked and arranged their meeting. Sally was to go to the Pennine Café, find a big corner table, order a coffee and wait. Amanda and Os would enter through Casualty then she would locate a staff locker room where she would remove her paramedic's greens, roll them up and carry them under her arm then join Sally. Os would do the same, locate Brian and join the other two. In the café Amanda would cram her boiler suit into the holdall on top of his then they would plan their next move.

He walked across the car park between the two women: 'Right, ladies. Hospitals are busy places so people like us wandering around shouldn't attract too much attention. Yes, we'll be on Candid Camera all the time but I don't really think anybody will be looking for us here – at least for a day or two. Yes somebody *may* recognize me as this terrorist wanted by the police, but I doubt it. Most people walking around in hospitals have other things on their minds. So, if we just behave ourselves and act like we belong we should be okay. Brian may be a little hard to find but I'm used to that. Any questions?'

'Nope.'

'Nope.'

'Good. See you around.'

He waved good-bye to Amanda when she stepped into the first Ladies they passed then he entered the nearby Gents. He exited a few minutes later looking a little rumpled from a day filled with escapes from exploding fuel bunkers, piloting small aeroplanes for the first time, assaulting paramedics and stealing motor vehicles.

The first place he looked for Brian was the staff canteen then he checked the Pennine Café, waving to the two women as he passed. His next stop was Casualty where he looked around the busy visitors' waiting area, still with no luck.

His last stop was the hospitality shop. He found Brian standing with his black computer bag slung over his shoulder salivating over a copy of *The Hackers' Yearbook*. His clothes were wrinkled and he needed a shave but this was not unusual. The magazine was opened flat and he was holding it up turned ninety degrees as though he was looking at a centrefold photograph of a young woman wearing no clothes, but when Os interrupted him he realized it was a chart detailing the relative performances of various laptops and netbooks.

Brian snapped the magazine shut when he realized who was watching him: 'Ossie Ossie wow am I glad to see you.'

Os stepped in front of him: 'Shush, shush. Not so loud. Remember I'm a dangerous fugitive. Nobody's supposed to know where I am.'

'Oh sorry Ossie –'

'Shut up – please. Don't use my name and don't speak above a whisper. This is important. If the wrong people discover us here, we're dead. I mean it! Truly. Dead! Got that? Okay? Quietly now and no names.'

Brian stooped over and hunched his shoulders as though in doing so his voice would not carry so far: 'Okay, Osss – sorry what can I call you anyhow I know I'll call you – oh gee I don't know what to call you – never mind I'll think of something so what's happening and what're you doing here and boy am I glad to see you 'cause I had no idea what was happening and –'

Os touched his arm again: 'It's okay, my friend – no names, remember – come with me and I'll tell you all about it.'

On their way to the Pennine Café they stopped at the main reception desk and Os gave the volunteer the keys for the Volvo telling her he found them in the car park where a visitor must have dropped them. They joined the other two for coffees, sandwiches and Amanda's and Os' first chance to sit and relax for many hours.

They ate and sipped in silence. Os sat back, looked around—confirming nearby tables were vacant.

He squeezed Brian's arm as he spoke: 'Folks, I may be stating the obvious, but I'm fully convinced that we are, to use the technical term, in deep shit.'

Brian was about to say something when Os squeezed his arm harder: 'Here's what we're going to do. The three of you are going to sit here just doing what you're doing while I have a good look around. Eventually they'll find us, and I think it'll take them at most two days, probably a bit less. I hope that gives our courageous chronicler here enough time to write her exposé with the able help of my loverly assistant. When that's done, we'll figure out how to get it to your friend, Livingstone. In the meantime, Brian – sorry – Horace –'

'Horace?'

'Yeah. How about "Horace Hacker" for a made up name? Clever, yes?'

'Only if I can call you "Dan".'

'Dan?'

'Yeah "Dan Dangerous: dastardly doer of –"'

'Horace –'

'Yes, Dan?'

'Shut up!'

'Yes, Dan.'

Amanda touched Sally's arm: 'Must be a guy thing.'

'Guess so.'

'– In the meantime – Horace – I'm going to find you a workstation where you two can do your thing without interruption. Big, busy hospitals like this one are full of nooks and crannies, closed wards, storerooms filled with obsolete linen and rooms full of dis-used beds, furniture, and all manner of interesting stuff. I'll do a recce of security here, how they make rounds – *if* they make rounds. Everything's cool for the next little while. See you soon.'

He opened his holdall, pulled the small, black box out and put it in his pocket, pushed himself away from the table, stood up, smiled a thoroughly unconvincing smile and left. The three looked at each other, around the room, back to each other and tried, without much success, to make small talk then they were silent. Over the next few minutes what began as a gentle trembling in Brian's right knee ended with his heel hammering up and down against the floor. The women tried to ignore it but this effort, as with the small talk, was unsuccessful.

Sally unzipped a compartment inside her case and held it up to him so he could see the Colt: 'That knee doesn't stop flying up and down, Horace, I'm gonna blow the bloody thing off.'

Brian's knee was still.

Os returned in an hour with a smile that was a little more convincing: 'Missus S, if you don't mind nursing another coffee, I've found someplace for these nice folks to work their magic. I'll be back.'

He kissed her on the cheek, patted her hand then led Sally and Brian out into the hall and towards an empty ward: 'I think you'll be okay here. There's a button checkpoint on the wall beside the door but I didn't see any inside. This means any security guard making rounds probably logs himself here at the door but doesn't go in. He may look in through the windows but we can deal with that. There's a CCTV camera covering this hall from the far end but since it's only one of many and this is a low-traffic area, we'll just have to hope nobody sees us and reports us as miscreants or ne'er-do-wells.'

They reached the door, he put his little black box next to the keypad, it beeped a couple of times and displayed a number that he entered. The door clicked open, they stepped in and closed it behind them.

He led them to a counter behind the nurses' station: 'If you set up here you won't be seen from the door. A single desk lamp will probably be okay, just turn it on once and leave it on. There's a toilet behind you and even the old rest room where you can have a little nap from time to time. Telephone works. All the comforts of home. What do you think, Horace, WiFi work in here?'

'Probably Dan anyhow WiFi's not the best not the most secure lots of computer points along the wall there maybe connect to the hospital's mainframe intranet vorld vide veb – something anything will do remember I'm the best there is.'

Sally patted her handbag: 'Just don't forget that knee, Horace.'

Brian shivered: 'She wouldn't really blow my knee off would she, Dan?'

'Might. Never can tell. Probably not. Long as you behave yourself, anyhow. Look, I need to get back to Mandy. Here's a mobile to use to contact me if you need something. I'll be back in an hour or so to see how you're doing. Best if you don't go in or out, so I'll bring in some food when I come back. Oh and I found a working kettle back there. I'll bring some tea bags and instant coffee. Milk? Sugar? what'll you have?'

Sally ordered a beef burger and some chips, Brian ordered two American hot dogs with mustard on toasted buns.

CHAPTER FIFTY-SIX

MILFORD CLEELAND WAS a good detective. When he was serving he was an honest copper but when he was offered early retirement he accepted it with the feeling there was more money to be had and less bureaucratic hassle working as an independent. And as an independent he quickly came to see the best-paid work involved assignments that sometimes went well over the line. Over time he succumbed: it was impossible to ignore the lure of big money.

He did, however, draw one particularly solid line he would not cross: he refused to do any wet work—this he always contracted out. He worked from an anonymous office on the second floor of a Victorian building near the intersection of Earl's Court Road and Old Brompton Road in West London—convenient to the sources of most of his assignments in Whitehall and Westminster but at the outer edge of Zone One where rents, if not reasonable, were still slightly less than obscene.

He was very good at finding people and right now he needed to find Doran, Stover and Tomlinson. He would not meet his sundown deadline but with Eddie Voigt's people on the job he would likely have good news for Darwin by the next day. He would just have to put up with his insults and tirades until then. After his return from Cheetham Hill he made several calls to contacts—old mates still serving—and although the processes he used might not have been as sophisticated as those of Brian Snapp or *Orwell*, they nonetheless counted as traffic and content analysis and most of the time they worked well.

He trawled through a sheaf of nation-wide reports of stolen vehicles: mostly cars, a few vans, two articulated lorries, four motorbikes, one ambulance, a John Deere tractor, three boats and, believe it or not, one aeroplane. His interest was in those that had been recovered—and when and where. The two bodies had *not* been found in the burned out fuel bunker so it was given they escaped. This bloody Doran was really starting to be a royal pain in the arse.

He was admitting a grudging respect for the man: he had not hurt anybody—well, except for Cantwell and that was funny when he thought about it—and he had not damaged any property—well except for the Sons of Damiens' workshop and at least two-hundred-thousand pounds worth of big shiny motorbikes—and from his perspective *that* was no great loss. While Darwin's anger and frustration had to do with the possibility his entire career, along with his personal reputation and the sources of much of his income were going down the drain, Milford's irritation was simply that Doran kept escaping—not good for his image as a competent private investigator.

He started making notes on his A4 pad—good old fashioned detective work. These consisted of locations and times, and possible links to Doran. He began with the cars and vans: the most likely escape vehicles, by highlighting those recovered. On this list he found nothing taken near the Hinton Skydiving Centre in Northamptonshire. The next choice for a man like Doran would probably be a motorbike; here, too, he found nothing. Using the same starting point, he quickly eliminated the ambulance, the tractor and the boats leaving him with just the aeroplane.

Bingo! A J3 Piper Cub. You fool, why didn't you look at that one first? Doran was a flier, as was the woman. He looked at reported times of theft and recovery, and they tracked perfectly. Having established this, the rest of the trail was obvious; well, Sherlock would have said it was obvious. Next two paramedics were assaulted, although not seriously, and their ambulance taken. A stolen ambulance was consistent with Doran's demonstrated sense of style. This vehicle was found abandoned four miles away. Times? check.

Next a blue Volvo S60. Times? check. Would Doran be stupid enough, once having escaped from them, to walk back into the lions' den? Well, maybe not so stupid as it first appeared. Not such a bad place to hide when you think about it from the perspective of the pursued rather than the pursuer.

Milford went back over his notes and concluded St. Gildas was the most likely place to start looking. Was this not akin to the aphorism about 'following the money'? A potential option was obtaining hours of CCTV images from their possible locations but this would take time. No, he could travel by train to St. Gildas and, depending on timetables, within three hours he could be on the job.

He thought about travelling immediately but decided to wait until morning; it would be easier to blend in with the mass of people filling hospital corridors during the day. His one problem was the verbal abuse he anticipated receiving from Darwin when he delivered his next status report. Just part of the job.

The taxi dropped him at the main entrance to St. Gildas Royal Infirmary at eight fifty-five the next morning. Although he never thought himself as a master of disguises, he nevertheless was dressed for success: jeans, trainers, light blue open-necked cotton shirt, a block casual jacket in burgundy and a dark blue baseball cap with a yellow number three on it. A tan canvas messenger bag with no logo completed his ensemble. In this he carried some tools of his trade including a Smith & Wesson Model 36, a half-box of 38 Special jacketed hollow point cartridges for same, three sets of hinged handcuffs, several fake photo IDs, a small digital camera and several face towels wrapped around all this hardware to keep it from clunking too much.

He looked like many of the hundreds of other visitors and staff coming and going. His job now was to wander around until he found any of the three people he was looking for. St. Gildas was a big, busy, teaching hospital and he was prepared to stay here the whole day and all night if necessary. He switched his mobile to 'silent' mode and started walking around.

At nine-ten the vibration in his pocket signalled the call he dreaded. Vituperation was ladled over him by his client. Darwin's upbringing, costly private education, profession and social status precluded any references to the sexual proclivities of Milford's mother or marital status of his parents at the time of his birth so he confined his remarks to his hireling's intelligence quotient as indicated by his inability to understand the precise meanings of simple English expressions such as 'before the sun goes down' and 'dead or alive'.

Milford grovelled appropriately and acknowledged he failed to meet the deadline agreed the preceding day. Without giving him any details of his location and his sub-contracting to Eddie Voigt for the 'dead or alive' provision of his assignment, he assured Darwin he was close to resolution and hoped to be able to ring later in the day to report a final, positive result.

Darwin, having exhausted himself with his tirade, was silent except for some heavy breathing until Milford reminded him that, contrary to the detective's decision, it had been *his* decision to lock the two in the fuel bunker and blow it up by remote control. This remark unleashed a second diatribe, more scathing, if possible, than the first.

Milford was desperately trying to figure out how to end the call when he decided it was time for some 'you're breaking up' action. He scraped his fingernails across the back of his mobile: 'I – can't – hear – you – very – –' and switched it off.

He started making his way around every part of the hospital open to visitors, looking for his targets. He had faced Stover and Doran—he would recognize them immediately; he had only a photo of Tomlinson for reference. He, of course, had no idea whether she was with them but since the disappearance of the two contractors sent to deal with her and her connection with this case, that was a possibility, so he was alert for her appearance.

The task was formidable: the hospital comprised nine-hundred and fifty-four beds, thirty-two departments and clinics enclosed in fourteen buildings spread over one-hundred and twenty-two acres all connected by an unspecified number of miles of corridors teaming with patients, visitors and eighteen-hundred and fifty staff. One and one third million outpatients and forty-nine thousand inpatients were treated annually.

Milford had no idea how many of these staff, patients and their attending visitors were present on the day but as he walked around, he felt like he was bumping into people on Piccadilly at the height of the tourist season. About the only positive connected with his search was the ease with which he could blend in. The plethora of reception and waiting areas for the various clinics also offered ample places in which to hide should his quarry turn around quickly to see if someone were following.

By nine in the evening his feet were tired and his head was buzzing from too many cups of over-sugared tea. He found a corner table in the Pennine Café with a view of the door and the entire room where he sat down with a newspaper, an apple and a bottle of what claimed on the label to be spring water—he had no more stomach for chips, doughnuts, sandwiches, fruit slices, flapjacks or carrot cake.

He was at that point in his search where Festinger's *Theory of Cognitive Dissonance* was coming up against his conviction this was where his targets *must* be hiding. He nursed his spring water until ten-thirty while reading yet more tabloid column inches on the so far unsuccessful efforts of several of the country's major police forces to apprehend the elusive and dangerous terrorist Oswald Doran.

As the number of patrons dwindled he left and went to A and E where he could rest his feet and spend the night without attracting any unwanted attention. At least for this surveillance he was not confined to a car with steamed up windows smelling of stale fish and chips or standing for hours in a freezing, darkened shop entrance smelling of stale urine. Thank God for small favours.

The night passed without incident and at seven-thirty the next morning he began another round of corridors and clinics.

CHAPTER FIFTY-SEVEN

SALLY AND BRIAN worked well together and, aside from his high decibel sighing, deep intakes of breath, subsequent exhalations and trembling knees, they were comfortable and productive.

He impressed her with his skills. All she needed do was give him a sender, receiver, date and approximate time, and within minutes he returned her a screen displaying any emails extant between the two. His ability to access almost any digital database she needed to examine was even more impressive, although this sometimes took longer. When Winifred travelled by train to her seminar in London and met Arnold for coffee, Sally was able to document this through her phone call to him and the trail of credit card transactions she left each time she punched in a PIN number or three-number security code.

Her preference for skinny lattes over cappuccini was noted. Naturally everything they were doing was illegal and none of it, as they say, would be 'admissible in a court of law', but that was for the editors' legal teams to sort out; their job was to document the wrongdoing and report it.

She was again ready to threaten him with damage to his kneecap when the keypad clicked and Os arrived with more food: 'Hi, campers. How we getting along?'

She typed a few more characters then looked up over the counter: 'Hello, Danny Boy. Hot food. Great. What time is it? Wow! Nearly ten. Time flies when you're havin' fun. Actually, we're doing okay. Couple more hours and I'll have everything I need to put it all together.'

'You decided yet how you want to deliver it?'

'Yeah. Most secure on a DVD delivered in person. No possibility of leaks that way – no chance somebody like our friend Horace Hacker here to intercept it or even get a look at it before its release to the great British public.'

'So that means we have to figure out how to get you from here to Wapping without your being spotted by the bad guys.'

'Something like that. What'd you have in mind?'

'I'm working on it.'

'You seem to say that a lot. Oh, by the way, this might interest you. Have a look at this trailer.'

She clicked on an icon and when her browser loaded, she entered the URL of her *Yahoo!* Homepage. She scrolled through the list of links for developing news bulletins and clicked on <u>Gang War In the Midlands?</u>

She shifted her laptop so Os could read the text: 'Greater Manchester Police are concerned about the shooting deaths of two men suspected of having connections with Harrison "Harry" Mabe, a prominent member of an organized crime family active in the Cheetham Hill area of the city. When questioned by reporters, a Police spokesperson declined to comment on whether this murder was connected with the stabbing death earlier this week of a member of the "Sons of Damien", a motorcycle gang based in North Lincolnshire.

'She did go on to say, however, that in the past bad blood between these two gangs, mostly having to do with territorial disputes over the control of the lucrative trade in illicit drugs in the Midlands, chiefly heroin and crack cocaine but also cannabis and Ecstasy, had several times spilled over onto the streets resulting in a number of deaths.'

Well done, Aidie. He smiled: 'Nuthin' to do with me, mate! Helpful, though, keep the cops busy and take some resources away from looking for us.'

He stepped back from the laptop: 'Listen up, folks. You two finish your work and try to get a little sleep. This corridor is almost deserted and I think I'd like to bring Amanda in so she can get some rest, too. I really don't think anybody's going to be looking for you tonight. I'm going to make rounds and see if everything's okay. I need to do some thinking because by tomorrow this time we need to be out of here and, Sally, you need to be on your way to London.'

He left the two, collected Amanda from A and E where she had been sitting nursing a cup of cardboard tea, reading a three-month old issue of *Hello* magazine and trying to look like a worried visitor, and returned to their sanctuary.

'Right. Night, night, you three. See you in the morning.'

CHAPTER FIFTY-EIGHT

THE NEXT MORNING at eight, Os turned the corner from a well-peopled corridor into the one leading to where his charges were hiding and he thought he spotted Milford walking briskly in the opposite direction. He turned around and shifted into 'tailing' mode. Moving left and right in the busy hallway to avoid bumping into anybody, dodging trolleys piled high with linen, breakfast services and other interesting-looking pieces of hospital arcana, he came close enough to the man to confirm he was Milford. He immediately turned the other way and hurried back to their refuge.

First things first. He delivered the croissants, butter and orange marmalade he was carrying to his guests then collected his paramedic greens from the holdall, telling them nothing about his spotting Milford, just that: 'he wanted to have a good look around Casualty'.

In unison the three queried his comment: 'We know something's up, Dan. Mind telling us what's going on?'

'No problem. Everything's under control. Sit tight. I'll be back.'

They did not believe him but knew he would tell them nothing more. They filled the kettle, switched it on and settled down to their breakfasts while he changed into his boiler suit.

Back in uniform he wandered through Casualty and out the automatic double glass doors to the row of parked ambulances. Now the adrenaline flow increased; he shifted into survival mode. His three charges were safe but he had to organize transportation out of the hospital and get Sally and her DVD to London. He soon found what he wanted: a Honda CR-V, 2.2-litre four-by-four, not really an ambulance, better described as a paramedic rapid response vehicle. This will do nicely. Now, where oh where are the keys kept and how much fuel in this little beauty?

A glance through the offside window gave him the answer to the first: the keys were in the ignition. That made sense for a big, busy casualty operation. The second was answered as quickly when he climbed inside and turned the key; the tank was full. These folks must have been Boy Scouts—remember their marching song: 'Be Prepared'. He checked a few more in the row to confirm each had keys in place. He went back inside, hoping for no call-outs for this one for the next little while. Never mind, if it were not available another one would have to do. There was one more thing he wanted do with Amanda before they left.

CHAPTER FIFTY-NINE

MILFORD STRODE TO the outpatient eye clinic having spotted Oswald Doran. Here were fifty patients sitting around waiting to be seen and as many nurses, technicians, specialists and assorted clerical types rushing about the warren of examination and treatment rooms. He judged this to be a safe place to hide while he contacted Eddie Voigt; Doran's running across him here would be a stroke of unbelievably bad luck.

He rang Eddie and told him he located Doran, that he had him under surveillance — now not strictly true — and it was time for Eddie to send around his associates. Eddie told him the people he trusted with this job were busy but would be available in a couple of hours. If Milford could keep an eye on Doran until then, they would be on their way.

Milford was not happy with this arrangement: he had not slept well on the chair in A and E, he was tired and after the work he had put in he wanted action *now*. They agreed to meet in the Pennine Café and he would recognize the four of them, each carrying a bulging, black holdall. The leader would be an evil-tempered man named George Barr who was not one of Eddie's permanent staff but a temp he called on from time-to-time for higher-risk jobs.

CHAPTER SIXTY

OS WANDERED AROUND Casualty until he found a small empty stand-up workstation complete with a wall-mounted telephone and a hospital directory taped above. He rang Winifred's number asking to speak with her and Vanessa told him she was in meetings in her office for the rest of the morning and she hoped it would be convenient for him to ring back after lunch. He thanked her and told her that would be fine. Good, she's in her office.

He found a small empty stainless steel trolley and rolled it through the department, keeping well out of the paths of people running in all directions. He collected supplies for his project. He found everything he needed then covered his load with a sheet of ubiquitous green linen. Nobody stopped him to question what he was doing or who he was. It's amazing what you can get away with so long as you act like you know what you're doing and that you belong.

He checked his supplies, replaced the linen cover and returned to where Amanda and the other two were waiting. They finished their breakfasts and were relaxing over their second coffees and teas when he came through the door pushing his trolley.

Amanda looked up: 'Okay, Mister Dan Dangerous, we've had enough of your mysterious comings and goings, sullen silences and cryptic comments. We've taken a vote and we've decided unanimously we're going to chuck our collective dummies out of the pram unless you tell us exactly what's going on. Now!'

'Whoa, campers, guess I'd better come clean, then. Update. Milford Cleeland has been spotted in the building, although I don't think he's seen any of us. Whether he has or not, it's time we're outta here. Transportation has been arranged. Sally, you packed and ready to go?'

'Yes, sir.'

'DVD burned?'

'Yes, Mister Dangerous.'

'A copy hidden in a safe place.'

'Yes, sir.'

She slapped the counter: 'Taped securely to the underside of this worktop with some gaffer tape. Should rest undisturbed here until we come back for it or until the NHS decides to re-open this ward which I think unlikely for a couple of years in view of the state of the economy.'

'Well done, thank you, Miz T. Horace, you ready to go?'

'Yep Mister Dangerous but can you tell me why the Americans call gaffer tape "duck tape" it doesn't make any sense why you would want to tape up a duck I don't understand?'

'Good question, Mister Hacker. We don't really have time to discuss it right now. And it has nothing to do with ducks, it has to do with *ducts* – important parts of American central heating systems. It's complicated. Missus S?'

'Yes, I'm ready to go but you still haven't answered any of our questions.'

'Well, remember I said we could probably hide out here for at most two days then we would have to go on the run. The time has come. The bad guys are closing in. I think we'll be able to get out of here safely and get Sally on her way to London. When that's done we just have to keep ahead of them for a little while until Livingstone Stanley exposes Darwin Cantwell, he calls off his dogs and the faeces truly hit the fan.'

'I'm still not happy with your non-answers – you sound like a bloody politician or hospital administrator – but if we need to get out of here fast then let's do it.'

'Well said, Missus S, but before we go you and I need to complete one more – *teensy-weensy* task – something I think you'll enjoy. I've done my sums and I'm confident we have enough time. So, if you can just put on your boiler suit, we'll be on our way.'

Amanda put on her paramedic greens and dropped the holdall at Os' feet: 'That's me – ready to go.'

He pulled the Uzi from the bag, checked the magazine, laid it next to his paraphernalia and re-covered it with the linen. He handed Sally the Glock and two magazines, then put the holdall on the lower shelf of the trolley: 'Okay, between this and your Colt you should be fine. I trust you to take good care of my friend Brian here. Mandy and I have something to do that should take us about an hour or a little more. You two sit tight. Immediately we come back, the four of us are gone.'

He turned to Amanda: 'Before we go, you and I are going to pay Miz Hyde-Davies a little visit. Oh, and I'm not planning to shoot her, the Uzi's just for effect. Although – if she really pisses me off –'

'This is *no* time for jokes!'

She put her hand on his arm: 'I really don't like the sound of this. What're you doing?'

'Some pain for her. I've planned some pain for her.'

She gripped his arm, her voice tightened and she started to cry. She was a confused mess of anger and sadness and frustration and fear: 'No, I *don't* want revenge – *I want my husband back!* But that can't happen can it? No? Then I just want out of this place. This is where he worked. This is where he was happiest when he wasn't with the girls and with me.'

She turned slightly to look directly into his eyes as her voice shifted subtly to concern for this quiet, confident, complex, loner of a man: 'There's a dark place you go to sometimes – a dark place where I can never follow. When it happens, I see a certain look in your eyes. I see it now. Tell me where it is you go?'

'Can't – please – just can't. Maybe someday – but not now.'

She squeezed his arm even harder but her face brightened and the tears stopped: 'Please, please – can we please just get out of here!'

He picked the UZI up from the trolley and put it back in the holdall. They switched off the lamp on the desk, collected their things and left.

CHAPTER SIXTY-ONE

TREVOR LaFARGE TRULY believed he might die—he was frightened for his life; this no longer had the character of a cliché. He escaped some fallout from George's anger when they raided Doran's house and found him absent; most of it had landed on the watcher who told him Doran was safely tucked up in bed. But from then he was one of George's un-favourite persons and hoped never to hear from him again.

This was not to be. He was working on a brief rumoured to have come down directly from Beattie's office; the Justice Secretary had embarrassed the PM and he wanted an excuse to oust her. Trevor sat at his desk trying to decide if her off-the-record admission she smoked one joint while a fresher at university could be turned into enough public outrage to ensure she would be forced to resign her cabinet post and moved to the back benches.

George rang him: 'Get your fuckin' ass down the pub, Trevor LaFarge, I want you here now!'

'But I'm in the middle of an assignment. Can this wait until –?'

'No, this can't fuckin' wait. You're not here in half an hour, I'm comin' to your office blow your fuckin' head off. Got that?'

'Yes, I'll be there.'

He entered the Flayed Ox with two minutes to spare, saw George at his usual corner table and went over without ordering a drink. He was determined not to show his terror, but his blink rate, dilated pupils and shaking hands contradicted his carefully rehearsed, business-as-usual question: 'Right, Mister Barr, how can I help you?'

'You know Doran's girlfriend? This Stover bitch?'

'Of course.'

'I mean you *met* her. You know what she fuckin' looks like?'

'Yes, I've met her. I know what she looks like.'

'Good. You're comin' with me. We gotta fuckin' job to do.'

'But I –'

'You what, Trevor LaFarge?'

'No – never mind.'

'No, say what's on your mind. You know I'm a reasonable man, just as long as you do what I fuckin' tell you.'

'No, it's okay. Where we going?'

'Well, you're gonna get a chance to meet her again. Maybe even get a chance to interview her for your newspaper. That is – hee, hee – if there's anythin' fuckin' left of her after Voigt's – *interviewed* – her.'

In the car park they climbed into a Range Rover covered in so much mud Trevor could not determine the paint colour. The only parts of the vehicle reflecting any light were the headlights and the crescents swept by the windscreen wipers. They drove to the Oubliette where George ordered Trevor into the rear seat then went into the pub. He returned with three men looking even bigger and scarier than he. Each carried a large, bulging, black holdall. They threw their bags into the rear of a dirty white van then one of them climbed into the front seat with George, the second in the back with Trevor and the third into the van. They drove madly out of the car park.

The front seat passenger slapped the filthy dashboard: 'Nice car, Georgie. Posh – travellin' in style. Where'd you find it?'

'Borrowed it from that charity place up the street, you know – where they collect sofas and shit for poor people.

You call me "Georgie" again I'll pull your fuckin' eyeballs out.'

'Sorry – George.'

'Told 'em they didn't gimme the keys I'd burn their furniture factory down. No problem – buncha fuckin' freaks and cripples! Same place we got the van. You okay back there, Trevor LaFarge?'

A thoroughly terrified Trevor mumbled everything was just fine. The man next to him tapped George on the shoulder: 'Mind telling me where we're going, George?'

'Job for Eddie. He needs two – three people done. You know that Doran terrorist guy been all over the telly? Him, his bimbo and maybe some fuckin' reporter broad.'

'When you say "done", you mean *done*?'

'Yeah, done, disappeared – disappeared for fuckin' good.'

'Great! Have some fun. Three of 'em? Yea! Haven't done anybody for a while now.'

Trevor thought his day could not get any worse then he realized why George wanted him with them. Enough. When the car slowed down behind traffic queuing for a roundabout he opened the door and jumped out. He rolled over twice then staggered to his feet and tried to run but the van screeched to a stop, the driver jumped out and caught him. George stopped the Range Rover and ran back to them, holding a Beretta 98G close to his leg.

He stepped around to the back of the van, opened the half-door and motioned to the driver: 'Throw this fuckin' piece a shit in here!'

Trevor was pushed into the van; before he could manage anything other than a squeal, George brought the pistol up and released the de-cocking lever: 'Bye-bye, Trevor La Fuckin' Farge. Have a nice day!'

He shot him twice in the head, depositing the entire rear half of it around the inside of the cargo space. Ignoring the startled looks of people in cars in the queue behind them, they climbed back into their vehicles and drove on towards the roundabout. Their delay lasted less than one minute.

They cleared the roundabout and George frowned: 'Shame about that. Too bad. He could've maybe saved us some time locatin' that Stover broad. Never mind. You just can't get good fuckin' help these days.'

Milford was panicking. His 'two hours or so' wait for Eddie's men was nearly up and he lost sight of Doran. He walked fast—almost trotting—from one end of the labyrinth of corridors connecting the public spaces comprising St. Gildas to the other without sighting him. He was not concerned these men had driven across the city on a useless journey, they were, after all, in his pay; he was frustrated he was wasting valuable time during which this elusive man might escape from him once more.

There was nothing for him except to keep walking and looking. Running around aimlessly was not working so he went back to where he spotted him in the morning and started a more methodical search: moving more slowly along the corridor looking through open doors and the windows of closed doors into wards, offices, laboratories, waiting areas and clinics—places he thought it likely a person might be sitting, trying to hide in plain sight.

Each time he moved along the corridor he extended his search farther and farther then started moving into smaller and less crowded hallways branching off this main one. He considered using one of his fake IDs, introducing himself to hospital security staff as a plainclothes policeman and asking for the opportunity to view their live CCTV feeds but decided this would take too long and involve too many people in this search he wanted desperately to keep secret.

He gave up. He decided to wait in the café, give the men he was meeting photos of Doran and Stover, and let them help. There was little else he could do except maybe ringing Eddie and asking him to send over more people. Under his present workload, any concern he had for further verbal abuse from Darwin concerned him not at all.

CHAPTER SIXTY-TWO

THEY WALKED DOWN the hall towards the corridor leading to A and E looking like two paramedics going about their business and two hospital visitors: one rumpled and worried, the other not nearly so rumpled or quite so worried.

They approached Casualty and Os stopped them: 'If you two will just wait here for a couple of minutes, your able and friendly team of paramedics will look for some transport.'

He and Amanda walked on into the busy area, turned into another corridor and returned pushing two wheel chairs: 'Okay, campers. As you know EU health and safety legislation requires that you're to be moved about in these things as long as you're in our care and we always strive to comply with EU legislation, so if you will just take your seats we can be on our way.'

Sally and Brian got into the wheelchairs, she laughing and he complaining, especially when Os wrapped them in blankets and piled Sally's case, their computer bags and Os' holdall on their laps: 'Now if you can just be patient for a little longer and look like you're really happy to be going home, especially you, Brian, we can get out of here.'

They wheeled their charges through Casualty, out through the sliding glass doors and along the row of parked ambulances. The Honda CR-V was still there—fuelled up and with keys in place. Os folded up the blankets and pushed the wheelchairs neatly back against a nearby wall while Sally and Brian climbed into the rear seats with their arsenal at their feet.

He and Amanda went into the front. He started the engine and she looked out at the wheelchairs: 'Shouldn't we return those?'

'Naw. Doesn't look like rain. Somebody'll be along to collect them eventually.'

Along with the clicks of seatbelts Sally asked a question: 'Ossie, pardon me for stating what is probably blazingly obvious, but isn't this rather silly transport for folks on the run trying to hide from not only the bad guys but most of the good guys, too? Wouldn't the Volvo've –?'

'Good question. A little while ago I casually mentioned – just a tiny hint – that we may have been spotted. Should anybody give chase, maybe, just maybe, this one'll give us that little extra oomph as we scurry across country, sirens, bright flashing blue lights and stuff. On the other hand –'

'Makes us a really conspicuous moving target – eh? "Attention all cars. Be on the lookout for a serial-killing terrorist cannibal driving a big, shiny ambulance with a huge number ten painted on the roof screaming southbound along the motorway."'

Amanda turned to her: 'Not a daft question at all. He's tried this once already and it didn't work that time either. I think it must be a guy thing – big, shiny, fast car as a substitute for a big – er – you know what I mean –'

Sally giggled.

Os half-turned to them: 'Yeah, careful, girls. It's just that – well when I was a little boy I thought my father and my mother were – oh, hell never mind. Let's just get moving.'

He pulled out of the parking space and drove towards the exit barrier. He picked up the card, lowered his window and stopped next to the control box where he swiped it to raise the boom. He glanced across past the control box at the vehicle coming in: a Range Rover of indeterminate colour covered in mud. When the driver of the Range Rover lowered his window to collect his ticket he looked across at Os and each recognized the other. George screamed as his boom came up and he accelerated, moving fast until he cleared the confining Armco beams to where he could U-turn and come after them. Simultaneously the boom in front of the Honda raised and Os accelerated. He watched in his mirror as the boom dropped and George made his turn with tyres smoking.

The driver of the dirty white van immediately behind the Range Rover could not reverse with traffic behind him or turn in the narrow space so he, too, collected his ticket to raise the boom and drive forward before he could follow George out. This gave Os a little time to clear the entrance and head for the motorway less than a mile away. He assumed George would crash the barrier arm instead of taking the time to pay his parking fee and he was right: in seconds he saw the Range Rover emerge from the entrance and turn into traffic with a dozen cars between them and with the van immediately behind.

'Well, ladies and gentleman, I guess that answers my question about whether we've been spotted or not. I don't know whether Cleeland's running this operation but either way there are now some genuinely bad people after us. We're in loads of trouble here. Let me ask you guys a deeply personal question – which one of you would like to drive for a while?'

The three responded: 'Don't look at me, mate. Nothing to do with me, mate. Why do you ask anyhow, mate?'

'Well, it's just I think there's going to be some shooting here in a little while. So the simple choice is yours – you want to drive or shoot at the bad guys.'

Amanda said she did not want to drive *or* shoot at the bad guys. Sally said she really did not want to drive but would *love* to shoot at the bad guys. Brian tapped him on the shoulder harder than necessary but understandable under the circumstances: 'I'll drive I mean I don't really want to drive and I never drove an ambulance before especially when there's bad guys probably with lots and lots of really big guns chasing us but I'm the best there is with "Transporter" and I play a lot of car chase computer games and anyhow I don't really want to shoot at anybody so yeah I'll drive.'

One would think Os had an advantage in the Honda. In addition to its being highly manoeuvrable, it was equipped with a siren, a klaxon and a combination of high intensity blue and white flashing lights, and these would help clear a path for them. He discovered screaming sirens and bright flashing lights can be something of a mixed blessing.

There are four observed and statistically significant responses to these stimuli: some drivers signal and pull to the side of the street immediately, some decide they can continue driving on while waiting until a more convenient space is available at the side of the street, some decide it is okay to keep driving just so long as they are moving faster than the overtaking emergency vehicle and some simple ignore them. A further problem for the pursuee, of course, is that if most drivers pull over, a convenient path is cleared for the pursuer. Os experienced all these responses while they drove.

They dodged traffic travelling in both directions, screeching through several intersections, finally reaching the M57 that soon became the A635. The Range Rover and the van were still a dozen cars behind, not able to close the gap.

Os addressed the three again: 'Right – now we're going to play some "musical chairs". Seatbelts off, headrests off and follow me, ah – one – and – ah – two.'

Brian and Sally switched places so Brian was sitting in the nearside rear seat. Amanda climbed over the back of the seat and settled in between the two. Brian crawled over the seat into the front. Then things really started to get interesting. With Os' foot fully down on the accelerator and switching from lane to lane dodging traffic as they flew along the Mancunian Way, he raised himself up so Brian could slide across under him and into the driver's seat.

Os released his grip on the steering wheel when Brian grabbed it then slid his foot off the accelerator so Brian took full control of the car. This was accomplished with minimum jerks and swerves, and they never came remotely close to crashing into anybody. Amanda and Sally switched places and Os climbed into the back between them. Sally climbed into the front.

Os slapped the back of the front seat: 'Wasn't that fun, boys and girls? Well done! I knew I could count on you. Brian, listen up. Stay on this A635 until you see signs for the A6140. We want the M60 south. Okay? Remember, we're paramedics answering an emergency call. We can go just as fast as we want – anywhere we want.'

'Okay this reminds me of a joke wanna hear it?'

Os looked at the women, smirked and shrugged his shoulders—he heard most of Brian's jokes, many times: 'No, I don't want to hear it – not really, my friend.'

'Well there's these two really old people are driving along listening to Wogan on Radio Two and the woman says "Oh imagine that Lester they're saying on the news there's a man driving the wrong way on the motorway" and Lester says "Not just one Mildred there's *hundreds* of them" ha – ha pretty funny – eh folks?'

'It's been a long time Since Wogan has been on Radio Two; he's retired.'

'I know that – it's an old joke.'

'We know it, too. Don't give up your day job, Horace.'

Os passed Sally's handbag containing the Colt to her then rummaged in his holdall and handed her the Glock, the two magazines and some cartridges. He then organized the UZI: 'Right, folks. Ready to rock 'n' roll!'

They travelled on through Openshaw and Droylsden, ignoring speed limits and lane restrictions. They even managed a short stint of wrong way driving on a one-way section and a modest distance on the pavement when traffic proved especially troublesome. Os was busy looking ahead to give Brian advice and keeping track of the two vehicles following them. Their pursuers had gained a little, there were now eight cars between but still not close enough for effective gunplay.

Sally turned to him: 'Where we going, Ossie?'

'We need to get across to Upton just south of Gainsborough. We're going to drop you at the train station in Doncaster.'

'Why Doncaster?'

'No time to get you to Manchester Piccadilly – wrong direction – it's a quick run down to London on the East Coast Line from there and anyhow it's on our way.'

Amanda tapped him on the arm: 'On our way to *where?*'

'On the way to where we can lose the bad guys for good. I have a clever plan; no time to tell you about it right now.'

'You're starting to give me the creeps. Every time you say that something very unpleasant happens to us.'

The Honda was new and well-maintained; the Range Rover and van were not. George was not able to get within shooting distance; sometimes they moved a little closer and sometimes Brian pulled ahead, putting more cars between them. South of the Audenshaw Reservoir when they turned onto the M67 towards Hyde, Os thought they lost their tail for good but near Godley he spotted them well back but still coming. Maybe the advantages of using an ambulance as a getaway car outweigh the disadvantages.

'Okay, Brian. When we run out of motorway, go straight onto the A57. Then at Hollingworth, go straight onto the A628. It'll be signposted "Barnsley". If we can just keep ahead of them until we get through Tintwistle, we can probably outrun them on the open road. We won't even need our siren and blue lights. By the time we get to the Dog and Partridge, we'll be free. Well, at least for a little while.'

'I've been meaning to ask you about something.'

'What's that, oh brilliant young computer wizard and getaway driver extraordinaire?'

'Is it "Tin-*twistle*" or is it "*Tint*-wistle" I'm never sure about that one what do you think?'

'I think you need to find a hobby, Brian. Maybe stamp collecting or tractor spotting. Anything. You have a girlfriend? Yes? No? I've never thought to ask.'

'No – no time for girlfriends computers are my only love.'

'Figures.'

Os was right. The road flattened at the crest near Upper Windleden Reservoir after their long, winding climb up from Tintwistle, and George and his friends were far behind.

CHAPTER SIXTY-THREE

MILFORD LOOKED AT the clock in the Pennine Café then his watch then back to the clock. Eddie's men should have arrived a half-hour ago. He wondered why they were delayed. He wanted to go walking about the hospital looking for Doran and Stover but he did not want to miss them. He rang Eddie and was told they left the Oubliette an hour before. Milford had never met George but had been told many times he was an evil-tempered son of a bitch. Eddie reminded him even a phone call asking his whereabouts might set him off.

'He's a nasty piece of work. If you value your goolies you never, ever question anything George Barr does! One time I saw him put a bloke's eye out just for asking when he was gonna get paid for a job.'

'Guess I'll have to take my chances, I need to know where he is.'

'Your funeral, mate.'

Milford thought about what he was going to say, took a deep breath and punched George's number into his mobile. The answer was what he expected: 'Whatcha fuckin' want, Cleeland?'

'Hello, George. Just wondered where you are.'

'Tryin' to catch up with Doran and that Stover bitch. What the fuck you think I'm doin'?'

'But I thought we were going to meet here at the hospital.'

'But Doran ain't at the fuckin' hospital you nobhead. I caught him drivin' outta the hospital in an ambulance. I'm chasin' him over the fuckin' Pennines, what're you doin'?'

'I'm waiting for you here. You're telling me you saw him leaving the hospital in an ambulance?'

'Even for a copper you ain't very bright, Cleeland. That's what I just said. Don't ring me again. When I catch 'em, I'll fuckin' let you know!'

A demoralized Milford switched off his phone and sighed. Once again Doran had escaped. His only hope now was George and his men would catch up with them and bring them back over the Pennines before he was due to ring Darwin with a status report.

CHAPTER SIXTY-FOUR

THE AMBULANCE DESCENDED from the crest of the Pennines towards Barnsley; here Brian negotiated several roundabouts, one sharp ninety degree bend and the high streets of several small towns: 'How'm I doing big guy?'

'You're doing just fine. Keep following the A628 signposted for Barnsley. Sirens and lights in these towns, please. We don't want to slow down too much.'

Brian pointed to a sign: 'Let me ask you another question why would you want to name your town *"Penistone"*?'

'Just keep driving. Forget *"Penis-*tone" – remember, bear left at the junction towards Barnsley.'

'Just asking jeeze can't a guy even ask a simple question?'

Os kept looking back and sometimes saw George's car far behind. They cleared Penistone, picked up speed and kept well ahead of the bad guys until they neared the M1. Here they negotiated two small roundabouts—ninety degrees right then ninety degrees left—before crossing the motorway on the Dodworth roundabout. He looked back and George had narrowed the gap to the original twelve cars.

He patted Brian on the shoulder: 'Okay, they're gaining on us but we're still fine. Now that we've crossed the M1 it's going to get a little scary. Just keep the speed up and I'll guide you through two big, busy roundabouts. Pay attention for the A635 for Doncaster.'

Siren screamed and lights flashed while they wove their way around many startled drivers in Barnsley, through the last roundabout and out onto the Road to Doncaster.

Os tapped Brian on the shoulder again: 'Right, my friend, put your foot down. We need to make a stop at the train station in Doncaster so our good friend Miz Tomlinson here can disembark and we need to be far enough ahead of these guys so they don't catch up with us there. They've gained a little on us but it's open country from here to the A1. Well, just a couple of roundabouts but you've demonstrated remarkable skill with roundabouts at high speed. Hasn't he done well, ladies? Let's have a big round of applause for Brian – Two Ps – Snapp!'

Sally clapped and cheered; Amanda managed nothing more than a slight smile. Os recognized the signs: she had had almost all the pressure she could handle.

He touched her arm gently: 'Just a little longer. I know it's tough. And I know my jokes don't help – *my* way of coping. I promise you, once we get Sally on that train and she gets to London, it won't be long until this is over. I know who's after us now and I know how to handle it.'

'I hope so. I appreciate all you've tried to do for me but I've had enough. I can't take any more. I wish we never started this. All this nonsense about "closure". I don't give a damn about closure, I just want some peace and quiet.'

'Promise – no more jokes, no more clever plans, no more smart-ass answers, no more silly disguises. You ask me about my dark place. When this is over I'll tell you all about it. The only thing I'll say now is maybe *I* could do with a little closure, too.'

She squeezed his hands tightly: 'Peace and quiet and my girls.'

'Peace and quiet and your girls. Promise.'

They crossed the A1 then flew into Doncaster, negotiating first St. Mary's then Markets roundabouts, under the Doncaster Centre and to the train station. Sally organized her laptop and case and was ready. Os thought they were far enough ahead of George to make their stop without his spotting it.

Sally cracked the door even before they stopped: 'See you around, folks. It's been grand. Read all about it in the evening papers. Brian, nice driving. Mandy, take good care of this lovable lunatic. Os – well, hell, Ossie, just keep being Ossie. Bye!'

She slammed the door and ran across the small car park in front of the station. Brian switched on the siren and lights and they screeched out onto Trafford Way: 'Where to Boss?'

'Straight across the next roundabout and follow signs for A638 sometimes signposted "Bawtry" and sometimes "Great North Road".'

'Make up your mind.'

'"Same difference" as the Americans might say.'

He turned to Amanda: 'From now on they're going to be gaining on us. There's probably going to be some shooting so if you can get in front and crouch down, that'll give me room to work back here. I promised no more jokes, but I think it's going to get messy. Okay?'

She was still quiet but calmer now. She even managed a little smile: 'Okay.'

She climbed over the seat and settled in next to Brian while Os pulled his Gerber from the holdall, strapped it to his ankle and checked both magazines for the UZI. They crossed over the M18 at Bessacarr and he could see the Range Rover and van gaining on them. They advanced to within eight cars of them. Both cars were following them—they must have missed Sally's delivery to the station.

CHAPTER SIXTY-FIVE

INTELLIGENCE GATHERERS, INVESTIGATIVE reporters, detectives and close protection security consultants are wary of events that at first look like amazing coincidences. Upon further examination they usually turn out to be causally related. In life occasionally sequences of happenings, intuition to the contrary, are *not* related. Os and his friends were about to be caught up in one of these.

While Brian was negotiating the roundabout over the M1 at Barnsley, Harry Mabe and fifteen of his heavily armed associates in three dirty white vans crossed the River Trent at Gainsborough and turned right onto the A156 headed for the farm near Upton where the Sons of Damien had their headquarters.

Coincidence or causally-related? Perhaps this event was triggered by Os' midnight ride to Cheetham Hill, otherwise, perhaps other than in its timing, this would have happened eventually without his input.

Activity such as this, certainly in the Western World, is usually managed in the dead of night but Harry decided his business might be more convincingly conducted in daylight. Besides, he planned to have completed his work well before the thinly stretched resources of the Lincolnshire Police arrived. At the village of Lea, Harry and his friends turned right onto the B1241, followed it for two miles, turned left onto an unmarked road then onto the rutted dirt track leading to the farm.

Immediately they left the tarmac they accelerated to the maximum speed the vans could manage on the unpaved road, reaching the cluttered yard in twenty seconds. In a well-rehearsed manoeuvre the two lead vans separated as they came into the yard and skidded to a stop at a one-hundred and twenty degree angle one to the other and with their front bumpers almost touching. The third slid sideways into the gap behind the first two, the third leg of an equilateral triangle not unlike wagons forming a circle in the American West of old.

They emerged from the vans with, literally, all guns blazing. The Sons of Damien, concentrating on the rebuilding of their ruined workshop, saw the vans coming but assumed these carried expected materials, supplies and volunteer help from sympathetic members of another club based near Whaplode Drove in the Fens. They were totally unprepared.

What followed approximated what one sees during a gang fight in a B-movie or a low-budget TV film. Well-prepared members of the Mabe Gang initiated the mayhem brandishing semi-automatic weapons including Colt 45s, Glock 17s, UZIs, Lugers, AK-47s and one 50 calibre IMI Desert Eagle. Startled Sons quickly retaliated with an equivalent number of Colts and Glocks supplemented by a couple of Webley 455s, several double-barrelled and pump-action shotguns of unknown bore and one 45 calibre Winchester Model 94—pre-nineteen-sixty-four.

In films, shoot-outs go on and on and on—seemingly for hours with hundreds of cartridges expended and with nobody's ever having to stop to reload; the gunfight at the O.K. Corral lasted thirty seconds with an estimated thirty shots fired. This mêlée was somewhere in between. Harry's men crouched down with their backs to their vans and shot at anything that moved. The Sons of Damien arranged themselves behind stacks of breeze blocks, piles of timber, heaps of rubble, rusting farm implements and the brick walls of several outbuildings.

One would have thought the city boys with no cover would have been easy pickings for the country boys hiding behind things but this was not the case. Every time a Son arose from behind a barricade high enough to try to get off a shot at a Mabe Man, the Mabe Man fired at him, driving him back down behind his cover. A couple of Sons tried reaching up and firing their pistols in the general direction of the vans without exposing their heads, again like one sees in films, but this resulted in nothing more than wasted ammunition, numerous holes in the sides of the vans and one wrist's being rendered incapable of further action. While the Mabe Men were firing outward from a central point, the Sons firing into them from all sides faced the possibility of hitting some of their own people in crossfire.

One Son climbed to the loft of a barn and was aiming at a Mabe Man from a window when he was dispatched with a shot from the Desert Eagle—the first fatality of the day. The wielder of the Desert Eagle spent too long lining up his shot and was brought down by a shot from the Winchester—the second fatality of the conflict. Mabe's Marauders versus Sons of Damien: one-all.

Their nearest neighbours one-half mile away were not too concerned about the noise; they were used to hearing this from time-to-time and it did not overly alarm them so long as the madness was limited to the farm and did not spill over onto their fields or nearby highways and byways.

Had it continued for more than an hour they might have called the police who probably would have responded slowly expecting participants to exhaust both themselves and their ammunition—and in the process eliminate permanently from their books many persons suspected of various serious crimes. Both the Greater Manchester police and the Lincolnshire Police—and no doubt other police forces around the country—would have been pleased to have the opportunity to link the weapons being discharged to the users and possible connections with other crimes.

Over the next half hour the Sons succeeded in eliminating one Mabe Man with a shot from a Webley 455 and with no wrist damage while a Mabe Man eliminated a Son with a well-aimed shot from a Luger. Mabe's Marauders versus Sons of Damien: two-all—clearly a well-matched contest.

All this changed when a Honda CR-V four-by-four painted like an ambulance came bouncing at high speed along the track and into the yard, slewing around the three vans, across the full length of the yard and out into the field beyond. Both the Sons of Damien and Harry's men paused for a moment to assess what was happening; the Sons assumed it belonged to Mabe's Men and Mabe's Men assumed the opposite.

Before either could respond, George's mud-covered motor charged into the yard. Several shots ruined the front tyres and it skidded to a stop just short of Harry's third van—the bottom leg of the triangle—then the fourth dirty white van—this one still carrying the body of Trevor LaFarge—slammed into the back of the Range Rover. Any further descriptions of what followed are rendered superfluous.

Os and his friends were ignored in the resulting pandemonium. This allowed them to drive leisurely across a large stubble field, locate a break in the hedge, pull onto the single-track tarmac—deserted under the early evening sunset—and park next to it. They climbed out, Amanda and Os removed their paramedic greens, they reorganized the holdall and Brian's laptop bag, and they started walking.

Os patted Brian on the back: 'Nice driving, my friend, *very* nice driving. And you'll notice, you two, that we escaped without any shots being fired. We didn't shoot at anybody and nobody shot at us. A good day's work!'

Brian was pleased. Amanda was not convinced: 'So, let me get this straight, Mister Oswald Aidan Doran, close protection security consultant – you're telling me that, although we're standing along the side of a deserted road in the middle of nowhere and the sun is sinking below the horizon as we speak, just because nobody has shot at us and we haven't had to shoot back at them, it's been a good day?'

'Something like that.'

'I'm not really sure I understand.'

'Well, think of it this way – for the first time in several days *nobody* is chasing us, instead the bad guys are killing each other. We're safe and Sally's on her way to London to tell your story.'

'So what do we do now?'

'We start walking. Eventually we'll come to Upton – hopefully big enough to have a place to eat where we can relax, chill out and, as the Americans say: "chow down". Let's be on our way. And you can forget about looking behind you: there's nobody following. Promise.'

CHAPTER SIXTY-SIX

GEORGE WAS THE exception: the one man who had *not* ignored the Honda when it careered through the yard and into the field. His obsession went beyond any payment by Eddie Voigt to capture these two and deliver them to Milford—he *wanted* Doran: he had a long-held score to settle with him. With the ménage à trois blasting all around him, he moved un-noticed inside the doorway of a small, brick shed. With everybody's attention directed towards the confusion in the yard he kicked out a window on the far side of the building and crawled out.

He made his way towards the field using straw bales, piles of rubbish and hedges as cover. Like Os he was a tracker of some expertise so he was able to follow the path of the ambulance across the field. And like any good tracker he had an ability to think like the tracked—where he was likely to go and what he was likely to do. With the Beretta stuck under his belt behind his back, a combat knife strapped to his leg and a Silver Stag knife with a three inch fixed blade in a sheath under his shirt collar at the back of his neck, he started walking.

CHAPTER SIXTY-SEVEN

AMANDA, BRIAN AND Os walked a mile into Upton and strolled up the high street until they located a chippie.

'Right, boys and girls, do we want some fish and chips, maybe washed down with a soft drink of your choice – mine's Irn-Bru, by the way – or do we want to look for some pub grub? Waddya say?'

His two charges voted for fish and chips so he dropped his holdall at their feet, went in and placed their order. When it was ready he pulled three tins from the cooler, paid and walked outside. They sat on a convenient wall, enjoying their meal while saying nothing as the sun went down. They savoured the peace and quiet. When they finished, Os collected their papers and tins, and put them in a nearby bin. Still nobody spoke or even suggested they move. He knew they needed to rest so he just let them sit.

They sat silently for an hour then he thought it was time they look for a bus before they stopped running, travelling either to Lincoln or Gainsborough thence to a train station. He was not sure what he wanted to do for the next twenty-four hours until Sally's story was out to the newsagents. The sun was down and a few scattered street lamps were winking on when they began walking leisurely down empty, quiet Main Street.

Perhaps he, too, needed a proper rest because he was caught completely by surprise. Later he wondered why George did not simply shoot him from the shadow of the hedge rather than choosing to talk. Maybe it was because he, too, wanted some sort of reckoning—to feel retribution—a need that would not be met if Os died without his speaking about it.

They were passing a ramshackle farm yard when George stepped out from behind the corner of a shed in front of them and into the light of a streetlamp, fifty feet away from Os and pointing the Beretta at him, holding it in both hands: 'Long fuckin' time no see, Doran.'

Os passed the holdall to Brian as he pushed him and Amanda behind him, raised his hands and, while continuing to look directly at George, screamed at them: 'Run. Back to the pub. Run. Get inside and *stay there*. Now run!'

Brian caught the holdall and the two turned and ran. George aimed the pistol at them, paused then turned it back to Os: 'Naw, might as well let 'em fuckin' go. It's *you* I want anyhow.'

Now they were out of effective range in the dark and still running. Os heard their steps fading and knew they were safe.

'Yeah, George – been a long time. Never hoped to see you again, not really.'

'We all thought you was fuckin' dead. How'd you get out of there anyhow?'

'Long story, I'll tell you about it if you're interested.'

'You gotta be fuckin' kiddin'. Not interested at all. Might be interested in why you did what you did but – naw – not fuckin' interested.'

'So, what now?'

'So now I kill you.'

'Why wait? Why haven't you done it?'

'Not sure, really. Don't know. Maybe just wanna see you squirm a little, beg a little – don't know.'

'Must have some reason.'

'Down on your knees. I want to see you beg!'

'Not going to do it. Not going to beg. You know me well enough to know that. Why should I beg? Haven't done anything to you.'

''Cause you think you're better'n me – you think you're fuckin' better'n me.'

'Don't know where you got that idea. Besides, that a good enough reason to kill somebody?'

''It'll do – it'll do.'

'Well, do it then. Just do it!'

As Os made his demand he stepped closer to George, short steps in time with his words. George made no attempt to step back. The gap was down to forty feet but still much too far for Os to rush him. He had no weapons: the Gerber and the Glock were both in the holdall. Unlike George, he carried no knife at the back of his neck. No weapons within reach: no sticks, stones or bricks lying near his feet—nothing. His only hope was to keep George talking as he stepped closer and closer to him and, of course, that George did not step back in time with him. He took another tiny step closer.

George waved the pistol then aimed at his right knee: 'One fuckin' step closer, Doran and –'

'I'm cool, George.'

Os looked hard into his face as he stepped back one pace. He watched the barrel of the Beretta come up and listened to the tone of George's voice. Both steady—neither wavering. So far, so good. If he had wanted to kill me he would have by now. I have no idea why but for some reason he's hesitating.

'So what now? What're you going to do now?'

Os was confused. In the time he knew George he had never seen him display any compassion, any empathy—let alone sympathy—for any living creature. He was a cruel man who enjoyed hurting people. He could not understand why George had not disabled him—hurt him—with a shot through a knee or elbow, or even a shot through the gut if his intention was to kill him here and now.

He tried to buy more time: 'You said I think I'm better than you. I don't follow. What do you mean by that?'

'In Africa. Why'd you fuckin' do that? Checkin' up on me – on what I did. Think you could do the job better'n me then just disappear into the bush? Don't understand.'

'Didn't want to see those people suffer anymore. No reason for what you did. We had our orders. You could've killed them clean. They didn't deserve *that*!'

George screamed as he gripped the Beretta in both hands and started to tremble: 'That's just what I fuckin' mean. You think you're –'

The shot from the shadows behind Os hit George high in the middle of the chest. He trembled but remained standing as his left hand came away from the pistol and his right arm slowly dropped to his side. Then he fell backwards. Os rushed forward, pulled the Beretta from his hand and shot him a second time in the chest. He dragged George into the shadows then turned and walked to where Amanda was standing, not moving, still holding the Glock in front of her in both hands. He took it gently from her, lowered her hands to her sides and led her to a low stone wall. He sat beside her and held both her hands in his. Neither spoke. Brian came out of the shadows carrying the holdall and his laptop bag and he, too, was silent.

They sat this way for ten minutes then Os spoke: 'Now we have to get out of here – right now. We must get to a bus stop and hope they're still running this time of night. Somebody's bound to have heard the shots and come looking. They'll find him eventually.'

He stood up and held her hand tightly; they began walking towards the bus shelter. They passed nobody on the street, neither driving nor walking. She started to shake all over.

They sat her down as far back in the shadow of the shelter as they could then looked at the timetable. If it were to be believed, they could board a bus to Gainsborough in a half-hour. He held her until the shaking stopped. He knew it probably would start again in a couple of hours but she was calm now.

Even Brian was starting to relax: 'I wonder where Sally is by now I guess she must be almost in London maybe she's already there talking to that editor friend what'd you say his name was Stanley Livingstone wasn't he the guy who discovered Africa?'

'No, his name's Livingstone Stanley and, no he wasn't the man who discovered Africa. Anyhow Stanley and Livingstone were two separate people. Livingstone was an explorer who went looking for the source of the Nile and –'

Amanda squeezed his hand as she began to sob and started trembling again: 'Oh would the two of you just shut up. *Just please shut up!*'

Os put his arm around her shoulder, pulled her head down against his chest and held her tightly: 'Bus'll be here soon and we'll be out of here. Brian, when it comes I want you to get on first, ask for a ticket to Gainsborough and pretend you don't know us. When the police start investigating they'll probably have a look at the CCTV from these buses so it's better if they don't think we're together. Okay?'

'Okay Ossie I mean – sorry Mandy – I talk too much –'

Amanda reached out and touched his arm: 'Sorry. Really sorry to yell at you. Not your fault. Sorry.'

CHAPTER SIXTY-EIGHT

MILFORD WAS FAR beyond 'dejected', sitting sadly in the Pennine Café, he was quickly approaching a state more accurately described as 'beyond all hope'. It was almost nine and he felt utterly helpless. Eddie Voigt was not answering his mobile; when he rang the message returned was 'This phone is not in service. Please try again later'. George was not answering his mobile; here he received the same message.

Any wandering around the hospital was a waste of his time unless Doran had cleverly contrived to escape from his pursuers and return to hide out once again in St. Gildas. No, such a move would have been beyond belief, even for him. He might as well go back to London and figure out what he should do next.

He picked up his holdall, walked to the main entrance and took a taxi to Manchester Piccadilly. There he boarded the next available train, not a direct route but one that took him through Stockport, Sheffield and further stops too numerous to think about before arriving, far into the night, at St. Pancras. He boarded his train, switched off his mobile, found a table seat facing forward, put his hardware-filled holdall on the floor under his feet and was sound asleep before the train cleared the station at Levenshulme.

CHAPTER SIXTY-NINE

AMANDA, BRIAN AND Os boarded a bus to Gainsborough and disembarked in the town centre fifteen minutes later. A short walk brought them to the train station where they boarded a train taking them through Retford and Worksop to Sheffield.

When Milford's train stopped in Sheffield, the three were checking into the Hotel Britannia Sheffield Centre.

CHAPTER SEVENTY

Darwin sat on a stool at the kitchen bar in his first floor flat in Montague Square not far from Baker Street trying to enjoy his breakfast when somewhere between the sliced mango and the fresh croissants he answered a call from Milford to learn it had all gone wrong: Amanda Stover and Oswald Doran had disappeared again. This was becoming truly tiresome. Throwing caution to the wind — damn the security risks, full speed ahead — he rang Wallace Weymouth on his landline to ask for an urgent meeting, hopefully before noon.

The response from Wallace was not what he expected: the two *had* been found but by the wrong people: 'Darwie, it's damnably bad news I'm afraid. At approximately five o'clock this morning the two were apprehended at the Hotel Britannia Sheffield Centre by Special Branch Officers operating under the joint command of NaTCSO and the South Yorkshire Police. They were alerted to their whereabouts by an observant desk clerk at the hotel –'

'Wally, this is a disaster of *monstrous* proportions. This was *not* supposed to have happened. They were supposed to have been captured by *your* people, not by actual police officers.'

'I know – I know.'

'So, what happened? No, never mind what happened, I'm not concerned about *that*. What, precisely, can we do – well, what can *you* do – to isolate these two before any more people know about this affair?'

'I can contact Stubbsie post-haste and get them moved, probably before noon, separately and in total isolation, from Sheffield to Paddington Green. Naturally since they have been apprehended under charges relating to undisclosed terrorist offences, they can be held without access to a solicitor or anybody else – no interviews or preliminary processing. We can hold them as long as you like –'

'Yes, yes, but what happens *next*?'

'Well, that's not for me to say, really – that's up to you. I'm sure Stubbsie can arrange it so absolutely nobody has access to them but you. You must know how these things work. What *you* choose to do with them is –'

'I'll speak with him about it. Maybe he'll have some suggestions. What I really want to happen is for them to be disposed of before they have any chance to tell anybody about this, but I suppose –'

'I know. But remember, it's not like in Thatcher's day. It's a shame, really. With modern forensic techniques, CCTV everywhere and almost everything joined up electronically, arranging suicides, poisonings and hit and run traffic accidents is not as easy as it once was –'

'Maybe the answer is simply to release them without charge and have them gunned down in the street in broad daylight. Beattie can make up something about somebody settling an old score with Doran. Messy – but certainly spectacular enough to stop anybody from looking in my direction.'

Darwin thanked his old school friend and returned to his breakfast. Why is it croissants, even freshly baked, never seem to taste quite as good as one anticipates they will be?

CHAPTER SEVENTY-ONE

DARWIN TRAVELLED BY taxi the short distance from his flat to the Paddington Green Police Station and was admitted to the below-ground-level cell where Os was held. He nodded to the custody sergeant who unlocked and opened the cell door then stepped back to allow the two privacy while still keeping them in view: 'Good day, Mister Doran. I trust the accommodation is to your liking?'

'Yes, thank you, Mister Cantwell. I've seen worse.'

'I'm sure you have.

'Your interference in my affairs has become noisome in the extreme. Throughout the morning I've been thinking about what I need to do to rid myself of your presence for good.'

'And you've decided?'

'I've decided simply to release you and Missus Stover without any charges and without any record of your having been arrested and detained. I've even decided not to subject you to any indignities like those you visited on me during your intrusion.'

'That's generous of you but I'm just a little curious about why. Bit risky from your point of view isn't it?'

'Why? My inference is that I know enough about human nature to conclude the story you're intent on telling the world is so preposterous nobody will believe a word of it – that is if you can find anybody prepared to print it. No, I've decided to return your holdall – sans some very impressive weapons and several well done fake passports, of course – and let the two of you simply walk away.'

'And that's it?'

'That's it. You will be permitted to keep the credit cards registered in your own name, some cash and the clothes you were wearing. What you do, where you go and whomever you tell about this mis-adventure is fully up to you. Since you have absolutely no hard evidence of anybody's wrongdoing, including mine, by all means tell the world.'

'Well, I guess, then, we'll be on our way. My one comment is that, as holding cells go, this one is rather comfy. I assume Missus Stover has been treated similarly.'

'Yes, as you will be able to confirm in a short time.'

He paused: 'May I give you some advice, Mister Doran?'

'By all means.'

'In spite of the way you have earned your living for a number of years now, you apparently have learned almost nothing about the way the world *really* works. All the people of the world are divided into two classes – the few of us who lead and the rest of you who follow. Occasionally the line between these two is blurred slightly but this hypothesis is overwhelmingly sound. And although you can defend yourself quite well in physical combat, you, as well as Missus Stover – and *Mister* Stover, for that matter – are followers. That is what you are and that is what you will always be.'

'And your advice is?'

'My advice is this – be content with your lot in life as a follower and leave important matters to those of us who are capable of understanding and who have the ability to lead.'

CHAPTER SEVENTY-TWO

Os THOUGHT ABOUT several suitably audacious replies then decided instead on quiet acceptance. Out on the street he could plan what he wanted to do next. The *Evening Tribune* would hit the newsstands within a few hours and their story would be told. No, best keep quiet and get away from this arrogant swine quickly.

His reply was measured, emotionless and polite: 'I'll think about it.'

Darwin nodded to the Custody Sergeant who led the two out and up to the front desk. Amanda appeared two minutes later. She saw Os and she looked relieved although puzzled. His slight nod signalled her to keep silent and she complied. The desk sergeant produced their holdall and handed him a clear plastic bag containing his credit cards, passport and cash.

There was no paperwork: no brown manila folders, no clipboards, no forms, no keystrokes, nothing to sign. Darwin walked them to the front door and stood silently as they exited the building onto the plaza at the intersection of Harrow and Edgware Roads. They walked down the steps and Os glanced back to see Darwin pull his mobile from his jacket pocket and make a call. He shifted the holdall to his left hand and took her hand with his right.

She squeezed his hand: 'I'm confused. I have absolutely no idea what just happened back there.'

'Just keep walking. Shoulders back and eyes straight ahead. Quickly now. I think I know what's going on but I need to concentrate. Tell you all about it in a couple of minutes.'

'As you've heard me say before, Oswald Aidan Doran, I *really hate it* when you say that!'

They turned and walked along Edgware Road towards Marble Arch. He squeezed her hand tighter: 'If you really hated that, you're going to be even unhappier about this. Or should I say, "more unhappy"? Never mind. I think we've just been set up. I believe our new best friend Darwin has sacked our clearly incompetent other new best friend Milford and he's bringing in some serious heavyweights to take us out.'

'Now I'm truly scared. When you say, "serious heavyweights" and, "take us out" do you mean what I think you mean?'

"Fraid so. I think our Secretary of State for Health has sent us walking down a London Street where in a short time we're to become the unfortunate victims of either a drive-by shooting or a dramatic hit-and-run traffic accident. I doubt we'll end up with radiation poisoning from our next cappuccini – that would take too long – or fatal jabs from the tip of a brolly – no rain forecast for this afternoon. No, I don't want to alarm you but –'

'Forget it – you've already done it.'

'– no, it's okay. Cantwell may think he's going to surprise us but remember, this is what I do for a living. He may think, as he says, he is one "born to lead" but he's on *my* patch now. I know more about what his so-called heavyweights are up to than they do. So – yes – be alarmed but – this I can deal with. Just be prepared to move fast and be ready to do exactly as I tell you without question and without hesitation. For now, though, just keep walking and let me concentrate on all these cars, motorbikes, vans, lorries and assorted people teeming around us.'

They crossed to the eastern side of Edgware Road and continued walking towards Oxford Street as fast as they could without appearing to be rushing. Occasionally they stopped and looked in a shop window to give Os time to see if they were being followed.

'I think there's too much traffic here for a spot of hit and run so my guess it'll probably be either two blokes on a motorbike or a lone walker with a pistol concealed under a newspaper. Sounds like a cliché but that's the way it's often done. A professional hit always involves two shots so that's a total of four and silencers aren't as *silent* as in the films, so he'll attract some attention. He'll either walk away and disappear into the crowd or jump on the back of a bike that just happens along.'

'This is really cheering me up. Almost more happiness than a girl can bear. Why didn't we just sit it out in those cells until Sally does her thing?'

'Good question. Don't really have time to answer it right now. Tell you all about it later. Quick answer is I think we're safer out here on the street than we would be in that station. Just keep walking.'

'I've yet to be convinced.'

They reached Marble Arch and turned left onto Oxford Street: 'Good news and bad news.'

'Shouldn't that be bad news and badder news, Ossie?'

'I'll ignore that. The good news is there are lots more people here – easier for us to blend in –'

'And let me guess – the bad news is there are lots more people here – easier for the people chasing us to blend in.'

'More or less. Seriously, though, with all these huge and busy shops along here there are lots more places for us to go when they catch up with us. We'll see.'

They walked along the north side of Oxford Street in the direction of Oxford Circus where they stopped to look in the window of a department store at some outrageous party dresses. They turned and Os looked behind them and confirmed the man he saw was following them; he moved when they moved and stopped when they stopped, keeping pace with them thirty metres behind. He carried a lumpy folded broadsheet under his left arm and Os concluded he was right-handed—the lump was an automatic of some sort with a silencer. To ensure Amanda's body language did not suggest they spotted him, Os said nothing but steered her into the store, across the floor and onto the escalator. They moved up to the second floor and their follower moved closer, keeping pace. They stepped off the escalator; Os tightened his grip on her hand and whispered: 'Okay. Remember a little while ago I said I wanted you to do exactly as I said and not ask any questions?'

'Yes but –?'

'Sorry, but I think that qualifies as a question. Right, here's what you're going to do. We're going to hurry a little as we walk among all these posh dresses and over towards those changing booths. I want you to take the holdall. When we get there, I'm going to let go of your hand and I want you to step quickly into the nearest empty booth, close the curtain and step up onto the seat so your feet can't be seen by anybody looking under it. I'm going to keep walking without breaking stride in the hope he won't notice you have –'

'He –?'

'I think that qualifies as another question but never mind, just keep walking. Once you get into that booth don't move until I come back for you. Okay?'

'Okay – but?'

'Not *another* question! Get ready.'

They came abreast of the entrance to the suite of changing booths, he passed her the holdall, smiled and gave her a gentle shove into the doorway: 'Have a nice day.'

He walked faster now, on into the handbag and glove department. He glanced back; his tail ignored her and stayed with him. He kept walking quickly across Handbags and Gloves planning his next move. He headed towards the shoe department, moving to his right so when he crossed into Shoes he was close to a projecting wall. He stepped around this wall and backed up against it, hoping to emerge behind his tail as he passed and before he spotted him. His success depended on his not appearing to know he was being followed. The man passed by the end of the wall close to Os and on his left. He paused for a moment as he looked ahead then to his left then to his right.

Os' left arm flashed out; he gripped the surprised man's right wrist, whipped him around and head butted him. The newspaper and pistol fell to the carpeted floor making less sound than the crack of his broken nose.

Os pulled him back into the corner, putting him into a sleeper hold while he dragged him backward through a door into a stockroom: 'You'll never make it as a Ninja, mate!'

He tightened his chokehold until the man went limp then stepped back out onto the floor to collect the newspaper and pistol. He backed through the door this second time, looked around and was pleased nobody, neither customers nor staff, had noticed either the few drops of blood on the floor or the foiled assassination attempt played out before them.

He looked over the silenced Walther PPK, stuck it under his belt in the middle of his back, searched the man then removed a sheathed combat knife from his leg and strapped it to his own. I'll bet Darwin will *really* be unhappy when he finds out what happened here. He finished his search; the man carried no more weapons.

Decision time: should he wait until the man recovered enough to tell him whether others were involved and, if so, how many, or should he just stuff him into a stock hamper, collect Amanda and go back to walking along Oxford Street? The upside was his possibly gaining some useful information; the downside was he might end up coming to the attention of somebody from store security. He chose the latter: now unarmed and injured this man was unlikely to do them any harm, and should there be more lurking out there, there were enough department stores between here and Oxford Circus to repeat this process.

He wandered around the stockroom, found a hamper and rolled it back to his corner. His assailant was stirring so he moved to option three: he snapped his neck, tipped him into the hamper, wheeled him into the lift, sent him to the basement, retrieved Amanda from the changing booth and they resumed their stroll along Oxford Street. Os hated contract killers and black ops goons, especially incompetents.

He was pleased—he read Darwin's intentions and the situation correctly, and dealt with it successfully. Now it was time to declare war on this obnoxious man and take him down. And not just take him down but be *seen* to be taking him down.

He made some assumptions. The first was he had been given back his credit cards so Darwin and his associates could monitor their transactions in real time and when they bought something their trackers knew their location. Second, since he let them walk out the door, their access to public CCTV imaging enabled them to track him and Amanda as they moved about the city. Whether they had placed a tracking chip in the holdall would not change anything. Next, the hit was to be very public—front page, six o'clock news: the whole world would see the Great British Public was finally rid of this notorious terrorist—absolutely nothing to do with Darwin Cantwell, The National Health Service, Sutton-Millhouse Medical Products or any ordinary citizens going about their lawful business and why would any reasonable person think otherwise? His fourth assumption was Darwin, with his 'born to lead' mentality, assumed Os was not capable of thinking on this level.

And this was the one question yet to be answered. Since he assumed his watchers did not have real time access to in-house CCTV systems for every store on Oxford Street, they saw him, Amanda and their hit man enter the department store, but only two emerge a few minutes later. Would they conclude from this their man had been taken out and, if so, would they have a backup plan: another operative, a Plan B?

Now more distress for Amanda: 'So far, you done good. One down and maybe a couple more to go.'

'I'm not even going to ask what you're talking about. If you're happy with the way it's going so far, don't give me any more useless, scary information, just tell me what we're going to do next – no, don't even tell me what *we're* going to do next, just tell me what you want *me* to do.'

'Good idea. I think it's time for a leisurely lunch.'

They passed through Oxford Circus and walked down Regent Street, turning right onto Vigo Street then left on Sackville Street until they reached Piccadilly. They walked along Piccadilly and found a restaurant Os decided would do for what he was planning. He wanted a place with a view of the street while they ate, their lunch would not take too long and they were seated by a man instead of a woman.

He assumed they were being watched, although he had not spotted anybody—maybe this lot were better than the last. The hit, when it came would be out in the street and not inside a shop or restaurant. Finally, he wanted them to spend long enough with their meal to make their watchers jumpy but not *too* jumpy.

They spent forty-five minutes with their panini, profiteroles and lattes then prepared to leave. When Amanda went to the ladies Os had a quick, whispered, conspiratorial word with their host while winking and palming him a twenty-pound note: 'I'm in a spot of bother here, mate, and I could use your help.'

'Certainly, sir. How can I help you?'

'Well – this rather awkward – but just as we got up to leave – I've spotted the lady's husband – just outside on the street. Would you mind awfully escorting us through the kitchen and out the rear door?'

The man smiled: 'Certainly, sir. I understand. Not a problem.'

Amanda returned, Os took her by the hand and followed their host out into the service area behind the building. A narrow yard led to Jermyn Street where they walked along to an alley taking them back to Piccadilly. He told her to wait within a little nook in the brick wall while he moved cautiously out far enough to see the crowd of people covering the pavements along this busy street.

He was unsure they were being followed but if they were, and if Darwin and his pals were monitoring real time CCTV images then their watchers were somewhere on the street waiting for them to come out of the restaurant. And if they were well organized it was likely there would be two, possibly one on either side of the street. He scanned Piccadilly in both directions and spotted both.

One was at the far side of the restaurant leaning against the wall and pretending to read a newspaper. The bulge of his shoulder holster under his loose jacket was not likely obvious to the casual observer. The second, on the other side of the street, also leaning against a wall, also reading a newspaper would be delayed by a few seconds when he crossed the four lanes of manic traffic. Whether they were in radio contact did not concern Os as he set them up.

He stepped back to Amanda: 'Okay, Missus Stover, it's show time! Here's what I want you to do and, as promised, I'm not going to give you any clues about what's going on. Just do as you're told, woman.'

'Right, captain. Orders is orders.'

She was calm; he touched her arm: 'I want you to move slowly up to the corner. Wait until a particularly large gaggle of tourists passes in front of the restaurant coming your way then step out in front of them and walk up to the window, pause and look inside as though you're expecting to see somebody you know. Immediately turn and shrug your shoulders as though you don't see the person you want to see, then walk, briskly now, back to this alley and move on down to Jermyn Street. Do not look at me as you pass, just keep walking swishing your lovely hips to and fro. Step into the nearest shop doorway and wait for me. Whatever you do, don't move until I come for you. I shan't be long – promise.'

'Didn't think you ever noticed my hips.'

'Why'd you think I invited you for that dirty weekend? Can't keep my hands off you much longer.'

'Promises, promises.'

She smiled then shuddered, squeezed his hand, kissed him on the cheek and turned to walk out onto the pavement, pausing at the corner.

The ruse worked. She disappeared from his view when he stepped well back into the nook. He waited for thirty seconds then she strode past him towards Jermyn Street, looking straight ahead. Their first watcher passed in front of Os; he was drawing his pistol: a semi-automatic with no silencer. They must really want to make a show of this. The man spotted Os and realized he had been set up but it was too late; Os gripped his right arm with his left hand, whipped his right hand around in an arc and crushed his windpipe. He pulled the man towards him, stepped aside and slammed his face into the brick wall then broke his neck.

He pushed the man back into the nook, collected his pistol, removed the magazine and chambered round then threw the lot into a convenient corner. He was not concerned about fingerprints or DNA. Although both Piccadilly and Jermyn Street were busy, nobody was in the narrow alley: his little adventure went unnoticed. So far, so good. He straightened up to wait for their other assailant.

With no people in the alley Os decided he wanted to send a more spectacular message with the second man. He appeared in the entrance a minute after the first and walked more cautiously, no doubt unsettled by the absence of his partner. His weapon was not drawn. Os pulled the Walther from behind his back and as the man passed him he grasped him by the shoulder, pulled him around and shot him quickly twice high in the chest. Os held him for three minutes until he lost consciousness then he crumpled to the pavement. He pushed him back into the nook on top of his associate.

He straightened up, slid the pistol back under his belt, tugged his jacket, picked up the holdall then walked down the alley towards Jermyn Street to Amanda.

CHAPTER SEVENTY-THREE

DARWIN WAS UPSET when his breakfast was ruined by the call from Milford and now into the afternoon his fortunes not only had not improved, they were deteriorating at speed. After his release of Stover and Doran, Leslie ushered him into a control room few knew about to watch the demise of his two nemeses. Instead he was entertained by a comedy of errors seldom seen in the history of institutionally-sanctioned wet work.

He watched them enter an Oxford Street department store followed by their first assassin only to see the two appear a few minutes later and their killer never to be seen again. He monitored their progress down Regent Street and into a restaurant on Piccadilly from which they failed to emerge, then saw them strolling down Jermyn Street an hour later. He watched in disbelief when they lured one then the other of this totally incompetent duo into an alley where Doran dispatched them with a professionalism Darwin had to admire even in his frustration and anger. Now they were out of immediately-available hit men.

He turned to his old school friend: 'What do you think I should do now, Stubbsie? This has to stop!'

'I'll have to think about this. Although I don't know this Doran character, he's quite a man. We could use somebody of his calibre on our list of contractors. Any chance we could –?'

'Don't be absurd. This man – and this woman, for that matter – know too much about things they shouldn't. To put it simply, I want them dead just as soon as possible and that's all I want to say about it.'

'Okay, well –'

'Well, is there *anybody else* we can call on to see to them? Surely somewhere out there is somebody capable of dealing with this man. He may be clever, he may be good at his job but he's not Superman – he's just a man.'

'Maybe we should've done them this morning when we had them.'

'Messy as it would've been, you're no doubt right. Too late to think about that now. What should we try next?'

'I have a contact in Manchester who knows some mercenaries—really ruthless men, scum of the earth, who can think like Doran – his sort of people. I know of one – man named George Barr. I'll make some calls. It'll take a little time, maybe half a day or so to set it up but it's the only reasonable thing I can think of at the moment.'

All interest in the progress of Doran and Stover around the streets of the West End having been lost, Darwin paced the small control room in frustration while Leslie made a call to his off-the-record contact in the Greater Manchester Police, to engage the services of Barr.

He continued to pace while Leslie made two more calls then turned back to him: 'I'm afraid this is going to take a bit longer than I anticipated. It seems that Barr has gone off the radar and there appears to be a serious three-way gang war brewing in Manchester between Harry Mabe, Eddie Voigt and a motorcycle gang based in Northern Lincolnshire –'

Darwin's pupils dilated as Leslie spoke, his intake of breath almost a squeak, he exhaled then pleaded: 'But I need some help here – now!'

'I know you do but there's nothing I can do until I can contact these people. I'm sure you don't want to use anybody local. Maybe sometime later this afternoon or into the early evening –'

'Yes – yes, but –'

'There's absolutely nothing I can do for the moment unless I re-issue the warrants and send the SWAT team and the NaCTSO lads – that's the National Counter Terrorism Security Office to you civilians – out again but I didn't think you –'

'No, I know what NaCTSO means, and you're right, I don't want any more people knowing about this operation. I'll just have to wait until –'

'In the meantime, you can't do any more here. Why don't you just get out of here for a couple of hours, go for a walk, have a coffee, read the papers – anything. Pacing around in here won't accomplish anything. Try to relax. Everything'll be fine.'

CHAPTER SEVENTY-FOUR

EVERYTHING DID *NOT* turn out fine for Darwin. He sat at a small, round table on the pavement outside a coffee shop on Edgware Road and before he unfolded the copy of the *Evening Tribune* he picked up from the counter next to the impressive, black and chrome machine where his cappuccino was brewed, paparazzi were already gathering around his flat in Montague Square, his palatial country home in Buckinghamshire, his offices in Richmond House and his offices in the Palace of Westminster.

Having been warned off by executives and senior editors, no reporters from the Beattie stable were chasing this fast-breaking story although some had been instructed immediately to prepare objective, honest, measured and carefully balanced rebuttals for these utterly absurd, scurrilous and thoroughly baseless allegations against some of our most highly respected, nay revered, duly elected public servants; honest, hard-working Whitehall mandarins; innovative captains of industry of unquestioned integrity; selfless hospital managers and administrators; our proud free press dedicated to fearless, honest and wholly unbiased news reporting, and police officers at every level throughout the land.

Paparazzi were also making their way to the head offices of Sutton-Millhouse Medical Products in Milton Keynes and to several large, prominent NHS hospitals named in the front-page report, including St. Gildas Royal Infirmary in Manchester. Darwin gently sipped his cappuccino while he slowly unfolded the paper.

CHAPTER SEVENTY-FIVE

OS AND AMANDA walked hand-in-hand to the end of Jermyn Street, turned right onto St. James's Street then left on Piccadilly towards the Green Park Tube Station.

She reached across and squeezed his arm with her free hand: 'Any idea what happens next?'

'No idea whatsoever. Depends on when Sally's story hits the headlines – which I hope will be in this evening's paper, soon to be out, I assume.'

'And if it isn't?'

'Good question. We'll just have to wait and see.'

'And in the meantime?'

'In the meantime, I think we'll just hop on the underground for a ride out to Heathrow and back.'

'Why Heathrow?'

'No particular reason other than it's a good long ride where we can rest our tired bodies – been a lot going on since five o'clock this morning. We'll get into the head end carriage and work our way to the front where we can sit with our backs to the wall with a decent view of people coming and going. Maybe try to contact Brian. Poor sod, bless his heart – probably going even more berserk than usual wondering where we are.'

'Ready to tell me what's going on?'

'Yep. Reckon you deserve some answers.'

Omitting some details, he told her about their three assassins and that they were no longer a threat. In his judgement for the moment there was probably nobody else on their trail—he doubted anybody would send *three* teams out at once although it was possible before long there would be another one after them. They boarded a train and settled themselves in for their journey.

They exited their train at Heathrow Terminal Four, walked out and up to the nearest newsagent, glanced at the front page of the *Evening Tribune*, smiled at each other, paid for it and walked back down to the platform. Os looked around as they walked and was convinced nobody was following them. They boarded the next train returning to London, again sitting in the head end carriage and settled back to read all about it.

This latest edition of the paper changed their circumstances entirely although they were not yet aware of this. Those immediately caught up in the turmoil that was the whole basis for this story had no further interest in the trials and tribulations of minor players such as Amanda Stover and Oswald Doran; much bigger issues were involved. These two were forgotten: any concern about their apprehension or ultimate demise vanished.

CHAPTER SEVENTY-SIX

DARWIN'S THOUGHTS WHEN reading about himself on the front page of the *Evening Tribune* were not that *he* did something wrong, it was the *reporter and editor* responsible for printing this tissue of lies were wrong. While it might be true somebody somewhere within the United Kingdom of Great Britain and Northern Ireland misbehaved in connection with this affair, he certainly had not; his conscience was clear.

He stated this hastily and tersely when pushing his way through the gaggle of reporters gathered in front of his London flat and this was what he planned to state at the press conference he called for early the next morning.

Some psychologists make a distinction between a psychopath and a sociopath; others use these terms selectively according to root causes for the condition. Antisocial personality disorder—ASPD—is today usually preferred instead of either. Two prominent symptoms are an 'incapacity to experience guilt' and a 'pervasive pattern of disregard for, and violation of, the rights of others'.

A person with ASPD is not only not uncomfortable telling lies, the assumption is this is a reasonable and acceptable way of behaving towards fellow human beings. Body language and non-verbals display no discomfort when telling porkies, to the extent a polygraph can be fooled. There exist no cognitive dissonances to be resolved. Darwin was the paradigm of this disorder.

What happened over the next three days is familiar to everybody who reads or watches daily news. On Day One Darwin held his promised press conference outside his flat—ostensibly impromptu but in fact carefully managed by Dirk Storm, a PR guru he engaged to deal with what he expected to be a paroxysm of unwanted media attention.

Mister Storm followed this immediately with an interview with a senior political reporter working for a commercial television channel owned by World-Universal News Corporation. He stated the allegations against Secretary Cantwell were almost too laughable to deserve a response but within the week his client would present evidence fully and unequivocally clearing his name. The reporter asked no difficult questions.

Within the hour a smiling Prime Minister stepped from the front door of Number Ten to a sun-drenched, temporary podium set up in the middle of Downing Street and issued a statement that his Health Secretary had his unquestioned—*one hundred and ten percent*—support and the allegations against him were obviously a pack of lies dreamed up by Labour to denigrate callously the Conservative Party and thus generate positive interest in their candidate for an up-coming by-election.

At a press conference called in Milton Keynes at Sutton-Millhouse Medical Products headquarters, Stephanie Wainwright, SMMP Chief Executive, reading from a prepared statement avowed they prided themselves on their extremely high quality standards and it was pure fabrication that any of their products were involved—the accusations were simply outrageous.

It was entirely possible this was the result of the actions of one of their competitors, jealous of their success in their securing massive contracts with the NHS year-on-year: 'Now Mister Gordon Milne, our Director of Operations, will take your questions.'

At a press conference called in Manchester at St. Gildas Royal Infirmary, Benton Goodrich, Chief Executive of the St. Gildas Foundation Trust, reading from a prepared statement avowed they prided themselves on their standards of care and it was pure fabrication any of the incidents described in the news reports could possibly have occurred in their hospital.

It was entirely possible this was the result of the fact that under the massive reorganization of the NHS managed under the aegis of the present forward-thinking Secretary of State for Health these lies were promulgated by a disgruntled executive or manager who was made redundant as there were always some narrow-minded individuals who objected to change: 'Now Ms Winifred Hyde-Davies, our Divisional Director, Paediatric Surgery and Specialist Medicine, will take your questions.'

At a press conference called in London at Scotland Yard, Sir Nikhil Saini, Commissioner of the Metropolitan Police Service, reading from a prepared statement avowed that the Met prided themselves on their extremely high integrity and non-partisan enforcement of the law and it was pure fabrication any serving officers were involved in any sort of cover-up or the leaking of sensitive information in exchange for money—the accusations were simply outrageous. It was entirely possible these scurrilous lies emanated from a disgraced former officer sacked for misconduct: 'Now Assistant Commissioner Leslie Grant-Stubbs will take your questions.'

Television news reports—for all channels except the one owned by World-Universal News Corporation—used the same file footage in their twice-hourly broadcasts: the Prime Minister, Stephanie, Benton, Sir Nikhil, Gordon, Winifred, Leslie and Marmaduke moving sequentially and in slow motion through the grand entrance of *Sans Soucis* and being greeted by a smiling Darwin either with warm handshake or kisses on both cheeks according to the guest's sex.

The single channel owned by Beattie used the same file footage in their twice-hourly broadcasts of a similarly smiling Darwin moving in slow motion through a hospital ward patting the heads of a sequence of unsmiling children swathed in bandages and with plastic tubes either affixed to their extremities or stuck up their noses.

On Day Two, while Darwin, along with Dirk and the PM continued to protest his innocence at several planned but ostensibly impromptu press conferences, leaders of the Labour Party and the Liberal Democrats called for the Secretary's immediate resignation and a full judicial enquiry into the affair. The *Evening Tribune* devoted further front-page headlines and many inside column-inches to detailed expositions of the affair, including verbatim transcriptions of numerous incriminating emails sent between named parties.

Phone hacking was illegal in ordinary circumstances, even in this effort to uncover wrongdoing at the highest levels, so Livingstone could not admit to it; he and Sally had to refer obliquely to text messages from 'sources who, for their own safety, wish to remain anonymous'.

Beattie's papers continued to support the Secretary in his heroic efforts to clear his tarnished name. His broadsheets and red-tops rehashed their headlines, text and photos of 'The Stover Incident' of two and a half years ago with many hysterical and unsubtle reminders Stover's widow was now implicated in the affairs of Oswald Doran, an armed and dangerous terrorist still on the run somewhere in Britain. The whereabouts of the two 'Daughters of Doctor Death' were unknown; they, presumably, had gone into hiding for their own safety and to conceal their shame.

Day Three began with the usual statement of his innocence by Darwin to the reporters gathered outside the entrance to his flat with the confident assurances his name would be cleared by the end of the day. At noon a smiling Prime Minister, stopped by a television reporter in the halls of the Palace of Westminster, reiterated his unwavering support for his beleaguered Secretary of State for Health.

At four o'clock Darwin stepped from the front door of Number Ten to issue a statement he had just tendered his resignation to the Prime Minister so he could spend more time with his family and the PM accepted it reluctantly. Further, he was resigning his seat in order to devote all his energies to proving he was innocent of all the charges being levied against him by the gutter press and the Labour Party. He was not ready to answer questions at the time but would be issuing a prepared statement later in the day.

One half hour later an unsmiling Prime Minister accosted by a television reporter in the halls of the Palace of Westminster commented he was saddened by the resignation of his Secretary of State for Health, that the country was losing a politician dedicated selflessly to the service of his fellow man and that he wished him well in all his future endeavours.

CHAPTER SEVENTY-SEVEN

AMANDA AND OS arrived back in London from their journey to Heathrow, exited the Piccadilly Line at King's Cross Station and walked across to St. Pancras. They went to the Undercroft; they bought sandwiches and coffees and settled themselves at a little table where they relaxed and Os kept a lookout for anybody still interested in apprehending or assassinating them. He saw nobody and hoped his assumption was correct: all interest was now elsewhere. Other than as an act of useless revenge, Darwin's eliminating them now would serve no purpose.

Neither spoke. They sat quietly and let tensions drain away—tensions begun what seemed like a long time ago when Trevor LaFarge knocked on her door and sent her back down that long, dark tunnel from which she had slowly been emerging—an emerging helped by this quiet, mysterious man.

She put down her sandwich and sipped her coffee: 'So – now what happens to us?'

'Good question. It depends on a number of things –'

'Such as?'

'Well, when you look at it strictly from the point of view of our duly appointed officers of the law – Wow! – your friend Ossie Doran has been a very naughty boy. He's kidnapped three citizens going about their lawful business, threatened two with torture and actually inflicted some on the third. He's – hell, do we really need to go into all this? Remember, you've not behaved too well yourself – the gunning down in cold blood of an innocent citizen going about his lawful business!'

'Still haven't answered my question.'

'Fair enough. Answer is, I don't really know.'

'Your best guess then?'

'My best guess is they'll just ignore us – pretend it never happened. These people have already been seriously embarrassed by Sally's report and if they come after us there'll just be more embarrassment for them. No, I think they'll just let us ride off into the sunset. But –'

'Yes? Usually there's no "but" with you. Usually it's just "trust me" or "I'm working on it". So, what about this "But"?'

'But – I still think it'd be a good idea if we just disappeared for a few days to a quiet corner of this Sceptred Isle until we see how things are going. Remember, too, we need to track down Brian. I have to assume he's still sitting in his hotel room in Sheffield thinking the worst and terrified that the bad guys have got us and soon will be coming after him.'

They finished their meal and he left her sitting and relaxing while he crossed Euston Road and found a shop where he bought a pay-as-you-go mobile phone, sim and top-up cards.

He came back to their table then realized his brand-new phone would not work until he charged the battery: 'Never mind. Surely somewhere around here there's a working phone box. Sit tight. I'll be back.'

He walked back out onto Euston Road and found a phone box near Midland Road that, believe it or not, was in working order and allowed him to use his credit card. He reached the hotel and a frantic Brian. He told him to relax, sit tight and they would be with him as soon as they could find a train to Sheffield. The bad guys were no more.

At eleven-thirty that evening the three exhausted comrades in arms were relaxing together in the Open Hearth, a bistro in the hotel where the walls were covered with huge photos of big, noisy, smelly, dirty, proper—*and* productive—steel mills. One sometime wonders why, along with the coal mines and car factories, they are almost all gone.

Os convinced the night manager their arrests were a case of mistaken identity and his proof of this was their standing before him, holdall in hand, a little rumpled perhaps, but smiling, safe and well, and not locked away in a cell somewhere. Since the NaCTSO and the South Yorkshire Police had been let into their room silently with a key card, unlike the old days no damage was done to their front door. The night manager's interest in increased occupancy outweighed his concern about his harbouring terrorist suspects in his hotel so he, reluctantly but only somewhat so, agreed they could return to their room.

Amanda showered and Os finished the charge for his shiny new mobile phone. He connected with Sally after several unsuccessful tries; she was lodged for the night in a B and B in Bayswater: 'It's only about one and a half stars but it'll do for tonight. So, what's new with you?'

'Oh, the usual. You know – dispatching bad guys, fighting crime, righting wrongs, saving the world – it's a dirty job but somebody's got to do it. Looks like you've made quite a stir in the world of investigative journalism.'

'Yep. Looks like it.'

'And we really appreciate it; it's certainly taken all the pressure off us.'

'No thanks necessary, my friend. All in a day's work. Been fun. So – now what?'

'Well, I could use a little more help. Are you headed for the house in the morning?'

'Yep. Looks like it. Plan to be back at the ranch sometime mid-afternoon.'

He felt the hullabaloo now surrounding Darwin eliminated any pressure on them, at least for the next few days, but he thought it best if Amanda stayed away from her house a little longer. Sally said Amanda was welcome at the farmhouse for as long as he thought necessary. She even suggested the girls, and Shirley, too, if they wished, came to stay with her: 'There's plenty of room and it would be nice to hear something in the house beside my own voice. And – as I have demonstrated, I'm quite capable of fending off unwanted visitors of any ilk – annoying reporters *or* seriously bad bad guys.'

When this conversation was ended, a thoroughly exhausted Amanda finished her shower and was sound asleep, wrapped up snugly and securely under an enormous duvet with the hotel's logo emblazoned across it.

Os turned out the lights and crawled into the other bed. Still feeling like Amanda's protector and not her lover—well, not just yet, anyhow—he drifted off to sleep thinking about what he needed to do while his girls were reunited and safely hiding out in the Pennines.

Assuming the bad guys had not discovered his lockup, he could affect another of his false identities and cruise around his and Amanda's houses, his office and the safe house for the next week confirming nobody was watching them. That done, then it was a good idea if he went into some hiding of his own until things quietened down. He planned first thing in the morning to track down Paul then he fell asleep.

CHAPTER SEVENTY-EIGHT

DARWIN'S FALL FROM grace was swift, spectacular and fully in the public eye. Following Sally's meticulously documented and sensational exposé in the *Evening Tribune* of the monumental web of bribery, corruption and incestuous relationships between politicians, the press, the police, NHS executives and the head of a major supplier to the health care professions, he retreated to his country home in Buckinghamshire to decide what he wanted to do next.

His friends deserted him; his wife travelled to Australia for an extended visit with her sister. Something to do with 'rats deserting the sinking ship': every time he rang an acquaintance or old school friend, regardless of the time or place each was 'simply too busy at the moment' to see him. The only people interested in his comings and goings were paparazzi who hounded him unmercifully wherever he went.

After he announced his resignation and the Prime Minister accepted it with regret, even the stable of newspapers and the television station owned by World-Universal News Corporation reversed fully their editorial direction and from then pummelled him with at least as much vigour as had the *Tribune*.

He was confused. Yes, it might be a few sentimental, misguided and overly-sensitive individuals were concerned a small number of hospital patients died unnecessarily and this resulted, apparently, in that Stover chap's suicide but, so what? nobody of any importance had died. Further, he had absolutely nothing to do with any of it.

His concern was not over his loss of income—between his personal fortune, properties and investments, even with the loss of his obscenely overstated Parliamentary and Ministerial expenses drawings and brown envelopes from the likes of Gordon, maintaining the way of life he had come to expect was ensured.

Rather it was his loss of standing within the society of which he had been a leading member throughout his adult life. Confusion emerged but it had nothing to do with any question of wrongdoing—of any collisions between 'rights' and 'wrongs'.

On the contrary, it was between *his* perceptions of his behaviour and what he felt must be those of the people who comprised the rest of the world. Human behaviour is not based on facts, it is based on every individual's perception of facts and these perceptions are wholly internal to each. Many people perceived he had done wrong while his perception was overwhelmingly he had not; for the first time in his life he questioned why he made some of the decisions he had.

CHAPTER SEVENTY-NINE

DIRK STORM SELDOM made house calls but Darwin had the potential to funnel much cash into his coffers for little work—and probably no useful results whatsoever; he was prepared to travel from his sumptuous offices on Albemarle Street in the West End to Aylesbury in the wilds of Buckinghamshire—wherever *that* was. He arrived at *Sans Soucis* by taxi at mid-day. They moved to the library.

Darwin was uncharacteristically unsure of himself: 'I need some help and I'm not sure to whom to turn. Since you are already familiar with my – situation – it only seems reasonable to ask you.'

'Well, Darwin – may I address you as "Darwin"? – you *do* seem to have found yourself in a bit of a pickle. In the words of one American novelist: "You seem to have been caught with your hand in the cookie jar."'

'Yes, yes – I don't need reminding of that! The question is whether you can help me or not and, if so, what do you suggest we can do?'

'I've been thinking a great deal about this on the train – beautiful house, by the way but – damnably inconvenient place to live, might as well be in Scotland. Give me Belgravia anytime. But – I digress. Sorry. Thing is, it would be absurd for you simply to deny you've been –'

'You mean you want me to actually *admit* to doing these things they're accusing me of?'

'Oh, no, no. Of course not. What I'm suggesting is –'

'Admitting to having done these things is tantamount to acknowledging that I actually *did* them –'

'Well, did you or did you not, contrary to the law, rules and regulations, accept pecuniary indulgences in exchange for decisions favourable to SMMP in the rewarding of contracts to supply the NHS with –'

'Yes, yes – of course, but what, exactly, has *that* to do with anything?'

'Let me ask the question another way – and, remember, this is not for publication. Think of it as well within the bounds of consultant-client confidentiality. Did you or did you not?'

'Well – yes. Certainly when you put it that way.'

'Then – while I'm not suggesting you admit to it, the starting point for our programme has to be that you recognize that you actually did it.'

'I don't understand.'

'Most people are stupid. Most people are wishy-washy. They can't make up their minds about even the most mundane decisions they must make every day just to get along. Why do think mass advertising campaigns are so successful and public relations consultants make so much money? Why do you think *I* make so much money? Simply because your average man on the street *wants* to be told what he knows. He doesn't want to think for himself, he wants somebody else to think for him.'

'I still don't understand –'

'We – you and I – can't go on television or to the papers and state with confidence you weren't on the take, that's all been documented by that Tomlinson woman. What we can do is tell the Great British Public they were wrong.'

'Oh, I see – well, at least I *think* I do.'

'That's right. I'll arrange a press conference where you'll make a statement. You'll tell them that although they may have read some things in the papers and heard some things on the television news about this apparently awkward situation, it's simply that they misunderstood what has been said about you. That even though it may *look* as though you have done some things that might seem to some people to be illegal or immoral, this is not the case. Because as ordinary people they cannot possibly understand the intricacies of public-service tenders, there is a strong possibility they have simply misinterpreted some of the facts.'

'I see – I see. Oh, but what about questions?'

'Questions?'

'Yes, Dirk, their questions – questions they might ask during the press conference?'

'Oh, Christ, Darwin, don't be absurd! You can't give them any opportunities to ask questions. This isn't about questions and answers, this isn't about "truth" or "facts", this is about telling them what to think. Questions!? Don't under *any* circumstances consider answering questions.'

They talked for another half-hour, agreeing details. Dirk would make all arrangements including writing the full text of Darwin's statement. When it was ready, the text, complete with stage directions, would be forwarded to him and he would rehearse it until he knew it by heart—pauses, eyebrows, smiles, frowns, gestures and all.

Then when it was convenient for both, he would travel to Dirk's offices in London and they would go through a dress rehearsal. Only when Dirk was totally happy with Darwin's presentation would it be announced. By the end of the speech, Dirk hoped listeners would have forgotten completely about Darwin and would be seen standing to attention ready to salute any Union Flag near to hand. About the only thing lacking was suitably stirring background music.

Telford Throckmorton, Solicitor and Senior Partner with the London-based firm of Philpotts, Philpotts and Seuss seldom made house calls but Darwin had the potential to funnel much cash into his coffers for little work—and likely no useful results whatsoever; he was prepared to travel from his sumptuous offices in Berkeley Square to Aylesbury in the wilds of Buckinghamshire—wherever *that* was. He arrived at *Sans Soucis* by taxi in mid-afternoon shortly after Darwin's meeting with Dirk. They moved to the library.

Darwin was still unsure of himself but slightly less so following his meeting with Dirk: 'I need some help and I'm not sure to whom to turn. Since you are already familiar with my – situation – it only seems reasonable to ask you.'

He leaned forward: 'What do we do, then?'

Telford paused, looked to the ceiling and back to Darwin, steepled his hands then he, too, leaned forward: 'We immediately file law suits for libel against that Tomlinson woman, the *Evening Tribune* and all Beattie's rags for impugning your good name.'

'I don't understand – if she told the truth –?'

'This is the law, remember – this has nothing to do with the truth. Even if what she wrote were true – and whether it is or not is not my concern – we can still bring suit under libel laws. We can claim she tried to defame your character by only printing part of the truth, omitting certain relevant facts, quoting out of context, stating her case in ways to suggest your actions were diametrically the opposite of what they really were –'

'But that makes no sense whatsoever.'

'Of course it makes no sense, man, it's the law. It's complicated. It's deliberately made complicated so ordinary folk don't understand it. That's what the law is all about.'

'But will it work?'

'It might – then again, it might not. It's a chance you have to take to try to clear your name.'

'And if it doesn't?'

'Well then, you'll owe the courts *and* me a great deal of money, and no doubt Tomlinson and the newspapers when they counter sue.'

'Doesn't sound like a very good deal to me.'

'It's not, but it's the best you're going to get.'

They talked for another half-hour agreeing details. Telford would draw up the necessary papers and send preliminary letters to Tomlinson and the editors of all the newspapers they planned to sue. When it was convenient for both, Darwin would travel to Telford's offices in London to affix his signature to relevant documents and to a handsome cheque payable to Philpotts, Philpotts and Seuss for the work done to date. Other than waiting for their day in court the only other order of business was to ask Dirk to arrange a second press conference to announce their impending lawsuits.

CHAPTER EIGHTY

BRIAN NEVER STOPPED working, either hacking or programming, and right now he did not feel like hacking. Ossie had disappeared. Brian could have found him, if he wished, by tracking him through the luminescent aether, that is assuming he left tracks and *everybody* leaves tracks these days, but Os said he wanted to be left alone for a while. Now with his other best friends Amanda and Sally resting at the farm at Hollow Meadows way up in the Pennines he needed something to do. Maybe a little rest and some peace and quiet for him, too. Time for some programming.

Recently he thought about enhancements to *Proust V1.0*, his traffic and content analysis and AI application. He wanted to link it to a voice stress analysis module, a blink rate module, one of those systems that tracks eye movement—the NLP folks really love those, a module he read about somewhere for monitoring and analysing body language and non-verbals, and a polygraph. He wanted to call it *V2.0*; and one would be able to read a subject's mind with it. Then with further enhancements to the AI module, he could use it to predict future behaviour: *V2.1*.

It was to be a great human resource management tool because a personnel person could analyse results of an initial employment interview and forecast accurately not only how well the applicant would fit into the job initially but also her or his entire career path.

This would save a great deal of money for businesses by enabling them to not hire losers or potential whistle blowers in the first place and thus avoid going through all that human rights nonsense foisted on them by the European Court of Human Rights, dealing with complaints about spurious health and safety issues, unfavourable tribunal results and successful lawsuits for unfair dismissal.

Police could use it, too. If a hoodie were brought in for questioning, they could divine not only what precise trouble she was bound to get into over the next few years but her entire lifetime of crime. This would save taxpayers much money because scarce police resources could be allocated in advance according to where crimes were going to be committed, and scheduling for magistrates and the CPS would improve dramatically because offenders could be locked up *before* they committed crimes.

The divorce rate could be reduced dramatically: every application for a marriage license would be refused those couples for whom it was predicted their union would fail.

With some solo brainstorming he thought he might come up with more applications for *V2.1*, but these would do until he finished preliminary programming and put it out for beta testing.

He worked on *2.0* and *2.1* when he had time since *1.0* went live so now he was ready for preliminary testing the week after he said goodbye to his friends. What he needed now was a suitable subject. He was pondering this when he heard a news item on the telly, a brief interview with Dirk Storm, announcing the next day Darwin was holding a press conference to denounce the scurrilous lies being promulgated about him in both the press and on television, and set the record straight.

When the great British public was made fully aware of the facts in this matter directly from Mister Cantwell himself, it was entirely possible after a short time out of the public eye he would be able to return to government in some yet unspecified capacity, perhaps as a non-elected advisor for military and defence procurement—the stain removed and his character unblemished.

Great, I can see how well this thing's going to work from a television image even though I won't have a chance to use the polygraph module. Never mind, needs must.

CHAPTER EIGHTY-ONE

Darwin delivered his much anticipated press conference on the pavement outside Dirk's office and it was an underwhelming disaster, so much so they decided not to schedule the second to announce their libel lawsuits. He stood behind a portable podium with the two little microphones standing on stalks like some alien creature's eyes. His presentation was abysmal: not only was he clearly attempting to recite a poorly prepared script, he did it badly.

His delivery was replete with unnatural pauses, his eyes darted from side-to-side and up-and-down in incongruous patterns, his hand gestures were totally out of sync with his verbal message, his breathing patterns looked and sounded like a drowning victim pulled from an abandoned, water-filled quarry just barely alive and his shoulders hunched and unhunched almost in time with his laboured breathing but not quite.

Brian was ecstatic; *Proust V2.1* exceeded his wildest expectations. Here, although he had not met him, he had the advantage of already knowing quite a bit about his subject and the program's assessment of Darwin's current mental state was consistent with everything Os said about the man. When he read on screen the forecast of Darwin's future behaviour he was so excited he had to contact Os and tell him all about it.

Brian decided to ignore Os' request to be left alone and phoned him; this was a story too good not to be told — and quickly. Os gave him *another* of his pay-as-you-go mobile phones for use in emergencies, so there was no tracking needed to find him. Was this a genuine emergency? Well, nobody was in any danger of getting injured or seriously killed but this certainly was something Os should know about.

He punched in the numbers and waited for a response: 'Hello, Brian, you're not supposed to be ringing me except in a dire emergency. What's your dire emergency?'

'Not an emergency well not a life or death emergency but boy oh boy do I have some interesting news for you where are you at anyhow and how're you doing you need to hear about this how soon can I come and see you?'

'Slow down, my timorously challenged young friend. I'm doing just fine. Relaxing and getting some rest. It was really peaceful and quiet here until just this second when this phone rang. What's up?'

'Well you know about *Proust* my AI program and remember I told you I was thinking about turning it into a mind reading program and how I even thought after it read somebody's mind it could predict their future behaviour well you know Cantwell gave that press conference a little while ago and –'

'You're not making much sense. I know Cantwell gave a press conference today, but I thought we were through dealing with him and he was out of our lives forever. He's not going to bother us anymore.'

'I know what you said but when he gave his press conference I thought I'd set up *Proust* and do an analysis of his speech that's *V2.1* not the original *V1.0* that you know all about so I – well it's kinda complicated but I'd like to tell you all about it because I think you'll really be excited with it and – heck can't I just come and see you I promise I won't stay too long and –'

'Okay. I'll tell you where I'm hiding out and you can come around but only for a short visit. I'm still on holiday, remember, and I still don't want to be disturbed.'

Os had assumed another of his false identities and his Slippery Rock disguise, and travelled by train to Wainfleet All Saints between Boston and Skegness where he checked into a quiet, out-of-the-way B and B. He chose this small market town for no other reason than he though it a pleasant place to hang out for a while; he stopped here once for a meal while driving around North Lincolnshire looking for a suitably obscure location to hide a client, a high-level foreign dignitary, from too much attention in connection with visits to several nearby RAF bases. He gave Brian instructions for the involved three-hour train journey from Manchester requiring changes in Doncaster and Grantham and myriad stops at interesting places along the way.

A grinning Brian knocked on Os' door about four hours later, carrying his computer bag and a small overnight case. Os was concerned when he saw the travel bag; he had planned, nay fervently hoped, his visitor was not expecting to stay for more than a couple of hours.

After his usual frenzied greeting, Brian opened his bag and extracted his netbook with as much speed and dexterity as he demonstrated at the keyboard: 'Wi-Fi?'

'Yes, Wi-Fi.'

'Great – wow! wait 'til you see this do you know anything about "antisocial personality disorder" that's "ASPD" for short anyhow the popular terminology used to be "psychopath" but then most people thought "sociopath" sounded more sophisticated and according to *Proust* Darwin Cantwell has ASPD and this is great because we already knew he's a real nutcase so *Proust*'s diagnosis confirms what we already know so that means my program had passed its first big test and I'm really excited about this and –'

'You're always really excited about *everything*.'

'I know but I'm really excited about this I mean really *really* excited.'

Now *Proust* was running on the netbook. He hit a few more keys to bring up the program's assessment of Darwin's present mental state: 'Sorry you'll have to read it on screen because I couldn't fit a printer in my bag anyhow we all need to learn to read stuff on screen and what's the sense of printing out stuff and wasting all that paper when we can read it just as well on screen well anyhow *I* can although some people still like to hold a paper copy in their hands but I think it's time we all got used to screens and not paper and –'

'Screen's just fine.'

Os pulled the netbook across and onto his lap and started to read. He was amazed at the accuracy of the program's assessment of not only Darwin's mental state but his world view as expressed by his behaviour: 'Wow! I'm impressed. Are you telling me you were able to achieve this just by looking at his presentation on a television screen?'

'Yep.'

'And you didn't input any information about him – about what we already know, or knew, about him, you just pointed your scanner gizmo thingy at his image on screen and this is the result?'

'Yep.'

'Scary, my friend, truly scary.'

'But wait ladies and gentlemen there's more –'

'What do you mean, "There's more"?'

'The best bit is this thing can read his mind and tell us what he's going to do next this program can predict his future behaviour.'

'I can't imagine *that*. I'll have to see it to believe it. Now you *will* have to use some paper. If you're going to convince me, I want you to make some predictions, print them out and seal them up in an envelope. When he does something specific you said he was going to do, you let me know about it and only then will I open the envelope. *Then* I'll believe.'

'No problem no problem at all.'

'Ready for some fish and chips?'

He shepherded his friend out the door and up the street to a chippie serving really tasty and crispy haddock caught earlier that day somewhere not too far off the coast. While they enjoyed their meal Os tried unsuccessfully to convince Brian he needed to be connected to his printer way back in Manchester to run off *Proust*'s predictions right away, not tomorrow. He could tolerate Brian's whistling, humming, deep breathing and sewing machine leg in the same room for brief periods but not for an entire night. Luckily he was able to book a separate room for the one night for his friend Horace Hacker.

CHAPTER EIGHTY-TWO

A DEVASTATED DARWIN retreated to *Sans Soucis* after his disastrous press conference to figure out what he was going to do next. He considered scheduling another session with Dirk but decided *that* would be a waste of time and money. He would no doubt prescribe more of the same: 'And that will be ten thousand pounds, please.' He thought about contacting Milford with orders to track down Doran and Tomlinson then realized any damage his renta-thugs might do would not change anything in his life other than sweet revenge.

That is if they succeeded at all: his track record to date against those two was not all that great; both had demonstrated amazing resilience to earlier efforts. But how sweet would revenge be anyhow? It would not improve his life in the least. No, for now he needed to withdraw into the safe haven of his library and try to think rationally about it. The papers for the libel lawsuits were still scheduled to be served; not he but Telford delivering the announcements to the waiting public.

The distinction between neurosis and psychosis is fine, most say blurred, and it is noted according to whether the subject can still function within social situations, perhaps with some awkwardness but function nevertheless, and if the carrying out of daily life activities is not impaired beyond an ability to cope with a minimal level of success. Thus the compulsive hand-washer obsessed with germs who can still go out to work each day is diagnosed as neurotic while one prevented from leaving the house has crossed that fuzzy line into psychosis.

And this withdrawal was the first, subtle sign of things to come for Darwin. He was *never* one to retreat, he was not one to shrink from confrontation; on the contrary he was recognized throughout the society in which he moved as one who always advanced in the face of the most formidable enemies.

His task now was to decide who, precisely, was to blame for his present state, since he was predisposed never to acknowledge the wrongness of any of his own actions. And although Doran and Tomlinson had to accept some responsibility for it, they clearly were not the cause of it; *that* must lay elsewhere.

When considering his options, although he was less confident than in the past, he kept searching. He was neither extremely left nor right-brain, he eschewed both flow charts and mind maps; instead he opted for several successive drams of fine, well-aged single malt, a highbacked, comfortable wing chair and a roaring fire.

By the time his third dram warmed his innards and the fire was reduced to a pile of glowing embers, he reached his conclusion: the root cause of this 'situation' he now found himself in was Winifred's inability to keep her mouth shut. With his trying to identify somebody specifically responsible for this fiasco, his conclusion was it was *she* who began this chain of events ending with his brooding in the dark, staring morosely and drunkenly into his dying fire.

Had she simply buried the information about those unexplained deaths—that tiny blip in her statistics, in the small print towards the latter pages of her quarterly operating report, none of this would have happened and life would be going on as usual. Nobody of substance really reads those reports anyhow. Having accepted this conclusion, he poured himself another drink, never mind the fire, and moved on to the next phase: he began thinking about an appropriate revenge, something consistent with his self image and world view.

⌘

He awoke with an impressive hangover as the earliest hints of dawn were lightening his library windows. He was cold. A few years earlier he succumbed to the recurring and persistent demands of a few close friends and his nagging wife, forsook totally his traditional values and agreed to the installation of central heating. His abandoning his traditional values had not, however, extended to management of the thermostat and other arcane controls so he never learned about its operation; this he had left to the servants.

He dismissed his housekeeper and gardener a week previously so if he wanted to rebuild his fire and have some breakfast he must do these things himself. It was not worth the effort. He stumbled to the kitchen and reheated the remnants of a carafe of coffee in the microwave then moved listlessly up to his dressing room where he switched on a convenient electric heater and prepared to shave. He looked in the mirror for a few seconds as though the decision were important, then chose to omit the shave from his morning toilet and move directly to the shower—the immersion heater was separate from the central heating system, so he had hot water.

After his shower he looked around for something suitable to wear for the day. The tan chinos and light blue button-down cotton shirt he found were not clean and certainly wrinkled well beyond his usually high standards but with his housekeeper gone he had no inclination to iron them himself even if he had the skill. A Cashmere jumper covered most of the shirt and he doubted where he was going anybody would pay much attention to the trousers. The brown tassel loafers were scuffed and in need of some polish but he was not concerned. He thought about making a breakfast of sorts but since his culinary skills extended only slightly beyond toast he decided it could wait; he was still feeling the effects of the thirty-year-old single malt of the night before; he was not all that hungry anyway. He finished the last of his now-cold coffee and drove fifteen miles to the Milton Keynes Hospital.

He had no medical training and his work as Health Secretary required even less exposure to the healing arts than one experiences during a basic first aid course but his contact with people like Winifred and Gordon provided him with enough knowledge to begin this project. The rest he could improvise. He arrived at the hospital, parked in one of the spaces reserved for doctors and entered the building through the ubiquitous double sliding glass doors into Casualty.

Now he had formulated a plan and was acting on it, some of his former bravado was returning; he even felt as though he was back in school engaging with some of his fellows in some outlandish, convoluted prank. He wandered around until he found a male staff locker room. He looked through white lab coats hanging on a rack and chose one that fit decently. It would have been nice to have been able to add a stethoscope to his ensemble but he saw none. Never mind, it would do.

He had enough knowledge of the way the world works to feel reasonably comfortable he could carry out this first stage of his project so long as he acted as though he belonged. He left the locker room and walked around until he found a small, empty stainless steel trolley then went looking for supply cupboards not surrounded by busy accident and emergency staff.

He looked through several glass-fronted cabinets and located the items he needed. Within half an hour he accumulated everything on his list. He covered these with a green sheet then went back to the locker room and parked his trolley in the hall next to the door. He rummaged through several unlocked lockers until he found a small holdall, tipped the contents onto the floor, loaded his supplies into the bag, threw his lab coat onto a changing bench and went back to his car.

Now he was hungry enough to enjoy a full English breakfast in the Eaglestone Restaurant before returning to his car. He ripped away the parking ticket firmly stuck to his windscreen, crumpled into a tight ball and threw it into a nearby hedge. He reached the exit barrier then realized he had no means of raising the gate.

Punching the button on the intercom he assumed his most authoritative voice: 'Doctor Smif from the tube department. I've forgotten my swipe card. Can you please let me out?'

The gate came up and he drove off.

He completed the one-hundred and fifteen mile drive to Altrincham in two and a half hours then spent another half-hour finding Winifred's maisonette. His headache and hangover were behind him now and he felt just fine.

To say Winifred was glad to see him would be inaccurate; it was not she was not happy to see him, rather she was confused about why he should want to see her at all. Her usually tidy and minimal maisonette was untidy and unminimal in the extreme and she looked as though she dressed for the day from the same heap of wrinkled laundry as had he. The two noticeable differences were she was not in need of a shave and the apartment was comfortably warm, no doubt because her central heating system was more easily managed.

Her hair could have done with a tidy-up. Uncertainly she offered him coffee: 'To what do I own this visit?'

'Well, I've been doing a great deal of thinking about this. At the moment you and I are both in – shall we say – "a state of flux" – and I thought perhaps if we worked together we might jointly be able to formulate a plan to –'

'I don't have the faintest fucking idea what you're talking about. "State of flux" my fluxing arse! Both our careers have well and truly gone down the shitpipe, our reputations are in tatters, most of the time paparazzi are hounding us unmercifully, our supposedly steadfast friends and associates have all deserted us, the PM is about to commission a judicial enquiry in which we two will play central rôles and as we speak the CPS are probably preparing warrants for our arrests on charges of criminal conspiracy, corruption, corporate manslaughter, bribery and perverting the course of justice. Just what sort of bloody plan did you have in mind?'

'I haven't seen any paparazzi about today.'

'No, you twat, because they've changed tactics. They're either hiding in the bushes across the street with telephoto lenses or somewhere in an internet café hacking into our phone messages and credit card purchases.'

'But at least we don't have to fight our way through them to get to our front doors.'

'No doubt because they're clearing a path for the fucking fraud squad to *break down* our front doors.'

'Surely it won't come to *that*?'

'Look around you, you bloody moron! Think about it for a moment. Just think about what's happening and what might happen next. Just try for once to get beyond that high-priced public school education of yours and think about what happens to real people in the real world. If you did, you'd know what's coming. I've seen the future and it sucks big time.'

'But with some kind of a plan –'

'About the only plan that makes sense right now is a plan to move to Brazil or Guatemala or Tasmania or anyplace in the bloody world without a bloody extradition treaty! That is, before they take our fucking passports away from us.'

Their conversation continued. As he argued for their formulating a plan and as he became more and more timid and vague, she became more and more angry, and more vociferous about the futility of any attempts to solve their problems.

The more he withdrew, the more she pushed. The more he pleaded, the more she stormed. The more he begged, the more she berated. The quieter he became, the louder she became. And despite her fabled mystical ability to read people's behaviour accurately, this time she mis-read him: she pushed him too far. With her sarcasm and derisive comments she moved him over that line from neurosis to psychosis; now he was ready to do to her what he had thought about before he left home and collected those things from the hospital; he now felt bold enough to carry it out.

They sat on stools at her kitchen breakfast bar. He stood and faced her then she stood, too. He grabbed her right arm with his left hand and slapped her hard across the face, quickly, three times. Before she could respond he dragged her into the bedroom, shoved her onto the bed and sat on her, straddling her stomach with his knees against her ribs and both hands on her shoulders. She was lithe and fit but she was confronted by a man in frenzy. She wriggled helplessly.

He looked around at clothes strewn across the floor, spotted several pairs of tights, took his hands from her shoulders, leaned over, reached down and grabbed a handful. She did not plead—she was never one to beg or plead, instead she sobbed.

Her bedstead was, as he expected, a modern design with gracefully curved wrought iron head and foot. How convenient. While still straddling her, he stretched out both her arms and tied them to their respective bedposts. She struggled but still said nothing. He spread her legs and secured her feet at the foot with more tights.

Her sobbing stopped: 'Why? Why are you doing this?'

He was calm now and any hint of timidity was gone: 'Well, while you were ranting and raving back there a little while ago I did, in fact, formulate a plan. And as you'll see over the next two hours or so, it's a very good plan, in fact a really grand plan that involves just the two of us.'

'You're not making any sense. Just what the fuck are you doing?'

'Tut – tut, my sweet – language! Your language is simply atrocious. Please try to maintain at least a minimum level of decorum, even in these times of trouble.'

'But this isn't getting us anywhere. This won't help us out of the trouble we're in.'

'Oh, but as you have so articulately pointed out, it's gone well beyond that. We're *not* going to get out of the trouble we're in – not now – not ever. So –'

'So?'

'So, I've decided I'm going to end it. Now just you wait and see what we're going to do. I don't know whether you'll like it or not but I think you'll agree it'll be rather effective and quite dramatic.'

Her sharp intake of breath suggested she was ready to scream. He put one hand over her mouth and grabbed another pair of tights: 'Now, now, no need for that. I thought we –'

She bit his hand; he yelped: 'Oh I really wish you hadn't done that. Shame on you. I guess – well, maybe – you're – maybe you just want to get on with it – to see what my plan is all about.'

He jammed the tights into her mouth then dragged a chair from in front of her dressing table across to the side of the bed and sat.

Her sobbing stopped. She tried to mumble through the gag then wilted down into the bed. Her trembling ceased and she looked at him in bewilderment tinged with terror.

He smiled at her then stood up: 'Right – what is it they say: "Resistance is futile?" Maybe you've finally realized you might as well relax so we can get on with it. But – now I think it's time for some refreshment. I'm not certain about your tastes in spirits but I'm sure I can find something.'

He walked into the kitchen and rummaged around, opening and slamming cupboard doors. The noise stopped and he returned with two brandy snifters and a nearly-full bottle of Drambuie: 'Fine. I think this should do us for the afternoon.'

With mock gentleness he removed the tights from her mouth and smiled: 'So, what do you think of my plan so far?'

She said nothing. He brushed the gag gently across her face: 'If you promise not to scream, we'll leave this out.'

She shuddered then nodded.

'Good. I'm glad we've had this little chat. Would you care for a wee dram, my dear?'

She shook her head violently from side to side.

'Suit yourself. Please let me know if you change your mind.'

'Why – why – why? Why are you doing this?'

'Well to put it bluntly and rather crudely: "You screwed me so now I'm going to screw you." Makes sense, doesn't it?'

'Doesn't make any sense at all. I never set out to screw you. I never set out to screw anybody.'

'You set out to screw everybody you come in contact with – either literally or figuratively you screw everybody you meet. I'm just returning the courtesy.'

She said no more.

He sat back, poured a liberal amount of liqueur into one of the glasses then sipped it as he stared down at her. He consumed this first then a second glass while he sat for an hour, silently; even managing a little nap for a few minutes. Throughout that hour she alternated between resignation and rage but forced herself not to beg anymore.

Finally he shuffled in his chair: 'Now I think it's about time for Phase Two.'

He filled the second glass and this time offered it to her. She refused again. He set it on the floor, paused for a few seconds, stood up and looked around, then poked about in dresser drawers until he found a pair of scissors. He looked at them as he opened and closed them—snip, snip, snip—then brought them down close to her face: 'Did I read somewhere that scissors are the choice of weapon in an overwhelming percentage of domestic murders?'

When he spoke the word 'murder' for this the first time, any defiance she displayed until now dissolved into primal fear—she appeared terrified. She no longer pleaded, she begged. He ignored her.

'Or was it screwdrivers? Silly me – I don't remember. It doesn't matter, really, does it? Of course the other metaphysical question to be asked is whether this might really be described as a "domestic murder"? After all, we're clearly not married – or even partners. Actually – we're not even friends. To be honest – I don't think you have any friends. Not really.'

He thought about considering whether she was capable of forming meaningful friendships with anybody, but in his drunkenness the matter was just too bothersome to ponder.

He waved the scissors in her face again then, snip—snip—snip: 'As you know there are all sorts of ingenious ways of murdering somebody in their home. Shall we count the ways? Um – let's see. We've already covered stabbing with scissors or screwdrivers. But these are boring and unimaginative when you think about it. No class – no creativity – no *style*.'

He put the scissors down, sipped more liqueur and smiled: 'Now here's one to think about. You might not know anything about this but if you mix chlorine bleach and caustic soda you can produce – voila – chlorine gas? Fascinating. Naturally you have to do it in a confined space like a bathroom or toilet, and obviously you need a supply of both chemicals but Wow! talk about being creative.

'Then, of course there's drowning in the bathtub but – again – pedestrian in the extreme – no imagination at all.

'What about fake suicide? Now that's better. All sorts of opportunities for lateral thinking – thinking outside the box, as they say. Few problems here though. Based on what I infer from murder mysteries and crime shows on the telly, this one has to be managed carefully so they don't conclude it's not suicide but rather murder.

'Speaking of murder, we're always hearing about the perfect crime and that it has never been committed. That's a patently silly conclusion. Stupid, really. According to *my* hypothesis the perfect crime has been committed many times – myriad times, probably. And because these are perfect crimes, we, in fact know nothing about them. Now what do you think about that? Ha ha!'

He paused and smiled another frightening smile—a rictus: 'Now that concludes my philosophy lesson for today. But I digress. Sorry. Back to business.

'And then there's ricin, cyanide, arsenic – a whole range of poisons – some fast-acting, some tediously slow-acting, some easy to obtain, some difficult. Oh, yes – then there's finely ground glass. Now *that's* slow-acting – might take years. What do you think, Winifred? Your choice – stabbing? drowning? gassing? fake suicide? poison? What floats your boat, my sweet?

'Tell you what. Maybe I'll just sit here quietly and have another drink while you think about it. While you think about all the interesting ways I might commit murder – how I might kill you. Torture? Well that's a totally different matter – haven't thought about *that* much. Never mind.

'No? Not interested in discussing it? Well, then, I reckon we'll just have to get on with it.'

Now she screamed—a piercing, wailing, high-pitched scream from one who was totally defeated, thoroughly cowed: 'Please, please don't do this. I don't deserve this. You're mad! You've gone totally mad. You've lost it completely!'

'Mad? I think not. Angry – well, yes I think it's fair to say I'm extremely angry. But mad – certainly not.'

'But me? Why me? I've done nothing to you.'

He paused and a vacuous expression crossed his face. He looked directly at her but he did not really see her—as though he was looking through her to something or somebody on the other side of her body; as though he was listening to a voice in his head and responding to it.

'Oh, but my sweet, of course you've done this to me. You're the one responsible for where we are today. All hope gone. No future at all for either of us. Now – no more screaming. Please be quiet – don't want to alarm the neighbours, you know. Just lie back and be prepared to take your medicine like a good girl.'

She shuddered and turned her head away from him.

'And now Winifred, my darling, I need to go out to my car for some things I brought with me. This, I can assure you, will be the final phase of our little project.

'I'm really sorry to have had to tie you up like this after we've been having so much fun but I don't really trust you. Come to think of it, I've *never* really trusted you. I don't know anybody who honestly does.'

He re-checked the ties then patted her tummy gently: 'Bye, bye. You just relax. Won't be long – promise. When I return – well I think you'll *truly* enjoy what I have planned!'

Her face was turned away from him. He grabbed her by the hair, twisted her head around savagely and kissed her roughly, ramming his tongue as far into her mouth as he could. She gagged as he pulled away. He giggled and she began to shiver. He left the room, closed the front door and walked down the stairs.

He returned a few minutes later with his holdall and a big smile: 'Okay, Winnie, now I promise you we'll *really* have some fun.'

She kept her face turned away and shuddered again. He saw none of the calculating sarcasm or anger she was noted for, only fear and rage now tinged with what looked to him as defeat. He slapped her hard several times across the face but there was no response: 'You don't seem to be enjoying our little game. I'm really sorry about that because I'm enjoying it immensely.'

She said nothing; then after a few seconds she tried to snarl but it came out more like a whimper. This time instead of slapping her he grinned and drew his hand gently across her cheeks, back and forth, back and forth. She cried, her pain dissolving into dread.

'Great body. Magnificent tits. Shame about that.'

'Shame about what? Shame about *what*? What do you want – what do you *really* want?'

'I thought you would have figured that out by now, woman. I want revenge, I want retribution.'

'But why?'

'Stupid question. I think. This is one of those situations where: "If you have to ask the question, you wouldn't understand the answer." Now I want you to shut up, or in your usually colourful language: "Shut the fuck up." I don't want to hear any more of your silly girly whinging. So, are you going to be quiet or do you want these tights stuffed in your mouth again? Or maybe you'd like my dick stuffed in your mouth instead. You decide.'

She shook her head. He smiled gently again. His face was placid: 'Good, then we'll just get on with it.'

He opened his holdall and placed its contents on her dressing table where she could see them clearly: four blood drawing kits complete with bags, tubing, pinch clamps and pre-attached venipuncture needles; four IV infusion sets with fluid filters, plastic tubing and hypodermic needles; four five-hundred millilitre bags of sterile water for injection; several rolls of adhesive tape in various widths, and a rubber tourniquet.

Each time he pulled an item from his bag her pupils dilated more. When she realized what he was going to do she screamed again. He said nothing but stuffed the tights in her mouth and bound them in place with a strip of adhesive tape. He began humming quietly—not any sort of recognizable tune; he hummed as he worked.

He looked at her: 'Goodness me, this won't do. Your arms are positioned all wrong. Damn – damn, damn, damn. Sorry – but I'm going to have to move you about just a bit.'

He fussed with the tights securing her wrists and ankles, and using some of his tape and with pillows stuffed behind her he positioned her so she was partially reclining with her arms secured at her sides. She could move her head from side-to-side and wiggle her feet but nothing more.

He pushed up the sleeve of her blouse and wrapped the tourniquet around her left forearm, took one of the blood drawing kits from the dresser, put the bag on the floor beside them and removed the sterile cap from the needle: 'Sorry, I really should use a sterile wipe – must prevent infection and all that but – never mind: where you're going it won't matter. Now, I'm probably not going to be very good at this – haven't had much practise at it. I might try to reduce the tension by saying something really humorous like: "Now you're going to feel a little prick," but – well, not really a *little* prick, certainly I don't think of it as such. Eh, what?'

He found a vein on the inside of her left elbow and tried to insert the needle. She winced at his amateurish attempts. On his third try he finally succeeded and when he taped the needle in place, removed the tourniquet and released the pinch clamp, blood flowed into the bag.

He fondled her left breast then leaned down and sucked it through her blouse: 'Lovely hooters, woman. You'd easily pass the pencil test or the BBC's female news presenter and weather girls elbow test. Now, I'd like a little more refreshment. None for you, though, my dear, not when you're donating blood.'

He confirmed blood was still flowing into the bag then poured himself another glass of Drambuie and sat back to admire his handiwork. The bag filled in fifteen minutes. He looked at the connection between the tubing and the bag and concluded he could not simply shift the tube to a new bag, he would have to insert a second needle. He pulled the needle out, closed the pinch clamp and reached for another kit. His second try was better but still caused her pain. He consumed more Drambuie while this second bag filled.

He removed the needle and stopped most of the bleeding with some adhesive tape then patted her arm: 'Sorry about this – it looks like we've spilled some blood on your very expensive-looking Irish linen sheets and Persian rug. As the Americans are fond of saying, I believe: "Shit happens." Right, I think that's about enough of that. I calculate you've donated at least a thousand millilitres of blood – more-or-less, perhaps. You're probably feeling a little faint but never mind. Now we're going to engage in a bit of fluid replacement therapy then you'll feel much, much better. Promise.'

He looked around the room: 'Damn, not a single IV stand in sight. Never mind; I'll think of something.'

He located a Ligne Roset Dimensions floor lamp in the far corner of the bedroom, dragged it across and positioned it to her right. He picked up three bags of sterile water from the dresser and showed them to her: 'Right, I believe this is standard procedure, isn't it? Must always have somebody check the intravenous fluid we're going to use so we don't make any mistakes. So, please nod if you agree this is sterile water and we're not making some kind of monumental mistake by infusing our patient with an isotonic fluid such as Hartmann's or something silly like that. Okay? Nice lamp, by the way.'

She writhed and twisted her head from side-to-side as far as her bonds would allow. She whimpered through the gag. Her eyes fill with tears.

He smiled again: 'It's okay, darling, just as soon as we get your fluid levels back up to where they should be, you'll feel much, much better. Now you just relax and let me get on with my work. Maybe close your eyes and have a little sleep.'

He hung the bags from the lamp then wrapped the tourniquet around her right forearm, connected one of the IV infusion sets to one of the bags then inserted the needle into a vein in her right arm, taped it in place, removed the tourniquet and set the drip control to full open. He looked at his setup and decided one needle would do: he could piggyback the second and third bags to the first through the ports used to inject medication intravenously.

With the three bags running he sat back to refresh himself with more Drambuie. She was sinking into unconsciousness. He slapped her face several times. She stirred and opened her eyes briefly then closed them listlessly.

When fifteen-hundred millilitres of sterile water were infused she was comatose and he was very drunk. He left everything as it was and went down to his car. He drove away and through his drunken haze realized he left behind his fingerprints and DNA. He was reminded of what he said to her: 'Never mind: where we're going it won't matter.'

He drove unsteadily onto Hale Road towards the M56. Next to the Manchester Airport Marriot Hotel he swung right at the entrance to the small roundabout and onto the northbound exit ramp. He was not wearing his seatbelt. When he reached the M56 he was travelling south on the northbound carriageway. He moved to the outside lane and increased his speed. When he was travelling at one-hundred and twenty miles per hour southbound he swerved across into the inside lane and drove head on into a heavily-loaded articulated lorry moving at sixty-five miles per hour northbound. The driver of the lorry was shaken by the experience but was otherwise unhurt.

Later when the Coroner opened a public inquest into the death of Winifred Hyde-Davies without summoning a jury, the pathologist's report stated: 'Post mortem results indicate death was caused by massive hypervolemia resulting in acute hyponatraemia followed by the onset of rapid, irreversible cerebral oedema. The likely cause was a rapid, intravenous infusion of a substantial amount of non-isotonic water.'

CHAPTER EIGHTY-THREE

MANY ACCEPT THERE is evil in the world but many also agree *most* people are not fundamentally evil, they simply want to get on with their lives. But in so doing, as Tolstoy said in *War and Peace*, events sometimes inexorably draw them in and they end up with their lives controlled by them.

An avalanche beginning as a few flakes of snow slipping away from their hold on the side of a mountain on a bright, sunny day, on its journey down the steep slope gains mass and momentum as it gains speed until it becomes an unstoppable force engulfing everything in its path—mountaineers, skiers, shepherds, walkers and those whose only attachment to the mountain is they live there.

So it is people initially with no evil intentions sometimes find themselves part of an occurrence of evil merely by being where they are at the time going about their daily business. When such people are sucked into an avalanche of evil not of their making, their efforts to cope with what is happening to them can be catastrophic, especially when these efforts collide with their very personal, hidden and deep-seated needs.

The tabloids headline writers, the reading public and columnists noted for their witty writing styles were facing a serious problem. They needed a clever and cynical name for the revelations about the deeds of prominent people beginning with Madison Tomlinson's sensational articles in the *Evening Tribune* and followed by the ingenious murder of Winifred and the spectacular suicide of Darwin.

They realized immediately the paradigm 'Gate' was 'Watergate'; they needed another name for this one. They first considered 'Son of Watergate' but two problems with it were it was quite pedestrian and it had too many syllables to generate amusing, spectacular and eye-catching red-top headlines. They thought about others, among them 'Sleazegate', 'Payolagate', 'Squalidgate', 'Labelgate', 'Rottengate' and 'Backhandergate'. With interest in the affair building daily and with all the people caught up in it frantically scheduling press conferences to place the blame securely with somebody else—*anybody* else—they finally settled on 'Scapegate'.

Editorials expectedly reflected the political and social leanings of their respective owners and senior editors. Conservative publishers commented on the surnames of some of the miscreants such as Kowalski, Milne, Hohenzollar, Schaffner and Patel with suggestions immigration policies of the last Labour government were responsible: they admitted so many foreigners to these Sceptred Isles Britain was no longer British—we were being overrun with huge numbers of unemployed *and* unemployable, non-English-speaking people who ate strange foods, wore weird clothes and probably moved here for no reasons other than offers of free healthcare and free bus passes for their elderly relatives who would be following immediately they obtained their subsidized council flats.

Soon one would not even be allowed to speak English when visiting certain council offices and before long all women would have to cover their faces when going about in any public place. Was it any wonder these crimes of the worst kind were being committed by immigrants with absolutely no understanding of our culture?

Newspapers with liberal-leaning editorial policies suggested this fiasco was the result of Thatcherism gone mad: a culture of everybody out for themselves, stealing everything not nailed down, particularly from the most vulnerable in our society, and if caught denying everything. Their editorials hinted this is what happens when our heretofore caring society stops providing little children with free milk and eliminates weekly bin collections and twice-daily post. Some of the blame could also be placed on Porsche-driving, Champaign-swilling city traders and their 'money for nothing' lifestyles.

What do you expect when you privatise electricity and water services and sell off our once proud automobile and steel industries to the Chinese, Indians, North Koreans and Albanians? Sunday-trading supermarkets gutted high streets throughout the land and with them any sense of respect for the Sabbath. Was it any wonder these crimes of the worst kind were being committed by people who had lost their way in our twenty-four/seven society, who valued nothing but money and who had absolutely no sense of our proud heritage?

Journalists on both sides conveniently ignored the fact the culture resulting in Scapegate was endemic for many years and over successive governments represented by both major parties. None of them suggested any lack of acknowledgement of personal responsibility for one's actions might have contributed to this disaster. They also conveniently ignored the part they, the Fourth Estate, played in this. And naturally while publicly denouncing this dastardly behaviour they were all covertly negotiating exclusive book deals for huge cash payments with the more prominent of the accused. Life goes on.

Paparazzi descended on them in droves, camping outside their workplaces—those who were still employed—and their homes. Children, parents, brothers, sisters, cousins, aunts, uncles, family friends, neighbours, former teachers and pastors were photographed and interviewed at every opportunity. Computers, voicemail systems and mobile phones were hacked. Cash changed hands for information, true or otherwise, and the irony of backhanders used to expose backhanders was totally ignored by the journalists involved.

When looking for scapegoats, people in positions of power and influence divide the population into three categories. Their first choices are naturally the vulnerable and helpless: those who have neither the disposition nor the means to defend themselves. These are sometimes crudely described as 'low hanging fruit': to be plucked with little effort and minimal cost.

Occasionally people in this category gain some support for their plights through petitions and blogs but they are usually unsuccessful. In the days of capital punishment these were the innocent ones hanged for crimes they had not committed. These folks never hire Dirk to represent them because they cannot afford his services and he would never be interested in being seen in their company anyhow.

Their second choices are low-level newcomers to the world of politics, the civil service, law enforcement or business. Although these cannot be described as vulnerable or helpless, they have not yet spent enough time in their vocations to build networks of people owing them favours or to create dirt-filled dossiers on their fellows. Being neophyte blame-gamers, rather than blatantly denying responsibility they awkwardly admit involvement but offer lame excuses: weakly acknowledging they acted without correct information or, even more weakly: 'I was just following orders.'

Their lack of political nous and ability to think quickly on their feet indicate they were never, in fact, destined for greatness anyhow so their sacrifices are no great losses to their professions. Former police officers in this category often end up as private investigators, junior members of Parliament sometimes go on to careers in reality television and those from business find themselves as game-show hosts or celebrity chefs. Dirk sometimes represents people in this category.

Failing to find any convenient targets within these two groups, their final, sometimes reluctant, choices are friends or peers. More challenging than the others, the results can be more rewarding because the thrill of bettering one's equals in the game of life is exhilarating indeed. There are, however, potential problems with this tactic.

First these folks *have* been in their respective positions long enough to build networks of people owing them favours and they *do* possess secret files on their fellows—stashes likely to include information on the very people seeking scapegoats in the first place. And they have attained a level of political acuity and sense of timing appropriate to their being able to create potentially damaging counter-offensives.

People in this category sometimes end up serving terms of incarceration in open prisons followed by seats in the House of Lords, successful careers as writers of trashy, best-selling novels, regular slots on late-night television shows commenting on political issues of the day or some combination of these. Some not ending up in the House of Lords have been known to return to the back benches or positions as non-elected advisors to ministers. Dirk makes an impressive amount of money representing people in this category.

The Prime Minister decided to mount an offensive campaign attacking people in all three categories. His immediate action, as is now nearly always the case with anybody in a position of power in a Western democracy—falling on one's sword is *so* out of fashion these days—was to pronounce solemnly: 'Nuthin' to do with me, mate!'

Winifred and Darwin were blamed in the first instance. They, both being conveniently dead, could not counter with any defences. This having been done promptly, competently and vigorously, the PM was still facing the problem of his very cosy relationships with most of the rest of the major players—this supposition supported, in part, by his featuring prominently in yet another slow-motion video of an entrance into *Sans Soucis* complete with warm, two-hand handshakes and chaste, two-cheek kisses.

He tastefully made no references to any part Bill Stover might have played in this affair; after all, even in these dire circumstances he still needed to maintain his very high standards.

He was, however, facing a problem of greater importance than choosing an appropriate name for this embarrassment. He was, as they say, on the horns of a dilemma. He was in office during one of the biggest tabloid headline generators to hit Westminster since the Parliamentary Expenses Scandal of two-thousand and nine. *Then* the results were confined to much embarrassment, some indignation, a few resignations, a great deal of posturing by the Opposition—that is, until it became clear more than a few from the Opposition were also implicated, demands it all be re-paid and criminal charges filed.

This time, to the public it looked as though *everybody* wielding any kind of authority—whether in politics, the civil service, the police, the news media or big business—was in everybody else's back pocket: a proper daisy chain. This time also, if both sober *and* hysterical news reports were believed, the results included the unnecessary deaths of an unknown number of hospital patients.

His dilemma was this: although he had neither labelled several thousand bags of IV fluids incorrectly nor ordered a cover-up when it was discovered, he was seen as one of the people involved simply because he and they were so closely linked. Thus his pronouncements of moral outrage and his commissioning of a judicial enquiry to identify and hold accountable those responsible might ultimately include him as one of those somehow involved in the affair. He had hoped to manage this with Parliamentary Committee hearings where he would have at least a modicum of control over witnesses called and questions asked but the scale of the disaster demanded a justice-led enquiry.

In this frenzy almost everybody forgot about Amanda and Os, particularly his active part in the affair. His offences included counts of affray, arson, assault, breaking and entering, discharging firearms in public places, flying a fixed wing aircraft without a private pilot's licence or filing a flight plan, impersonating a paramedic, kidnap, murder, storing Semtex in a private residence without appropriate authorization or concerns for health and safety, torture, using false identities, vehicle theft and purporting to be an alumnus of Slippery Rock University of Pennsylvania.

Those within law enforcement agencies considering filing charges against him, obtaining warrants for his arrest then tracking him down and serving them were, for the most part, facing the same dilemma as the Prime Minister: their pursuit of him might expose their own wrongdoings. Further, under the circumstances, their highest priorities were saving their own skins—resulting ultimately in more generous consultancy fees for Dirk and anonymity, certainly for the short term, for Os.

A few intrepid journalists tried to interview Brian but soon decided everything he said or even suggested made no sense whatsoever—even quoted fully out of context, as is not unusual with the more creative and less scrupulous investigative journalists. None of it was deemed either newsworthy enough to excite readers or quotable enough to sell papers.

Some succeeded in tracking down Amanda at Sally's farm but when presented with the business end of her Purdey 12 bore they went away immediately they arrived. They were not successful in finding Os at his Wainfleet All Saints hideaway but then they did not really try that hard to find him; many, particularly several senior editors, were in pursuit of some low hanging fruit of their own.

The most sympathetic judge the Prime Minister could identify to chair the enquiry was Sir Morton Fennimore deBruce, Lord Justice of Appeal of England and Wales. He was a keen supporter of the Conservative party and conservative policies in general. To the PM's knowledge he had never appeared on video entering *Sans Soucis* or any other stately house and his cash contributions to Conservative election campaigns were carefully laundered through anonymous offshore accounts.

Old school ties were closely guarded and he was *never* seen dining discreetly in expensive West End restaurants with influential people, power brokers, celebrities, king makers or Dirk. He was squeaky clean, and his views on flogging and hanging were well-known. The PM hoped the judge's objectivity would render him immune from any perceived connections with the events under investigation.

The brief was *supposed* to be limited to the deaths caused by incorrectly-labelled IV fluids, the rôles SMMP and NHS executives and managers responsible for procurement played in the affair, and the efforts of the late, disgraced Health Secretary to cover it all up. But by the time the enquiry team sat for their first session the avalanche was already gathering speed down the mountainside; the PM was unable to stop its advance or deflect its course away from his closest associates and ultimately himself.

The first witness called was Stanley Kowalski and his testimony was characteristic of the whole messy business. He was not strictly low hanging fruit, he was more accurately described as second tier, but his work in quality assurance made him an attractive candidate on which the entire debacle might be blamed and there the matter would rest. But it was not to be.

If his questioning and testimony had been carefully managed this might have been possible had it not been for his unanticipated, hysterical, hyperbolic description of a late-night encounter with a madman named Melvin Gibbs—tastefully omitting only the accident to his trousers. During the account of his interrogation he admitted he told Gibbs he was ordered by his superior, Gordon Milne, to falsify QA records to bury all information about bags of incorrectly labelled fluids. The immediate results of his testimony were: first, a search initiated for Melvin Gibbs and second, the order of witnesses amended and Gordon called to testify next.

Gordon referred the Lord Justice to Bahrat Patel and he in turn referred him to another, thence to another, then another in a series that finally ended several weeks later with Darwin. Somewhere along the way another mystery man, Thornton Gilrey, was mentioned. Within this sequence, Leslie, Wallace, Marmaduke and Milford were also included. Subpoenas were issued for Gibbs and Gilrey, but investigators working for the enquiry failed to find either. Verbal testimony was supported throughout by emails, diary entries, phone records, credit card receipts and CCTV images, some of which were even obtained legally and thus might be admitted in evidence at later criminal trials.

Material collected from witnesses' waste bins was accepted as admissible, although this was recognized as being messy and further deemed underhanded by the more reputable reporters and bloggers. Sir Morton became increasingly uncomfortable when the growing list of persons of interest included people closer and closer to the Prime Minister. His training and experience as a barrister, however, enabled him to control his body language to hide most of this, certainly from the casual observer, although it is likely anybody well experienced in reading subtler non-verbal clues might have noted his distress.

At the close of testimony each day the PM was a little unhappier with what he *and* everybody else was hearing. His dread of Prime Minister's Questions was becoming palpable. He decided it was time for a massive and visible diversion. Ideally it would have been an external threat to national security around which major political parties could converge, thus at PMQs the Opposition would be forced to offer some weak words of support before beginning their weekly tirade over Scapegate.

He finally concluded, in consultation with his Downing Street chief of staff, cabinet secretary, principal private secretary, press secretary and two highly-paid, non-elected advisors the public are not supposed to know anything about, a project like this would be entangled within too many threads outside his control. Instead he needed to invent an initiative into which he could introduce enough controversial elements to swamp PMQs and with prospective costs high enough to anger every back bencher in the chamber to the point of apoplexy. Were he to come up with something truly imaginative, Scapegate would be consigned to no less than page thirteen of any tabloid worthy of the name and life could get back to normal.

After long discussions and lateral thinking, brainstorming, mind mapping and thinking outside the box, he and his advisors settled on a project they named the Happy Society: an ambitious endeavour the aim of which was to make the life of every citizen of the United Kingdom of Great Britain and Northern Ireland supremely happy.

They appointed a study group to investigate the proposal and determine how happy citizens presently are. Next they commissioned research projects at several prestigious universities into the nature of happiness and how it can be measured and achieved. Questions were raised about why their investigation into people's happiness preceded definition and measurement, but politicians have never been concerned about minor details such as these.

They decided on a three-pronged approach: a series of neighbourhood meetings introducing people to the programme, creating happiness academies throughout the land where gifted children from all ethnic groups and economic backgrounds would be trained as happiness practitioners and establishing degree-level courses in happiness studies.

Later they planned to introduce a fourth addition: happiness apprenticeships for unemployed school leavers who had demonstrated an inability to meet minimum standards of achievement in maths and literacy—everybody acknowledges today studying grammar is a complete waste of time and nobody needs to know algebra anymore anyhow. Immediately they completed their preliminary proposal they commissioned a highly-paid advertising agency to devise a logo, develop a marketing campaign and create eye-catching brochures, posters and promotional videos to be aired throughout the day on television. The entire programme was to be financed with funds made available from cuts in defence, social and health services budgets.

The diversion worked well for several weeks. Revelations during their sworn testimony highlighted the close links and personal congress between the PM and prominent members of the establishment such as Wallace, Leslie and Marmaduke with the implications he must have known *something* about the cover-up, but the furore over the absurdity and high costs of the happy society programme replaced most interest in Scapegate by the public and the Opposition during PMQs.

That is, until two unfortunate things happened — unfortunate certainly for the Prime Minister. First, his driver during his travels up the M1 with Darwin succumbed to the temptation of the offer of an obscene amount of money from one of the red tops for details of their conversation during that ride and revealed all in a Sunday exclusive.

Second, a personal email to the PM from his press secretary discussing some of the minutia connected with the creation of the Happy Society was made public and within it a humorous reference to another email by an earlier spin doctor who suggested: 'It's now a very good day to get out anything we want to bury.' The Prime Minister's position became untenable.

Then the clichéd faeces hit the proverbial fan. One day before the PM was to testify before the enquiry, the Leader of the Opposition initiated a Motion of No Confidence in the Government. She had the unlikely support of thoroughly disgruntled Conservative back benchers who decided it was worth the probable dissolution of Parliament and a hastily-called election to rid themselves of this pesky person who was clearly out of control.

Not only was he trying to move them too far to the left of their traditional values, his actions—or more accurately his inactions—in the face of this scandal had drawn too much attention to their revered old boy networks. They were confident they and the party would survive and re-emerge looking like the Tory party of old with their dark corridors intact—traditional values and all. Lord Justice deBruce agreed to suspend the hearings temporarily until this unpleasantness was addressed.

The speed with which the Government was brought down, Parliament dissolved and elections held is amazing when one considers the government of the United Kingdom is recognized as one of the most stable, if not *the* most stable parliamentary democracy in the world, debates surrounding free vote issues and Prime Minister's Questions notwithstanding. The time when the Leader of the Opposition tabled her Motion of No Confidence until she assumed office as the new Prime Minister was one month.

With the Leader of the Labour Party now in charge of things, Lord Justice deBruce's enquiry resumed with the former Conservative Prime Minister as the next witness to be called. The dilemma confronting him earlier when Scapegate first appeared was a minor inconvenience compared with what he was facing now. Now he was under oath: sworn to tell the truth, the whole truth and nothing but the truth. How was he going to be able to deny knowledge of the Scapegate cover-up and the more profound issue of fraudulent procurement practices when this would require his contradictions of the testimonies of earlier witnesses? He thought help might be available from an unexpected source: Stephanie Wainwright, Chief Executive of Sutton-Millhouse Medical Products. He considered modelling his testimony on hers.

As had been noted earlier, the subtleties of organizational dynamics, particularly the dynamics of large, amorphous groups such as political parties, the press, civil service and the big commercial enterprises with which they all interface daily are fascinating. Organizations evolve according to the values and ethics of people who are active within them; over time the organizations themselves assume the values and ethics of those in positions of power—these evolve into the 'culture' of the organization.

And much of what happens is governed, managed, controlled, not by a set of written rules and regulations but by things unsaid—what has been described as the 'informal organization'. People entering organizations are made clearly aware through nudges and winks that things are done, *must* be done, in certain ways, and they who fail to comply fail to remain in the organization. Nothing is in writing, no direct orders are ever given; if conclusions and recommendations in a report are not according to what an executive expects, the underling is ordered quietly and privately to: 'Recheck your figures. I think you'll find that department is overstaffed by forty-one percent rather than the twenty-nine percent you reported.'

Although Stephanie headed an organization whose entire culture was built upon a foundation of lies and fraud—contracts were awarded not based on cost and compliance with specification but based on her brown envelopes containing more used five-pound notes than those of her competitors—she could testify honestly she knew absolutely nothing about it. *She* never ordered anybody to falsify anything, just as *she* never ordered anybody to render up baksheesh to the likes of Winifred. She was responsible for an organization within whose culture these actions were not only encouraged but demanded; those who could not or would not comply must seek employment elsewhere. Unlike others she could state truthfully: 'Nuthin' to do with me, mate!' because she had never given the order.

These revelations came, she assured the Lord Justice, as a complete surprise to her, she was appalled by these incidents of nefarious, probably criminal behaviour, those responsible would be found and punished, and she vowed that upon her return to her office lessons would be learned and nothing like this would ever happen again. She and Marmaduke were reading from the same script: his responses to questions about phone hacking and payments to police informants by reporters throughout his newspaper empire were startlingly similar.

But the difference between her position and that of the former Prime Minister was while there was no documentation or evidence linking her to the mis-deeds by any trails—paper, electronic or even anecdotal, for him there was. She was careful enough never to have left any tracks at all; he, in his public school arrogance, had. In addition to his driver's testimony, emails, telephone recordings and meeting notes detailing communications between him and many of the principal players in this disaster were entered in evidence. Aside from Darwin's embarrassing encounter with the lawnmower, during his ride up the M1 to Toddington Services and then after, the PM was continually, fully apprised of developments. Under oath he could not claim not to have known about what was happening without perjuring himself.

He had three choices. He could keep protesting his innocence, claiming everybody else was lying. Politicians have used this tactic; even in the face of overwhelming evidence to the contrary, swearing on their mothers' graves they are right and the rest of the world is wrong. This works for somebody with enough stamina and chutzpah to keep screaming: 'You're wrong – you're wrong – you're wrong!' louder and louder until the questioners give up and go away. He could acknowledge he did wrong and offer his profound apologies. Politicians rarely do this, only when forced by circumstances to step out their front doors to waiting reporters to explain why they tendered their hasty resignations—or just before they disappear for a few months into one of Her Majesty's secure hotel accommodations.

Finally he could assert that, yes, it *looked* as though he was involved but all was not as it seemed: these scurrilous allegations were the result of a massive conspiracy of left wingers, Europhiles, Green Party supporters, animal rights activists, pro-life groups, several militant labour unions, the Liberal Democrats, the SNP, UKIP, the BNP and a couple of splinter groups keen on reinstituting the death penalty, all bent on hounding him from office.

There was too much hard, consistent evidence on record for his choosing option one. He was not yet ready for option two; this is more often the choice of those on the second tier, and as a former resident of Number Ten, he was clearly third tier. This left him with option three—ignoring options four and five: suicide or a permanent move to Argentina under a false identity; few Western politicians of any stature have resorted to either of these since the end of World War II.

He went on the attack but his efforts failed. The Lord Justice refused his request to read a prepared statement prior to his questioning, reminding him he was answering a subpoena rather than a voluntary invitation to appear, as would have been the case with a Parliamentary Committee hearing. Each time he tried to respond to a question from either the Lord Justice or the senior barrister leading the council team by launching a tirade against members of the alleged conspiracy against him, he was reminded to answer directly and refrain from making unsubstantiated comments not related to the question.

He ended up looking and sounding almost as awkward and unsure of himself as had Darwin during his last, disastrous press conference. He now understood that answering questions with non-answers is easy when facing reporters or constituents, but almost impossible when facing experienced barristers.

The avalanche swallowed him up, rolled over him and left him in a shivering heap at the bottom of the mountain on whose summit he had recently stood. Even his enemies privately acknowledged he was caught up in events rather than his having been the cause. His tragic flaw was to misinterpret the philosophies of Hobbes, Hume and Locke, and assume once elected to high office one's responsibility to the electorate was fulfilled: then one's responsibility is to the state and not the individual.

He believed, as have many in the past and likely will many in the future, what sometimes appears as a few injustices to the common man are justified in the pursuit of what is perceived as the common good. And as an organization assumes the ethics and values of those in power within it, so, constitutions notwithstanding, the common good becomes that defined by those in power within the State.

CHAPTER EIGHTY-FOUR

BRIAN WAS HAPPY. He watched TV news reports about the deaths of Winifred and Darwin then opened his envelope to review *Proust's* predictions. He knew its contents but was still pleased to read it again—impressed with its accuracy and detail. He was the paradigm left-brain man and enjoyed reading and re-reading anything he wrote to see if he could improve it and to remind himself what a clever guy he was.

Proust predicted Darwin would go mad, sooner rather than later, murder one or more people and commit suicide. Brian was keen to pay Os another visit but meanwhile he wanted to run a similar analysis on the Prime Minister. Here, too, he preferred face-to-face analysis but on-screen would do; it worked well enough with Darwin. Brian set up his monitoring equipment, booted up *Proust*, turned on his telly and waited for the PM's next pronouncement of shocked moral outrage at the things people were saying about him. He considered ringing Os then decided to wait until it completed its analysis, read the PM's mind and made its predictions. What the PM was doing over the next few weeks was important; the next few years could wait. Brian wanted to visit Os again when his prophesies were shown to be accurate.

He entered his predictions into a Word file—no paper this time—just as television news presenters were announcing the tabling of the Motion of No Confidence and the possibility the Government would be brought down, Parliament dissolved and elections called. I'm a really clever bloke, maybe it's time to see about flogging this package to the MI6, the CIA or the Chartered Institute for Management of Human Resources.

CHAPTER EIGHTY-FIVE

OS WAS READY to move. Every Sunday since his arrival in Wainfleet All Saints he bought a copy of the *Sunday Times* and scanned the Business to Business section of the classified ads looking for a listing that had nothing to do with anybody's trying to sell anybody anything. Any Sunday now he expected to see a cryptic ad—meaningless to everyone but him—telling him where to contact his friend Paul Adler.

Even in this age of electronic miracles, an ad in this widely-circulated Sunday broadsheet is still an effective and low risk way of communicating; *Orwell* would not spot it unless the same ad ran for too many weeks thus enabling that amazing application to identify a link from the ad to the person who placed it. He heard nothing to the contrary; he hoped Paul was hiding safely somewhere and not under a pile of earth or the recently-poured concrete floor of a new industrial building, having met a sticky end at the hands of Cantwell, Cleeland or some of their friends at MI5.

Os followed news reports closely in the weeks taking the United Kingdom of Great Britain and Northern Ireland from the beginning of the set of revelations called Scapegate through the Happy Society to the dissolution of Parliament and a newly-elected Labour Prime Minister. He correctly anticipated the reading, some might say 'fickle', public would soon forget about a terrorist named Oswald Doran and any potential threat to the security of the nation.

He was confident neither Harry Mabe nor Eddie Voigt would be spending any time looking for a connection between him and their recent unpleasantness, and the death of George Barr had caused little fuss in either the tabloids or on TV news programmes. Nor was he concerned about any threat from the Sons of Damien. He needed to do one more thing before he came in from the cold and that was to ask Brian to monitor chatter for a week to confirm nobody was still out there looking for him. He was suffering from cabin fever and even a visit from his manic pal was something stimulating to look forward to.

He rang Brian: 'Good afternoon Brain – two Ps – Snapp creator of the world's *original and only* mind-reading software program you can become the first in your neighbourhood to beta-test it ring me for a confidential consultation and full particulars references provided on request how can I help you?'

'Hello, Brian, what's the "mind reading program" bit all about?'

'Oh hi Ossie how're you doing it's really great to hear from you when can I come and visit you and "mind reading software" is all about *Proust* you remember?'

'It's nice to hear from you, too. Yes, I remember. In answer to your first question, I'm doing okay – just fine really, although I'm getting a little bored. And in answer to your second question, I need a favour that'll take you about a week to see to and when you've done that, then I'd really like you to pay a visit.'

'Sure just tell me what you need and as you know I'll be glad to waive my usual fees for an old friend gee I'm really glad you called what can I do for you and does it have anything to do with *Proust* because I would really like the chance to –'

'No, nothing to do with *that* but it does require your finely honed and world class hacking skills –'

'"Finely honed and world class" I like that can I use that one in my testimonials –?'

'Yes, certainly. Feel free to use it but first things first.'

'Fire away big guy.'

'Right. I'm ready to get back to my life and my friends but I need to confirm nobody's looking for me, for you to see what kind of messages, if any, are winging their way through the airwaves that might suggest either our friends in high places or their renta-thugs in not so high places are interested in finding me and doing me harm.'

'Easy-peasy oh inscrutable one any place in particular you want me to look or just a thorough scan of the aether? you know emails routine phone calls encrypted phone messages and stuff like that well as you know when it comes to the encrypted stuff sometimes I can't decipher *all* of it but I can tell you where it's from and where it's going you know what I mean –'

'Yep, anything you can find. My guess is with all the other things going on these days they've probably forgotten about me, but I need to be sure there's still nobody out there trying to track me down and kill me – or you or Sally or Amanda, for that matter.'

'You got it yeah I hope there's nobody trying to kill me and I'll get right on it can I ring you next week?'

'One week's just fine. No need to ring, just come by next Sunday afternoon. I'll expect you whenever you can book a train. That is, unless you come across anything really interesting – or scary – in which case, please ring me on the spot.'

'"So it is written so it shall be done" I saw that in a movie one time about some pharaoh in ancient Egypt or Babylonia or someplace and every time the pharaoh gave his trusted advisor an order to do something the trusted advisor said "so it is written so it shall be done" catchy isn't it?'

'Say "Goodbye", Brian.'

'See you next Sunday have a nice day goodbye.'

CHAPTER EIGHTY-SIX

NEXT SUNDAY OS received the two pieces of information he needed to leave his hideout expecting nobody was going to try to murder him. His *Sunday Times* included Paul's classified ad and Brian arrived at his door telling him he found nothing in the aether suggesting anybody was looking for him. After seeing Brian onto a train taking him back to Manchester, he pulled another pay-as-you-go mobile from his holdall, rang Paul's number and heard a recorded message.

'You've reached the world headquarters of Ascendit Vestrum. There's nobody here to take your call at the moment so please leave your name and number after the tone and we'll get back to you within the next twenty-four hours.'

Os heard the click indicating Paul had picked up his phone: 'It's about bloody time, Paul. Where the heck are you and how're you doing?'

'I might say the same to you, Ossie.'

'Able to sit up and eat solid food. And you –?'

'I can play the violin now, which is interesting because I couldn't play it before.'

'Right, where are you and can I come and see you?'

'Hiding in plain sight, one might say –'

'Might one?'

'Yep. B and B in Earl's Court. Seedy but squalid, no bedbugs and no stars at all beside the door of this place, but the great thing about it is nobody around here asks any questions if you put down cash. Lost in the crowd – you know what I mean. Hell I could have registered as Ed Gein and nobody would have batted an eye.'

'So where and when can we meet?'

'How about tomorrow afternoon at two or so, tube station, Earl's Court Road entrance?'
'Great. I'll be there. We'll do lunch.'
'Do lunch? You need to get out more, mate.'
'You're right about that. See you then. Bye.'
Os put on his trainers and went for a run; Paul put on his trainers and went for a stroll through the madness and wonder of Earl's Court.

They did lunch: finding a place somewhere between frantic fast food and genteel, leisurely dining where they could sit and chat quietly and with a modicum of privacy—there are establishments in Earl's Court catering to a broad spectrum of tastes. That they were sitting less than five-hundred metres from Milford Cleeland's former office—his being at the time on remand for certain actions relating to Scapegate—was nothing more than a coincidence.

Through their starters they talked about what happened to each of them since their last phone contact. Through their main courses they agreed most of the pressure was off, nobody was intent on tracking either of them down and it was probably safe to leave their respective hideouts and get on with their lives. Then during their sweets, they were ready to talk about finding employment and whether they might work under their own names or if they had to assume new identities.

'Paul, I'm really sorry to have dropped you in all this mess.'
'Not your fault, mate. Not really. Yes, you asked for my help but I could've just as well said "No."'
'Yeah but not only have you lost your job, you've had to go on the run.'

'Not really. Well, yeah I've lost *that* job but hell it was just a two-year contract – think of that. These days even spies are on short-term contracts – no pension – no holidays – no chance for any kind of promotion – nineteen-year-old fast trackers are in charge – you know what I mean. What the hell's this world coming to? Is *everybody* free-lance these days?'

'Speaking of free-lance, any bright ideas about how you're going to earn a crust, or me, too, for that matter?'

'Been thinking about that – been thinking a *lot* about that as you might expect. Friend of mine, he's from Thames House, too, another short-termer, by the way, is thinking about putting together a private intelligence gathering group – sort of a civilian GCHQ-type operation. The kind of thing that'd interest you. More brains than muscle, if you know what I mean. What's it you're always saying: "Prevention is better than detection"?'

'Don't have the faintest idea what you're talking about.'

'Simple, really, when you think about it. Bring together the best hackers and traffic and content analysis people you can find, team them up with some old-timers like us with bags of field experience and offer your services to anybody who needs good intelligence to do whatever it is they want to do.'

'Still not sure what your friend has in mind.'

'Let's say an oil company thinks there might be the potential for a new field to open up somewhere off the Shetlands or the Gulf of Mexico or someplace. Immediately they start doing any kind of investigating, all the competition gets wind of it and start their own investigations. It would be really useful for the original company to know what they were up to.'

'Interesting, but –'

'But?'

'I see all kinds of problems – or potential problems, anyhow.'

'Such as?'

'Well first, won't most of what he's doing be illegal? Isn't this just plain old industrial espionage dressed up in a posh frock to make it look legitimate?'

'Not necessarily. He's not talking about sneaking into the competition's offices in the dead of night and rummaging through file drawers to steal their trade secrets. No, he's not proposing anything more than what private investigators do, or *should* be doing, most of the time anyhow – walking around, asking questions, looking at stuff that's out there in plain sight – what the good PI, any detective worthy of the name or competent investigative reporter, does all the time – and putting it all together.'

'So what makes this one different?'

'Difference is he wants to organize it properly, state-of-the-art monitoring equipment and sophisticated analysis software. Keep it all legitimate – well, maybe except for some of the hacking, proper contracts with legitimate companies doing legitimate stuff. You know what I mean.'

'But what about possible conflicts of interest? What's to stop this guy from selling his services to both sides?'

'Again, no different from your ethical PI – no decent investigator takes money from both the wronged wife *and* the straying husband. Well, not at the same time anyhow.'

'Point taken. Any muscle – no muscle, no muscle at all then?'

'Some, maybe. He's also talking about linking all this to some very discrete close protection work. Oligarch sailing the world in his hundred-metre yacht with a few of his friends might need to deal with Somali pirates – that sort of thing. But, again, based on intelligence. Hopefully staying away from places where they shouldn't be anyhow, places where they know there's bound to be trouble. You know what I mean.'

'So he – and you, for that matter – think you can turn this into a profitable business?'

'Yep. Imagine this – way back in the sixties, hell's fire, that was in the *last* century, wasn't it? Sorry, I digress. Way back in the sixties when Walt Disney was planning to build Disney World in Orlando he set up a raft of dummy companies to buy the land he needed for that venture. He was able to get his hands on over twenty-seven thousand acres before anybody figured out what he was up to. His aim, naturally, was to acquire the land at reasonable prices before the speculators knew what he was doing and drove up prices. Now, imagine you were a local mover and shaker who owned some tracts you wanted to, shall we say, divest yourself of at a handsome profit. Wouldn't it really have been nice to have some intelligence about what Ol' Walt had in mind?'

'Makes sense. When and where?'

'Soon – maybe within the next three to six months. Where? He's not sure yet but probably here in London or environs, certainly somewhere in the UK although he's also talking about possible field offices wherever. Depends on how long it takes him to pull together the talent he needs. Interested?'

'Yeah, why not? I'd like to have a talk with him. Oh – was that what the "Ascendit Vestrum" bit was all about?'

'Yep – more or less. Just trying it out. What it sounded like when somebody picked up the phone.'

They talked about some of the pros and cons of this venture then, into their coffees, stopped talking, both fiddling awkwardly with cream and sugar, and staring past each other to the far walls.

Os put down his spoon and sat back: 'Would you look at the two of us – forty-one years old and –'

'Speak for yourself. Remember, I'm only thirty-nine, not an old guy like you –'

'Minor detail, minor detail. I ever tell you about my brother?'

'Nope, not that I remember.'

'Three years younger than me. Never travelled anywhere except for a couple of holidays in Spain. Married the girl next door. Four employers in his entire life, even counting part-time jobs when he was at uni. Steady jobs all his life. Has lived in all of five houses, none more than three miles from where he spent his second birthday. Goes to church every Sunday. Pillar of the community. Never went to war, never been shot at, never killed anybody. Sometimes I wonder what my life might have been like if I had chosen that path.'

'Is he happy – is he truly happy?'

'Don't really know. Yes, I guess he is – I guess they are. Yes, I think he's happy. He and I were never all that close. Never talked about any of this.

'Here I am, "no fixed abode" as they say, no two days in a row the same, no religion – no belief in God – no belief in much of anything except myself, when you come to think of it. Other than a very few trusted friends like you, nobody to regularly play golf with on a Saturday or darts down the pub on a Thursday night. Proper loner.

'So – just like I sometimes look at him and think maybe it might be nice to have that neat, tidy, ordered life he has, does he ever look at me and think it might have been nice to have the sort of adventures I've had? Is an "ordered life" the same as a "boring life"?' Sometimes I ask myself if he ever looks at his life and wonders what it might have been like to live like me.'

'Wow! You're, as they say, "waxing philosophical" here, old friend. I'm not sure I see your point.'

'My point, is – is it worth it – *has* it been worth it? Have the good times been worth the bad times?'

'Don't know, mate, just don't know. Can't say – really. Lyrics of a couple of songs come to mind. *The Rose*, Bette Midler – Conway Twitty did a nice cover, too. Anyhow, whether it's been worth it is really up to you and what you've decided you want to do with your life. Some of us will climb to the top of a hill just to see what's on the other side, some just walk on by the hill and aren't all that curious about what's on the other side –'

'And aren't there some who just stand and look at the hill, wonder what's on the other side, never make the climb to the top but spend the rest of their lives cursing themselves for not having tried?'

'Yep, I guess there are a few of those, too. But maybe we – you and me – are more like Kenny Rogers' *Sweet Music Man*. Somewhere deep inside us is something that drives us to do what we do. Maybe we don't really have a choice – and we certainly don't know *why*, it's just who we are.'

He paused: 'I don't know. Shite, Ossie, how'd we get into all this?'

'Maybe you're right – maybe a waste of time to ask about the "Whys?" maybe we just have to accept that it *is*.'

They sat back, looked at each other, smiled, and agreed the time for introspection was over.

CHAPTER EIGHTY-SEVEN

AMANDA, SALLY, SHIRLEY and the girls were sitting around Sally's huge, cluttered pine table in her huge, cluttered kitchen enjoying a leisurely breakfast when they heard the knock. Their lives were so relaxed now Sally no longer reached for the Colt when anybody came calling. Shirley, Louise and Anne returned recently from Canada and they were spending their time enjoying each other's company.

Sally went to the front door and returned towing Os by the hand — followed immediately by boisterous greetings and hugs all around, ending with an impressive group hug.

Sally rearranged chairs to make room for him: 'Coffee and something to go with it: full English? Continental? American pancakes and sausage with loads of maple syrup? Sorry, all out of Hollandaise so no eggs Benedict on the menu.'

'Coffee'll do just fine, thanks.'

Sally poured his coffee as they continued their comments about how happy they were to see each other.

At a convenient break in the conversation Os spoke: 'Right, ladies, two things. First, I'll give you an update on what's happening out there in the big, bad world, then I think we need to think seriously about what we're all going to do next.'

Louise: 'Does this mean we have to go back to school?'

Os: 'Yep. 'Fraid so.'

Anne: 'Bummer and double bummer!'

Os told them about his work with Brian and what he was doing on his own, and that he was convinced they could go back to their own homes without anybody's bothering them, neither reporters harassing them nor any law enforcement agencies seeking their apprehension. He had been doing discrete surveillance on their houses and found nothing to suggest they were being watched.

'So, Mandy, maybe it's time for you and me to change the locks on our respective doors, tidy up our abodes from the recent unpleasantness, lay in some provisions and try to get back to some kind of normality.'

He winked at Anne: 'Then we need to get over to school and see about getting the two of you re-enrolled.'

'Yuck! and ugh! We liked it better this way. Mummy's maths and computer classes were fun – well, almost – and Sally's English and geography classes were really great!'

'Ah, my sweets, but what about history, biology, philosophy, psychology, archaeology *and* anthropology?'

He winked again and turned back to Amanda: '¿Qué?'

'Good timing. Day before yesterday I rang the building society and, believe it or not, they've kept my job open for me. So, yes, I think it's time to go home.'

They chatted for another half-hour then Amanda and Os left in his hire car for their locksmithing and housekeeping chores. In the evening Os dropped Amanda off at Hollow Meadows then drove back to his own house for the night.

The next day he returned his three girls and Shirley to their homes. Shirley said she felt okay about being alone and she would be just fine; she was happy to be back in the peace and quiet, surrounded by her familiar things. Amanda was still not too comfortable being on her own with the girls; Os agreed to spend the night on the sofa: 'But just this one night, Missus Stover – it's time you got back on the horse.'

'Yes, I know, Mister Doran, but you're nice to have around.'

⌘

Through the week Os visited Amanda, the girls and Shirley at what to them seemed like random times and for trivial reasons. His aims were two. First, to see they were settling in well and not looking out fretfully from behind the curtains every time they heard an unusual noise outside. But his second intention was subtler: had they been keeping track, they would have noted his visits were becoming shorter and further apart. He was quietly removing himself from their lives so they could get along without feeling the need for his protection.

Towards the end of the week during one of his visits he suggested it would be nice to have a meal at the Brindle Cow. Shirley thanked him for his offer but said she was enjoying her own quiet company so much she declined and hoped they all would enjoy themselves. When Os mentioned the restaurant, Amanda asked when they were planning to get back to their gliding. He hesitated awkwardly then said it would be soon.

They ate on a Saturday night and a good time was had by all. Their recent adventures were drifting further into the past and as they were becoming less recent, the four were able to talk more freely and without the fear and uncertainty they felt when those adventures were happening. They laughed and sometimes talked over each other in their excitement. Some details were missing from this conversation: those having to do with Os' dispatch of the three hit men and Amanda's killing of George Barr.

Some details were repeated several times to the accompaniment of more chuckles: the theft of their uniforms and ambulance from the two thoroughly bewildered paramedics and their hiding in plain sight at St. Gildas. The only time it all went quiet was when Anne giggled and reminded them of the time she asked Mummy if Ossie was going to be their new daddy. This passed after a short, awkward silence and they got back to the business of enjoying themselves.

He drove them home and Amanda asked him in for coffee; despite all they had been through together, there was still a subtle, unspoken distance, an unexplained formality between them that bothered her when she thought about it. The girls were seen to bed and the two of them sat on the sofa—television off, it had never been turned on—quietly sipping their coffees and not saying anything beyond that it was great just to be sitting on a sofa quietly sipping their coffees without having to worry about anybody's looking for them, chasing them, knocking on their doors at weird hours, writing horrible things about them in the papers or trying to kill them.

She put her cup down on the low table, took his cup from him and set it next to hers, turned to him and took both his hands in hers: 'Right. It's been a wonderful evening – the four of us together – talking, joking and laughing – a really nice evening, but every so often when you weren't looking I caught you staring off into the distance.'

'But –'

'No "Buts!" – going off into that far place of yours.'

He hesitated and looked away, then back to her: 'I have to go away for a while – Canada – Paul's found us both jobs in Canada.'

'Canada? Talking about "far places". Wow! When and for how long?'

'Soon. Within the next couple of months. How long? This first project is three months.'

'Wow! Wait until Anne hears about this – "bummers" and "double bummers"! Why Canada?'

'I need to get away for a while. Off the radar. Even though nobody's seriously looking for me for the moment here –'

'I don't want you to go – *I really don't want you to go*!'

'Have to –'

She squeezed his hands tightly and started to tremble: 'But you can't –'

'Have to.'

'No, you don't. What you *have to do* is stay here with me and the girls. This is where you need to be.'

'It's where I *want* to be, but I can't, I just can't.'

'Can't or won't? What's driving you away? Why would you leave these three women who love you?'

It was the first time the word had been spoken by either of them. They were silent for a few seconds then he pulled his hands from between hers and gripped them in his: 'A while ago you asked me about my dark place and I promised you someday I'd tell you about it. I reckon now's the time.'

'Whatever it is, it can't be that bad, can it?'

'It's bad, believe me, it's *very* bad.'

'Tell me.'

He stared at the black television screen for a few seconds and squeezed her hands even tighter: 'You remember I told you I spent some time in Africa?'

'Yes, but you never told me anything about it.'

'Never told *anybody* about it. Nobody knows about it except George Barr.'

'George Barr! What in God's green earth has he got to do with it?'

'Please – please. Listen! It's something I can't bury – I can't make it go away, *it just won't go away*!'

She sat back and relaxed a little: 'Okay, promise. No more interruptions.'

'Chad, south-western Chad, Logone Oriental region, a "region" is something like a county or province. Chad, one of the poorest and most corrupt nations on Earth. The governor of the region, Negue Odingar, local mover and shaker, own private army and all that goes with it, hired twelve of us including George. At first, I thought he was a genuine revolutionary serious about reform. You know, the usual thing in certain parts of the world, somebody who wants to bring about change for the better.

'Build a power base, form a viable opposition to a corrupt regime, take over the government in a coup d'etat then build on that. But I was wrong – deadly wrong. As it turned out he was nothing more than a warlord with his own bunch of thugs who wanted to take control of the region and turning it into his own little kingdom.'

'So, when you found out, why didn't you just get out?'

'Well, you see, that's the problem with being a mercenary. You're hired to do a job. No loyalties, no rules, no higher authority than the person who's hired you. His friends are your friends; his enemies are your enemies. When it comes right down to it, you're a hit man, a contract killer. Somebody hires you to kill people and you do it.'

'Still doesn't answer why you didn't get out. Surely you could have somehow just faded away, disappeared.'

'That's what I finally did but right before that it turned ugly – really, truly ugly.'

'How ugly?'

'I'm coming to that. Please just let me keep talking until I get through this.

'I'd made my decision. I'd had enough. Although none of us ever talked about it, we all *always* kept our passports with us and a stash of American Dollars, Sterling or both. Just in case, you know. Good anywhere in the world. So, yeah, if you choose to you can sneak away in the night and if you're careful you can make your way back to civilization, hopefully before you get caught by the people who hired you.

'Anyhow – maybe Odingar was interested in building a power base, winning over the local people, planning a bright future, a brave new world, but not at first. What he was bent on doing first was eliminating anybody who opposed him and this meant anybody who didn't agree with his line and anybody who supported President Déby. He had no time for winning anybody over, if they didn't see things his way he simply killed them. And that's what we got caught up in. He had hired himself a band of elite killers – identify a village that backed Déby and destroy it. Simple as that. And when I realized this I wanted out as fast as possible.

'Not that difficult, really, well not the logistics of it all anyhow. Remember, I'm trained to survive anywhere – live off the land – evade capture – all the stuff you see on TV and in the films. It's what I do, it's what I *can* do, it's what I *have* done, it's me.

'And the thing to realize is you can't make any preparations. If you try to prepare, no matter how careful you are, one of your comrades will know you're up to something. So one morning you wake up and tell yourself: "Today's the day," you pat your pockets to confirm your passport and cash are there, you check that nobody's looking and you walk off into the bush.

'Odingar had been sending us through some villages looking for what he called "traitors". Usually by the time we got there the men had gone, sneaked off to wherever, nobody there but the women and children. We had orders not to kill any women or children, just burn the village and move on. But this one time we caught them unawares. Odingar's man in charge ordered us to round up all the males between the ages of ten and seventy and herd them out of the village. There were twenty-three of them – twenty-three! He ordered six of us on to the next village down the line and ordered the other six, with George in charge, to see to them.

'So – the six of us left, headed off down the red-clay track. We could hear the shooting behind us. For me that was it. I told the others I needed to, as they sometimes say in that part of the world, "ease myself" and stepped off the road into the bush. They naturally kept walking, expecting me to catch up. I didn't. In the bush I dropped down away from the road and went the other direction, back the way we'd come. As I went along I heard George and the other five moving above me on the road. They were laughing and joking – twenty-three people "seen to" and they're joking about it.

'When I got close to the village, I found the tracks and followed them out and down into a steep, narrow ravine, and there they were. All twenty-three of them lying at the bottom of this ravine. But he hadn't killed them, he'd gut shot them. All twenty-three of them lying at the bottom of this ravine screaming and moaning in pain.'

He squeezed her hands even tighter: 'You know what "gut shot" means?'

'Only what I see on the telly and in films. You get shot in the stomach and it takes you a long time to die.'

'Yeah – long time – painful – extreme pain. If you're lucky you get it in the stomach or a major artery and you either bleed out or stomach acids get into your blood stream and you're gone in about fifteen minutes. Painful but it's all over in a quarter of an hour or so. Otherwise it can take you hours, sometimes a whole day to die. That's what George was – he enjoyed making people suffer. Not his enemies, these people hadn't done anything to him, he just wanted to hurt them simply because he liked to hurt people.'

'So what did you do?'

'I had no choice. There was absolutely no way I could help them. Whether I got caught or not, whether I got them some help or not, they were all going to die. All I could do was stop their suffering. Even if there was a hospital nearby, and there wasn't – obviously, it wouldn't have made any difference. They were dying.'

She leaned towards him, knowing what was coming but dreading it nonetheless.

'I was going to shoot them in the head – quick, clean, but thought the others were still close enough to hear gunshots. So I snapped their necks. Starting with the youngest, one-by-one, I snapped their necks. Twenty-three boys and men and I broke their necks.'

He squeezed her hands so hard it hurt her then tears filled his eyes and he started to tremble. He said no more. She pulled her hands from between his, pulled him to her with his head on her shoulder, wrapped her arms around him and held him tightly until he stopped trembling. She said nothing; she just held him.

He relaxed a little, sat back and wiped his eyes: 'It took me ten weeks to find my way out. Eight hundred miles. I threw my rifle and ammunition away and started walking. By day, by night, hiding in the bush, moving on. I walked west into North Cameroon, through the Mbang Mountains then into Nigeria. Once into Nigeria sometimes I was able to hitch rides in lorries. Lots of people on the move in Nigeria, almost everybody's always moving – going somewhere. Bit of Sterling will get you just about anything.

'I finally made it to Benin City where I was safe. I had made it. There's a big brewery in Benin City – Guinness.

Friend of mine's head of security there. He took me in. To get out of the country and back to Britain I needed a visa and a work permit stamped in my passport. Easily enough done – in Nigeria they call it "dash". My mate gave my passport to the company fixer and for some of my American Dollars he went off to Abuja and returned two days later with the necessary stamps in it.

'Scariest bit of the whole thing wasn't worrying about big snakes in the bush, it was sitting there in my mate's compound for two days without my passport. From then on every step was easier. On one of his trips to Lagos his driver dropped me off at the Sheraton Hotel in Ikeja. British Airways desk there, plane ticket to Heathrow, little more dash to the customs and immigration guys at the airport and I was on the plane for home.'

Then he was silent. Over the next few minutes he gradually relaxed but said nothing.

Finally she spoke: 'I have nothing to say. I'm not going to say *anything*. And I'm certainly not going to say something really stupid about putting it behind you. The only thing I will say is that I'm here. That's it – just that I'm here.'

Then she was silent, too. They sat, side-by-side on the sofa holding hands and saying nothing. Finally he felt her quiver and as he turned to her, he saw the tears in her eyes.

'You're not coming back, are you? You're not coming back *ever*?'

'I don't think so, I don't think so. Maybe – if the wounds heal – maybe – if the demons go away – maybe – if the nightmares stop – maybe. But I don't think so. I don't think the wounds are ever going to heal. You ever see *Rambo*? Of course – everybody's seen *Rambo*.'

'Yes, I've seen *Rambo*.'

'Not too far from the truth, really – man so damaged by war, by what he's seen, by what he's been through, by what he's *done*, that he can never come back – he can never, ever live like a normal human being again. Never, ever free of what's happened to him. A man terrified of letting people in – letting people into his life – letting people love him.'

'But where does that leave me? And the girls? And don't give me any schoolgirl crap like "Oh, you'll get over it," or some bullshite about "You'll get over me or you'll find somebody else, etcetera, etcetera, etcetera!"'

He did not reply. He stood up, pulled her up and they walked, hand-in-hand to the door. He turned and faced her: 'I have to go now. Tell the girls I'm thinking of them.'

He opened the door and stepped out still holding her hand. He looked at her for a moment then looked away into the darkness, dropped her hand and closed the door.

She threw the bolt, walked back into the sitting room and sat down. There were no tears, just an all-pervading emptiness. She had not felt such emptiness since her husband left her.

EPILOGUE

THE DEAFENING SILENCE from behind her told Louise Stover at the very least they were not going to die. Her instructor said nothing since they took off. She would turn sixteen in three weeks and then she would be allowed to fly solo.

She rolled out of her turn at six-hundred feet above the ground instead of where she should have been: at three-hundred. The overwhelming silence continued. They hit the ground at fifty-five knots, she applied the wheel brake and they rolled to a stop. The right wing dropped slowly to the ground.

Finally, a quiet response from the back seat: 'That wasn't a landing – that was an *arrival*.'

Louise said nothing.

They climbed out then pushed the glider to the edge of the runway where they waited for the tractor to retrieve them.

While they waited her instructor smiled a motherly sort of smile: 'Great flight except for that little bit at the very end. Another couple of weeks and you'll be ready to go off on your own.'

Louise smiled a daughterly sort of smile: 'Must try harder.'

'From now on all your flights should be with a senior instructor. You'll need to be ready for the big day!'

'I'll be ready, Mummy.'

Theirs was the last flight of the day, the sun was below the horizon, dew was fast rising and mist was collecting on the canopy. The tractor arrived and Louise picked up the tail, swung the glider around in line with it then hooked up the tow rope. She took the wingtip from Amanda and they started back towards the hanger.

The towrope tightened and the two began walking side-by-side but then Amanda slowly dropped back until she was all alone, feeling the cool air on her face and the damp grass beneath her trainers. It had been a good day—a great day—but it was now, between the last landing and the closing of the hanger doors when the bittersweet memories sometimes swirled around her with an intensity causing her to gasp: the only two men she ever loved had gone away.

Then, for a little while, she needed to be alone. She looked at Louise, tall and beautiful, and growing taller and more beautiful each day. She thought about Anne. Bubbly Anne, still missing her daddy and sometimes crying in the night, and giggling squeamishly when she talks about dissecting a frog in biology class. Last week she solemnly announced she wants to be a doctor—a heart surgeon. A heart surgeon, indeed. The lights in the clubhouse came on; the swirling ceased.

THE END

INJURED OR SERIOUSLY KILLED

A brutal murder A cynical conspiracy A web of hatred

'People of my class don't lead troops into battle, people of my class send other people into battle. People of my class send other people out to be killed.'

'But – why? – *why*?'
'Enough questions for now. Time to get on with our entertainment for the afternoon. Now – where was I? Oh, yes, the Boger Swing. As I was saying –'

George Pendragon, ruthless Tory grandee, will do *anything* to guarantee a Conservative majority at the next general election. Henry Lovell, bigot, anti-Semite and white supremacist, will do *anything* to keep England English, Christian and white.

Together they hatch a devious plot to achieve their separate aims but it goes horribly wrong when Os Doran is drawn into their schemes.

Lord Pendragon uses his connections at the highest levels within the government, police and security services to ensure his links to Lovell remain hidden forever.

But when Doran threatens them with exposure, Pendragon sets out to destroy him using a secret government black ops team while Lovell contracts with a crime boss to murder him.

How will Pendragon, the paradigm cynical power player, achieve his aims through his hidden connections within the corridors of power? How will Lovell survive the madness brought on by his raging paranoia? How will Doran escape these two different faces of evil?

An Os Doran thriller   www.RiisMarshall.co.uk